A Conspiracy in Belgravia

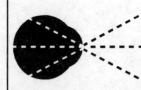

This Large Print Book carries the
Seal of Approval of N.A.V.H.

THE LADY SHERLOCK SERIES

A Conspiracy in Belgravia

Sherry Thomas

THORNDIKE PRESS
A part of Gale, a Cengage Company

Farmington Hills, Mich • San Francisco • New York • Waterville, Maine
Meriden, Conn • Mason, Ohio • Chicago

Copyright © 2017 by Sherry Thomas.
The Lady Sherlock Series.
Thorndike Press, a part of Gale, a Cengage Company.

ALL RIGHTS RESERVED

LIBRARY OF CONGRESS CIP DATA ON FILE.
CATALOGUING IN PUBLICATION FOR THIS BOOK
IS AVAILABLE FROM THE LIBRARY OF CONGRESS

ISBN-13: 978-1-4328-4696-1 (hardcover)
ISBN-10: 1-4328-4696-5 (hardcover)

Published in 2018 by arrangement with The Berkley Publishing Group, an imprint of Penguin Publishing Group, a division of Penguin Random House LLC

Printed in the United States of America
1 2 3 4 5 6 7 22 21 20 19 18

*To Kerry, who has been a true champion
for these books*

PROLOGUE

Thank goodness for a blatantly obvious murder.

Inspector Treadles did not say those words aloud — that would be disrespectful to the deceased. But he most certainly entertained the thought as he made his way, Sergeant MacDonald in tow, to the house where the body had been found.

After the taxing irregularities of the Sackville case, a run-of-the-mill murder would be calming and restorative. He looked forward to gathering clues. He looked forward to questioning witnesses. He looked forward to assembling an account that would serve as the crown's evidence.

He looked forward to handling every aspect of the work on his own, without needing to turn to anyone else for help.

The district was unexciting, the streets without character, the houses unimpeachable in their blandness. Inspector Treadles was beginning to like this case more and more, even as in the back of his mind, a voice whispered that it was all he was good for: the utterly ordinary. The cases that required only dull, plodding work.

Grimly he pushed the thoughts away. They were for the small hours of the night. At the moment his time and his mind belonged to the business of the Criminal Investigation Department. And he would show his superiors that with or without Sherlock Holmes, he was a capable and effective man, an asset to any police force.

"That's the place ahead," said Sergeant MacDonald.

They were on a street that could have come from anywhere in the ring of suburbs that surrounded London: macadam lane, two- and three-story brown-brick buildings, a newsagent's at one end and a pub at the other. A constable had been stationed at the murder site, outside the front door. As they approached, curtains fluttered in nearby houses.

A hackney drove past and came to a stop. A man alit.

"Is that . . ." murmured Sergeant Mac-Donald.

It was. Lord Ingram, Inspector Treadles's esteemed friend — a little less esteemed these days, perhaps, given his association with "Sherlock Holmes."

Lord Ingram stood by the side of the hackney and helped a lady descend. No, not a lady, a fallen woman, one who had never seemed remotely bashful of either her past or her present.

They saw Treadles, exchanged a glance with each other, and came toward him.

"Inspector, Sergeant, how unexpected," said Lord Ingram. "Trouble in these parts?"

Treadles noticed that his friend was less warm than usual in his greeting. Had he read the tension in Treadles's jaw and deduced his discomfort in the presence of Miss Charlotte Holmes? It was natural that as a friend to both, he might feel himself constrained. But Treadles couldn't help a sense of injury, a feeling deep down that Lord Ingram would choose Miss Holmes over him any day of the week.

"I'm afraid I'm not at liberty to discuss police matters," he said, hating the stiffness of his voice.

A tall, red-faced man emerged from the house. "Ah, Inspector Treadles," he said loudly. "You are here. The body's inside and it's not pretty."

"Let me not keep you from your work." Lord Ingram nodded. "Inspector, Sergeant, good day."

He and Miss Holmes returned to the hackney and drove away. Inspector Treadles stared after them. He had no idea how they had learned of the crime when he himself had been informed less than an hour ago, but he had a presentiment that their involvement in the matter was only beginning.

And he did not like it.

ONE

Sunday
Six days earlier . . .

This is an account of a remarkable man named Sherlock Holmes.

No, no, too *unremarkable* an opening. Miss Olivia Holmes scratched out the line.

Let me recount a tale of woe and vengeance.

Better, maybe. At least a little more intriguing.

The origin of our story lies decades ago, in a paroxysm of violence and betrayal. Let your mind leap over the tumult of the Atlantic Ocean into the vastness of the New World. Past the cities on the East Coast of the continent, past the farms and homesteads of its tamer interior regions.

Now you have come to the edge of the frontier. The land beyond is harsh; survival is uncertain. But you have come too far. You have no choice but to forge ahead.

Livia tapped the end of her pen against her lower lip. This was a fair enough beginning, if she did say so herself. The setting was clear. The sentences were muscular. And when she read the whole thing aloud — as all good stories should be — she detected a pleasing cadence to the syllables.

Was it possible she could actually do it, compose an engrossing story inspired by the feats of her sister Charlotte?

The day before, Charlotte had assured her that she was fully worthy of the task. Livia hadn't been able to sleep a wink. As she'd stared at the dark ceiling, the story had come to her in flashes: a grassy, mountain-ringed oasis in an arid, hostile landscape, a wagon train laden with weary yet hopeful families headed for California, a massacre brewing in the hearts of Utah Territory militiamen who feared persecution and loathed outsiders.

If she did manage to give birth to this story, it could very well go on to be featured in a respected and widely read publication. How gratifying would it be, from her neglected corner in whichever Society drawing room, to hear those guests who never had any use for her discuss her narrative with astonished admiration.

Livia imagined the warm satisfaction she would feel, a snug, enduring sense of well-being.

She took a bite of bacon and consulted the travel handbook she'd borrowed from the circulating library. It was imperative that she give a correct description of Utah. Inaccuracies on the part of Sherlock Holmes's chronicler could diminish readers' opinion of the great detective, and she must not let that happen.

The problem was, she also couldn't paint too complete a picture, as even the handbook only offered patchy information. She would have to be vague about the exact location of her setting — somehow cobbling together one or two descriptive paragraphs — then pivot onto the doings of her characters.

Except she didn't know yet who those characters ought to be. The victim would be a girl — that much was clear. But what about the eventual avenger who swooped in decades later to punish the culprits? Would that person be a woman or a man? And those culprits, who were they?

According to Mr. Mark Twain, whose account of the Mountain Meadows Massacre first gave her the idea of a story of vengeance, nine men were indicted afterward, but only one was tried in a court of law. Those who escaped justice, naturally, made for good targets for a vigilant avenger. But eight targets were too many — two or three seemed more reasonable.

Did that mean she also had to reduce the scale of the massacre to account for the smaller number of killers? Or would it be all right to say more of them had been lawfully punished? According to the records, only children younger than seven were spared — and taken in by nearby families. If her avenger was one of those children, it would add an entire other dimension of complication to the story. Could an older child, an adolescent perhaps, have crawled away during the night and escaped?

Livia rubbed her temples. Now she remembered why she never proceeded beyond a few pages in any story: too many decisions to make. Often she wished that her life weren't so constricted, that she could make more of her own choices. But staring at the still largely empty sheet of paper before her, she was reminded that no, Charlotte was the one who wanted to make her own decisions. She, Livia, merely wished the world would be served up on a platter, cut to bite size and seasoned exactly to her liking.

A housemaid entered the breakfast parlor. Livia slammed her notebook shut. But the maid only set an ironed copy of the paper on the table and left silently.

Livia swore under her breath. Why was she always so jumpy? Why couldn't she be calm and majestic instead?

She reached for the paper. More specifically, the small notices at the back of the paper. She especially enjoyed the ones in code, secret transmissions between lovers who didn't dare communicate openly.

The code they employed tended to be simple letter substitutions, frequently no more complicated than shifting the entire alphabet one letter over. Some aspired to a bit of sophistication. A series of notices that started a few days ago, for example, had taken the extra step of converting already substituted letters to numbers, according to where they stood in the alphabet.

A rather distressing set of messages they were, too, a discarded lover dispiritedly yet doggedly trying to get a response from the faithless beloved.

Or at least that was how Livia interpreted

the messages. She didn't believe the sender would receive the hoped-for response, but she couldn't help but check each morning to find out whether the unrequited transmissions were still ongoing.

She almost didn't see her sister's nom de guerre in print. But something made her glance back at the columns of newsprint she had skipped.

STRANGE NOISES IN THE ATTIC? THERE IS ALWAYS SHERLOCK HOLMES

In June of this year the death of the Honorable Harrington Sackville brought to notice one Mr. Sherlock Holmes, self-styled consultant to the Metropolitan Police. Since then, Mr. Holmes has made his services available to the public. Which leads to that most reasonable question: What exactly has he done for the man on the street — or, for that matter, the lady in the parlor?

One gentleman, Mr. S_____, enthused that Mr. Holmes helped him decipher clues from his beloved concerning her birthday present. A lady, Mrs. O _____, claimed that Mr. Holmes located her lost ring. A trio of elderly sisters declared he was instrumental in easing their minds concerning mysterious noises in the attic, which did not emanate from spirits communing via Morse code, but wood-boring insects carrying out their daily routines.

When asked about Mr. Holmes's overwhelmingly domestic private consultations, an official at Scotland Yard answered, "How Sherlock Holmes chooses to spend his time is not the Metropolitan Police's concern." The same official refused comment on whether Scotland Yard would seek Mr. Holmes's assistance in the future, except to note that his advice is not needed on any current cases.

After an exciting arrival on the scene, has Sherlock Holmes's great promise already faded into the tedium of uncovering household curiosities? Thunderous murders to the life cycle of deathwatch beetles?

Only time will tell.

"Oh, what drivel!" exclaimed Penelope Redmayne, as she finished reading the newspaper article aloud.

"I concur," said her aunt, Mrs. John Watson, the lady of the house.

They both looked toward the third occupant of the table, a young woman in her midtwenties. She wore a dusky pink day dress with a ruffled collar of starched white eyelet lace, which perfectly set off her shiny blond curls, large blue eyes, and generous lips. The same lace, in three tiers, also fell from her cuffs, the trailing edge of which brushed against the tablecloth as she spread a pat of butter on a freshly baked muffin.

She did it with great concentration — Miss Charlotte Holmes, Mrs. Watson had realized from the very beginning, took her food seriously. In fact, given her pleasantly plump form and the suggestion of a second chin — her features were lovely but her face would never be praised for its bone structure — one might easily suppose that Miss Holmes thought of nothing else except her meals.

Miss Holmes took a bite of her muffin, her expression intense with pleasure. But when she spoke, her voice was cool and measured. "I enjoyed the article. The timing is good — we will not need to spend on advertisement this fortnight. And frankly, the writer's thrust is no less advantageous to our interests. Household curiosities are the backbone of our enterprise. There must be a number of men on the street — and ladies in the parlor — who have decided against consulting Sherlock Holmes because they chiefly know him as someone who advises Scotland Yard on murders. Now that they understand Holmes is happy to help with domestic oddities, they are more likely to come forward."

She glanced down at the muffin, as if debating whether to drench it with even more butter. The term *Maximum Tolerable Chins* popped into Mrs. Watson's head — it had come up the first time they sat down at the table together, the benchmark for whether Miss Holmes ate as she wished or gave in to the lamentable necessity to curb her appetite.

With visible regret Miss Holmes set down her butter knife. "Besides, I think highly of uncovering household curiosities. They remunerate well and do not endanger any-one."

"Hear, hear!" said Penelope cheerfully.

Mrs. Watson flattened her lips. "I still do not like the snide tone of the article."

"Then you should be glad the writer is unaware of Sherlock Holmes's actual gen-der, Aunt Jo." Penelope tapped the offend-ing broadsheet. "He clearly means to imply that Sherlock Holmes's genius has been emasculated by Londoners' everyday prob-lems. Imagine if he learns Sherlock Holmes is but a woman going about easing the minds of old widows. Why, it would nullify said genius altogether."

Miss Holmes took a small bite of her muffin. In a different young woman this gesture might be interpreted as delicacy of comportment, but Mrs. Watson suspected that Miss Holmes was only trying to prolong the pleasure of a single muffin, since she wouldn't be indulging in another one.

"We are in no danger of that," she said. "Even if I stand in the middle of Trafalgar Square and solve problems on the spot, there will be a large segment of the population who will believe that I am being supplied answers by secret means — and by men, of course."

"But don't you wish credit for your accomplishments?" asked Penelope.

Another tiny nibble on Miss Holmes's part. "I've only ever wanted to put my abilities to use — and be respectably compensated for my work."

Her equanimity could be interpreted as laudable maturity, for one whose circumstances had changed greatly of late. But Miss Holmes was also not prone to the kind of careening emotions most people either took for granted or suppressed from habit.

In fact, sometimes Mrs. Watson had the impression that Miss Holmes examined a situation as a dressmaker might measure a customer, and then cast an eye over a catalog of responses the way the dressmaker considered bolts of silks and velvets.

It was not calculation so much as . . . The closest analogy Mrs. Watson could think of was that of a foreigner who didn't learn English until an advanced age. Through perseverance and a great deal of practice, the foreigner had achieved a passable grasp of the syntax, grammar, and vocabulary of this mishmash of a language. But a conversation would always be a trial, what with all the idioms and quirks of usage just waiting to ambush the non-native speaker.

"Miss Holmes," said Penelope, leaning forward with eagerness, "given that you are about to have more clients, would you be willing to put me to use this summer? I'd be delighted to show people up to the parlor at Upper Baker Street and bring in the tea tray. I, too, have a resolute lack of contempt for domestic mysteries and quotidian oddities."

Mrs. Watson sucked in a breath. She wished Penelope had asked her first before posing the question directly to Miss Holmes. But more importantly, the business of Sherlock Holmes was not all domestic mysteries and quotidian oddities: Mrs.

Marbleton's recent case, for example — suffice to say it did not involve little old ladies befuddled by noises from the attic.

"And, of course, my true ambition is to play Sherlock Holmes's sister," continued Penelope. "I might not have appeared on stage professionally, but my aunt can testify that I staged performances for her in the nursery and made for a convincing Juliet — and an even better Lady Macbeth."

Miss Holmes glanced in Mrs. Watson's direction. "Mrs. Watson is in charge of the assignment of duties. I am sure she'll let you know, should we need an assistant on Upper Baker Street."

"Aha, you saw through my scheme. I was hoping to bypass my aunt's strictures." Penelope grinned cheekily at Mrs. Watson. "But I see now I must level a mountain with nothing more than a soup ladle. It's a good thing I have a temperament built for Herculean tasks."

Without waiting for Mrs. Watson to respond, she rose. "I'd better go change into my walking dress. We'll need to hurry if we want to get in our daily constitutional before it rains again."

Left alone at the table, Miss Holmes continued to nibble while Mrs. Watson nursed her cup of tea. She felt uneasy. A note from Lord Ingram had come this morning, letting her know that Miss Holmes had seen through their deceit — that Mrs. Watson hadn't stumbled upon an exiled Miss Holmes by accident, but had been tasked by Lord Ingram to help this young woman in need.

But Miss Holmes hadn't said anything about the matter, nor had Lord Ingram expected her to. *I do not believe she holds it against us — certainly not against you,* he had written. *But I felt her disappointment: She had averted disaster because of whom she knew before her fall from grace — and not because life had turned out to be fundamentally gentler than she had supposed.*

Mrs. Watson hadn't known Miss Holmes as long as Lord Ingram had — she could not sense either ire or disappointment in the young woman. And this made her anxious. She held Miss Holmes in the highest regard and was loath to alienate her, however unintentionally.

But how to broach the subject? How to reassure Miss Holmes that her affection and camaraderie were genuine without coming across as protesting too much?

Miss Holmes finished her muffin — and everything else on her plate. "If you will excuse me, ma'am," she said with her usual placidness, "I will also change and get ready for our walk."

"Did you see the article in the paper about Sherlock Holmes?" asked Inspector Treadles's wife as she worked his necktie.

He had. "No, I must have missed it. What did it say?"

Alice flattened her lips. "Nothing worth reading, really. Quite snide about his everyman — and everywoman — clientele and their less-than-shocking problems. Shouldn't it be a given that the general public doesn't wade hip-deep in dramatic criminality?"

She patted the finished knot and looked up at him, her hazel eyes more green than brown. "And that official from the Yard who gave the statement doesn't come across any better. One would think Scotland Yard would be more grateful."

He had been the official who had given the terse statement. That she did not know it only made her remark cut deeper.

"What else could anyone from Scotland Yard say besides something bare-bones and obvious?"

Did he sound defensive? Or more defensive than he ought to be?

Her gaze was curious, baffled, and — was

it possible? Was there, however slight, a trace of suspicion? "I believe I'll write to Miss Holmes and let her know that I think the article is utter rubbish."

No, you will not *write her.*

He swallowed the words.

By the end of our meeting I knew I would never think lightly of her again, he had confessed to his wife shortly after encountering Miss Holmes for the first time. But he had never told Alice the truth — that there had been no Sherlock Holmes, ever, only a woman possessed of a brilliant mind.

A woman who was no longer acceptable in polite society.

But why should he be so cruel? Why not let Alice enjoy the illusion of the great consulting detective, flexing his deductive prowess from his sickbed, tenderly surrounded by a gaggle of concerned women?

She cupped his face. "Is something the matter?"

Mere weeks ago he had thought himself the most fortunate of men. He had the favor of his superiors, the respect of his subordinates, and the love of the most perfect woman alive. Not to mention a direct line of transmission to Sherlock Holmes — a magnificent boon for his career.

To be sure, God had chosen not to gift

him with children. Nevertheless, he had been filled with gratitude for everything he had been given. And then Sherlock Holmes had turned out to be a woman with loose morals and no remorse. And Alice, Alice had let it be known that she had aspired to helm Cousins Manufacturing, the great industrial firm that had been her father's life's work.

Treadles would never have guessed. She was intelligent and well read, not to mention competent and organized. But ambitious? Ambitious far beyond her lot?

Of course there was no danger of her running Cousins Manufacturing — she had been candid about her father's refusal to consider her for the business. And in any case, the firm was now in the hands of her brother.

Yet her revelation had sent him through various stages of shock, anguish, and grief. *Why do you want things I can't possibly give you? Why must you desire power and unwomanly accomplishments? And are you, in the end, also not who I thought you were, not the one I loved and respected?*

"Of course nothing's the matter," he said, after a delay perhaps a fraction of a second too long. "Why do you ask that?"

She worried a corner of her lower lip, as if

wondering whether to say anything. "You've been a little distracted lately."

"Sometimes I come back from work a bit tired."

She studied him another moment, then smiled and kissed him on his cheek. "In that case, we'll make this Sabbath a true day of rest."

He couldn't be sure whether she believed him — or chose to let it go for the moment.

She walked to her vanity table and put on her Sunday hat, an elaborate confection as architecturally complex as a Gothic cathedral. "Oh, I almost forgot. A note came from Eleanor while you were in your bath. Barnaby isn't feeling well. She asks that we postpone our Sunday dinner until next week."

Barnaby Cousins, the man currently at the head of Cousins Manufacturing, and his wife, Eleanor, were two of Treadles's least favorite people. And the feeling was mutual. While Mr. Mortimer Cousins, his estimable late father-in-law, had been alive, the entire family had met each week after church for Sunday dinner. After his death, the joint Sunday dinners had become less and less frequent, once a fortnight, once a month, and now, once every two months.

"Are we going to meet quarterly hence-

forth?" Not that Treadles minded not seeing them, but still, the insult of it.

Alice slid a long pin through the crown of
her hat; her eyes met his in the mirror.
"That was also my first thought. But when
they've wanted to bow out of Sunday dinners before, they've always said that *Eleanor*
wasn't feeling well. This is the first time
Barnaby has been cast in that role and a
part of me wonders whether it's true, that
he really is ill."

Treadles shrugged into his coat. "You're
not going to drag me to call on him, are
you?"

"No, but *I* might, in the evening." She
smiled at him again. "You put up your feet
and enjoy your day off, Inspector."

Charlotte Holmes stood before the window
of her room and took in the greenery of
Regent's Park across the street. A soft mist
drifted across the lake, which was just visible beyond a colonnade of mature trees,
heavy with rain and foliage.

She relished a good winter downpour, but
she enjoyed a summer shower almost as
much — that is, when she had a proper roof
over her head and no pressing concerns
about losing said roof.

Odd to realize this, but she was in a finer

town residence than any she had ever occupied.

Her father, Sir Henry Holmes, baronet, had once owned a house in London. But that was sold well before Charlotte had her first Season. Every year Charlotte's mother, Lady Holmes, lamented the loss. Oh, how much better it would have been to arrive at one's own house, rather than a hired property.

The houses they hired were in more fashionable parts of the town than Mrs. Watson's, but that made them expensive — and never large enough for Lady Holmes's needs. A dinner of more than sixteen was out of the question and proper balls were daydreams. The best they could do for dancing was to push all furniture out of the drawing room and pray that gentlemen who dared to waltz were skillful enough not to crash their partners into other guests.

Those houses did not offer views or the latest advances in plumbing. And certainly not electricity, which she was still slowly coming to terms with. Her parents never employed a cook as fine as Madame Gascoigne or a butler as efficient as Mr. Mears. She had, in fact, never had a room to herself.

Charlotte had the unnerving sensation

that she did not deserve such good fortune — or at least, that she hadn't earned it. And she did not know how to reconcile herself to the fact that the seed of this good fortune had been bestowed upon her by Lord Ingram, whose aid she had not sought, even in her most desperate hour, because she had not wished to be indebted to him.

But now she was, always and forevermore.

The rain had started only after they'd returned from their walk, during which Miss Penelope Redmayne, with steadfast cheerfulness, worked on Mrs. Watson's resistance. Mrs. Watson remained resistant. Charlotte had maintained — without any effort, it must be said — her complete neutrality.

At the moment Mrs. Watson enjoyed a respite from Miss Redmayne's determined appeal: The ladies were at church. Charlotte had not been to church since she ran away from home. God likely wouldn't mind if she stepped inside His house — Jesus voluntarily associated with women of less-than-pristine repute — but His followers tended to be less magnanimous.

In any case, she had a prior appointment, one she hadn't mentioned to Mrs. Watson.

Umbrella in hand, she made her way to 18 Upper Baker Street. The house belonged to Mrs. Watson and was usually let to a tenant. But recently it had been turned into a dwelling for the fictional Sherlock Holmes, who was stricken with a mysterious illness that left him bedridden and incommunicado by ordinary means, leaving his sister as the oracle with whom his clients must consult, in order to gain his great and terrible insights.

Normally Charlotte played the role of the sister, though Mrs. Watson had also, on occasion, taken the part.

The parlor of 18 Upper Baker Street was of a good size, furnished with comfortable chairs clustered around a fireplace. The air held whiffs of whisky and tobacco, enough to hint at a masculine presence, but not so much as to put one in mind of a public house. There was also the scent of convalescence, of camphor and linseed oil. And floating serenely above it all, the fragrance of flowers, courtesy of the fresh bouquet that always bloomed on the seat of the bow window.

At precisely eleven o'clock, the doorbell rang — Lord Bancroft, like his brother, possessed exquisite punctuality, one of the few traits they shared.

"You look well, Miss Holmes," he said, as he settled himself into the seat she offered, his tone somewhat surprised.

Charlotte had timed a kettle to boil over the spirit lamp for his arrival. Now she warmed a teapot and set two spoons of first-growth Ceylon leaves to steep. "Thank you, sir."

In some ways he was the antithesis of his brother. While Lord Ingram radiated physicality and magnetism, Lord Bancroft was devoid of any personal charisma. But instead of being forgettable, the consensus was that those stuck next to him at social functions emerged mere shadows of their former selves.

His "blandness" consisted of a singular lack of warmth, a dogged social persistence, and a heavy application of skepticism. Livia had been his dinner companion once. She was obliged to answer questions for hours on end, from the Holmes girls' practically nonexistent education to all the minutiae of a parliamentary election in their rural borough, in the wake of their father's unsuccessful attempt at standing for office. Lord Bancroft had demanded that she source each fact and justify every opinion, while he played devil's advocate and asked why she didn't believe in the exact opposite of what she did.

Livia, who already suffered from a lack of confidence, came home in tears, convinced that she was the stupidest and most ignorant creature alive.

His social conduct did not stem from malice, but obligation as he understood it: One ought to keep the conversation going at table, and keep it going he would. But he had few interests and no hobbies, did not want to inform anyone what they should have learned from books and newspapers — and of course could not possibly recount to mere debutantes the clandestine work he did on behalf of the crown.

And so he asked questions of those with whom he socialized, men and women alike. Charlotte had heard gentlemen swearing foully after an encounter with him, because he had interrogated them on their management of estate, friendship, and horseflesh, and they had come away feeling as immature and incompetent as Livia had.

Charlotte, on the other hand, got along well with Lord Bancroft. She sourced her facts and was not particularly attached to her opinions — opinions, by their very nature, were subject to change. Possessing neither the desire to please nor the need to impress, she answered his questions as long as he had questions to ask and when he ran out of them, she was happy to eat in silence.

As she did now, nibbling on a slice of

excellent pound cake while Lord Bancroft looked around the parlor.

"Pleasant surroundings," he said, after a while. "And very fine pound cake."

"Thank you," she said.

Many people, women especially, she had observed, responded to a compliment by explaining what they had — or hadn't done — to merit it. But with Lord Bancroft, simple, unembellished answers were the way to proceed, unless one stood ready to verify the provenance of one's chairs by producing affidavits from long-dead carpenters and upholsterers — or to admit that said chairs were inexpensive reproductions manufactured in Leeds.

Though in this case, she was half tempted to say something about the pound cake, which deserved every praise. She touched the side of the teapot, gauging the temperature of the brew within. "You wished to see Sherlock Holmes about something, my lord?"

"Was that what I wrote in my note? No, I have come to see you, Miss Holmes."

The evening before, in delivering Lord Bancroft's message, Lord Ingram had said, half jokingly, *I was always afraid this day would come. That Bancroft would discover you for your mind.* Charlotte, on the other hand, had not been as sanguine. Lord Bancroft was accustomed to solving his own problems. He had vastly more resources than Inspector Treadles. And most likely he rarely thought of women as useful outside their biological functions.

His tone, a peculiar mix of pushiness and hesitation, further solidified her suspicions. But she only folded her hands in her lap. "Oh?"

"We were all dismayed when you left home," he began. "It was reassuring to learn that you had landed on your feet."

He looked at her; she poured him a cup of tea. "You take it black, if I recall correctly."

"Yes."

She added cream and sugar to her own tea while gazing at him with her usual lack of facial expression, which was almost always misinterpreted as a look of sweet hopefulness.

He took a sip. "But of course the situation is still highly irregular."

She remained silent, stirring her tea.

"Ash tells me that you have been to the house near Portman Square."

Ash was what Lord Ingram's intimates called him. Recently, when 18 Upper Baker Street had suffered from a bout of house-breaking, they had met, along with Inspector Treadles, at the house Lord Bancroft referred to.

"Yes, I have."

"He also tells me you had a positive impression of it."

The place had boasted the most . . . exuberant interior she had ever come across, a combination of color blindness and willful abandon — and she would have liked it just fine if its excesses had been pared back by a half dozen or so orange-and-blue cushions. "There was much to admire about the decor."

It was a gaudy zoo, and she enjoyed gaudy zoos.

"I had once hoped we would dwell there as husband and wife."

And so it begins. He would now propose that they dwell there as man and mistress.

"I still entertain the same hope," he said.

Her teacup paused on its way to her lips. In fact, she had to set it down altogether. Had she heard him correctly? "My lord, I am no longer eligible."

"You are no longer welcome in Society, but as you are of sound mind the Church can have no cause to consider you ineligible for matrimony."

Matrimony. It wasn't easy to surprise Charlotte, but Lord Bancroft was coming danger-ously close to flabbergasting her. "You are most kind. Nevertheless, I remain ill-suited to marriage."

"But you are not ill-suited to me. I would be happy to never be invited anywhere again — you would serve as a good excuse. I would be happy to never indulge in small talk again — I have a feeling you share that sentiment. And I will be busy and away from home a great deal — not something most brides look for in a groom, but for you it would count as an added attraction, no doubt."

Whatever his faults, he was an intelligent and honest man.

"I am not a rich man, but I can provide comfortably for a wife. By marrying me, you will not rehabilitate your reputation completely. But at least you will be received by your family again. That must count for something."

She didn't believe in being grateful for marriage proposals — men did not pledge their hands out of the goodness of their hearts. Even so, she found herself inclined to consider this particular union, at this mo-ment in time, on sentimental rather than rational grounds.

With a small shake of her head, she pulled

herself back to reality. "I am honored by your gesture, sir. But I take it you would require me to give up my friendship with Mrs. Watson, as well as my practice as Sherlock Holmes."

"It will not be necessary to cut Mrs. Watson. She was an acquaintance of our father's. Ash is on excellent terms with her and even I have crossed paths with her on occasion. She strikes me as a sensible woman, not one to exploit your position to promote her own. I do not see why you shouldn't be able to call on each other in the future, provided it is done discreetly.

"As for the business with Sherlock Holmes, I understand Mrs. Watson has invested in the venture. If you feel that she has not received a sufficient return against that initial outlay, I will be more than happy to compensate her as a part of our marriage settlement."

In other words, she was to discontinue as Sherlock Holmes, consulting detective. "I thank you most warmly, my lord, for the honor of —"

He raised a finger, forestalling the *no, thank you* part of her answer. "However, given that mental exertion gives you pleasure, I shall be happy to supply the necessary exercises. After all, I come across them on a regular basis."

He opened a leather portfolio he had brought, extracted a slender dossier, and set it before her. "These are but a small sprinkling of items that make their way to my desk. Do please examine them at your leisure."

And with that, he rose and saw himself out.

Two

Charlotte and Livia Holmes approached life very differently.

Livia viewed everything through a lens of complications, real and imaginary. From where to sit at a tea party, to whether she ought to say something to the hostess if her table setting was missing a fork, her lugubrious and plentiful imagination always supplied scenarios in which she committed a fatal misstep that destroyed any chance she had at a happy, secure life. For her, every choice was agony, every week seven days of quicksand and quagmire.

Charlotte rarely resorted to imagination — observation yielded far better results. And while the world was made up of innumerable moving parts, in her own personal life she saw no reason why decisions shouldn't be simple, especially since most choices were binary: more butter on the muffin or not, run away from home or not, accept a man's offer of marriage or not.

Not necessarily easy, but simple.

But Lord Bancroft's proposal . . . She felt like a casual student of mathematics faced with non-Euclidean geometry for the first time.

Her marriage would be a boon to her family. Her parents might be deeply flawed individuals who could not be made content by any means, but her continued status as an outcast certainly increased their unhappiness, both now and in the long run. They cared desperately about their façade of superiority — and as shallow a façade as it was, to them it remained infinitely preferable to being seen for their true selves: two middle-aged, less-than-accomplished people in a loveless marriage, their finances in tatters, and without a single child they could count on for comfort and succor.

Henrietta, the eldest Holmes sister, had distanced herself from her family almost before she returned from her honeymoon. Bernadine, the second eldest, had never been able to look after herself. Livia despised both her parents. And Charlotte, of course, had delivered the worst blow, a sensational and salacious fall from grace.

Should Charlotte regain her respectability, even partially, her parents would be able to walk around with their heads held high again — or at least without an overabundance of shame.

And it wasn't only her parents. Charlotte's infamy affected Livia's chances at a good marriage. Livia had scoffed at the idea, declaring herself the biggest obstacle to matrimony that she would ever face. But Charlotte could not be so blithe about it.

Moreover, if she did marry Lord Bancroft, then she could provide shelter for Livia, who would no longer face daily belittlement from their parents. And Bernadine, too, if at all possible — she couldn't imagine that the atmosphere at home was conducive to Bernadine's well-being.

On the other hand, marrying Lord Bancroft would make her Lord Ingram's sister-in-law, a situation so fraught even Livia's imagination might prove unequal to the ramifications. Not to mention, he clearly required her to give up her fledgling enterprise — and she was rather attached to the income it generated.

She bit down on another slice of pound cake, her appetite for rich, buttery solace even greater when faced with intractable dilemmas.

Suppose she persuaded Lord Bancroft to settle five hundred pounds a year on her . . .

She would have an independent income — enough to look after Livia and Bernadine. She would still be able to see Mrs. Watson. And if he should indeed prove the wellspring of intriguing and diverting cases . . .

She picked up the dossier he left behind.

It contained six envelopes. She unsealed the first envelope and pulled out a sheet of paper.

In 18_____, Mr. W., a young widower whose wife had perished in childbirth, traveled to India to take a civil service position in the Madras Presidency. A few weeks after his arrival, he attended an afternoon tea party. Taxed by the heat — even though the rainy season had arrived and temperatures were cooler than they would otherwise have been — he sat down on the veranda and closed his eyes for a nap.

The party dispersed. As the family dressed for dinner, a servant informed the mistress that a sahib was still on the veranda, asleep. The lady of the house went to rouse him and, much to her shock, found him dead.

Mr. W. had no connection to power, prestige, or fortune. He held no position whereby his removal — or his cooperation, for that matter — would have given anyone any noticeable advantage. And in his personal life, he was vouched to have been timid and trouble-averse — no criminal tendencies or unwise dalliances.

How and why did Mr. W. die?

India. Monsoon. The answer seemed much too obvious.

Charlotte dug further into the envelope and found a folded strip of paper that said *Clue* on the outside and a smaller envelope marked *Answer.*

The clue read, *Mr. W.'s death was declared an accident.*

Well, that settled it. She opened the *Answer* envelope.

The physician who examined Mr. W.'s body found puncture marks on the latter's wrist. Common kraits, highly poisonous snakes indigenous to India, sometimes enter dwellings to keep dry during monsoon months. Mr. W. was not the first, nor would he be the last, to be bitten in his sleep and never wake up again.

Snakebite, as she'd thought. She studied the sheets of paper and the typed words. The case might be old, but the construction of case-as-puzzle was recent. And it was meticulously done.

Not by Bancroft, obviously — he was too busy for that. A minion, then, one with access to the archives. What had been Bancroft's instruction? *Reach in and grab the first few records?*

She shook her head. She was being unfair. Bancroft dealt with real life, and real life seldom made for particularly intriguing puzzles. Not to mention, the construction of puzzles was an art. A minion who had no prior experience in said art — and who had never met Charlotte Holmes — could very well consider Mr. W.'s case, as it was presented, a first-rate conundrum.

She opened the next envelope.

On the last Sunday of January 18 ___, the S_____ family did not attend Sunday service. Mr. S. was a laborer, Mrs. S. a housewife who took in washing. They were poor but devout. Neighbors knocked on their door after church, concerned that they might have fallen ill. No one answered.

When the neighbors at last entered the dwelling, they found the entire family — husband, wife, and three children — dead in their beds.

What was the cause of death?

Where were the S_____ family? Had they been in England, Charlotte would hesitate longer, but if they lived on the Continent . . .

This case also came with a clue, which read, *The S_____ family resided in Minden, Germany.*

A guinea said that they perished from carbon monoxide poisoning.

The incident took place in a cottage, which happened to be the end house in a row of cottages, located directly above a disused mining shaft. All five members of the household, along with two cats and a caged songbird, died overnight. In the cottage opposite, also an end house, the occupants also fell ill, and they, too, lost family pets that night, though the humans eventually recovered.

The theory is that harmful gas from the mine shaft seeped upward through the dirt floors of the cellars. The cellars were fitted with doors that opened to the outside, but in the case of both houses, they had remained closed during the preceding weeks — it was winter and the families did not want cold air coming up into the house. The neighbors, when questioned, recalled that members of both families had complained of headache and nausea for a while. It then came to be viewed as a matter of luck. Similar conditions, similar dangers. One family succumbed, the other survived.

Charlotte would have thought it was simply due to insufficient ventilation for the stove — the composition of coal on the Continent made it more likely to emit carbon monoxide as a by-product of under-aerated combustion.

So . . . *slightly* more interesting, but hardly stimulating.

She had the next envelope in hand but made herself put it down. There were only six envelopes. No point finishing everything at once.

Instead she went to the bow window and picked up the slender volume that lay on the window seat. *A Summer in Roman Ruins*, Lord Ingram's account of those adolescent days he spent exploring the remnants of a Roman villa on his uncle's estate. It contained an oblique reference to their first kiss, but that wasn't the only hint to her presence.

There was also, for example, this particular passage:

One day, I unearthed a stone object, nearly three feet across and a good ten inches thick, perfectly circular except for a protuberance that appeared to be a handle, except it was far too short.

Clearing the encrusted dirt from the surface of the object revealed a groove that had been etched around the circumference of this large disk, and straight down the center of the protuberance. Not a millstone then, as I had originally supposed.

The function of the artefact baffled me, until someone better read came along with a copy of Bede's Ecclesiastical History and pointed to references of vineyards in olden times: It was a grape press — and the protuberance the spout from which grape juice would flow into a receptacle.

Grapes? He had frowned. *Here?*

She showed him the exact paragraph where the Venerable Bede described vines growing in various places in Britain.

What happened to all those vineyards?

Perhaps the climate or the soil turned unsuitable. Perhaps the plague wiped out everyone who knew how to work vines. Or perhaps French wines were simply better and cheaper, and it made sense to uproot the vine stock and grow something more profitable.

He was quiet for some time. *My godfather owns some vineyards in Bordeaux. I've visited them. Hard to imagine that landscape here.*

Did you frequent any patisseries when you were in France?

Don't think so — don't like sweet things. He glanced at her. *You like French pastry?*

I like the description of them. But I've never had croissants or mille-feuilles or cream puffs.

You still wouldn't have tasted them even if I'd visited every patisserie in Paris.

But at least you would have been able to describe them.

I've had croissants. They aren't bad. But I don't remember anything particular about them.

She'd sighed and picked up her book again.

But two days later, she'd walked into her room to find a box of croissants, mille-feuilles, and cream puffs.

Neither of them ever mentioned the pastries, but this was the next paragraph in the account:

I hadn't much cared for the consumption of books, preferring sports and the more physical aspects of excavation. But that moment I realized ignorance would ill serve me — and that if I wished to continue in archaeological endeavors, I must study the history passed down on library shelves, in addition to that evidenced by objects left behind by the long departed.

She closed the book softly.

No, she didn't wish she'd married him — she was ill-suited to marriage, after all — but she did wish he hadn't married someone else.

That he hadn't married the former Alexandra Greville.

The doorbell rang. Charlotte raised her head. Mrs. Watson and Miss Redmayne would not yet have returned from church. Lord Bancroft had left nothing behind. And she herself had no other clients scheduled for the day. Who could it be?

A courier stood on the doorstep, an envelope in hand. He respectfully inclined his head. "I've a letter for Mr. Sherlock Holmes."

"I'll take it to him."

The courier tugged his cap and left.

The envelope was of a familiar weight and material, the linen paper crisp yet strong. Charlotte also recognized the typewriter that had been responsible for the name and address on the front — typewriters, especially those that had been in use for a while, produced letters almost as identifiable as those written by hand.

Lord Ingram. They'd spoken in person only the evening before. What could have compelled him to send a letter by courier so soon afterward?

Dear Mr. Holmes,
I apologize for interrupting your day of rest, but I am in desperate need of help.
I beg you will receive me at four o'clock this afternoon.

Mrs. Finch

The handwriting on the note was not Lord Ingram's. Nor was it one of the scripts that he, an accomplished calligrapher who had taught Charlotte everything she knew about the forging of penmanship, had developed.

Her spine tingled. There was someone else in Lord Ingram's household who could have legitimately used the typewriter in his study and the envelopes that had been ordered from London's best stationer.

His wife.

"Papa, have you ever danced all night?" asked Lucinda, Lord Ingram's daughter.

Lord Ingram smiled, amused by her question. "No. I've danced half the night, but never all night."

They were in the nursery, back from church, and about to have their Sunday dinner together. Carlisle, his younger child, was playing intently with a boxful of wooden blocks. Lucinda enjoyed the blocks as much as Carlisle did, but for the moment she was not yet done with her plants.

Small terra-cotta pots crowded the sills of the nursery's three windows, holding a dozen different seedlings. Lucinda had been observing them for the past week, measuring their height, counting the number of leaves, and making drawings in her notebook to help her better recognize the plants at different stages of growth.

She wrote down the numbers of leaves for a sunflower seedling. "Why haven't you danced all night?"

"Because dances and balls usually don't last that long. By three o'clock in the morning most people want to be in bed, even those who love dancing."

Lucinda counted leaves on another sunflower seedling, the last of her experimental subjects. "I want to try dancing all night. Miss Yarmouth said I could once I'm married — she said I could do anything I wanted once I'm married — but Mamma said it was all nonsense."

It had been a long time since Lord Ingram asked his wife what she thought of marriage, either in general or in specific. "You'll be able to do more of what you want when you are older, whether you are married or not."

"Miss Yarmouth said I can be married at sixteen. Mamma said she won't let me. She said she'll have a word with Miss Yarmouth." Lucinda looked up, worried. "Is she going to dismiss Miss Yarmouth?"

Lord Ingram watered the last seedling — that was his task as her "prime assistant," as she'd dubbed him. "I shouldn't think so. But Miss Yarmouth's idea of marriage . . . I don't know anyone else who thinks of marriage as unlimited freedom."

"Mamma said I might hate it. And I won't be able to unmarry."

Who recoiled more from the state of their marriage, Lord or Lady Ingram? Until this moment, Lord Ingram had never been able to decide on an answer. Now he knew it was his wife, by a hair.

"It definitely isn't easy to unmarry."

An annulment would render his children illegitimate. And even if he'd had grounds for a divorce, it was a breathtakingly scandalous — and damaging — process.

Lucinda closed her notebook. "Why do Mamma and Miss Yarmouth think so differently about the same thing?"

"It's like asparagus. You can't get enough of it; Carlisle hardly ever touches his. Nothing is for everyone."

"What about you? What do you think about it?"

He'd been expecting the question — this was where the conversation had been inexorably headed. Still he flinched inwardly.

He set aside the watering can, sank down to one knee, and placed his hands on his daughter's shoulders. "I think it's the best thing I've ever done. Do you know why?"

She shook her head.

"Because it brought me you — and your brother." He kissed her forehead. "Now let's eat. I hear we'll have asparagus again."

"Something has come up," said Miss Holmes as she served herself a generous portion from the trifle bowl at the center of the table.

They had been talking about Penelope's friends from medical school who were shortly to arrive in London. Penelope was intent on organizing a tour of the Scottish Highlands. Mrs. Watson, in between listening to her ideas, pondered whether she ought not to make some changes to the house's public rooms. They were so very somber, full of deep blues and joyless browns. Practical to be sure — the soot in London would turn everything dark and grimy in time. But perhaps a new wallpaper with leafy designs on a stone-hued background might serve as a compromise?

Miss Holmes's announcement yanked her out of this pleasant reverie of colors and patterns. "What is it?"

Miss Holmes spooned a whipped-cream-cocooned blueberry into her mouth. "At four o'clock a new client will be calling. She knows me. I have a sneaking suspicion that she might also know Mrs. Watson by sight, even if they have never been formally introduced. So Miss Redmayne, provided she can keep a secret, must take on the part of Sherlock Holmes's sister."

Penelope's dessert spoon hovered above her own serving of trifle. She glanced at Mrs. Watson. They had come to a stalemate concerning the role Penelope would or wouldn't take with regard to Sherlock Holmes. Miss Holmes's request broke the deadlock.

Mrs. Watson grew alarmed — Miss Holmes would not give up her neutrality unless something extraordinary had happened. "I thought we had no appointments for the day. Who is this client?"

"Lady Ingram," said Miss Holmes.

Placidly.

Mrs. Watson exchanged another look with Penelope, now slack-jawed in astonishment.

Three years ago, during intermission at the Savoy Theater, Lord Ingram had come to Mrs. Watson's box to pay his respects. As he was about to leave, her eyes happened to alight on Miss Holmes in the auditorium, headed for her own seat.

Oh, look at that young woman in rose moiré, Mrs. Watson had exclaimed. *She must be the most darling girl in attendance tonight.*

Lord Ingram glanced down. *That's Charlotte Holmes, the greatest eccentric in attendance tonight.*

Mrs. Watson had been incredulous. *That sweet young thing? Are you sure, sir?*

Her friend had smiled slightly. *I'm quite certain, madam.*

The theater's electric lights dimmed — the next act was about to begin. Lord Ingram took his leave. But Mrs. Watson remembered that smile, a fond smile that said, *The stories I could tell.* No doubt the stories would have been delightful — yet

Mrs. Watson had felt strangely dejected for the rest of the evening.

It was only the next day that she had been able to articulate why she had been so affected: In that smile had been a wistfulness that encroached on regret.

Mrs. Watson had not brought up Miss Charlotte Holmes again. Neither had Lord Ingram, until he came to see her the evening of Miss Holmes's unfortunate "incident," and asked for her help.

Mrs. Watson knew then that her instincts had been correct all those years ago. She had no doubt that Miss Holmes reciprocated Lord Ingram's sentiments: When these two young people had been alone in the same room, despite their reserve — or perhaps because of it — the tension had been palpable. Mrs. Watson, sitting in the next room and pretending to look after the nonexistent Sherlock Holmes, had departed hastily, her own face flushed from the latent heat of their unacted-upon desires.

How then, did Miss Holmes manage to utter Lady Ingram's name with such ease — such casualness, almost? Even Mrs. Watson, who considered herself not ungenerous of spirit, could not speak or even think of that woman without a swell of hostility.

But this was not the question she posed

to Miss Holmes. "Lady Ingram does not realize that you are Sherlock Holmes?"

"It would appear not."

"Did she say why she wished for a meeting in her letter?"

Miss Holmes dug up half a strawberry from the decadent depths of her trifle. "No, only that she urgently needed one."

"And she sent it to Upper Baker Street? How did she know the address?"

"My guess is via Mr. Shrewsbury. I have heard now that the mystery behind his mother's death has been solved, he's told certain parties that he's been to see Sherlock Holmes. It would not have been difficult for Lady Ingram to ferret the address from him without disclosing that she wanted it for herself."

A silence fell. Penelope blinked slowly, as if unable to believe what she'd heard. Miss Holmes ate with great solemnity and concentration, giving every appearance of encountering this most familiar dessert for the very first time. Mrs. Watson took sip after sip of water and tried to convince herself that she ought to trust the decision Miss Holmes had already made.

After all, that extraordinary mind was usually allied to a lot of good sense and pragmatism.

"I can't help but feel that we should *not* see Lady Ingram," she heard herself state emphatically. "She is known to us and we are known to her, or at least Miss Holmes is. If hers is a problem she wanted Miss Holmes to know, she would have told Miss Holmes. Instead she chose to put her trust in a stranger. Shouldn't that tell us that she values her anonymity in the matter?

"What if her concern has to do with Lord Ingram? Does the confidence we owe her outweigh our duties of friendship to him? What if we learn something that he would want to, indeed, *deserves* to know? Worse, what if his wife's disclosure should prove detrimental, were he to remain in a state of ignorance?"

Miss Holmes did not deviate from her imperturbable self, but Penelope stared at Mrs. Watson with more than a little concern. Mrs. Watson realized that her voice had risen a good half octave. That instead of giving calmly reasoned objections, she had let herself be carried away on a current of righteous dismay.

For a minute, everyone busied herself eating. Then Miss Holmes set down her spoon.

"By seeking an appointment with Sherlock Holmes, Lady Ingram has already informed me, however unwittingly, that she has a problem. Knowing what I do about her, I have a fair idea of the nature of the problem. Suffice to say that it does not involve Lord Ingram, except in the sense that she is his wife and any problem of hers ought to concern him, too.

"Moreover, by putting her hope in Sherlock Holmes, Lady Ingram makes it clear that she has no one else to turn to. Not at this moment. Not with this problem. If we do not help her, no one will. Purely on a humanitarian basis, it would be cruel to turn her away.

"As for what duties we owe Lord Ingram, since her problem does not relate to him, except peripherally, it would be no moral compromise to keep her confidence." Miss Holmes looked down momentarily. "Lord Ingram is my friend and benefactor. I wish him nothing but success and happiness. But the estranged wife of my friend is not my enemy. If she were a stranger knocking on Sherlock Holmes's door, would she have been denied help in her hour of need?"

Unfortunately, Lady Ingram was no stranger. And by accepting her as a client, they would become interlopers in an already unhappy union. As much as she admired Miss Holmes's principled stance on not abandoning anyone in need, Mrs. Watson could not possibly imagine any scenario in which they ended up doing more good than harm.

But she didn't know how to change Miss Holmes's mind without a draconian invocation of authority: *I finance this operation, therefore my word is law.* She couldn't see herself acting in such a heavy-handed manner, certainly not on the day after the young woman learned that Mrs. Watson had first helped her at Lord Ingram's behest. If anything, Mrs. Watson was keen to reassure her that their partnership — and friendship — was genuine, an expression of mutual respect and affection.

Mrs. Watson sighed.

Miss Holmes must have sensed her capitulation. She picked up her spoon, gathered the last bit of trifle from her bowl, and consumed it with her characteristic mixture of gourmandise and wistfulness.

Now she addressed Penelope. "I trust in Mrs. Watson's discretion. May I count on you also, Miss Redmayne, to refrain from broaching this subject to anyone outside the present company?"

Penelope, to her credit, did not answer immediately. She thought for a while. "I don't believe I've ever made such promises before, but I'm beginning to see now why

Aunt Jo doesn't want me to be too deeply involved in Sherlock Holmes's affairs: Even when there is no actual danger, the matters that are brought to the attention of Upper Baker Street can be ethically challenging."

She thought for a moment longer. "But it seems today I'm destined to play a part and I promise you that nothing I learn will be repeated to anyone outside this room."

"Thank you, Miss Redmayne," said Miss Holmes. "We are ready for Lady Ingram, then."

"Excuse me, miss, but is this yours?"

Livia looked up. A young man stood before her, holding out a book.

The rain had stopped some time ago. The clouds, instead of remaining thick and sulky, had parted. And the young man, framed against freshly rinsed trees and a blue-enough sky, appeared as cheerful as any summer afternoon she had ever known.

Livia didn't mind cheerful people, as long as they didn't tell her to cheer up, which, alas, they did more often than not. And they probably thought her petulant and ungrateful when she didn't seize on the chance to burst out of her shell.

She glanced down at the book he proffered. *The Woman in White*. How odd, she had taken that title from the circulating library two days ago. Had even hauled it to the park, in case the other book she'd brought turned out to be less than engrossing. But her copy was safe in her handbag, wasn't it?

She patted her handbag and it was, well, not empty exactly but most certainly devoid of full-length novels.

"Ah — yes, I believe that is mine. But I've no idea how I lost it."

Surely it should have been in her bag all this time — nothing else seemed to have fled.

"Not a problem at all, miss." The young man handed the book over. "An excellent reading choice, if I may say so."

Livia forgot all about how *The Woman in White* had magically disappeared. "Do you think so, sir?"

She was sure of very few things in life. And one of those few happened to be the types of books she enjoyed, none of which, alas, were the least bit improving. Charlotte could at least defend her choice of reading as encyclopedic; Livia, well, all Livia wanted was a solid stretch of time away from her own life. And she was surrounded by people who disapproved of such transport.

An excellent reading choice were words

that she had never heard spoken in *her* direction, with regard to *her* reading choices.

"Oh, yes." He grinned. His full beard made it difficult to gauge his age — he could be anywhere from twenty-two to thirty-two. The corners of his eyes crinkled but his skin was otherwise smooth and unlined. "I read it a while ago. Sat down and never got up till I was done."

"That sounds promising."

"Of course I sat down at about nine o'clock in the evening, you see, and intended to read only for a short while before bed. But the next thing I knew, it was dawn. And I had to get ready for the day!"

"Oh, dear!"

"I know, but I don't regret it. There's nothing like the pleasure of a book that pulls you in by the lapels and doesn't let go until *The End.* God gives us only one life. But with good books, we can live a hundred, even a thousand lives in the time we are allotted on this earth."

Livia was not prone to feeling such things, but she could kiss the young man for the sentiments he'd so eloquently expressed.

"And what about this one then?" Eagerly she showed him the book in her lap, which she'd only just started. "It's by the same author."

"*Moonstone?* I liked that one, too, but it wouldn't have kept me up all night reading." She must have appeared disappointed, for he held up a finger. "However, a good friend of mine prefers *Moonstone* to *The Woman in White.*"

"Oh, how fortunate that you know someone who enjoys the same books you do. My father only reads history and my sister only things that impart knowledge. I pestered her for a long time to read *Jane Eyre,* and she did, finally, but I don't think she much cared for it."

Charlotte had little use for fiction: She would rather not deal with people altogether if she didn't have to, real or imaginary. Livia, on the other hand, actively preferred literary characters to real-life acquaintances: Tom Sawyer stayed forever young, Viola always retained her spunk, and Mr. Darcy could never turn out to be a hypocrite who was also disappointing in bed.

"Well, *I* thought *Jane Eyre* was splendid," said the young man. "What an indomitable spirit in our Miss Eyre. And it turned out all right for her, too!"

"Precisely. I told my sister she needed to be more grateful that such a book exists. So many novels about women either feature stupid women who make bad choices and then commit suicide when it all goes awry, or subject virtuous women to terrible misfortunes and then, to add insult to injury, have them die of consumption anyway."

He laughed. He had lively brows and warm, dark eyes. "Goodness, I've never thought of it that way, but you are absolutely right."

Livia could only be glad that she was already sitting down — her knees would have buckled otherwise. Nobody, but nobody had ever told her that she was "absolutely right."

About anything.

And the sensation zipping along all her nerve endings — as if she were taking on solidity and existence for the first time, as if until now she had been an apparition, drifting in the shadows, a mere shimmer under the sun.

From the other end of the bench, her mother snorted.

Lady Holmes and Livia had come to the park together. Lady Holmes, her penchant for laudanum tippling more pronounced than ever in the wake of Charlotte's scandal, had quickly slipped into open-jawed slumber, her cheeks slack, her parasol listing hard to the right, like the headsail on a capsized sloop.

Don't wake up. Don't wake up!

Lady Holmes snorted again and drew a few agitated breaths. Then her entire person slumped further. Livia exhaled, relieved to be spared her mother's suspicions, thrilled that she wouldn't drive the young man away with her unpleasantness.

"I mustn't impose any longer, miss," said he, inclining his head. "I hope you enjoy both of Mr. Collins's books. A very good afternoon to you."

THREE

Mrs. Watson was not proud of herself.

She and Lady Ingram had never been introduced, but Mrs. Watson, like Miss Holmes, suspected that Lady Ingram knew of her existence and could recognize her on sight. Therefore, there was no reason for her to be anywhere near 18 Upper Baker Street during Lady Ingram's call.

Especially since she had been the one to protest that they ought to have nothing to do with Lady Ingram's problem.

Yet here she was, exactly where she had no business being, rearranging books on the shelves and plumping cushions that were already plenty plump, while Miss Holmes checked on the camera obscura.

A camera obscura was usually a box with a pinhole at one end that allowed in light, which rendered as a reversed and upside-down image. When that image in a box fell upon light-sensitive material, voilà, photography.

Here "Sherlock's" entire room had been turned into a camera obscura. The wall opposite the door had been painted a thick white, the window fitted with two sets of black shades — in addition to the curtains already in place — to block out all exterior light. The pinhole, an opening the size of a guinea, was set in the center of a round frame that, although made for a picture an inch and a half across, was itself at least six inches wide and so ornate and protuberant that no one ever paid attention to the image it ostensibly displayed.

The frame was one in a group of six, to lessen the chance that it would be noticed. Although Miss Holmes had never been particularly worried about it. She pointed out that their clients already knew they were being observed by someone in the next room, so they could scarcely protest that an unobtrusive method had been devised for said observation.

Penelope was still at the other house, getting ready. Mrs. Watson debated with herself whether to take advantage of her absence and ask a few questions.

Miss Holmes, returning to the parlor, settled the debate for her. "You aren't certain, Mrs. Watson, that I harbor enough goodwill toward Lady Ingram to truly want to help her."

On the evening Mrs. Watson offered Miss Holmes the position of a lady's companion, Miss Holmes had been shocked that the older woman still wished to spend time with her, after Miss Holmes had laid bare not only the facts of Mrs. Watson's life but the most closely held secret of her heart. Miss Holmes had been sure that no one wanted to be around someone who could see through them so transparently.

Belatedly Mrs. Watson realized that since then Miss Holmes had refrained from practicing her powers of deduction on Mrs. Watson. Until this moment.

"Perhaps it would be more accurate to say that I'm not sure *I* harbor enough goodwill toward her for any philanthropic purposes."

Miss Holmes pushed the chair that would be offered to Lady Ingram a few feet farther from the pinhole. "I feel no animosity toward her."

But she is what stands between you and the man you love. Between you and happiness. "I find it difficult to achieve such equanimity. She is the wife of a young man I dearly adore and admire — and she has not made him happy."

"One could also argue that he hasn't made her happy," Miss Holmes said, moving the chair for "Sherlock's" sister a corresponding distance.

Mrs. Watson blinked. There was fairness and there was high-minded fairness, but Miss Holmes's defense of Lady Ingram shot past both and landed directly in false equivalency. "She married him for his money."

"For a woman raised to be purely ornamental, marriage is her livelihood. If Lady Ingram hadn't married for money she would have been a fool."

Mrs. Watson stared at Miss Holmes, who smiled a little. "I do apologize, ma'am. My sister Livia has told me repeatedly how useless I am when she wishes to rail against someone. Instead of echoing her sentiments, I analyze the situation from different perspectives."

Together they shifted the tea table. "So you truly don't despise Lady Ingram?"

Mrs. Watson still found it difficult to believe. Or did Miss Holmes feel guilty toward Lady Ingram, because Miss Holmes was now the object of Lord Ingram's affection?

"For making rational choices for herself? No, I do not despise her. I do not applaud her, but I do not find her decision to marry the richest man interested in her reprehensible."

"Even if —"

The front door downstairs opened: Penelope had arrived for her performance as Sherlock Holmes's sister.

"Even if her rational choice hasn't led to marital felicity for Lord Ingram?" Miss Holmes finished Mrs. Watson's question, as Penelope bounced up the steps. "Let us not forget that he isn't without blame in the matter."

Before Mrs. Watson could protest that Lord Ingram's conduct had always been above reproach, Penelope sauntered into the parlor.

Lady Ingram was slightly older than Miss Holmes.

In fact, Mrs. Watson knew the woman's precise age, as her husband had once given extravagant balls in honor of her birthdays.

He still did: Lord Ingram was not the kind of man to publicly repudiate his wife, by either deliberate gestures or the deliberate absence of certain other gestures.

This year's ball was coming up soon, the last major event of the Season. But Mrs. Watson no longer sent anonymous bouquets in honor of the occasion. Nor did she ask Lord Ingram whether he still gave his wife lavish gifts.

Lady Ingram was still a remarkably good-looking woman. But Mrs. Watson remembered a time when she had been heartbreakingly beautiful, with luminous skin, wide eyes, a perfectly placed beauty mark at the corner of her mouth, and a smile that conveyed just a hint of vulnerability — the sadness of the innocent, upon finding out that the world was a deeply heartless place.

Little wonder that Lord Ingram had been wildly in love with her. He was born a protector and she had aroused every last one of his protective instincts.

She had not aged badly — at mere weeks short of twenty-six she had barely aged at all. But her face had changed: Her lips had become thinner, her complexion chalkier, her jaw squarer and more prominent. And she resembled not so much her older self as a less ravishing sibling.

Or at least upside down she did.

Her inverted image on the wall, almost life-size but not quite, moving, speaking — Mrs. Watson felt as if she were in an uneasy dream.

In the parlor, Penelope was all effusive welcome — the girl was a better actress than

Mrs. Watson had given her credit for. Lady Ingram sat down, rather stiffly, in the seat that had been indicated. That lack of suppleness resulted from the birth of her younger child, a back pain that never completely went away.

"Won't you take some of this pound cake, Mrs. Finch?" Penelope addressed Lady Ingram by her alias. "Very good stuff."

"Thank you, Miss Holmes. I'm quite all right," said their caller.

Her voice, at least, had retained its original loveliness, a sweet contralto with a hint of huskiness.

Some back-and-forth on the weather took place. Then Penelope, her image also upside down, part of her skirt almost invisible against the darkly stained wood of the bedstead, set down her teacup and folded her hands in her lap. "You wrote to this address directly, Mrs. Finch. Should we assume you have already spoken to someone who had dealings with Sherlock?"

"That is correct."

"May I also assume that you know the situation of my brother's health?"

"Yes."

"Would you like some reassurance that despite his physical handicap, his mental perspicacity remains undiminished?"

Their caller hesitated.

Penelope did not wait for her answer. "That is a yes, then."

Hurriedly the ladies-in-hiding pulled up the black window shades and removed the rug that had been pushed up against the bottom of the door to keep out the light that might seep in from the crack. Penelope knocked, and when Mrs. Watson had given a "Come in" in a broad Yorkshire accent, she entered, retrieved a notebook, and returned to the parlor.

Back at her seat, she took a minute to peruse what had been written inside the notebook, which gave Mrs. Watson and Miss Holmes time to again block all light from the room. The images on the wall, of Penelope reading with great concentration and Lady Ingram sipping uncertainly at her tea, gradually returned.

"My brother thanks you for your trust," said Penelope, eventually. "You've come on a delicate matter and he would like to assure you, Mrs. Finch, that every word spoken on these premises will be held in the strictest confidence."

Lady Ingram fidgeted. "Thank you."

"My brother feels it's safe to say that you hail from very respectable stock. But that respectability hasn't always been accompanied by as solid an income. In fact, he hazards that your parents often found themselves in financial straits. But you married well and have known only ease and stability since."

An upside-down Lady Ingram bolted out of her chair, her head sliding past the skirting board to the floor. "Does Mr. Holmes know who I am?"

"Yours is not an unusual reaction to Sherlock's powers of deduction," Penelope answered calmly. "He is able to perceive a great deal based on your attire. Your visiting dress is from the House of Worth — the workmanship is impeccable. A married woman who has a wardrobe from Monsieur Worth has either deep pockets of her own, or very generous pin money from her husband.

"Your dress dates from two seasons ago and has since been altered to keep up with the whims of fashion. Your hat, however, is from this season, Madame Claudette's, also a first-rate establishment. Which tells us that you have not become less well off, but that you are still holding on to thriftier habits you developed in your parents' house, that of modifying garments rather than getting rid of them wholesale at the end of a season."

Lady Ingram sat down slowly. "I see."

"Given your personal frugality, we can assume that you have not come to see Sherlock on a matter concerning money. Were it a problem about your children or your household, you would not have sent a letter without a return address. Clearly you do not wish for anything concerning this matter to reach your residence. That implies a problem that, if it becomes more widely known, could cause embarrassment, at the very least. Possibly much worse.

"Which leaves two possibilities. Either you feel a certain apprehension with regard to your husband or you are here to see Sherlock about a man who is not your husband."

Mrs. Watson's fingers dug into the sides of her chair. Miss Holmes had already said earlier that it wouldn't be about Lord Ingram, which meant . . .

Lady Ingram bit her lower lip. "I'm surprised Mr. Holmes did not name the exact reason I'm here."

"Sherlock wishes only that you should have confidence in his ability, Mrs. Finch, not to tell you why you have come to see him."

Had Mrs. Watson received Lady Ingram and uttered this exact sentence, she would not have been able to prevent her words from dripping with judgment. Penelope, who adored Lord Ingram just as much, somehow managed to sound only reassuring and matter-of-fact.

"Very well then," said Lady Ingram, taking an audible breath. "I have come to consult Mr. Holmes about a man, and that man is not my husband."

Beside Mrs. Watson, Miss Holmes picked up a slice of plum cake and took a bite. Mrs. Watson stared at her. Lady Ingram could potentially reveal information that would give Lord Ingram grounds for divorce. Were he a free man, he could marry Miss Holmes. Yet the latter seemed far more interested in cake.

"As Mr. Holmes inferred, I am advantageously married," said Lady Ingram. "That is the consensus and you will find no disagreement from me on that point. Pedigree, wealth, and good form — my husband possesses them all in abundance.

"But . . . perhaps I should tell you something of my girlhood. Mr. Holmes is again correct here: My parents were in a perilous state of finance. We couldn't afford anything. And yet because of our name, because we were offshoots of an illustrious family, appearances had to be kept at all times.

"I have two younger brothers. For as long

as I can remember, it had been my duty to marry well, so that they would not go through life under the same yoke of penury. But I'd hoped for a miracle. That we would, out of the blue, find ourselves beneficiaries of a generous settlement by some distant relative we'd never heard of. Not because I was a romantic who disdained the idea of marrying for money, but because I was already in love."

Mrs. Watson sucked in a breath. Miss Holmes continued to graze on her plum cake, as if in their parlor sat a little old lady who couldn't find her favorite slippers.

"He was poor — not to mention illegitimate," Lady Ingram went on, her voice turning softer, dreamier. "But he was kind, sweet and sunny in temperament, and appreciative of any drop of good fortune that fell his way. We met when he was an apprentice bookkeeper. His ambition was to be an accountant in London, to be successful enough to comfortably support a wife and a family.

"A simple life, that was all he wanted. And I found it impossibly appealing. Very little in my own life wasn't about pretenses. To give a dinner meant that the rest of the month we subsisted on bread and thin soup. Another piece of my mother's jewelry must become paste before my father can have a new coat. One year we were so short on funds that we hired out our house and lived in a hovel, while telling everyone that we'd taken off for a tour of southern France and Italy.

"I yearned for the honest, uncomplicated life he envisioned for himself. How wonderful it would be to live as ourselves, complete nobodies who wanted only the shelter we found in each other. But of course my parents were apoplectic. My father said he would never be able to hold up his head again if it was known his daughter had married a bastard. My mother was horrified that I would be so selfish as to let my brothers suffer, when I could ensure a far better future for them.

"I was bitter. My beloved was . . . He apologized. He said he'd always known it was a futile dream and he should never have let himself hope, however briefly."

In spite of herself, Mrs. Watson felt a pang of sympathy. She, with her history on the stage, had been an irregular candidate for marriage. But her husband had been the last surviving member of his immediate family. What if his parents had still been living? Would they have been distressed about his choice? What if he'd had siblings who took offense that he would bring such a woman into the fold? It would have made their marriage an agonizing choice — and he had been a man with an independent income, not a young girl trained from birth to defer to the will of her family.

Lady Ingram was silent for some time. "In any case, six months later I was in London for my first Season. Another few months and I was married. Before my wedding, we agreed that after I became another man's wife we would not meet or write to each other. I also told him I would not seek his news, as to do so would be . . . I did not believe my husband would have been pleased to learn that I kept a close eye on the doings of an erstwhile sweetheart.

"But we did settle on something. Each year, on the Sunday before his birthday, at three o'clock in the afternoon, we would both walk by the Albert Memorial. And that would be how we would know that the other person was still alive and still well enough to be up and about."

So much for Mrs. Watson's hope that Lady Ingram would give her husband grounds for a divorce. If this was all Lady Ingram had done, it would take a far more thunderous moralizer than Mrs. Watson to condemn her for her conduct — at least with regard to this "erstwhile sweetheart."

"We followed our agreement strictly. Once a year we passed each other before the memorial, with nothing but a nod." Lady Ingram laced her fingers together. The column of her throat moved. "This year he was not there."

Mrs. Watson's hand came up to her own throat. Miss Holmes nibbled some more at her cake.

"If for some reason one or both of us could not make it, the agreement called for us to put a notice in the *Times*. Every year, in the weeks leading up, I always scan the notices religiously and save the papers, in case I miss something. As soon as I went home that day, I looked through all the papers again. Nothing.

"I had no idea what to do. It has been more than six years since I last spoke to him. I don't know where he lives or what he does for a living. I don't know whether he's still a bachelor or married with children. I've put notices in the papers but have heard nothing. I'm plagued with terrible thoughts, wondering if he is . . . no more, but I can't bring myself to go to the General Register Office to search for a death certificate.

"Of course, the far more likely explanation is that he outgrew a youthful infatuation — in fact, every year I was surprised to see him. But it isn't as if he would fear recriminations on my part, if he were to declare that he no longer wished to see me. In fact, it would be only natural, if he'd met someone else."

"But that he never sent word has you worried," said Penelope.

"It's entirely out of character for him to break a standing appointment in such a brusque manner." Lady Ingram touched the cameo brooch at her throat, as if seeking to draw strength from it. "And then I saw the article about Mr. Holmes in the papers. I'd thought he only consulted on notorious criminal cases. But the article made it plain that he would also help those of us with less sensational problems."

"A problem is a problem. My brother does not turn away clients because their problems fail to meet a threshold of notoriety or sensationalism." Penelope handed Lady Ingram a plate of cake, which the latter meekly accepted. "Now, if I understand you correctly, you would like for us to look into this gentleman's disappearance."

"Yes. I already suspect the worst. So nothing you learn will shock me. But I want to know with some certainty whether he has passed away unexpectedly, whether he has married and no longer wishes to continue our acquaintance, whether he has been imprisoned or sent abroad, et cetera, et cetera."

"To do that we will need to know as much as you can tell us about him," Penelope said decisively. "His name, to start. His last known domicile. Names of employers, landladies, friends. Leave nothing out."

Lady Ingram closed her eyes briefly. "His name is Myron Finch."

The name meant nothing to Mrs. Watson, but Miss Holmes stilled, a slice of plum cake stopping halfway to her lips. In another woman Mrs. Watson might not have noticed such a pause. But for Miss Holmes, this was a sizable — seismic, one might say — reaction.

In the parlor, Lady Ingram poured forth a torrent of ancient information concerning Myron Finch. In the bedroom, Mrs. Watson wrote on a piece of paper, *You know this man, Miss Holmes. Who is he?*

Miss Holmes considered the note. For a long moment Mrs. Watson had the impression that she meant to brush the question aside, but then she uncapped a fountain pen and wrote back.

Mr. Finch is my brother.

FOUR

"I haven't liked her too much," said Miss Redmayne. "But now I feel sorry for her."

Lady Ingram had departed, leaving behind only a whiff of perfume, of the essences of neroli and gardenia.

Mrs. Watson sighed. "Her parents should not have demanded that she marry for money, rather than love."

They were softhearted creatures. Charlotte, on the other hand, was almost as slow to sympathize as she was to condemn. She did not despise Lady Ingram for watching out for herself in the marriage mart, but neither did she think better of the woman after a tale of woe and lament. After all, it didn't change anything she did subsequently.

"I'm sure her parents would have preferred for her to marry for both love and money," she said from the window, watching as Lady Ingram's hired trap pulled away.

"But failing that, money is more reliable than love. Money does not devolve into ennui and regret, as romantic sentiments often do."

"Do you mean to say you *don't* fault her parents?" asked Miss Redmayne.

"Given that marriage presented her sole path to greater wealth and respectability, they acted in the only logical fashion. Had they defied the norm and given her their blessings, they would have been the ones held accountable by everyone, including Lady Ingram herself, should her marriage to Mr. Finch have proven less than successful."

But even if she had married Mr. Finch, would that have made any difference to Lord Ingram?

In those years immediately after he first learned that he was not the late Duke of Wycliffe's fourth son, but the product of an affair between the duchess and one of the country's most prominent bankers, he'd been hell-bent on proving his own respectability. He would still have married *somebody* — nothing made a man as respectable as the possession of wife and children.

So in the end, none of it made any difference to *Charlotte*.

"Miss Holmes, you are the most unromantic soul I have ever met — and I like that," pronounced Miss Redmayne. The next moment she leaped up. "Oh, goodness, look at the time. We are to meet with the de Blois ladies and I haven't even opened the book they gave me for my journey home from Paris. Better take a quick look — in case they ask about it this evening."

She ran off. Mrs. Watson and Charlotte followed, at a more sedate pace, out of 18 Upper Baker Street. They were not dressed for walking, but Charlotte did not protest when Mrs. Watson, instead of going home — a stone's throw from Sherlock Holmes's office — bypassed her own front door and headed for Regent's Park across the street.

Mrs. Watson didn't ask any questions until they stood on the edge of Boating Lake, beside a large weeping willow. "You once mentioned an illegitimate half brother, Miss Holmes. The same Mr. Finch?"

Charlotte reached out and touched a trailing branch. The sun had emerged a while ago, but the finely serrated leaves were still damp from earlier showers. "It is unlikely for there to be more than one illegitimate man named Myron Finch working as an accountant in London."

"You never said why you chose not to seek his aid when you were in desperate straits."

A breeze rippled across the lake. The willow swayed, the motion of its foliage as sinuous as that of a woman shaking out her hair before a lover. "I didn't want to leap from one man's keeping into another's, for one thing. Not to mention . . . I didn't trust that he wouldn't immediately call on my father and tell him where I was."

"Was there a rapport in place between father and son?"

"I do not believe so. But he did send a letter not long after we arrived in London for the Season."

Sir Henry had happened to be away that day. Livia and Charlotte had a standing appointment to ransack his study and read all his letters whenever they had a suitable window of time. Sir Henry and Lady Holmes often chose not to tell their children, or each other, the truth of any given situation. Their two youngest daughters snooped so as not to be kept in the dark.

"In his letter, Mr. Finch expressed gratitude for the support my father had given him over the years. He stated that he was now in the accountancy profession in London, living in quarters befitting a gentleman, with prospects of greater success in the future. He begged for no intimacy and gave no hint that he wished to call on my father or vice versa. But that he'd written at all was shocking, especially to my sister, who did not consider it to be either discreet or seemly.

"I came away with the sense that Mr. Finch was not at all averse to some kind of cordial relationship with my father. And that was the reason I didn't go to him, other than not wanting to burden him and not wanting to burden myself with a possibly meddlesome brother."

Mrs. Watson furrowed her brow — then quickly undid the motion. Charlotte smiled to herself. Mrs. Watson was in no hurry to add to her wrinkle count, even though her husband was long dead and she needed no longer fret about appearing too old next to an eleven-years-younger man.

"Are you worried for him, your brother?" she asked.

Charlotte hesitated. Was she worried? She hadn't thought so, yet the question felt unexpectedly weighty.

"As Lady Ingram said, it's far more likely that he no longer wishes to see her than that he has fallen victim to mishap or misfortune," she answered. "So no, I am not apprehensive on his behalf. But I am beginning to be curious. Very curious."

■ ■ ■ ■

The de Bloises were a pair of students
Penelope had met in medical school. The
elder one, Madame de Blois, had been
widowed by the time she was twenty-one.
Instead of setting her sight on remarriage,
she decided to seek an education. The other,
Mademoiselle de Blois, was Madame de
Blois's late husband's cousin. Inspired by
Madame de Blois's example, she'd followed
the former to medical school.

They were elegant, opinionated, and very
French. Mrs. Watson enjoyed meeting them,
but it was obvious that the young people
wished to enjoy their own company. Madame de Blois promised to act as a stern
chaperone and return Penelope home at a
most appropriate hour; Mrs. Watson and
Miss Holmes bade them good evening and
walked out of the hotel.

Mrs. Watson was about to climb into her
waiting carriage when Miss Holmes said, "I
know a place 'round the corner, a lovely tea
shop that I couldn't afford to go into the
last time I was in the area."

Mrs. Watson glanced at her in surprise.
But it was only half past six, the sun still
high in the sky, and they had no other press-

ing business. "Then let us take our patronage there."

She and Miss Holmes had first met at a tea shop near the General Post Office, an unpretentious place for harried clerks to wolf down a plate of scrambled eggs before they headed home. This St. James's tea shop was a far more sophisticated establishment, reminding Mrs. Watson of the sleek, mirror-walled Parisian patisseries where she and Penelope had indulged in café au lait and slices of apple tart when she'd visited the dear girl the previous autumn.

And it must have a French pastry chef on the premise, for they had similar offerings in large glass cases. Mrs. Watson ordered a small pear tart; Miss Holmes took an entire plate of miniature concoctions.

"Lord Ingram's godfather used to have a patissier in his employ," said Mrs. Watson. "Imagine that. What luxury."

"Oh, I have imagined it many times, ma'am."

Miss Holmes had asked for black tea, for once — to better set off the taste of the pastries, perhaps. Or perhaps because one must pay the penance for all those Parisian *délices* by forgoing any additional sugar and cream.

"Anyway," she continued, "Mr. Finch lives

in a residential hotel on this street."

Mrs. Watson started — and was forcefully reminded that although Miss Holmes might sometimes have her stomach first and foremost on her mind, one should never assume, not even for a second, that it was ever the *only* thing on her mind.

"Did we pass it?"

The area was rich with snuggeries suitable for bachelors with a decent income. Some of those establishments sat cheek by jowl with family hotels such as the one on Jermyn Street that hosted the de Bloises; others were situated on quieter streets, indistinguishable at first glance from private dwellings.

"No, it's at the other end of the street. Black front door, white window trims, white stone and stucco exterior — identical to its neighbors. I'll point it out when we leave."

Their waitress arrived with tea and temptation. "Anything else for you, mum, miss?"

"Thank you for the prompt service," said Miss Holmes, unobtrusively sliding a coin into the waitress's hand. "Have you a minute?"

"Of course, miss."

"We are from Dartmouth and we don't know much about London. But my brother is an architect and says that for a man of his profession, there is no place to be but London. So we are here to look for a nice place for him, with good people nearby, in the hope that he won't fall in with the wrong crowd."

"Ah, you'll want Mrs. Woods's place then," said their waitress. "It's right down the street. I've never been inside, me, but Mrs. Woods — she looks after them there and she's mighty proud of her gentlemen. Old Dr. Vickery comes here from time to time for a bite to eat. Lovely man, he is. He's had first-floor rooms there for years, ever since his wife died. They do your plain cooking and your washing — much easier for a man that way."

"Just down the street, you say?"

"Second from last if you go out that way, on the north side. But you wouldn't know to look at it, that's the kind of superior place it is."

"Oh, this is sounding better and better. How do we apply for a place? Will we be able to speak to this Mrs. Woods and see the establishment for ourselves?"

"That I don't know, miss. I do know you'll have to be lucky to get in. Mrs. Woods doesn't have rooms to let very often. Once she said that her gentlemen only leave when they marry or die — and they don't seem willing to do either!"

They all laughed at that. "Too bad. The place sounds perfect for my brother."

"Oh, don't you worry. There are plenty of good places near here. But Mrs. Woods does run the tightest ship, she does."

"Would you happen to know how much a set of two rooms costs?"

"That would depend. The house isn't divided up all the same. Dr. Vickery's place has three rooms and a private bath and I heard from Mrs. Woods's girls that he pays two pounds eleven a week. Your brother can probably get two rooms on the second floor for half that much."

"That seems reasonable. Have there been any vacancies recently?"

At establishments such as Mrs. Woods's, the bills were usually settled weekly. If Myron Finch had been missing since the previous Sunday — as Lady Ingram believed him to be — by now Mrs. Woods would assume that he had vacated the premises.

"No, I don't believe she's had any vacancies recently."

Did this mean he wasn't missing, or was Mrs. Woods *that* subtle in her advertising methods? "Superior" residences were quieter about their rooms for let, preferring to maintain an air of *not* being available to the public.

The waitress departed to look after other patrons. Mrs. Watson let Miss Holmes have two uninterrupted minutes to enjoy her miniature éclair before suggesting, "You could simply call on him. You are his sister, after all."

"I would rather not publicize my involvement. Most likely something unforeseen has come up. When conditions change and Mr. Finch is once again able to contact Lady Ingram, they might interact to a greater extent than they have in a very long time. I don't want it to come out that Charlotte Holmes visited Myron Finch immediately after Lady Ingram called on Sherlock Holmes. That might be enough for her to put two and two together."

"What will we do, then?"

Miss Holmes considered a tiny, boat-shaped tart filled with a glossy dark mousse, the last remaining delicacy on her plate. "Do you think Mr. Mears might already be back?"

The servants had Sundays off — or in any case, the hours after church. Some employers preferred that they be gone from the house if they weren't rendering actual service. Mrs. Watson gave her staff the freedom to go out and enjoy the city, or to stay in and spend their time reading in bed or socializing in the servants' hall.

Mrs. Watson had met Mr. Mears, her butler, during her days in the theater, and though he had worked more behind the scenes, he had also acted in a number of productions.

By the time they reached home, Mr. Mears had indeed returned from his outing to Kensington Gardens, where he had spent a pleasurable afternoon sketching the fountains at the head of the Long Water.

Together, they decided that he ought to take on the role of Mr. Gillespie, Sir Henry's solicitor, visiting Mr. Finch to inquire whether the latter had heard from his wayward half sister. After a short but intense rehearsal, Mr. Mears, now sporting a pair of wire-rimmed glasses, departed for his command performance, with the understanding that the matter was to be kept strictly confidential.

The drawing room fell quiet. Mrs. Watson felt self-conscious. Earlier, there had been photographs taken of her in various stage costumes on the mantel, the display shelves, and the occasion tables. They had been put up when she realized that Miss Holmes would soon find out where she lived — and that she had better match the realities of her house to its description in the tall tale she'd told the younger woman: that she couldn't find a lady's companion because respectable candidates took one look at those stage photographs and fled.

But of course she'd had to take those down when Penelope returned. Poor girl had never seen most of them — young people had a remarkable lack of interest in the lives of their elders, preferring them to be like the walls of a house: holding up the roof and keeping out the elements, but otherwise completely ignorable.

The absence of the photographs, of course, underscored the fact that Miss Holmes had not been told the truth, from the beginning, about Mrs. Watson's involvement in her life. Had still not been told much of anything, though she had no doubt already deduced every last detail.

Was it possible that she was angry at Lord Ingram? Was that why she had decided to help his wife? Mrs. Watson would never attribute malice to Miss Holmes, but sometimes anger, especially anger of the unacknowledged variety, seeped beneath other decisions. All other decisions.

"A penny for your thoughts, Miss

Holmes," she heard herself say.

Miss Holmes, who had been standing by the window, looking out to the park, turned around halfway. "I was pondering the system of territoriality among street merchants — the division of spots, the length of tenancy, and the rules of succession."

The hawkers? There were always a half dozen of them selling boiled sweets and ginger beer near the entrance to the park. "What I meant is, have you any thoughts on Mr. Mears's chances of success?"

"He is certain to learn something."

"Enough to answer Lady Ingram's query outright?"

"That we will know soon enough."

"What if this case doesn't resolve itself quickly?" Mrs. Watson gave voice to her true fear. "What if we must come face to face with Lord Ingram while still carrying on this investigation, on behalf of his wife, for the whereabouts of the man whose existence is the cause of his marital infelicity?"

"The cause of his marital infelicity was his haste and lack of self-knowledge," said Miss Holmes quietly. "The revelation of his true parentage brought on a paroxysm of self-doubts. Instead of facing it, he opted for marriage and fatherhood, believing they would erase the doubts — highly unlikely that any marriage contracted under such mistaken assumptions would have led to domestic contentment."

Little wonder that as a younger man, Lord Ingram had not courted Miss Holmes. In fact, Mrs. Watson wasn't sure that present-day Lord Ingram would have been able to bear this verdict without flinching.

"But otherwise I understand your concern, ma'am," continued Miss Holmes. "We cannot betray Lady Ingram's confidence. Yet to keep her confidence appears as if we are betraying Lord Ingram. But please understand that, in this case, appearances are merely appearances. Were he to know everything, the situation would still remain what it is. He cannot undo the past, he cannot prevent Lady Ingram from fretting about Mr. Finch, nor can he demand that Mr. Finch leave his wife alone, since that is exactly what the latter is doing, willingly or not."

She turned back to the window. "We might as well leave Lord Ingram out of all consideration and carry on as before."

■ ■ ■ ■

Dear Charlotte,

You must have seen the execrable article in the paper about Sherlock Holmes. My word. The Sackville case is barely solved — thanks to *your* insight and audacity — and they would already pour slop on Sherlock Holmes's good name, because he dares to help ordinary people with problems that perplex *them*?

I would have ripped the paper and thrown the shreds into the fire, had there been a fire lit. Am now determined to make your nom de guerre a hero for the ages, with such invincible, godlike mental acuity that no one would ever dare publish another word about him in disrespect.

The problem, as always, is that it is easier said than done. Not sure how to proceed on my magnum opus, I turned to reading the work of others, in this case, novels by Mr. Wilkie Collins. And the oddest thing happened.

Mamma and I went to take some air in the park. She fell asleep and I opened one of the books to read, only to have a gentleman return the other one to me, which should have remained securely in my handbag.

But never mind that. He had read both of those books. And we had a brief but gratifying conversation on books and reading.

Of course it would be just my luck that when I at last cross paths with a man I would like to know better, he should turn out to be someone I have no hope of ever seeing again. How I wished you had been there. You would have given me his name, address, and genealogy.

And then he could disappoint me at leisure.

Oh well.

I hope it has been an uneventful Sunday for you.

Love,
Livia

Livia dropped her pen back into the inkwell and glanced at the other occupant of the room. Bernadine sat with her back to Livia, her face practically pressed into the far corner of the room, wordlessly spinning small wooden cylinders that had been strung on a string.

It would feel like an insult if Bernadine was capable of it. Or if she hadn't already been sitting in this exact same position when Livia had entered the room.

Bernadine had been almost eighteen when she learned to use a spoon. And she wielded that spoon on food that had already been cut into small pieces with no more grace and accuracy than a two-year-old. But that had been progress for Bernadine, mind-boggling progress.

Three days after Charlotte left, Bernadine had stopped feeding herself, once again needing to be spoon-fed. And Livia, who thought she'd given up on Bernadine long ago, had wept, hard, racking sobs that would not stop, all the despair in her heart condensing into a singular misery.

Charlotte was doing better these days. But Bernadine had yet to recover any lost ground.

Livia glanced at the untouched bowl on a stool next to Bernadine. She glanced at Bernadine, seated on the floor, staring at where the walls joined, barely two feet away from her, and felt a burning desire to be out in the wildest, most sweeping space in all of Britain.

It was going to be a long evening.

FIVE

Mrs. Watson couldn't stop shaking her head.

Miss Holmes had brought up the previous week's papers from the domestic offices in the basement of the house: Newsprint, terrifically useful for all kinds of household purposes, was never thrown away. And it didn't take her long to find and decipher Lady Ingram's messages to Mr. Finch.

M, are you well? Your silence worries me more than your absence. I pray for your health and well-being. A

M, a word is all I need. Let me know you are well and you need say nothing else. A

M, I can neither eat nor sleep. Please do not keep me in ignorance. A

M, my heart still flickers with hope, but the flame thins daily. A

M, am I truly never to hear from you again? A

"These are all the notices?" asked Mrs. Watson, still shaking her head.

Miss Holmes nodded. "The first one appeared on Wednesday and the last in today's paper."

Such an escalation of despair, even as each subsequent message grew shorter and shorter, like an old woman shrinking under the weight of her years.

"I wonder if she held out as long as she could against this need to know exactly what happened," murmured Mrs. Watson. "And perhaps once she gave in, she couldn't stop: The lengthier his silence, the more she needs him to respond."

In recent years, Lady Ingram had always appeared extraordinarily self-possessed, as if her skin were not made of flesh and blood, but an adamantine, unassailable substance. The hurt and desperation in her appeals, however, made Mrs. Watson recall the debutante with a hint of sadness in her eyes.

Love, the saboteur of all defenses.

A soft knock came at the door. Mr. Mears. Mrs. Watson's heart thumped. It was embarrassing how much she needed to know the truth of the matter. And downright shocking how much she wanted to tell Lady Ingram that Mr. Finch had been abed with a broken limb, drifting in and out of a laudanum haze. "Do come in, Mr. Mears. Do you have news for us?"

Mr. Mears had put away the wire-rimmed glasses and removed most of the pomade he'd put into his hair for the role. Now he once again resembled the elfin young man Mrs. Watson had first met, when she herself had been a grass-green girl, overwhelmed by the raucousness and sheer indifference of London.

"I introduced myself to the landlady as solicitor to Mr. Finch's father. She didn't doubt I was who I said I was and was very complimentary to Mr. Finch. She thought him a fine young man, courteous and personable and no trouble at all to his landlady. But according to her, he has gone on holiday — left two days ago and isn't expected to return until Sunday next."

"Holiday? Where?" But that was impossible. "He *isn't* incapacitated?"

"Nothing Mrs. Woods said would indicate that he wasn't in the finest of health and spirits at the time of his departure. She didn't feel herself at liberty to disclose his precise destination but mentioned that he had promised to fetch her a souvenir."

"What about his bills?" asked Miss Holmes, her fingers tented together under her chin.

"He paid up in full before he left — reduced rates of course, since he wouldn't need cooking, washing, or attendance while he was away."

Miss Holmes's brow furrowed, a barely perceptible crease. Mrs. Watson asked a few more questions, but the answers she received were all variations on a theme: No one at Mrs. Woods's saw the least need to be concerned for Mr. Finch's well-being.

Mr. Mears withdrew to enjoy the rest of his Sunday. Mrs. Watson paced the length of the room, utterly befuddled. If Mrs. Woods was correct — and there was no reason she wouldn't be — this meant that Myron Finch had been very much in London Sunday a week ago and could easily have walked by the Albert Memorial for a fleeting glimpse of his beloved. That he had gone about his normal life for several days afterward before gallivanting off to his holiday clearly indicated he was not bothered by the breaking of a long-standing tradition.

"I guess you were right not to worry, Miss Holmes. But this was the last thing I expected."

When Miss Holmes didn't reply immediately, Mrs. Watson chuckled self-consciously. "You'll probably tell me that expectations are squirrelly things — better not to have them."

Miss Holmes rolled a pencil between her palms. Her hands were a little plump and looked remarkably pliant. "I try not to expect people to be who I wish them to be, rather than who they are. But the kind of expectations you speak of, ma'am, deal with probabilities. I have nothing against those. Without them, it'd be difficult to mark anything as out of the ordinary."

"So you agree this is out of the ordinary?"

Miss Holmes spun the pencil between her fingers, a blithe motion. In contrast, her features were drawn, colored not with the bewilderment Mrs. Watson saw on her own face each time she passed the mirror on the wall, but a somberness that verged on disquietude.

Compared to someone like Penelope, whose brows waggled and danced and whose lips stretched into hundreds of exaggeratedly eloquent shapes, Miss Holmes's expression could seem as unchanging and inscrutable as Mona Lisa's. But Mrs. Watson was becoming more skilled at reading the minute deviations.

Earlier in the day Miss Holmes had not been worried about her brother. She had been surprised by the connection between Lady Ingram and Mr. Finch but had viewed the latter's absence as but another quotidian oddity one quick explanation away from being no oddity at all.

But now she had changed her mind.

"Perhaps we should question some of our assumptions," she said.

It took Mrs. Watson a good minute to even see her own assumptions. Her eyes widened. "We assumed that because Lady Ingram has been fervent in her devotion to this young man, he must love her to the same extent. Perhaps he has been showing up yearly more out of pity than passion. Perhaps he has been hoping that Lady Ingram would come to her senses and put a stop to these rendezvous — that way he'd be able to maintain an appearance of having never rebuffed her. But over time it became too great a burden. Instead of informing her he no longer wished to participate, he struck a decisive blow."

Miss Holmes appeared contemplative. "That is certainly one assumption we must now question. I wonder what else we have accepted as given that perhaps we shouldn't."

"Good gracious. Do you think we ought to question whether he loved her at all? She said that her family sought to maintain appearances above all else. It's possible that he was a social climber who didn't realize that her family's financial situation was so precarious. It's again possible that he had maintained this yearly not-quite-contact with her out of a hope that she might stop being so fastidious about the boundaries of marriage and either undertake an affair with him or furnish him with introductions that will allow him into milieus that provide rich targets for a fortune hunter."

Her heart ached for all the ways it could have gone wrong for the former Alexandra Greville. For all the ways things could go wrong for any woman, really.

"Do you suppose, ma'am," said Miss Holmes, "that Mr. Mears's report is sufficient evidence to bring before Lady Ingram?"

Mrs. Watson didn't know whether it was disconcerting or reassuring that Miss Holmes didn't seem to feel any pity for Lady Ingram. "I can tell you right now that Lady Ingram will not accept this account. Even I have trouble accepting it and I've known Mr. Mears for more than thirty years."

Again, only the smallest movement in the muscles of Miss Holmes's face, but Mrs. Watson felt the consulting detective was relieved that the case was not yet at an end. "We will bide our time until Mr. Finch's return then — and see if he truly is as cheerfully unrepentant as his choices suggest."

"A week is an eternity for a woman waiting on news of her lover."

Mrs. Watson saw herself standing on the veranda of her small bungalow in Rawalpindi, after the Battle of Maiwand. It had been a hot day. Waves upon waves of heat and humidity battered her, and yet she'd grown colder with every passing minute.

Miss Holmes studied her, as if she were witnessing the exact same thing. Then she walked to the sideboard, poured a glass of whisky, and brought it to Mrs. Watson. "I'll see what I can learn in the meanwhile."

Livia muttered a curse at herself as she slipped out the back door of the house.

Now she regretted telling Charlotte about the young man from the park. *Now* she wished she hadn't so blithely left the letter in its designated hiding spot for Mott, their groom and coachman, to post when he went about his duties on the morrow. Why hadn't she realized sooner that it was a stupid idea to mention the young man at all, let alone state so plainly — in writing, no less — that she wished she could meet him again? She might as well wish to reconnect with the drop of rain that fell exactly on the tip of her nose and made her laugh when she was ten years old.

And she would have about as much chance of success!

At least it was dark and no one would see her: Lady Holmes was already abed; Sir Henry had gone out again. A narrow lane separated the handkerchief-size gardens behind the houses and the row of stables that held the residents' cattle and carriages. The air was thick with the odors of horse, straw, and horse droppings, topped with an incongruous note of sweetness from a neighbor's profusely blooming honeysuckles.

She knocked on the door of the Holmes stable and prayed that she wouldn't have to pound on it with both fists before Mott would hear. To her surprise, the door opened quickly.

"Is everything all right, Miss Livia?" asked Mott.

He was about thirty years old, a man of dark hair, medium height, and somewhat stocky build. Charlotte once mentioned that she thought him nearsighted, but he had yet to drive a carriage into a lamppost.

Livia squeezed past him. It wouldn't do for her to remain outside the door — she would be that much more easily seen in the light spilling out. "I need my letter back, Mott. You still have it?"

A nonplussed Mott closed the door. "Yes, miss. I'll fetch it."

He climbed up to the loft that served as his lodging, the ladder squeaking with his every step.

The place smelled of leather polish, wheel grease, and ammonia. Livia looked around. She hadn't been in here since shortly after Charlotte ran away, to ask for Mott's help in getting her letters to Charlotte and vice versa. It was as tidy as she remembered. A town coach — hired for the Season — occupied one side. The other side was taken up by four stalls, but only two were occupied, a pair of fidgety bays that were also hired for the Season. Stirrups and coils of ropes hung from large wooden pegs; an array of brushes, scrapers, and homemade pastes lined an uneven-looking shelf.

Mott came back down the ladder, her letter clasped between his lips.

"Thank you," she said, when he handed her the letter. And then, without much hope, she added, "Have you spoken to my father about staying on with us?"

Mott, like the carriage and the horses, was hired only for the Season: Appearances must be maintained, and someone had to drive Lady Holmes and her daughters about town. At home in the country, they shared a gardener-groom with their nearest neighbor and drove themselves.

Normally Livia did not inquire into prospects of continued employment for members of the staff. Her parents were not easy or kind and she had become inured to the coming and going of servants. But Mott had been truly helpful this summer.

And he didn't seem to dislike her, which made him rather extraordinary in her eyes, since most people didn't care for her particular kind of high-strung self-consciousness. Still, it had been an act of desperation on her part, asking him to speak with Sir Henry about his chances of remaining with the Holmeses beyond the Season. But he was now her only ally and she didn't want to rusticate in the country for nine months without a single person she could count on.

"He ain't been in a proper mood lately," said Mott.

Livia couldn't disagree with that assessment.

One would think her father would be thrilled to be cleared of all suspicions with regard to the death of his erstwhile fiancée, with whom he had been heard to argue in the hours shortly before her sudden demise. And to learn that it was his good fortune to have been jilted by Lady Amelia Drummond after all, as the Sackville affair had shown her ladyship to have been of singularly questionable character and judgment.

But no, Sir Henry had been furious instead.

According to Charlotte, he felt outraged that a woman of such inferior moral fiber had rejected him. And he was further incensed that as she was already six feet underground, he couldn't possibly berate her as she deserved.

As a result, there had not been an opportune moment for Mott to approach Sir Henry.

Nor was he very likely to find one before the end of the Season.

"Well, don't give up hope," said Livia, more for her own benefit than his.

Mott opened the door for her. "I shan't, Miss Livia."

Lord Ingram met his wife on the stairs — he was headed up to the nursery to say good night to his children, and she had just come from there.

"My lady," he said, keeping his voice free of inflections.

She nodded coolly. "My lord."

Over the years they had come to a domestic arrangement that enabled them to spend as much time apart as possible, while still ostensibly living as man and wife. They took their meals separately, simple enough when she had her morning cocoa in bed and he availed himself of luncheons at his clubs. And during the Season it was particularly easy to avoid each other at dinner: Whether they dined out or hosted dinner parties at home, it was Society's unspoken rule that such occasions were not for chitchat between husband and wife, but socializing with others.

With regard to the children, too, they had come to an unspoken agreement: He breakfasted with them on weekdays and took them out Sunday afternoons; she lunched with them on weekdays and had the nursery to herself Sunday evenings.

She would have tucked the children in bed just now — had she managed the feat five minutes sooner, as she usually did, they would not have run into each other. Come to think of it, she had also been late coming back home this afternoon. He didn't mind spending more time with his children, but it was uncharacteristic of her to be less than punctual.

She descended past him, her steps impatient.

"Did you use the typewriter in the study, by the way?"

He did not say *my typewriter* or *my study*. But she must have heard something to that effect. She turned around. "Would you like me not to, in the future?"

"You are at perfect liberty to avail yourself of anything in this house. I was only curious — you do not ordinarily require a typewriter."

"Sometimes I wish for my correspondence to be typewritten," she said, her tone civil but distant.

He wasn't sure what had led him to ask the question in the first place. Something about his wife felt different of late. Charlotte Holmes would be able to tell him exactly what constituted that disparity; he, not blessed with Sherlockian faculties of observation, had to rely on his gut, which didn't tell him how or why, but only that he should pay attention.

Was it possible she was having an affair? He had yet to betray his marriage vows; he didn't think she had either. Not to mention that for a while now, he'd had the impression that romantic entanglement was the last thing she was after.

But did it behoove him to be more watchful, in case she gave him grounds for divorce? Would he actually put those grounds to use? Was he hardened enough to tear his children from their mother, who, despite her flaws as a wife, had always been a caring parent?

And if he was never going to divorce her, what would he gain by finding out whether she might be having an affair?

"I wish you a good evening, Lady Ingram," he said.

Charlotte walked into her room, shut the door, and leaned back against it, a hand over her face.

It had been a long, strange day, from Lord Bancroft's proposal to Mr. Finch's non-disappearance. And to think, only a little more than twenty-four hours ago, she had kissed Lord Ingram. Very briefly, to be sure, but the first time in more than a decade, a moment of stark, all-engrossing heat.

Events were easy to deal with. Emotional responses, less so. They were not crisp or factual. They mutated at will. They expanded to fill all available space in one's consciousness and left no room for anything else.

And no clarity with which to think.

The situation with Mr. Finch was too incongruous to be normal. But between Lady Ingram's anguish, Mrs. Watson's distress, and her own discomfort with having Lady Ingram as a client, Charlotte couldn't pin down exactly what was bothering her.

It was as if she were trying to listen to someone timidly tapping out a message in Morse code on the window, in the midst of a hailstorm.

She pushed away from the door. The dossier from Lord Bancroft lay on her bed. She pulled out the next envelope.

A cipher: a page of uppercase letters with no breaks.

The clue informed her that it was a Vigenère cipher. Vigenère ciphers had been in use for centuries but were first solved only a generation ago. Mr. Charles Babbage, who managed the groundbreaking feat, did not publish his methods. But Charlotte, with a mind in search of use and a great deal of time, had made Livia compose several Vigenère ciphers, so she could learn how to decode them on her own.

And what she learned was that solving Vigenère ciphers was an experience best compared to being kicked in the head by a distempered mule. Repeatedly — because not only was it brain-crackingly difficult, but the long, drawn-out process could not be made shorter or less tedious.

Lord Bancroft believed *this* to be the kind of mental exertion that would give her pleasure?

To be fair, before she knew exactly what solving Vigenère ciphers entailed, she had thought so, too.

At least now she knew that Lord Bancroft had instructed his underling to select difficult cases for her — and that most certainly counted as a point in his favor.

A Caesar cipher, despite its majestic name, was a simple one, in which each letter of the plaintext was replaced by another letter a fixed number of positions up or down the alphabet. In a Caesar cipher with a right shift of 2, for example, A was replaced by C, B by D, and so on.

The Vigenère cipher incorporated the principle of Caesar ciphers. First, Charlotte constructed a *tabula recta,* a twenty-six-by-twenty-six square that represented all possible letter-to-letter substitution schemes.

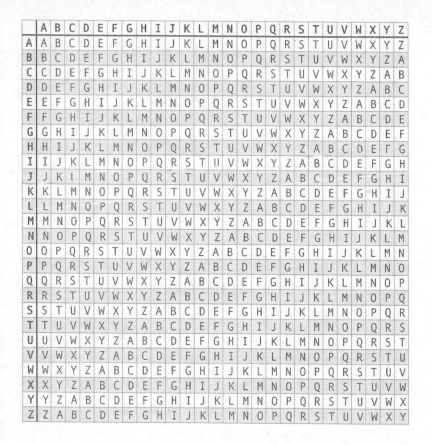

	A	B	C	D	E	F	G	H	I	J	K	L	M	N	O	P	Q	R	S	T	U	V	W	X	Y	Z
A	A	B	C	D	E	F	G	H	I	J	K	L	M	N	O	P	Q	R	S	T	U	V	W	X	Y	Z
B	B	C	D	E	F	G	H	I	J	K	L	M	N	O	P	Q	R	S	T	U	V	W	X	Y	Z	A
C	C	D	E	F	G	H	I	J	K	L	M	N	O	P	Q	R	S	T	U	V	W	X	Y	Z	A	B
D	D	E	F	G	H	I	J	K	L	M	N	O	P	Q	R	S	T	U	V	W	X	Y	Z	A	B	C
E	E	F	G	H	I	J	K	L	M	N	O	P	Q	R	S	T	U	V	W	X	Y	Z	A	B	C	D
F	F	G	H	I	J	K	L	M	N	O	P	Q	R	S	T	U	V	W	X	Y	Z	A	B	C	D	E
G	G	H	I	J	K	L	M	N	O	P	Q	R	S	T	U	V	W	X	Y	Z	A	B	C	D	E	F
H	H	I	J	K	L	M	N	O	P	Q	R	S	T	U	V	W	X	Y	Z	A	B	C	D	E	F	G
I	I	J	K	L	M	N	O	P	Q	R	S	T	U	V	W	X	Y	Z	A	B	C	D	E	F	G	H
J	J	K	L	M	N	O	P	Q	R	S	T	U	V	W	X	Y	Z	A	B	C	D	E	F	G	H	I
K	K	L	M	N	O	P	Q	R	S	T	U	V	W	X	Y	Z	A	B	C	D	E	F	G	H	I	J
L	L	M	N	O	P	Q	R	S	T	U	V	W	X	Y	Z	A	B	C	D	E	F	G	H	I	J	K
M	M	N	O	P	Q	R	S	T	U	V	W	X	Y	Z	A	B	C	D	E	F	G	H	I	J	K	L
N	N	O	P	Q	R	S	T	U	V	W	X	Y	Z	A	B	C	D	E	F	G	H	I	J	K	L	M
O	O	P	Q	R	S	T	U	V	W	X	Y	Z	A	B	C	D	E	F	G	H	I	J	K	L	M	N
P	P	Q	R	S	T	U	V	W	X	Y	Z	A	B	C	D	E	F	G	H	I	J	K	L	M	N	O
Q	Q	R	S	T	U	V	W	X	Y	Z	A	B	C	D	E	F	G	H	I	J	K	L	M	N	O	P
R	R	S	T	U	V	W	X	Y	Z	A	B	C	D	E	F	G	H	I	J	K	L	M	N	O	P	Q
S	S	T	U	V	W	X	Y	Z	A	B	C	D	E	F	G	H	I	J	K	L	M	N	O	P	Q	R
T	T	U	V	W	X	Y	Z	A	B	C	D	E	F	G	H	I	J	K	L	M	N	O	P	Q	R	S
U	U	V	W	X	Y	Z	A	B	C	D	E	F	G	H	I	J	K	L	M	N	O	P	Q	R	S	T
V	V	W	X	Y	Z	A	B	C	D	E	F	G	H	I	J	K	L	M	N	O	P	Q	R	S	T	U
W	W	X	Y	Z	A	B	C	D	E	F	G	H	I	J	K	L	M	N	O	P	Q	R	S	T	U	V
X	X	Y	Z	A	B	C	D	E	F	G	H	I	J	K	L	M	N	O	P	Q	R	S	T	U	V	W
Y	Y	Z	A	B	C	D	E	F	G	H	I	J	K	L	M	N	O	P	Q	R	S	T	U	V	W	X
Z	Z	A	B	C	D	E	F	G	H	I	J	K	L	M	N	O	P	Q	R	S	T	U	V	W	X	Y

If she were writing the cipher, this would be the point at which she chose a keyword.

To encode the sentence CHARLOTTE IS SHERLOCK, with the keyword HOLMES, she would write the following:

CHARLOTTEISSHERLOCK
HOLMESHOLMESHOLMESH

In coding the first letter C, one consulted column C, row H of the tabula recta. The next letter was to be found at the intersection of column H, row O. The process was repeated as many times as there were letters in the original message. In the end, the cipher text would read:

JVLDPGAHPUWKOSCXSUR

But since someone else had chosen the keyword for this cipher, Charlotte must first find out what it was. She examined the huddle of letters that formed the cipher text, looked for repeated sequences, and counted the number of letters between each iteration of the same sequence — to help determine the length of the keyword.

By the stroke of midnight, her temples throbbed. Mr. Babbage, in fact, had turned down the opportunity to decipher King Charles I's coded letters — probably because his head still ached from the Vigenère ciphers.

She rose and walked to the window. Almost immediately she saw Lord Ingram in her mind's eye. Winter, two months after his wedding, at a house party in the country. She had come upon him outside, on a snow- and mistletoe-draped terrace. He had been smoking, his head tilted back, blowing a leisurely stream of smoke into the air.

His eyes had been closed — and he had

smiled at the overcast sky. At what he believed to be a benevolent universe.

"Hullo, Holmes," he said, his shoulders relaxed, his eyes still closed, and a trace of smile still on his lips. "Aren't you going to ask me how I knew it was you?"

"You'd tell me because no one else would stand here without saying anything."

He laughed and opened his eyes. "It's you all right, Holmes." He took a drag on the cigarette. "You look different. Have you lost weight?"

She had. "No," she said. "You look happy. Marriage must agree with you."

"It does indeed." He was magnanimous in his happiness, refraining from reminding her that she had warned him against this particular match. "You should give it a try."

He and his wife had come back only a few days ago from their honeymoon, their return more than a fortnight late. They had arrived at the house party in the afternoon but had not made an appearance at dinner. Lady Ingram was said to be a little under the weather.

Charlotte felt as if she had been harpooned. "You're going to be a father, aren't you?"

Present-day Charlotte turned away from the window.

It was the most joyous she had ever seen him. She'd never trusted that joy, but to look back, knowing exactly how false its foundation had been, how ephemeral its soap-bubble brightness . . .

She marched back to the desk and re-immersed herself, almost gratefully, in the mind-pulverizing tedium of the Vigenère cipher.

SIX

Monday

Livia didn't mind music. But she would enjoy a soiree musicale much better if she could dance — or read. Dancing, however, was not to be had, and reading would be profoundly frowned upon. So she had no choice but to listen, bored, irritated, and worried — her usual state of mind — as the soprano warbled on.

When the broad Italian woman hit another glass-scratching high note, Livia simply had to get out. She had taken care to sit in the back of the drawing room, at the edge of a row of chairs. Her mother glared at her as she rose. Livia headed toward the cloakroom — she didn't need to use it, but Lady Holmes would be less likely to follow if she believed Livia had gone to answer a call of nature.

When she was far enough from the drawing room, she leaned against a half pillar in the passage. Whose house was she in? Oh, what did it matter? The Season was drawing to a close. Soon London would empty, and Livia would take part in the exodus.

Usually, by this point in July, despite the disappointment of having once again failed to secure a husband, she would be more than ready to return to the country, so as not to be obliged to constantly smile, nod, and make pleasant conversation, in a futile quest to prove herself worthy of that holy grail, matrimony.

But this time Charlotte would not be coming with her. This time she would truly be all alone.

At the sound of approaching footsteps, she straightened hastily. A woman turned the corner from the direction of the cloakroom. Lady Ingram. She had arrived late to the soiree, after the first piano recital had already begun. But the hostess had been overjoyed to see her and had hovered about her for an indecent length of time.

Lady Ingram appeared equally startled to run into Livia. "Miss Holmes."

"Lady Ingram."

They had rarely spoken to each other before. Lady Ingram surrounded herself with women who were as cool and sophisticated as she. And the power of their combined beauty and influence was such that Livia was afraid to go near. She was invisible enough as it was without placing herself in the shadows cast by such luminosity. And she was also proud enough not to want to be seen as a hanger-on, someone who would never be accepted into the group but was allowed to exist at its periphery, a barnacle on an otherwise sleek ocean liner.

There was a moment of awkward silence. Then Lady Ingram said, with a small smile, "I don't know about you, Miss Holmes, but I, too, prefer singing that doesn't threaten to pierce my eardrums."

Livia was astonished. This woman was almost . . . approachable. Who was she? "And here I thought I gave a convincing impression of someone who needed to visit the cloakroom."

Lady Ingram laughed softly, not with ridicule but with understanding. For some reason Livia couldn't shake the impression that there was something else to her expression. A weariness, perhaps.

Fatigue.

"Are you well, Miss Holmes?"

The question arrived so unexpectedly; Livia felt almost . . . ambushed. "Ah, I am — tolerably well. You, my lady?"

"Also tolerably well, I suppose." Was that

an ironic curve to Lady Ingram's lips? "And Miss Charlotte, have you any news of her?"

Since Charlotte had run away, other than ladies Avery and Somersby, Society's leading gossips, no one had brought her up in front of Livia. Her parents might argue about Charlotte with each other, but they didn't involve Livia in those discussions. Even Lord Ingram, Charlotte's most trusted friend, had refrained from speaking her name, the one time he had called on Livia, shortly after Charlotte had made her escape. Livia had been the one to do so, feeling as if she'd broken a cardinal law.

But now Lady Ingram asked about Charlotte. Without malice. And conversationally, as if Charlotte had gone on a trip to Amazonia, rather than fallen through the floor of ignominy.

Lady Ingram, of all people.

Charlotte, being Charlotte, had no particular feelings toward Lady Ingram. Lady Ingram, on the other hand, had always been less than friendly to Charlotte. It was Livia's belief that in the days of antiquity, Lord Ingram had rather relished those displays of frostiness on the part of his future wife. But Lady Ingram had never warmed up to Charlotte, not after she had secured Lord Ingram's hand in marriage, not even after their estrangement. In fact, her coolness toward Charlotte had become even more pronounced after everyone learned that she had married her husband solely for his inheritance. This Livia had never understood: Why this antagonism toward his friend when she didn't even want his love?

Perhaps Lady Ingram had at last realized that Charlotte had never been a threat to her position. Perhaps that Charlotte had been ruined by a different man gave her a better sense of Lord Ingram's propriety of conduct all these years. Or perhaps Charlotte's downfall had been so extreme, her fate so unknown — at least to the general public — that even Lady Ingram was moved to a measure of pity and concern.

"I'm — I'm afraid not," said Livia, belatedly realizing she still hadn't answered. "We've had no news of her."

"And that's the worst, isn't it, the waiting?"

Livia was taken aback to see Lady Ingram's throat move, as if she weren't merely being polite, but was recalling — or even experiencing — her own agony at the disappearance of a loved one. At being left behind to drown in uncertainty and despair.

"You are right about that, ma'am."

Lady Ingram smiled. "If you'll excuse me,

Miss Holmes, I believe I'm needed at home."

Long after they had parted company, Livia still saw Lady Ingram in her mind's eye, her smile full of regret and desolation.

Tuesday
Charlotte rubbed her eyes.

Livia was the night owl in the family, able to stay up for forty-eight hours at a stretch and need only a brief nap before she was good as new again. She also skipped meals without feeling the effects of an empty stomach. Charlotte, on the other hand, adhered to a rigorous schedule: She needed to be fed 'round the clock and enjoyed her sleep almost as much as she enjoyed her food.

Therefore, Charlotte was not accustomed to scraping along on four hours of sleep. But that was all she'd had the past two nights thanks to the onerous Vigenère cipher from Lord Bancroft's dossier.

But better that than lying in bed thinking about Lord Ingram, Lady Ingram, and Mr. Finch. Not to mention Lord Bancroft's proposal.

She rubbed her eyes again. She must look lively. Sherlock Holmes's next client was already here. The parlor door opened and

Mrs. Watson ushered in Mrs. Morris.

Mrs. Morris, according to her letter, was married to a naval captain currently at sea. In his absence she had decamped to London to look after her aging father.

The aging father had been a physician in his prime: The handbag Mrs. Morris carried was larger and sturdier than the usual ladies' accessory and would have served capably as a doctor's bag in its former life. In fact, it must have been a doctor's bag very recently — it was new enough to have been acquired within the past year.

So the good doctor had retired not long ago — and since he wouldn't have invested in a new bag knowing he was quitting the practice, the retirement must have been a somewhat abrupt decision.

As Mrs. Morris set down the rain-flecked bag, Charlotte noticed that she wasn't wearing a wedding ring. Nor did her ring finger show the telltale mark left by a ring that had recently been taken off for cleaning.

"Mrs. Morris to see you, miss," said Mrs. Watson.

Charlotte shook hands with the woman, who was in her midthirties, pretty in an anemic fashion, her demeanor eager but brittle.

The usual pantomime ensued. Tea was offered. Mrs. Watson left to sit with "Sherlock Holmes." This was usually the point at which Charlotte asked her clients whether they needed proof of Sherlock's deductive powers. But to Mrs. Morris she wasn't sure whether she ought to mention anything she had observed.

Regulations to the contrary, for as long as there had been a navy, the wives of naval officers — not all of them, but the more intrepid ones — had gone on tours of duty with their husbands. And if Mrs. Morris didn't care for life as one of a handful of women sharing cramped quarters with an overwhelmingly male population, she could always travel to ports of call where her husband would be spending considerable amounts of time ashore.

But Charlotte wasn't convinced that Captain Morris was in fact at sea.

Or that Mrs. Morris was staying with her father solely because she wished to look after the latter.

She had arrived on foot. But the debris clinging to the soles and edges of her boots made it clear that she hadn't been slogging through the streets of London. Rather, she had taken a walk in Regent's Park. A vigorous one, too, judging by the grimy streaks on the inside of her boots, which could only have been made by herself.

It was not pouring outside — that had happened during the small hours of the night, while Charlotte was still bent over the Vigenère cipher. But it was drizzling and had been for a while. Would a woman who thought this a good day for a brisk walk in the park shy away from traveling the world with her husband?

More importantly, she was wearing her second-best pair of Wellington boots.

If one didn't count the pair Henrietta had left behind when she got married, Charlotte didn't have galoshes — not even in the country, as she preferred to enjoy rainy days from inside a firmly shut window, with a cup of hot cocoa by her side.

Livia, however, lived in her Wellington boots. And she had a second-best pair, which were ancient and used when she was certain she'd face plenty of sludge on her walk. As opposed to her best pair, donned when she suspected she might encounter, but still had hopes of avoiding, muddy puddles.

Even Livia brought only her best pair to London.

Would a woman who was only visiting bring her second-best pair?

"You mentioned in your letter, Mrs. Morris, that you learned about my brother from Mrs. Gleason, who came to see him not too long ago."

"That's right. Mrs. Gleason and I belong to the same charity knitting circle and she had nothing but high praise for you. So yesterday, when I couldn't possibly go another moment without speaking to someone about my fears, I thought of you. Thank you for seeing me so soon."

They could scarcely make her wait, when she wrote that she was afraid for her health, and possibly even her life.

"Not at all. Given that you've spoken to Mrs. Gleason, I assume you are familiar with how I help my brother in his work."

"Yes. Mrs. Gleason's account gave me every confidence in Mr. Holmes."

"Excellent, now how may we help you?"

"I believe I told you that when my husband is at sea, I stay in London with my father," began Mrs. Morris. "London is a livelier place, of course, but I also promised my mother, before she passed away, that I would always look after my father. Her own father, you see, retired at sixty and promptly went into a decline.

"My father was a very successful physician. He and his old housekeeper, dear Mrs. Foster, retired at about the same time. The new housekeeper, Mrs. Burns, came highly recommended. And I can't complain about her work. But —" Mrs. Morris twisted her handkerchief. "But with my father home so much, I'm afraid, well, I'm afraid it has led to designs on Mrs. Burns's part."

"Oh?"

That simple prompt seemed to provoke a fit of uncertainty. Mrs. Morris reddened, swallowed, and twisted her handkerchief some more. "I hope Mr. Holmes doesn't think me ridiculous. After all, even as great a mind as his can't prevent Mrs. Burns from wooing my father. But that isn't all she is doing. I've reason to believe she's trying to poison me."

Charlotte had more or less expected such an account: To someone in Mrs. Morris's position, danger was more likely to arise from inside her own household.

"What brought on this particular concern?" she asked.

"I know I don't look it, but I'm in exceedingly robust health — everyone will tell you that. I never have the sniffles, never need smelling salts, never have any aches and pains at all. My father says that I can eat rocks and horseshoes without being the worse off. But this week I felt awful twice, both times after eating biscuits made by

Mrs. Burns. And no one else in the house was the least bit unwell."

Charlotte poured herself another cup of tea. "Please describe the circumstances of each occasion."

"The first time was five days ago. I came home from calling on some acquaintances and took coffee with my father. A housemaid brought the biscuits. I handed the plate to my father; he took his pick and I took mine. We spoke for some time about our day. I didn't eat the biscuit until we were almost about to rise from the table. By the time I reached my room, ten minutes later, I was in agony."

"What were your symptoms?"

"My throat burned. And I don't mean that it was scratchy. The whole of the back of my mouth felt as if it had been flayed raw with a rough rope. I hurt so much I could scarcely breathe."

"How long did your symptoms persist?"

"An eternity. Though the clock insisted it wasn't more than two hours."

"And what did your father think?"

"He was at loss for an explanation. I didn't run a fever, didn't have enlarged lymph nodes, didn't exhibit other aches and pains or any gastrointestinal symptoms. I was fine before and I was fine after: I ate well, I moved well, and I slept well.

"He consulted his books for half a day but in the end wondered if I wasn't simply reacting to London. He said that in his practice he came across men and women who suffered from headache, shortness of breath, and general malaise. If he couldn't find any pathological explanation for their unwellness, he encouraged them to spend some time in the country, where air and water are both less polluted. More often than not, they improved.

"I was skeptical and pointed out that I'd been in London for two months. Shouldn't I have reacted to it sooner? He said the effects could be cumulative — that sometimes people who have lived in London for decades find that they suddenly can't tolerate the city anymore.

"So we discussed the matter — at length, I would say. But I didn't worry. After all, I was probably overdue for some kind of unwellness. But when it happened again, just as inexplicably, I grew afraid that someone in the house might be conspiring against me."

"When did it happen again?"

"The night before last. Mrs. Burns usually lays out biscuits and coffee at about quarter to ten. I had the exact same symptoms as I got into bed and spent a horrible few hours clutching at my throat, my poor father by my side. At breakfast we were discussing it again when Mrs. Burns came into the room. And I swear to you, Miss Holmes, I swear that she refused to meet my eyes."

Mrs. Watson didn't have a housekeeper, so Madame Gascoigne, her cook, made cakes and biscuits for the household. Today her contribution was a plate of thin, crispy, saddle-shaped almond biscuits — *tuiles,* she'd called them, which must be French for *exceedingly delicious.* Charlotte picked up another one. "Why do you think Mrs. Burns has designs on your father, Mrs. Morris?"

"Almost as soon as I arrived for my visit, I felt her hostility toward me. I am friendly by nature and got along well with my father's old housekeeper. Mrs. Burns, on the other hand, has been curt whenever I try to engage her in conversation."

Mrs. Morris paused to eat a *tuile.* "I asked my father what he thought of her demeanor and he said he found her perfectly agreeable. Now, Miss Holmes, you must understand, I have been raised not to make unreasonable demands of the staff. I don't know whether you've noticed my boots —

they are not my best pair. My father would consider it imposing on the staff if I wore my best pair knowing that they would get muddy, and then handed them over to a maid, expecting them to be made spotless again.

"Since my arrival in London, I have folded myself into the routines of my father's house and made sure to cause minimal disruption. So Mrs. Burns has no good reason to dislike me, and yet she clearly does. Is it not natural to assume, then, that she sees my presence as an obstacle?

"I also learned from my father that she wasn't always a woman of the serving class. Her own father was a doctor, too, but he died from drink and in debt. Again, is it not natural to assume that she would want to raise herself back to the station she had once enjoyed? And to remember that she would have some familiarity with poisons and such?"

Charlotte nodded slowly, but it was only to buy time to eat the *tuile* in her hand before she went on with her questioning. Not sleeping enough made her hungrier.

"What kind of biscuits did Mrs. Burns serve, Mrs. Morris? And were they the same both times?"

"They were dessert biscuits both times."

"And your father didn't suffer either time?"

"My father likes currants in his biscuits. I despise them. Mrs. Burns makes two batches of the same biscuits, one with currants, one without. We never eat each other's biscuits. Besides, it would defeat Mrs. Burns's purpose if she accidentally killed him, wouldn't it?"

Charlotte adored currants. After all, plum cake, that great English misnomer, was characterized by the addition of half a pound of currants for every pound of flour. Livia, however, was in complete agreement with Mrs. Morris where currants were concerned.

"Have you spoken to your father about your suspicions?"

Mrs. Morris sighed. "It would be no use. He would think me unkind for having such thoughts. In fact, once, when I pointed out that Mrs. Burns might have her cap set on him — jokingly, of course — he was sincerely baffled. To him Mrs. Burns was everything a woman in her position ought to be. He couldn't remotely conceive that she might be strategizing to become the lady of the house one of these days."

"I see. I assume you brought the rest of the biscuits, Mrs. Morris?"

"I did — I saved them. I understand Mr. Holmes was able to deduce, in the Sackville case, that something else had been substituted for strychnine. Will he be able to tell if any noxious substance had been added in these biscuits?"

Charlotte had bought a few chemistry sets in her time, but she was no trained chemical analyst. That didn't mean Sherlock Holmes couldn't be — clearly, Mrs. Morris already believed him to be proficient in that capacity.

"It will reflect in our fees but it can be done."

"Thank you," said Mrs. Morris, sagging with relief. "I can't thank you enough."

"In the meanwhile," said Charlotte, "I trust you won't eat any more biscuits at home."

"Have no fear. I will not touch *anything* served in that house."

Mrs. Watson returned to escort Mrs. Morris out — and to assess fees in the ground-floor room that had been turned into a small office. As they headed down the stairs, Charlotte stuck her head out of the parlor.

"Do excuse me, Mrs. Morris. My brother has a question for you."

"Yes?"

"Are you prone to seasickness?"

Mrs. Morris blinked. "No, not at all. I enjoy ocean voyages."

"Thank you," said Charlotte, and closed the door.

In the days immediately preceding their departure for the country, both Sir Henry and Lady Holmes made a number of appointments with tailors, milliners, modistes, haberdashers, and conveyers of other fine goods. They always regretted their splurges upon receipt of the accounts. But an entire Season surrounded by their wealthier peers and all the luxuries that poured into the heart of an empire never failed to eradicate memories of past regret.

This ill-considered frenzy of acquisition usually depressed Livia: another year without a proposal, another year closer to irreversible spinsterhood, and here were her parents, squandering the money that could be used to put a roof over Livia's head in her old age, nudging her another step closer to that cabbage-eating, dingy boardinghouse-dwelling future that loomed ever over an unwanted woman without any means of support.

But at least today it meant that she, too, could be out of the house, browsing the shelves at Hatchards, dreaming of a collection of her own, so many books that the entire house would smell of leather, paper, and binding.

"Excuse me, miss, but is this yours?"

Livia spun around. Good heavens, it really was him, the young man from the park the other day, except he wasn't holding anything out toward her.

He grinned, his brown eyes warm and crinkled at the corners. "Already looking for more books? Have you finished those two Collins novels?"

"Yes, I have, as a matter of fact."

"And do you agree with me or my friend on their merits?"

"Your friend, most certainly. *Moonstone* is superior to *The Woman in White.*"

"No!" After that cry of mock horror, his smile was back in full force. "In that case, we must read something else in common and see if our opinions converge better the next time around."

Her heart thudded. Was he implying that she *would* see him again? "Have you any titles to recommend? I intend to read more books along the lines of *Moonstone* and *The Woman in White.*"

"There is a German book from a while ago, *Das Fräulein von Scuderi.* Very dramatic stuff. There are also some stories by Mr.

Poe, the American."

"Oh, please don't recommend 'The Murders in the Rue Morgue.' "

"Never! Not the blasted orangutan. I was angry for days afterward."

"Me, too!" concurred Livia wholeheartedly. "My sister had to listen to endless grumbling on my part. And if Mr. Poe weren't already dead, I'd have written him a strongly worded letter — and paid for the transatlantic postage to make my displeasure known."

He laughed. To her disbelief, Livia found herself laughing with him, unabashed glee coursing through her veins. Dear God, it felt good to finally speak to someone who understood the affront that was the blasted orangutan.

Their laughter subsided. For a moment, neither of them said anything. Then he asked, "If I may be so forward, miss, what inspired your interest in this genre of stories?"

Because she had nothing to lose, she told him the truth. "I hope to write a similar story, but better, of course."

"Please do! Will you divulge a thing or two of the plot?"

"Well, I want it to be a revenge story. A spate of mysterious deaths, a genius who

143

strides in to untangle the web, and then, the revelation of a terrible wrong from decades ago, now avenged."

He gasped. "You mean, a variation on the Sackville case, with the involvement of that man. Now why can't I remember his name?"

"Holmes."

"Yes, Sherlock Holmes. You must write it. I will be the first one in line to buy a copy."

Charlotte had said she believed Livia could write such a story. But Charlotte never voluntarily touched fiction. This young man, however, was a connoisseur. And he wanted to read her — as of yet non-existent — work.

"And will you stay up all night reading?" she heard herself ask.

He gazed at her. "Not likely. I will finish reading by bedtime, so I will most likely go to sleep wishing I could read it again for the first time."

She swallowed. She must be red; her face, her throat, and even her ears felt scalding hot.

He gazed at her another moment, then bowed and left.

Livia trudged up the stairs to her room, closed the door, and flopped down on the bed.

After her first meeting with the still-nameless young man, she had felt a secret excitement — ruthlessly tamped down, of course, exemplified by her midnight jaunt to retrieve the letter about him from Mott. Nevertheless, that excitement had lingered, as if she already knew, somehow, that she would run into him again.

But now she was only dejected, convinced that they had exhausted their lifetime allotment of chance encounters.

Why hadn't she introduced herself? Well, because she had been taught from birth that it wasn't proper to meet anyone, men or women, but especially men, except via a trusted mutual acquaintance who could vouch for everyone involved. She'd never minded the stricture before because she didn't enjoy meeting people. But now her unthinking obedience had robbed her of any chance she might have at . . .

At what?

She stared at the ceiling and cursed under her breath. And then, louder. The house was silent. Her parents hadn't returned yet. She could hear footsteps and some soft, muffled words from Bernadine's room — one of the maids must be trying to coax her to eat.

Livia rubbed her face. Why did she do this? Why let her imagination run away on the merest hint of anything? A man spoke to her for two minutes and she was ready to rip London apart to present him with a proposal of marriage.

It was not going to happen. None of it was going to happen. She needed to forget her fanciful conjectures, get up, and check on Bernadine. But the thought of facing Bernadine's own kind of despondency only made her wish she could sink deeper into the mattress.

The door to her room creaked. Charlotte entered in a striking white day dress with purple polka dots on the bodice and purple stripes down the sleeves, a peaked straw hat trimmed with a matching purple plume in her hand.

Livia sighed — she hated for Charlotte to see her like this.

The next moment she bolted upright. "Charlotte! What are you — wait, that was *you* with Bernadine? You can't stay! Mamma and Papa will be back soon."

"I'll leave in a minute."

Charlotte glanced around the room in her usual unhurried manner, before she looked back at Livia with a steady, attentive gaze.

No one would ever label Charlotte tender or loving, and yet Livia had always been at ease with her little sister. She used to believe it was because Charlotte was so peculiar that she herself felt normal. But she'd been dead wrong.

Charlotte knew everything about Livia — and Charlotte did not want Livia to be anything other than who she was. And Livia had not realized how much she needed it until she met the young man and was reminded of what it felt like to be accepted.

"Are you all right, Livia?" Charlotte asked quietly.

Tears, out of nowhere, prickled the back of Livia's eyes. She wasn't all right. She hadn't been all right. And she didn't know if she would ever be all right for any sustained period of time.

"I manage," she said. No point elaborating — Charlotte already knew the truth.

"And Bernadine, has she been like that since I left?"

"Some days."

Livia wasn't lying. Some days she couldn't bring herself to go into Bernadine's room.

Charlotte nodded — and did not immediately say anything else.

Her silence. How Livia missed the companionship of that soft, calm silence. And perhaps this was where she reciprocated Charlotte's acceptance: She never demanded that Charlotte speak but always waited for it, trusting that when Charlotte had something to say, she would.

Which she did, presently. "You haven't written since we saw each other on Saturday."

"I've been reading — to study how other people write stories with plots involving strange and mysterious events."

Charlotte nodded again, walked to the window, and looked out.

Livia's alarm returned. "Anyone coming back?"

"Not yet." Charlotte turned around. "I take it you don't wish to tell me about the man."

Every muscle in Livia's body seized, yet she felt as if her arms and legs were flopping wildly, uncontrollably. "I haven't been introduced to any man."

Which was God's truth, even if it was far from the whole truth.

"No, you haven't," said Charlotte.

Silence again, but not such a soft, calm silence anymore. Livia had no idea what to do. Should she lie? Should she confess? Or should she continue to stare at Charlotte, saying nothing?

Charlotte sat down on the windowsill, the same one she had occupied the night of her scandal, immediately before she told Livia that she would be running away from home. "Actually, I came to ask you for a favor."

"Wh— I mean, *of course.* Anything."

Anything to get the subject away from the man to whom Livia had not been introduced.

"It's about Lady Ingram."

"Wouldn't you know it, I met her last night at the soiree musicale Mamma dragged me to. I couldn't believe it, but she was very decent to me — said she understood exactly how much I wanted to escape all that yodeling. She even asked about you."

Was this effusive enough an answer for Charlotte to forget what they were talking about before?

"She did?"

Charlotte didn't raise a brow or the volume of her voice, but Livia thought she heard a note of surprise.

"Yes, rather nonchalantly, too. None of that look-all-around-then-lean-in-and-whisper business."

Charlotte didn't speak for a minute, as if needing time to digest this unexpected nugget of intelligence. "What do you think of Lady Ingram?"

Livia shook her head. "Women of her kind make me nervous — they are so sure of themselves. I don't know that I ever think

149

about them so much as I pray they don't think badly of me."

It took only a passing glance from someone like Lady Ingram for Livia to be acutely conscious of her shortcomings. Or it could be said that she was already acutely conscious of her shortcomings and that a whiff of disdain from any quarter, real or imagined, heated that general anxiety to a froth of self-scorn.

"What I meant was, do you believe she ever loved Lord Ingram?"

What an odd question from Charlotte, who had never commented on that marriage. Had rarely brought up Lord Ingram in conversation, in fact, despite their long-standing friendship. Sometimes Livia wondered about the two, but it was usually to speculate on whether Lord Ingram might be secretly in love with Charlotte: She was fully prepared to accept that Charlotte had never felt the slightest twinge of romance in her twenty-five years on earth.

"I don't know that Lady Ingram ever loved her husband, but I do remember thinking that she seemed awfully pleased with the match. Not to an unseemly degree, mind you, but still. I envied her that happiness."

"Our envy always lasts longer than the

happiness of those we envy."

"Oh, I'm not entirely sure about that. Her happiness lasted a good long while — at least it seemed so to me."

Charlotte cocked her head to one side. "What if it was all a pretense?"

"It was, wasn't it? She only married him for his inheritance."

"No, I mean, what if that happiness was all a pretense? What if she'd never been happy to marry him, even in the beginning?"

"Why are you interested in Lady Ingram, all of a sudden?"

Charlotte glanced out of the window again. "I'm going to tell you something that I learned recently, but you can't say anything to anyone else."

"You know I have no bosom bows eager to receive gossip from me. But very well, I won't tell anyone. What is it?"

"I have heard that before she made her debut, Lady Ingram had been in love with someone else. Someone unsuitable."

Livia sucked in a breath — and was almost sad she didn't have a group of lady friends before whom she could dangle this juicy tidbit. "How unsuitable?"

"As unsuitable as our brother would have been."

"We don't have a —" They did have a brother. Charlotte had found that out. But it was one of those things that Livia tried to forget: She knew the kind of man her father was, but before such tangible evidence, she still felt as if she'd been punched in the kidney. "Who told you that?"

"I'm not at liberty to reveal that right now. I understand that ladies Avery and Somersby still seek you out to ask for my news. If you see them again, will you please ask whether they know anything of Lady Ingram's romantic past? Subtly, of course."

"Of course."

"Thank you." Charlotte came forward and squeezed Livia's hand. "I must leave now. But don't forget, I'll look after you — and Bernadine."

After she was gone, Livia stared at the door for a good long while.

She wanted to believe that Charlotte could fulfill that promise, but everything stood in the way.

Everything.

Charlotte had seen the burned letter the moment she walked into Livia's room.

The problem with her parents treating their servants with scant respect or consideration was that the servants returned the favor by doing as little work as possible. In better households, even during warmer months, when no fires were laid, the grates would be swept out daily. But not so in the Holmes residence.

And so the carbonized remains of Livia's letter had stayed in place, the original curled mass having since crumbled from gravity, small ash-edged bits blown about the grate from the daily airing of the room.

What had she written about? Their parents? Bernadine? Charlotte failed to see any reason why concerns about either should give Livia such pause as to destroy the letter altogether. And Livia's despondency had felt both newer and keener than her usual gloom.

So it was something that affected her personally, something that upon reflection she couldn't, after all, bring herself to tell Charlotte.

Livia's reaction had confirmed Charlotte's hypothesis. That Livia should have met a man who piqued her interest — well, it was what she was in London to do. The problem lay in what she'd said.

I haven't been introduced to any man.

Society was structured to prevent young ladies from meeting men who hadn't been first approved by those around them. It was not a watertight system, but by and large it did what it was supposed to do. Charlotte, while she retained her respectability, had never conversed with a man who hadn't been vouched for by a known third party.

And as far as she knew, neither had Livia.

So where had this man come from? And what did he want?

From her parents' hired house, Charlotte made her way to the laboratory of London's best chemical analyst and delivered Mrs. Morris's biscuits. That afternoon, she met another client at 18 Upper Baker Street. The rest of the day she again devoted herself to the odious Vigenère cipher. It was past one o'clock in the morning before she held in her hand the completed table of distances and could conclude with confidence that the keyword was five letters long, given that the vast majority of the distances between repeated sequences of letters had been multiples of five.

There was little satisfaction in the discovery. Her eyes felt gritty, her head light — as if she'd been drinking. But she had no intention of stopping, even though she needed to get up the next day for work.

The unsettling sensation in her stomach about Mr. Finch's nondisappearance. The pointed guilt she felt toward Lord Ingram. The pressure to marry Lord Bancroft that had, all of a sudden, reached a crushing point. Livia was not well. And Bernadine, Bernadine had regressed to an appalling degree. Charlotte had but to say one word and everything would improve drastically.

One word.

She bent her head to her notebook and began the next step in the deciphering.

SEVEN

Thursday

Penelope let herself into the house, humming bits and pieces of remembered tunes.

A light was on in the afternoon parlor. Was Aunt Jo waiting up for her, after all? Penelope had told her not to do so: After the performance, she and her friends would repair to the de Blois ladies' hotel and enjoy a late repast.

The clock on the wall told her that it was two minutes past midnight. Yes, she was late, but two minutes was a negligible amount of time, under the circumstances.

She poked her head into the afternoon parlor, except it wasn't her aunt who sat there, but someone with a loose blond braid and a cream dressing gown heavily embroidered with poppies and buttercups.

"Miss Holmes, you are up late."

Miss Holmes turned around. "Miss Redmayne, did you enjoy *Mikado*?"

156

"I did. I think Mademoiselle de Blois enjoyed it even more, though. She was afraid her English wouldn't be good enough to understand everything, so she purchased a copy of the libretto ahead of time. I was worried that might ruin the fun, but she loved it."

"Always surprising, isn't it, what people enjoy?"

"But you never appear to be surprised at all."

"It's my face — takes rather a great deal of feeling to move it. Shock, rather than surprise. And while I'm frequently surprised, I'm not usually shocked."

Now Penelope was curious. She had no idea Miss Holmes could be shocked. "So what does shock you?"

Miss Holmes thought for a moment. "I'm surprised when people are not me. I'm shocked when they are not them."

"You mean, we are so much who we are that it's staggering when we do something truly out of character."

"Yes. Normally when people are shocked by someone, it's because they didn't know that person sufficiently well. We are asked to judge one another on such things as parentage, attire, and demeanor, as substitutes for character. So we know others primarily by how they present themselves in public, which is often the furthest thing from who they are."

Penelope opted to be cheeky. "So when you ran away from home, the only people knocked speechless were those who'd had no idea who you truly were."

Miss Holmes did not appear at all offended. "Exactly. And those who had every idea of my character were no less dismayed, but probably thought — seethingly — *Stupid woman. I knew this would happen.*"

"Lord Ingram. Would he have thought that?"

Her aunt would be appalled at her forwardness. But Penelope had long ago decided that while the meek might inherit the earth, the nonmeek enjoyed far more interesting conversations — to say the least.

Miss Holmes's lips curved. "I'd be shocked to the core if he didn't."

"Speaking of Lord Ingram . . ." Penelope walked up to the desk and tapped her fingers on the paper. "Is Lady Ingram still sending coded messages to Mr. Finch?"

Miss Holmes flipped the open notebook on the desk a few pages back, then nudged it toward Penelope. "I keep track of all the coded messages among the small notices. These are hers."

The top of the page gave the construct of the cipher: *Numbers 1–26 correspond to letters. Resultant letters need to be left-shifted seven places in the alphabet.* Below that, each day's coded message had been copied down and deciphered.

M, I still await your answer. A

M, I will not give up. A

M, please give me a signal. A

M, are you all right? A

"What's in the rest of the notebook?" Penelope asked. "The other coded messages?"

Miss Holmes nodded. "So I'll know when a new one comes up — in case Mr. Finch responds."

"That must have taken a great deal of work."

"It consumed some time, especially in the beginning. But the codes tend to be unimaginative."

The latest edition of the paper was on the desk, opened to the small notices, which had been carefully marked. The majority of them were not in code and almost all of those had a small dot next to them, likely indicating that no further investigation was warranted. One coded message had the letter A next to it — from Lady Ingram, presumably. Most of the other coded messages had small squares to the side, which probably marked that they were "unimaginative."

Three notices, however, were unusual enough to merit question marks. "What's unusual about this one?"

"The plaintext of the cipher is in German. It may not mean anything — but it's different from the others, so I keep an eye on it."

The second listed five different kinds of flowers. "And this one?"

"My guess is it's code for which horses to bet on."

The third notice was also in plaintext. *And many among them shall stumble, and fall, and be broken, and be snared, and be taken.* "Is that an actual biblical verse?"

"Isaiah 8:15."

"You know that from memory?"

Miss Holmes shook her head. "I consulted a reference book that indexed all the verses in the Bible."

"And why is the verse in the paper in the first place? Did the fire-and-brimstone crowd pay for it?"

"I can't say."

Penelope went to the sideboard and poured herself a glass of soda water from the gasogene. "Now I wish I'd paid closer attention to the notice columns. So much eccentricity and clandestineness in that space."

"My sister Livia has long been a devotee. She was the one who first taught me about substitution ciphers. But she doesn't have the patience for more complicated codes."

"Patience is an overrated virtue. It's much more fun to have what you want now — especially since there is no guarantee that a longer wait will produce better results."

Miss Holmes was quiet for some time. "Do you see Lady Ingram as the patient kind?"

"No. Well, I didn't, in any case. But I suppose she has proved herself extraordinarily patient, at least in one sense. An entire year's wait for one fleeting look? That is downright painful."

Penelope took a sip of her soda water — she liked how the bubbles tickled the roof of her mouth. "Although it could be said that her arrangement was dictated by circumstances, rather than temperament. Still, if it were me, I might have grabbed Mr. Finch by the lapels when he passed by and compelled him to give me his address and whatnot."

"I meant," said Miss Holmes softly, "do you think Lady Ingram will wait calmly and uncomplainingly while Sherlock Holmes works?"

Penelope laughed ruefully. "Ah, that. Well, I don't see it. She is posting daily notices in the papers, even as Sherlock Holmes works."

"In her position I would, too. The papers have far greater reach, empirically, than does Sherlock Holmes, whose only advantage is that he is obliged to report his findings, unlike Mr. Finch, who can ignore the notices until the presses run out of ink." Miss Holmes carefully folded the paper. "But this makes me wonder. How does Lady Ingram manage all these notices? Surely she can't be going every day to the papers."

"She can do it easily via cable. Text and money can both be wired."

"But that would still require her to make daily trips to the post office. A woman like her attracts attention. She can't keep going to the same post office, and she can't use the locations most convenient to her — her code isn't difficult to break and she would hardly want word to get out that she's sending desperate pleas via the papers."

"She can send her personal maid," suggested Penelope. "She must have one."

The lady's maid enjoyed a closer rapport with her mistress than most of the other servants, given that her services were of such a personal nature. And since she typically did not follow the lady around on her calls or errands — that was the purview of the pair of footmen matched in height, for the households that could afford them — she could act with a far greater degree of anonymity.

"The lady's maid she had when she first married had served Lord Ingram's mother for many years," pointed out Miss Holmes.

"Hmm, that would present difficulties, if the maid feels greater loyalty to him than to her."

"Then again, I don't know whether she still has the same maid. It was years ago. But in any case, does Lady Ingram strike you as the kind to trust a servant with matters that are so personal?"

Penelope drained her glass. "Not really. But we've learned, haven't we, that we don't really know her, which makes it difficult to say what would be in character for her, and what wouldn't be."

"You are right," said Miss Holmes slowly. "At this moment we can't say anything with certainty."

Saturday

The table of distances was, in fact, the easier part of the deciphering. Once Charlotte settled on the length of the keyword — five letters, in this case — she still had to test each of the five positions. To test a given position, she started with T, the most commonly used letter in the English language. Working backward from that, she decoded every fifth letter in the cipher text, then recorded all the letters and their frequencies, to see whether they conformed to the relative ratio of letter usage for the English language.

It wasn't easy in theory and it was ten times more troublesome in practice, as this particular piece of text had noticeably fewer O's than she would have expected, skewing the general proportions.

But in the end she managed. The keyword was TRUTH. After punctuation had been inserted, the deciphered text read:

MUCH THAT REMAINED IN THE AN-
CIENT VALLEY HAD BEEN RANSACKED
BY RAIDERS IN LATER CENTURIES.
THE RUINS WERE A SAD SIGHT, DE-
CREPITUDE SANS GRANDEUR, AN IN-

SIPID PAST THAT INSPIRED LITTLE BEYOND A GLOOMY SIGH. WE WERE GLAD AS WE DEPARTED, LEAVING BEHIND MOUNDS OF RUBBLE AND THAT GENERAL AIR OF MOURNFUL-NESS. ONWARD! LUCKY FOR US, OUR NEXT DESTINATION, A THOUSAND YARDS EASTWARD AS THE HAWK FLIES, WAS AS MAGNIFICENT AS THIS ONE WAS INFERIOR. THE GRANITE EDIFICE MUST HAVE BEEN A PALACE IN ITS HEYDAY AND THE TREASURES WITHIN MUST HAVE BEEN ASTONISH-ING. MY FRIEND, PRAY EXCUSE MY BREVITY. LET ME DIG INSTEAD AND WRITE AGAIN WHEN I HAVE UN-EARTHED ARTEFACTS AND OTHER ARCHAIC GEMS.

Her work matched with the answer that had been provided. But since no background information had been given, she had no idea what she was looking at. She could only hope there had been actual "archaic gems" involved, their worth in thousands of pounds. Otherwise the work involved in the encoding would have been a pure waste, a manifestation of paranoia rather than any true need for secrecy.

She would have liked to take a nap — it

was only eleven o'clock in the morning but she felt as if she had been awake for more than forty-eight hours. The de Blois ladies, however, had arrived for a call. Twenty minutes later, Charlotte, Mrs. Watson, Miss Redmayne, and their visitors were out in Regent's Park for a promenade, taking advantage of clear air and bright sky after several days of intermittent drizzle.

Mrs. Watson cast fretful glances in her direction once in a while. Charlotte had kept to her room a great deal, even taken her suppers there once or twice. And when she did appear for meals, she had been happy to let Miss Redmayne take charge of the conversation, and spoke rarely unless first spoken to.

Mrs. Watson no doubt believed she had been preoccupied by thoughts of her half brother's disappearance, Lord Ingram's marriage, and the connection between the two. Certainly, from her perspective, it should be difficult for anyone to think of anything else.

But at the moment Charlotte wasn't thinking of those things at all.

The decoded text of the Vigenère cipher. Something about it compelled her to examine it more closely. This minute.

"If you will excuse me, ladies. There is

something I must attend to." She barely remembered to shake Madame and Mademoiselle de Blois's hands, before pivoting around for Mrs. Watson's house.

In her room, she took out the deciphered text again. What was it that kept scratching at the back of her head? Ah yes, the words *as the hawk flies.* If the author wished to convey that the place was a thousand yards distant in a straight line, then why not say *as the arrow flies*? Or *as the crow flies,* since hawks wheeled and circled, but crows were said to take the shortest path?

Not to mention, no one measured distances in thousands of yards.

The noticeable lack of O's came to mind — instead of constituting around seven point five percent of the letters, the O's in this passage accounted for just under three percent. What if *hawk* had been selected because the writer of the message hadn't wished to put a word that contained the letter O at that particular point in the passage?

She picked up a pen and underlined all sixteen of the O's. They seemed most heavily clustered around the middle of the passage. But if there was a significance to the pattern of their distribution, it wasn't obvious. She stared at the passage for several more minutes, then took a blank sheet of paper and copied the text, but this time all in lowercase.

Sometimes a different perspective helped. Not this time.

She tried various methods — it wasn't as easy to hide a hidden message in plaintext, but it could be done. She examined the cross bars on the t's and the dots on the i's to see whether they formed legible Morse code. They didn't. She looked at the punctuation marks she had added and varied them to see if they signaled anything. They signaled nothing.

She got up and walked about the room. When that failed to trigger any fresh perspective, she went down to the kitchen. Madame Gascoigne was pulling a batch of madeleines from the oven — a treat for the ladies when they returned from their walk.

Charlotte absconded with half a dozen of the madeleines. She sat down at her desk and examined the plaintext message again, stuffing the first still-hot madeleine into her mouth. As the little cake disappeared into her stomach, her brain suddenly . . . sprouted.

Of course. Now she saw the error of her ways. She had been so consumed by the Vigenère cipher that she — horrors — hadn't been eating properly. A quick glance at the mirror told her that she was down to only one point three chins. No wonder her brain was so slow and unwieldy, like a steam engine on the last shovel of coal.

Two more madeleines and she felt like a new woman.

The O's. What if they weren't letters? What if they were instead numbers?

Zeroes.

And if they were zeroes, that would make the I's or the L's ones.

According to her notes, I's were over-represented, acceptable given that the other vowels must compensate for the shortage of O's. But L's, like O's, were underrepresented. And when she thought about the distance measured in thousands of yards . . . What if the cipher writer had been trying to avoid more reasonable units such as miles or furlongs, which would have put an L where it did not belong?

She made a fresh copy of the plaintext and underlined all the L's and the O's.

Much that remained in the ancient val_l_ey had _been ransacked by raiders in _later centuries. The ruins were a sad sight, decrepitude sans grandeur, an insipid past that inspired _litt_le bey_o_nd a g_loo_my sigh.

We were glad as we departed, leaving behind the mounds of rubble and that general air of mournfulness. Onward! Lucky for us, our next destination, a thousand yards eastward as the hawk flies, was as magnificent as this one was inferior. The granite edifice must have been a palace in its heyday and the treasures within must have been astonishing. My friend, pray excuse my brevity. Let me dig instead and write again when I have unearthed artefacts and other archaic gems.

The L's and O's, once converted into ones and zeroes, respectively, made a string of numbers thirty-one digits long: 1111101001100110010100001001010
She translated it into Morse code, dashes for ones and dots for zeroes. But no matter how she parsed the resultant sequence of dots and dashes, they refused to make any sense. And if they, too, were a code, then she didn't have a long enough sequence for decoding.

Deciphering, a science and art only for those with no fear of ending up in any number of blind alleys.

She nibbled on the next madeleine, hoping this wouldn't turn out to be a six-madeleine problem, because she had hopes of stowing away the last two for a late-night snack. But what else was she to do with a passel of ones and zeroes?

She stopped midchew. Ones and zeroes, when used in a binary system, could convey other numbers. The calculation might be a bit tricky. To convert a thirty-one-digit binary number, she would need to calculate powers of two up to the thirtieth, which promised to be a sizable number. Nevertheless, it would be much, much easier than cracking a Vigenère code — orders of magnitude easier.

But what purpose would the resultant number serve?

She could take out any passage from any book or newspaper, underline the L's and the O's, turn them into ones and zeroes, and arrive at a binary number.

Her gaze went around the room and landed on an item she had recently bought, a well-made object at once beautiful and very, very useful.

Hmm. She might just know what to do if she had *two* numbers.

EIGHT

As Lord Ingram Ashburton's hansom cab approached Mrs. Watson's house, his attention was ensnared by the middle-aged nanny pushing a perambulator.

A nanny out and about in these parts was a perfectly common sight. Mrs. Watson's house faced a large, verdant park. At any point during the day there could be nurses, nannies, and governesses taking their charges for some fresh air. The thing was, he was almost entirely sure that this particular nanny had been selling cigarettes and boutonnieres two days ago, when he last passed before the house — but did not, in the end, choose to ring the doorbell.

He didn't ring this time either.

Before his vehicle had come to a full stop, Charlotte Holmes, clad in a burgundy-and-cream-striped dress, stepped out of the front door, a cream parasol in one gloved hand, a burgundy handbag in the other, the whole ensemble capped off by a toque festooned with jaunty burgundy feathers.

On another woman, this would have been dramatic. On Holmes, it passed for austere — he was far more accustomed to seeing her in sartorial concoctions that featured endless yards of laces, fringes, *and* ruffles, a mobile ribbon stand of a woman.

"May I offer you the use of a conveyance, miss?" he said.

She couldn't possibly have been expecting him, but judging by her perfectly composed expression, one would have had reason to conclude that he stopped before Mrs. Watson's house at this hour every day to present the use of a for-hire carriage. "Thank you, sir. You may indeed."

To the cabbie she said, "Portman Square, please."

Lord Ingram raised a brow. Bancroft kept a house near Portman Square. No one lived there except for a small staff, as the house served more as a meeting place than a residence, except to provide an occasional refuge for Bancroft's shadowy regiment of intelligence gatherers who needed a padded chair for an afternoon or a bed for the night.

"You have business to conduct, Holmes?" he asked once she had settled down next to him.

The rules of Society being what they were, he and Holmes rarely found themselves alone and in physical proximity. A hansom cab could theoretically hold three stick-thin individuals, but as she had never been stick thin, the spread of her skirt touched his trousers, provoking unmistakable sensations up and down his nerve endings.

"I may have business to conduct, depending on whether I locate the necessary resources. Or it may turn out to be nothing."

He glanced out the window. The woman with the perambulator was gesturing at a hackney for hire that had been parked at the edge of the street. The hackney turned itself around and was now fifty feet behind them.

Holmes must have noticed his preoccupation but asked no questions. Indeed, why ask questions when she could draw her own, frequently more accurate conclusions at a glance.

He had never told her how unnerving it was to be so transparent before another, especially someone who was, most of the time, as opaque as a brick wall.

The nearest intersections to Mrs. Watson's house were in the shape of elongated X's: The roads in the vicinity met at haphazard angles. To turn south and head in the direction of Portman Square, the cab would round one of those ship's-prow-shaped junctions, which would put them out of sight of the hackney for half a minute or so.

Lord Ingram instructed the cabbie not to make the turn on Upper Baker Street — that would put them too close to Sherlock Holmes's address, which might be watched, too. The cabbie drove a little farther west and coaxed his mare left. The moment they were shielded from view of the other carriage, Lord Ingram tapped his walking stick against the top of the cab. "We are getting down here."

He tossed the cabbie a coin. "Head for Piccadilly."

Streets approaching one another at acute angles meant that town houses along their lengths also met like two sides of a wedge, with only a narrow opening for the carriage lane. They slipped into the carriage lane and were immediately hidden by houses that faced the street.

He allowed them to emerge once he was certain the hackney had passed, still following the now-decoy hansom cab. They walked to the intersection, hailed the next vehicle for hire, and made for the house near Portman Square.

The vehicle happened to be another hansom cab, when he would have wished for the larger hackney. Holmes did not wear perfume, but up close, she emanated an almost imperceptible aroma of cinnamon and butter, so faint that he could never be entirely sure he wasn't imagining it.

"That probably wasn't someone following you," said Holmes, patting her forehead with a lacy handkerchief. "You wouldn't lead such a person to Mrs. Watson's front door. Was the house watched then?"

He told her about the nanny who had, forty-eight hours earlier, been a seller of boutonnieres and cigarettes.

"A great many individuals have been interested in my movements since I left my parents' house," she mused, her demeanor unconcerned. "Didn't you once tell me that Bancroft sometimes had his underlings followed by other underlings, to test their general alertness?"

He sucked in a breath. "Have you become an official underling to Bancroft?"

She gazed out of the window, her attention seemingly caught by the wares of a hawker who sold boiled sweets. "Not yet, but he would like me to be. You must know that he proposed."

He did know, as a matter of fact. It was

the reason he'd wished to call on her, to gauge the likelihood that she would become his sister-in-law. A ghastly possibility, but one for which he blamed himself: He still believed that he could have stopped her scandal from erupting in the first place, even though the exact measures he could have taken remained somewhat elusive.

"You're considering the proposal," he said.

He had never known her to reject a proposal reflexively. She always thought seriously about each, then declined just as seriously.

"I'm working through the inducements Bancroft offered." She retrieved an envelope from her handbag. "One of which happens to be a Vigenère cipher."

A *Vigenère* cipher? Sending Holmes a Vigenère cipher was akin to gifting her a cubic yard of cake — just because she enjoyed a slice a day didn't mean she wanted to eat only that for days on end.

On the other hand, Bancroft could not have better signaled his respect for her abilities.

She passed him a piece of paper. By habit he glanced behind himself — there was no window between them and the cabbie perched on the back of the hansom cab. And the enclosure that protected the passengers from the elements was more than enough to prevent eavesdropping — which was before one took into account the general din of the city in the middle of the day.

"Do you recognize this passage?"

He read the vaguely archaeological paragraph. "Never seen it before."

"It's possible that the plaintext, too, contains a code." She handed him another piece of paper, this time with all the L's and O's underlined. "If they stand for ones and zeroes, they can represent a binary number."

Instead of looking at the paper, his gaze remained on her a moment too long. It was all too easy, at times, to believe that she never felt anything, that inside her rib cage beat not a heart but the metronomic device of an automaton. But this was not one of those times. Today she gave off clear signals of a hunter on the prowl, quietly excited about her quarry.

She tapped her finger on the sheet of paper, directing his attention where it ought to go. "If I separate the text into two paragraphs at the most reasonable point, I end up with two binary numbers. When I convert them into denary numbers, these are what I get."

512818 and 2122.

"You'll have to tell me their significance."

"I would add a zero to the beginning of the second number."

A zero at the *beginning of* the second number? But one could add a string of zeroes before any given number and not change a —

"You mean like this?" He took out a pen and made some changes.

51'28'18
0'21'22

Latitude and longitude.

She smiled. He blinked. She was around sixteen or seventeen when she learned to smile for company, but she never took the trouble for him.

A fortunate thing.

Once, he'd commented on the high number of marriage proposals she had received in the course of eight London Seasons. She had replied, only half jokingly, that all the credit lay with her bosom. He, on the other hand, was of the opinion that gentlemen, while heartily appreciative of her fine décolletage, were actually besotted by something else: her quality of concentration.

When Holmes gave her attention, she gave with such thoroughness, as if no one else mattered, as if no one else *existed*. The poor sod might realize, much too late, that she now knew his every last secret. But the next time he was caught in the gaze of her large, limpid eyes, even with those intellectual alarm bells clanging in his head, he still couldn't help but feel more important, more recognized, more *seen* than he had ever been in his life.

Not to mention, not every poor sod realized her powers of observation.

Lord Ingram had witnessed, more often than he cared to recall, the expressions of marvel and bliss on the faces of men who had been the recipients of that attention. Then, when she smiled, all the inadequacies they'd ever known were swept into a great big bonfire of strength, confidence, and will to conquer.

"Very good," she said. "This is somewhere in the vicinity of London, if one assumes that the latitude is fifty-one degrees north. The longitude is close enough to the meridian that east or west shouldn't matter greatly."

Lord Ingram also couldn't recall the last time — if ever — she'd said *Very good* to him.

"It's my understanding that at the house near Portman Square," she went on, "Bancroft has a store of maps, among them highly accurate ones of London marked with longitudes and latitudes to the second."

Caught in the gaze of her large, limpid eyes, he needed a moment to answer. "He does."

She smiled again. "Bancroft does have some uses after all."

Lord Ingram, too busy putting out bonfires, did not reply.

The place indicated by N 51°28'18", E 0°21'22" was close to the mouth of the Thames, in the parish of Chadwell St. Mary. N 51°28'18", W 0°21'22" marked a spot near High Street in Hounslow, a small town that had once been at some distance from London, now swallowed up by that insatiable metropolis.

Two more unremarkable patches of ground could not be found nearby.

"Were you expecting landmarks?" asked Lord Ingram.

Holmes walked slowly around the large map table, the hems of her skirts swishing softly. "I didn't expect landmarks, but I *was* hoping for them. After all, any two paragraphs in the English language would give sufficient L's and O's to form binary numbers — and any number of binary numbers would result in denary numbers that resemble longitudes and latitudes."

She promenaded one more round, her fingers trailing along the beveled edge of the table. She had kissed him twice — upending him both times — and he still couldn't decide whether she enjoyed human contact. But she seemed to be interested in the texture of inanimate objects: the pile of a velvet-covered cushion, the cool surfaces of a stone wall in a field, the smoothness of each individual grape in a freshly snipped bunch.

"I suppose I had better go take a look at these places."

"It will be almost impossible for us to go to Tilbury and return in less than four hours," he pointed out. "I have an appointment before then. Better we try the location in Hounslow first."

She did not fail to notice the pronoun he employed. "No doubt you also prefer that I don't head to Tilbury on my own afterward, without you."

"No doubt."

When she didn't say anything, he added, "I am not asking to insert myself everywhere you go. But this business originated with Bancroft. Should you prove correct, should there be more to this cipher than even Bancroft knows, then you would be wading into uncharted territory. And it's only proper to take precaution when entering uncharted territory."

She came to a stop. "All right. I promise I won't investigate the other location unless you accompany me."

A *promise*? And *two smiles* before that?

If one disregarded the business with Roger Shrewsbury, Holmes would be considered a sensible person. But her sensibleness didn't extend to giving him any pledges — he had expected to content himself with knowing that she had heard his words of caution.

"What have you been up to, Holmes?"

She met his gaze. "Only the business of my clients and this Vigenère cipher. Mrs. Watson will tell you that I barely left my room this week."

The problem when dealing with a once-in-a-generation caliber of liar was that her countenance never lost its earnest innocence — and hers was an exceptionally earnest and innocent face. "You are up to something — you are never this accommodating. Have you found a way to siphon funds from my account to bankroll some misadventures as Sherlock Holmes?"

"Yes."

An answer of serene sweetness. He shook his head. "Very well. I won't inquire too deeply. But I know I'm right."

"I'm sure you are," she said, her face bent to the map on the table. "Now shall we to Hounslow?"

He ought to have left well enough alone.

Another man would have been delighted to be smiled at. Another man would have been happy to have extracted a promise. But he'd had to do the uncalled-for and question why. And now the silence had descended.

From time to time, someone at his club would complain about the wife or the fiancée who wouldn't stop talking and he would have to restrain himself, not to say something biting — and far too revealing — about how lucky the man was.

One could ignore aimless chatter. One could not ignore silence.

His house was often silent, a pointed absence of affectionate speech. He had become inured to it, but it was always a reminder of the mistakes he had made, of hopes and dreams that had become as withered as yesteryear's gardens.

With Holmes it was different. With Holmes the silence was taut with if-onlys. With hopes and dreams he dared not indulge in, not even in the secrecy of his own heart. Because he was a married man. Because that was an unalterable reality. And because he was afraid to find out that he had read her completely wrong.

That what he had heard in the overtures and codas of their silences, the arpeggios, the crescendos, and the occasional discordance, had all been in his own head. That their two kisses had been mere experiments to her, and her proposal to become his mistress had resulted from mere pragmatism and conveyed more of a desire not to be indebted to him than a desire *for* him.

That she truly possessed a mechanical heart, no more capable of engaging in higher emotions than an abacus could produce poetry.

Which made it all the more difficult to decide whether there was a new component to the silence today, an uneasiness apart from the usual tension. Was it at all possible, this nuance upon a nuance, or was it as far-fetched as finding an additional code in the solution to a Vigenère cipher?

He was glad when they got off the train and into a hackney. Not the entirety of the forty-minute journey had been mired in charged silence. Some of it had been productive silence: They had performed calculations to arrive at a rough estimate of the distance represented by one second of longitude at their current latitude.

A very rough estimate, given that to simplify the calculations, they supposed the earth to be perfectly round, rather than the oblate shape that it actually was. But they let that assumption stand. All they needed was an idea of how far from the point on the map they ought to search — to allow for errors on the part of everyone involved: the surveyors, the mapmakers, the cipher writers, and they themselves.

They started on a street that overlaid the spot specified by the decoded denary numbers. It possessed no features to suggest that anyone would take the trouble to create an elaborate cipher to hide its location. In fact, the entirety of Hounslow, its heath aside, could be used to illustrate the word *unexceptional.*

Not to mention they had no idea how old the cipher was. If Bancroft had taken something out of the vault from a generation ago, this part of town could have looked very different. If memory served, Hounslow had fallen into a decline after being passed by the railway. And only when another rail line came through did the community experience a revival.

Holmes snorted softly, sounding unimpressed with herself.

He looked at his pocket map, on which he had demarcated the search area, and told the cabbie, "Take us to all the surrounding streets. We want to see the whole area."

They discussed how much of the area they wished to see, retreading much the same ground that had been covered when they'd performed the calculations. He was treating her lark of a quest with far too much seriousness — but better that than to lapse into silence again.

They passed yet another street. Brown brick houses, narrow doors, postage-stamp-size picket-enclosed front gardens that displayed a general lack of horticultural talents.

As they turned onto the next street, Holmes said, "Someone is coming out of a house in that lane we just passed. Perhaps I can ask a few questions."

It seemed unlikely that a random neighbor would be privy to secrets that required several iterations of ciphering — or confirm that no such secrets existed — but Lord Ingram relayed the directions to the cabbie.

By the time they turned back onto the lane, three men stood outside. The one with his back to the houses was in uniform: a policeman.

"Interesting," murmured Holmes. "This I did not anticipate."

They alit. All three men turned in their direction. Now here was a development *Lord Ingram* did not anticipate: He knew two out of the three men, Inspector Treadles and his colleague Sergeant MacDonald, of the Criminal Investigation Department of the Metropolitan Police.

He exchanged a glance with Holmes. She appeared as unmoved as ever, but he could feel his own heartbeat accelerate.

Lord Ingram and Inspector Treadles had been friends for years — they shared a passion for archaeology. The inspector had known *of* Holmes for a while but had met her only recently, for the Sackville case. The successful untangling of the case had made Holmes's name and it had also made the inspector look good both in the papers and to his superiors.

Therefore, as surprising as this reunion was, Inspector Treadles should be glad to see them.

A flicker of displeasure crossed the inspector's face. This jolted Lord Ingram. Almost as shocking was the tightness with which the man held himself, as if preparing for an assault.

"Inspector, Sergeant, how unexpected,"

said Lord Ingram, far more restrained than he would have been otherwise. "Trouble in these parts?"

"I'm afraid I'm not at liberty to discuss police matters," replied his friend, his voice flat.

A tall, red-faced man emerged from the house. "Ah, Inspector Treadles," he said loudly. "You are here. The body's inside and it's not pretty."

Lord Ingram didn't know why this should stun him — Inspector Treadles primarily investigated murders — but stun him it did.

He hoped he did not betray too much agitation when he said, "Let me not keep you from your work. Inspector, Sergeant, good day."

They drove to the nearest telephone station, which happened to be on the premises of a high street shop. The apparatus itself was located inside an armoirelike structure, with a large pane of glass on the door — a silence cabinet.

Charlotte was interested. She had never used a telephone — neither her parents nor Mrs. Watson had one. But it would have been the height of impropriety to squeeze into the cabinet with Lord Ingram — not that she hadn't done worse with Roger

Shrewsbury — so she stood outside at some distance and waited.

He had his back to the glass door, the earpiece pressed close. The silence cabinet wasn't entirely soundproof. Occasionally she caught a few syllables that didn't make any apparent sense — he was probably speaking in code.

When they met, she had not foreseen that he would become a clandestine agent of the crown — forgivable since at the time, she hadn't been aware such entities existed. But she had soon concluded that his would not be an easy life.

He had been well-built and athletic even then, a young man with an assertive, lupine stride. His scowls were already legendary — at least among the children who knew him. And the rumors that had circulated about him . . . They would have made him at once the cleverest and the stupidest boy who ever lived, the most impulsively passionate and the most chillingly callous.

But then she saw him with her own eyes. Noticed the mud that stuck to his boots even after he had scraped them — and the traces of dirt that still clung to the lateral folds of his nails even though he'd scrubbed them until his fingertips were reddish and raw. Whatever he'd been doing, when nobody could find him, he hadn't been making love to saucy maids.

She didn't discount the possibility that he might be burying them — even though none had been reported missing. But then she traced the mud on his boots to the old quarry on the property and the unexpected Roman site he was painstakingly excavating.

By himself.

She was well aware of the whispers that he was not his father's son but the result of his mother's affair with a Jewish banker. And she was fairly certain that he didn't know it yet — not officially, in any case. Which didn't mean he hadn't sensed the looks or the whispers that stopped when he entered a room, only that he could still pretend it was about something else.

But perhaps he was nearing the end of his ability to pretend. Perhaps that was why he had secluded himself amid the ruins of an ancient villa, reading the lives of the dead.

He was sensitive. And he believed himself to have been somehow responsible for the disgrace attached to his birth.

In this he had not changed in all the subsequent years. Another man would have turned on his wife, believing, with sufficient reason, that his affections had been preyed upon. He had continued to extend every courtesy and generosity to Lady Ingram, even as they grew ever further apart, because of this deep conviction: If there was any blame to go around, then some of it must belong to him.

Was it possible that he would absolve himself of that culpability if he should hear something of what Charlotte had learned of his wife? Could Charlotte, in the end, render him this one favor, for everything he had done for her?

Lord Ingram emerged from the silence cabinet. "Would you like to take a walk?"

She blinked. He had never asked whether she wished to go for a walk. "On the heath?"

Hounslow Heath was probably the town's only claim to fame, other than that it had once been a major stop on the carriage road.

"Yes. It's a good day and we could both do with more exercise," he said in all seriousness.

But then the corners of his lips curved.

"Ha," she said.

"Ha, of course. You will have had a walk with Mrs. Watson today, and fifteen minutes on your feet counts as an active day for you."

"It must be a sound philosophy, as I am in glorious health."

"That is called youth and you will pay for

192

your sedentary habits sooner or later. But since I am a terrible friend in this regard . . . would you like to sit for a while? I understand there's a place down the street that has won some renown for its Devonshire cream."

"God bless terrible friends. Yes to the Devonshire cream, of course." She waited until they had left the shop before asking, "What will Bancroft do?"

"Pull a few levers of power. His people, perhaps he himself, will inspect the house. And needless to say, before the end of the day, someone will also have seen to the site in Tilbury."

"Why are you herding me to a tea shop, then?"

"Bancroft has asked if you wouldn't mind staying nearby for some time. I have a feeling he plans to further woo you by letting you inspect the site."

Death was all around them. Modern medicine, for all its advances, had yet to find a way to prevent vast swaths of the population from being felled by everything from influenza to septicemia. Charlotte had viewed the bodies of a number of neighbors and relatives, so she was no stranger to corpses. But this would be a first.

"He would let me view the murdered man?"

Bancroft, by proposing to her the second time, had proved himself no ordinary man. But she had no idea that he was this unconventional. Could they suit each other, after all?

"It is generally agreed upon that Bancroft has no chivalry," said his brother.

"What about you?"

"Haven't you always told me that chivalry should only be practiced on those in need of assistance and not on those perfectly capable of assisting themselves?"

"When did you start to listen to me?"

"I often listen to you, Holmes. I don't always announce it when I do."

Lord Ingram was the most fair-minded man she knew — and it was a fair-mindedness that arose from a sincere desire to put himself in the shoes of another, unlike her general neutrality, which was composed largely of logical distance.

And sometimes, that logical distance came under assault from irrational sentiments. She had told Mrs. Watson that it would have helped him not at all for Sherlock Holmes to turn down Lady Ingram — and she believed it still, absolutely. But when he was open and honest with her — and it couldn't be easy for him to be that way . . .

She felt rotten.

"Did it bother you to see Inspector Treadles?" she asked.

He glanced at her askance. "Have *you* taken up the practice of chivalry? Since when are you concerned as to whether something bothers me?"

"Do excuse me. I meant to say, I saw that Inspector Treadles's demeanor gave you pause."

"Only because it was largely directed at you. Has he conducted himself in a similar manner before?"

"I wouldn't say he'd expressed outright displeasure toward me earlier, but the trend was clear. It was obvious that when he last bid me good-bye, he'd hoped not to see me for a good long while."

"Why? He owes much of his recent success to you."

She only looked at him.

He shook his head. "He can't be this kind of a man, can he? He respects women."

"He respects women he deems worthy of respect — I am no longer one in his eyes. He is not pleased that he has helped and been helped by a woman he cannot respect. And he cannot think as highly of you as he had earlier, because my lack of respectability seems to have made no difference to you."

"What kind of a friend would I be if I'd cut ties the moment you were no longer acceptable to the rest of Society? And why should he be offended that I didn't do it?"

She shrugged. "There are men like my father. It is not enjoyable to number among his female dependents, because he is selfish and because he disdains women in general — or indeed anyone who is any different from him. And then there are men like Inspector Treadles, an excellent person by almost all standards. But he admires the world as it is and he subscribes to the rules that uphold the world as it is. For him then it's the principle of the thing. Anyone who breaks the rules endangers the order of the world and should be punished. He does not ask whether the rules are fair; he only cares that they are enforced.

"Someone like me, who has broken the rules blatantly without seeming to have suffered any consequences — I am an affront, a menace to the order that he holds dear. Worse, his opinion is immaterial to me and he cannot do anything about it. It must chafe at him. I only hope his wife fares better, if she ever breaks any rules he deems important."

"But he loves her!"

"I'm sure he does. Let's remember, however, that he also admired Sherlock Holmes, until he discovered Charlotte Holmes's transgressions."

At Lord Ingram's pained expression, she added, "I am not saying that he is a completely draconian man who will always put his principles above the people in his life. Only that for him, questioning what he believes — what he believes so deeply he doesn't even think about — would be more painful than breaking his own kneecaps with a sledgehammer."

Lord Ingram looked as if he was about to reply, but something — or someone, rather — caught his attention. "That's Underwood, Bancroft's man."

Mr. Underwood, large and rotund, moved with surprising agility. He came to a stop at their table and bowed. "Miss Holmes, his lordship awaits you."

Mr. Underwood also had a message for Lord Ingram, who glanced at it, frowned, and said to Charlotte, "Do please excuse me, Miss Holmes. I trust I'll have the pleasure of your company again before too long."

"Good day, my lord — and I do hope so."

He had given his standard parting line,

but hers had been a few words too long —
usually she stopped at *Good day, my lord.*
He narrowed his eyes before he bowed and
left.

Charlotte followed Mr. Underwood to a
waiting town coach.

The street where they were deposited was
neither cheerful nor oppressive. It was
simply part and parcel of a place built for
function, rescued from outright tedium by
an occasional window box of blooming
pansies, or a set of shutters newly painted a
sky blue, in defiance of the murky air of the
city, which would soon turn it a much
grimier shade.

The house itself was a nonentity. Its tiny
plot of land, delineated by a low brick wall,
contained two bushes, pruned but not
meticulously so. The door opened into a
small entry, a space for coats and umbrellas
and muddy galoshes — but any mud that
had been tracked in earlier had been cleaned
away, and the vestibule was empty except
for a walking stick that hung on a hook on
the wall.

Mr. Underwood guided her into a sparsely
furnished parlor, where Lord Bancroft sat,
a tea service on the low table beside him,
along with a handsome Victoria sandwich.

Lord Ingram ate everything set down

before him and didn't care greatly whether the food was exquisite or barely edible. Lord Bancroft, on the other hand, shared with Charlotte a sustained interest in dinners — and breakfasts and luncheons and teas.

Moreover, he was the sort of fortunate man who could eat what he pleased without having to worry about exceeding Maximum Tolerable Chins. In fact, Charlotte suspected that the more he ate, the leaner he became.

"Ah, Miss Holmes," he said cheerfully. "Have you been enjoying yourself with my brother?"

Another man might have said it snidely. Lord Bancroft was not that man: He had not asked Charlotte to love him, only to marry him — and therefore her spending time with his brother, a married man, was of no concern.

He and she were more alike than she had ever realized before.

"It has been an interesting day," she answered. "Are you having me followed, by the way, my lord?"

"My dear Miss Holmes," said Lord Bancroft without the least hesitation, "you know I can never answer such queries. A bite with your tea?"

"Yes, thank you."

She'd had a scone with Devonshire cream at the tea shop, but it would be remiss not to try the Victoria sandwich. The kind of pastry a man could come up with on short notice — and with a dead body in the house — said a great deal about him.

The sponge was fresh and light, the strawberry jam between the layers the perfect combination of sweet and tart. Chased with a cup of beautifully brewed tea, it was absolutely flawless.

"No one ought to work without being properly fed."

Charlotte couldn't agree more if she tried. "This is certainly being properly fed."

Lord Bancroft looked pleased. "I take it you are ready to work then, Miss Holmes?"

"Lord Ingram gave me the impression that you would like me to see the body," said Charlotte cautiously.

She braced herself to hear Lord Bancroft clarify that there were no such plans, but he said, "I understand you can tell a great deal about a person from a look. I assume it might also work for corpses."

He really meant for her to see the victim — and no mention of anyone's delicate feminine sensibilities.

"I can do that," she said, scarcely able to keep wonder and eagerness out of her voice.

"But it always helps to have greater context. What can you tell me about the victim or the circumstances?"

"You'll first allow me to apologize, of course, for this unpleasantness. The Vigenère cipher, as well as the other riddles that had been repurposed for your leisure, came from an archive of cases deemed to have been thoroughly investigated — of no further interest whatsoever to the crown.

"Now, obviously I'm grateful to you — I much prefer knowing that something nefarious is going on under my nose, if this is what it is, and not a coincidence. But I would be lying if I didn't acknowledge that I am also mortified and more than a little miffed that my courtship present has led to a dead body, of all things."

"No harm done. I would much rather that my efforts shed some light on this man's death than that they only resulted in solving a code someone had already deciphered ten years ago."

"That's how Ash thought you would feel, but still, it's good to hear it directly from you. Now to answer your question. The Vigenère cipher began life as a cable about ten years ago, before my time. It originated in Cairo, though it's also possible that Cairo had served as a relay station and the actual telegram had been sent from a smaller locale in the region."

Charlotte would not be surprised if Bancroft had agents in telegraph relay stations all over the empire.

An operator in a relay station listened to the telegraph sounder and wrote down the Morse code as it clicked and beeped, before sending the message further along the line. When a message had been relayed, the operator would have a copy in hand, which made it easy to hand off.

"The sender is named Baxter, the recipient, a C. F. de Lacy residing at a small hotel in Belgravia. According to the notes in the original dossier, it was decided by those responsible at the time that the telegram must have been communication between overly mistrustful archaeologists — or men who call themselves archaeologists but are simply modern-day grave robbers."

"So no one was sent to the hotel to check the register?"

"We have limited funds and therefore limited manpower — in fact, much of my work involves trying to obtain more funds. I imagine the hapless men who worked on the cipher were crestfallen that it turned out to involve no foreign state secret or dastardly plot against the throne. They recommended that an eye be kept on the papers for any big archaeological discovery. But as far as I can tell, no one bothered to follow through with that."

She had always thought Lord Bancroft recruited his little brother to have at hand someone he could trust absolutely. But now she wondered if there hadn't been budgetary reasons: Lord Ingram, as a gentleman, would not expect to be paid — or even reimbursed — for his troubles.

"So now, ten years later, we have trouble unearthing anything. The hotel where de Lacy stayed? The hotel keeper died eight years ago. The premises were sold and made into a block of flats. The records of the old hotel were disposed of, so there is no means of tracking this Mr. de Lacy, even if that had been his real name. About Baxter we know even less. My subordinates are checking to see whether we have other records of them, but they are not hopeful."

"When Lord Ingram and I arrived on the scene, there was already a policeman guarding the property — and the C.I.D. had become involved. How did that happen?"

The determined ordinariness of this house — or any of its neighbors — should not have inspired a bobby to peek behind the curtains.

"It's curious how that came about. This morning, the nearest police station received an anonymous note, concerning nefarious activities that have taken place at this address, which the note alleged to have involved a number of innocent and helpless children."

Charlotte's ears perked up. It was not very long ago that the city had been gripped by just such a case. "The constables jumped to, I imagine."

"Indeed," said Lord Bancroft, "a contingent from the station flew out to investigate the premises. When no one answered the door, they forced open the entrance at the back. There were no children, nor any sign any had ever been in the house — but a dead body isn't the worst consolation prize."

Charlotte supposed not, if one had been seeking evidence of villainy.

"The police looked about and decided to hand the matter over to the C.I.D. Inspector Treadles arrived on the scene. You and my brother arrived on the scene. And the rest you already know."

"Not all of it. Was Inspector Treadles asked to leave?"

"Of course not. Inspector Treadles is fully involved with the case. He believes that the body will be transported to the coroner's.

And it will be. But first you have a look, Miss Holmes."

"Certainly. But before we proceed, can you tell me whether Simmons is still serving Lady Ingram?"

"My mother's old maid Simmons? Yes, she's still there. She came into some money last year. We thought it was time to buy her a retirement gift but she decided to stay on, in the end. Said she wouldn't know what to do with herself if she retired."

"I see."

Lord Bancroft cocked his head. "Any reason you remembered Simmons all of a sudden?"

Charlotte shook her head. "No, no reason at all."

He raised a brow but only said, "Then, shall we?"

When Charlotte was five, her grandfather, an old man with jolly demeanor and sad eyes, visited the Holmes household. He arrived a hearty man, if one who liked to complain of arthritic joints. A week later he was laid out on the dining table, dead.

Late at night Charlotte had stolen down to the dining room to study the cold and stiff body of the man who had slipped her an orange bonbon after every meal. It would be years before she realized that the constricted sensation in her chest was nothing more — or less — than sadness. But she did understand right away, in the light of a guttering candle, that she did not fear the dead.

The man who now lay underneath a dust sheet had not had the good fortune to pass away in old age, surrounded by family, on a comfortable feather mattress. Instead, he had been strangled, his still-young face grotesque with desperation, as if even at the very end he still couldn't believe that he had met such an unkind fate.

She pulled out her magnifying glass.

"May I take a look at it?" asked Lord Bancroft.

She handed it to him. The magnifying glass was solid silver mounted with an openwork design of foliage and scrolls. But hidden among the leafy swirls, if one looked closely, were tiny silver cakes, muffins, and molded jellies.

"I thought I'd seen a drawing of such a magnifying glass in my brother's expedition notebook a few years ago," said Lord Bancroft. "Did he give this to you?"

"It was a birthday present."

Lord Bancroft turned the magnifying glass over a few times. "What is this?" he asked, pointing to a rather unimpressive bit of light green glass at the tip of the handle.

"To me it looks to be a tessera from a mosaic. Perhaps something Lord Ingram has dug up."

"It could be very old — he once excavated a minor Roman site," said Lord Bancroft, a speculative gleam in his eyes as he handed the magnifying glass back to her.

"It could very well be from that site — I've never asked him," answered Charlotte, being at once perfectly truthful and completely evasive.

She had recognized, upon first glance, that this small piece of cloudy glass, polished and rounded for the mounting, had come from the remains of a Roman villa, where it had been, long ago, part of a floor mosaic in the atrium.

The site of her first kiss.

The magnifying glass had been delivered via the post, rather than in person or via courier. The accompanying note wished her many happy returns and made absolutely no reference to the glass tessera. Her return note had been equally brief and equally quiet on the matter.

And yet it had been the beginning of those charged silences that had come to characterize all subsequent interactions between

Lord Ingram and herself.

She knelt down and examined the dead man from top to bottom, paying special attention to his hands and the soles of his shoes. Mr. Underwood helpfully turned him over, so she could inspect his dorsal side.

"I'd like to see this man unclothed."

Mr. Underwood wheezed a little and glanced toward Lord Bancroft, who said, with no appearance of surprise or consternation, "Will you oblige Miss Holmes, Mr. Underwood?"

"Yes, my lord."

"We've looked for tailor's labels but found none," said Lord Bancroft to Charlotte, as Mr. Underwood divested the dead man of his garments.

After a few more minutes, Charlotte rose and said, "I don't know that I can tell you much more than you already know, my lord."

"And what is it that I already know, pray tell, Miss Holmes?"

"You know that he wasn't killed on the premises — or at least not inside this house. There was a struggle — he has blood and skin under his nails and dirt and grass embedded in the treads of his soles."

"I have indeed deduced as much."

"His clothes are of inferior material, indifferently tailored and too large for him. But you are certain they do not indicate his place in the world because his hands are white and soft and these rough garments do not reek as you would expect them to.

"You would have confirmed your suspicion by looking at his underlinens, which happen to be of merino wool: hygienic, comfortable, and completely at odds with the rough image his outer garments conveyed — or sought to convey. Same goes for the shoes, which, though not bespoke, are of an excellent quality and workmanship."

"Indeed. Now, you said that you can't tell me *much* more than I already know. So what do I not know yet?"

"This suit was bought at a secondhand shop — probably in an effort to conceal himself from those who did not mean him well. And not a secondhand shop in Kensington that a lady's maid who has been given castoffs might take her wares to, but the kind you find in Seven Dials and other such districts."

When she had been low on funds and looking for some clothes that would not appear out of place on a secretary, she had frequented a few resale shops. The problem had been that the halfway decent garments still cost too much and the cheaper stuff looked like dishrags.

"I've had occasion to browse in some of the less . . . prestigious of these establishments. This suit has been through the resale shops a few times. Inside the left sleeve, there are five stitch marks done in brown yarn. Inside the right sleeve, three similar marks in blue yarn. Different shops use yarn of different colors to mark items that come through — it helps them track how popular an item might prove to be.

"And what makes this particular item so popular that it went through such places eight times? One would think that it could scarcely be worn eight times before the seams came apart."

"Under certain circumstances the use of a garment does not add much to the wear and tear. The front of the suit is made of serge, not the best I've seen, but presentable enough and durable enough. The back, however . . . if it isn't shoddy that has been ground up and rewoven, I would be very surprised."

"A suit with only a front side presentable. Are you telling me this is funeral attire for the poor?"

"It's what I would conclude."

"Did our corpse rob a grave then?"

"Judging by how many times this suit has

circulated, I would say no. It's quite possible that the family of the deceased removes the suit and sells it back to the shop, to save some money. Or the grave diggers might have. In either case, I would guess that our man had no idea that he'd donned a funeral suit."

Only to have it become prophetic.

"What else can you tell me, Miss Holmes?"

"That depends, my lord. What did you do with his pocketbook and his watch?"

"He had no wallet on his person. I do have his watch in my possession."

The watch had been made by Messrs. Patek, Philippe, and Co. Monsieur Patek had invented the stem-winding mechanism that did away with winding keys. The company had been a well-known name ever since the queen had bought two of their watches for herself and Prince Albert at a London horological exhibition thirty-five years ago. And their dedication to quality had not waned since: If Charlotte's memory served, their watches were awarded the special prize at a recent competition held at the Geneva Observatory.

This watch had been beautifully cared for and appeared new at first glance. Only on close study with her magnifying glass could she see the minor dents and scratches that came with the simple passage of time, inevitable for any item used on a regular basis. She opened the back, and then the cuvette, the inner lid that protected the precise and complex arrangement of gears and springs that moved the dials. Neither the back nor the cuvette bore any inscriptions.

"Our man was an orphan."

"The watch can tell you that?"

"How did you come by your first fine watch, my lord?"

"A gift from my late father."

"With an inscription inside, I imagine?"

"An exhortation to the dutiful life."

"This is easily an eighty-guinea watch. And our man, who looks to be only twenty-eight or so, would have barely come of age when this watch was made. To be that young and acquire a watch that bears no inscriptions? It suggests to me that he purchased it himself, rather than that it was a gift from an elder."

"And if it had been his own choice, then it might also explain the care he took — it was his first significant purchase as a man, something he meant to carry with him for a lifetime," mused Lord Bancroft. "But why then didn't he put his own initials on it?"

"I thought that odd, too, and I can't offer you a reason."

"Anything else you can tell me from the watch?"

She shook her head.

He looked a little disappointed.

"At the moment, the watch relays nothing else helpful. But I *can* tell you that he tried to leave a message about his fate."

"How?"

"Does Mr. Underwood carry the necessary implement to remove the lining of the jacket?"

Mr. Underwood did — a pair of small, sharp scissors that gleamed in the light. The cheap lining was removed to show nothing in particular. But Charlotte ran her hand over the rough black shoddy of the back and said, "Ah, I think I know what this is. It's rice that had been doused in ink — then the individual grains were applied to the fabric."

Cooked rice, when in contact with any kind of surface, stuck to it with an enormous tenacity as it dried. And dried grains of cooked rice were hard as pebbles and almost as indestructible.

"Is it possible to make a rubbing of the jacket?" asked Charlotte. "I believe we are dealing with braille."

Mr. Underwood performed the task, his motions quick yet delicate. Charlotte examined the resultant sheet of paper and wrote down the message.

MY KILLER IS DE LACY ON BAXTERS ORDER

De Lacy and Baxter, the two names that had been associated with the coded telegram that had brought Charlotte to the vicinity of the house in the first place.

Lord Bancroft exhaled. "Miss Holmes, you have given me much work to do."

Then he looked at her and said, "Thank you."

Lord Ingram had always treated Charlotte as an equal. But theirs was a complicated bond, constricted by circumstances and abraded by a number of disagreements over the years.

Now Lord Bancroft, too, treated her as an equal. He and Charlotte shared no long-standing friendship, but they were also free of any burdens of the past.

It was . . . most certainly interesting.

She smiled at him. "I wish you luck in your endeavor, my lord. Now if you will kindly arrange for a carriage to take me to

the train station — I promised Mrs. Watson
I'd be home by tea."

NINE

"There you are," cried Mrs. Watson, bolting up from her chair, when Miss Holmes stepped into the afternoon parlor. "Where have you been?"

She hadn't meant to ask that question — certainly not in that tone. Miss Holmes was a grown woman and she was neither Mrs. Watson's child nor her employee.

But her abrupt departure this morning from the park, her terse note that said only *Headed out. Will be back for tea,* and the fact that she, a woman who was never late for cake and sandwiches, was a whopping three quarters of an hour late to said tea —

"I was five minutes away from running to the nearest telephone, to let Lord Ingram know that you are missing."

Miss Holmes could have been hit by a carriage or robbed of her cab money. But the possibility that had truly frightened Mrs. Watson was that she might have been taken by her own family, stuffed into a railcar, and shunted to the country, never to be heard from again.

Such abductions had happened when Mrs. Watson was young. They still happened. And what could anyone do, when it was the family who acted as judge, jury, and jailer?

Miss Holmes stood very still, her skirts wrinkled, her ringlets droopy from humidity. She looked at Mrs. Watson unblinkingly, and Mrs. Watson found that she couldn't read the younger woman's face at all.

Uncertainty gnawed at Mrs. Watson. Had she been too shrill? Had she given offense? Had she overstepped the bounds of friendship?

"I'm sorry, ma'am," said Miss Holmes softly. "I didn't mean to be so late."

Relief washed over Mrs. Watson, relief and a measure of mortification that she hadn't put a stronger leash on her anxiety. "No, I should apologize. Do please excuse me for acting like the old worrywart that I am."

Miss Holmes shook her head. "I was on my own for a short while — I have not forgotten what that was like. The life I lead now is a luxury. You make that life possible, ma'am. I'm sorry that I made you worry, but I'm not sorry that I have someone who worries for me."

It dawned on Mrs. Watson that Miss Holmes wasn't speaking only of this moment. She was also addressing the fact that, unbeknownst to her then, Mrs. Watson had first approached her and offered her aid at Lord Ingram's behest.

And she wanted Mrs. Watson to know that it did not affect her commitment to their partnership — and their friendship.

"Oh, you're back, Miss Holmes!" Penelope flounced into the room. "How do you do?"

They all sat down. Almost immediately, Miss Holmes turned the conversation to what Penelope had done this day with the de Blois ladies. Penelope gladly related their little adventures while Miss Holmes listened attentively. Mrs. Watson, who had already heard an account of Penelope's day earlier, pondered that a stranger could so swiftly become such an integral part of her existence that it was difficult to remember how she had lived before their meeting.

Polly, one of the housemaids, came with the tea tray. Usually Mr. Mears attended at tea, but he was in Gloucestershire for a niece's wedding and a grandnephew's christening, and not expected back until late on Tuesday.

"Does this mean we'll need to wait until Wednesday to verify that Mr. Finch has returned from his holiday?" asked Penelope, pouring for everyone.

"Another two days shouldn't make too much difference," said Miss Holmes.

Mrs. Watson wished she could be as detached. Each day since Lady Ingram's call had felt like an age of the world and she had been wondering with increasing urgency how they could have more news sooner. She did have another man in her employ. Alas, Lawson, her groom and coachman, was no actor. She supposed she could ask Rosie and Polly whether they knew anyone in service in that area, but the likelihood of any useful answers coming from that direction seemed infinitesimal.

"I have an idea," announced Penelope.

Miss Holmes lifted the sandwich plate toward her. "Let's hear it."

"Thank you," said Penelope, taking three of the finger sandwiches. "At medical school, Mademoiselle de Blois organizes visits to districts in Paris where people can't afford to see doctors or buy medicine. But we also go to the wealthy arrondissements, to speak with women in service. In the bigger mansions we would first call on the housekeeper to make the arrangements. But at a smaller household, if we arrive when they are not too busy, we might speak to everyone right away over a cup of coffee."

"You propose we carry out a similar visit to Mrs. Woods's staff?" asked Miss Holmes.

"I daresay that would give us more solid intelligence on Mr. Finch than another call by Mr. Mears, pretending to be a solicitor. And I wouldn't even need to lie. I will be exactly who I am, a medical student trying to do a little good on holiday. And I can visit more than one house on the same street, so that Mrs. Woods won't feel that her place has been singled out."

Mrs. Watson gazed at this dear, dear child, her lively confidence, her mischievous audacity — and worried. Lady Ingram's heartbreak and the moral quagmire of the situation with regard to Lord Ingram aside, to Penelope this was still all fun and games. But Mrs. Watson had seen how quickly a case could turn from merely intriguing to actively dangerous.

She hadn't wanted Penelope to be at all involved in the consulting detective business. But now that the girl was, she didn't want to clip Penelope's wings, just as she didn't want to curtail Miss Holmes's freedom of movement, no matter how much the latter's longer absences unsettled her.

"It's a good idea," she said. "But you shouldn't go by yourself. I'll come with you."

They spent the rest of tea planning the specifics of their semi-ruse. In the end, it was decided that Miss Holmes would go with them, too, but under disguise. "You might still have to call on Mr. Finch in person at some point," Mrs. Watson pointed out. "Better not for the servants to see you come in from both the service door and the front door — it might give rise to suspicions."

The arrival of the post saw a tidy stack of missives for Penelope from her other friends and classmates. Delighted, Penelope excused herself to wallow in her reams of correspondence. Miss Holmes, on the other hand, seemed disappointed.

"Were you expecting a letter?"

"I haven't heard from my sister in a while," said Miss Holmes. "I did see her on Tuesday. And I did ask her to gather some intelligence on Lady Ingram for me. But it's unlike Livia to wait until she'd accomplished that in order to write me."

She fell silent, then murmured, rather cryptically, "I do say too much sometimes, especially on matters that are better off not brought up."

While Mrs. Watson pondered whether she should ask Miss Holmes to explain herself, the latter sighed. "Anyway, there is something I need to tell you, ma'am, something to do with Sophia Lonsdale."

Mrs. Watson sucked in a breath. "I thought we agreed we wouldn't mention her again by that name."

Like Miss Holmes, Sophia Lonsdale had been exiled from Society for her indiscretions, albeit a generation before. She had returned to England from abroad and consulted Sherlock Holmes. And *that* had led to a cascade of events that no one could have foreseen.

The world believed Sophia Lonsdale to have died many years ago, and she had come to Charlotte under an alias. At the end of *l'affaire Sackville,* Mrs. Watson and Miss Holmes had decided that she must have had an important and desperate reason to stage her own death — and that they would not compromise her safety by tossing her real name about willy-nilly.

"I wonder that she hadn't given herself away," mused Miss Holmes. "Pattern of action can be as recognizable as speech or handwriting. Here's a woman who tries to accomplish goals without betraying her involvement. What if her husband saw the newspaper reports, remembered that one of the central parties had been a close friend of hers, and suspected that she might have had a part to play?"

"The husband who thinks she is dead?"

"What if he already had some inkling that her death was a ruse?"

Mrs. Watson tensed. "Have you heard from her, Miss Holmes? Is she in trouble?"

"I haven't heard from her at all, but Lord Ingram has reason to believe that someone — or more than one person — has been watching your house since earlier in the week."

Having Sherlock Holmes offer his services to the public had been Mrs. Watson's idea. An exccedingly splendid idea, she had believed. But all splendid ideas came with their inevitable drawbacks. The undertaking, engrossing and rewarding in the main, had also been at times more than a little troubling.

"I didn't tell you this," continued Miss Holmes, "but after the Sackville case, I went to Somerset House and looked into her marriage record, since the desire to escape from her husband seemed the most likely reason for her to counterfeit her death. His name is Moriarty. I wrote to Lord Ingram and asked if he knew anything about this man.

"He in turn asked Lord Bancroft. And according to him, Lord Bancroft was discomposed by the mention of that name and warned Lord Ingram in no uncertain terms to refrain from getting mixed up in any business with Moriarty."

"And you think it's this Moriarty fellow who is having the house watched?"

"It seems to me the most logical hypothesis."

Mrs. Watson waited for Miss Holmes to continue. After a while, it became obvious that Miss Holmes was waiting for a reaction from *her*.

"I hope she stays safe, Mrs. Marbleton," she said, using the alias Sophia Lonsdale had given them.

Miss Holmes studied her. "You aren't worried for yourself?"

Before Mrs. Watson could answer, she shook her head. "Of course, what was I thinking? You worry primarily for others."

"Not out of altruism, mind you. I worry about others because I don't know whether they'll be able to handle the difficulties life drops into their laps. As for me . . ." Mrs. Watson shrugged. Her niece was grown, her mate dead, her servants looked after in her will. What did it matter to her that Sophia Lonsdale's husband wished to watch her doors for some time? "As long as it doesn't affect you or Penelope."

"I expect nothing will happen to either Miss Redmayne or myself. Or you, for that matter." Miss Holmes fell quiet for some time, not the opulent silence that seemed to be her natural habit, but a contemplative one. "For which I am grateful, as you are an indispensable advisor."

Mrs. Watson was feeling a little sorry for herself. Widowed, in the autumn of her life, her only relation away much of the year. But oh, such warmth radiated through her at Miss Holmes's words, as if she'd swallowed a drop of sunfire and now glowed from within. True, certain beloved phases of her life had come to an end, but with Miss Holmes's arrival, a whole new vista had opened up. And for one who had tended her years with care, autumn need not be a season of scarcity or regret — but one of harvest and celebration.

She leaned forward an inch. "Have you an hour to spare, Miss Holmes?"

Charlotte was curious. Mrs. Watson had asked not only for an hour of her time, but also whether she had some garments in her possession that allowed for easy movement. Her tennis costume had been packed by mistake for the London Season — tennis was a game for the country — and had remained in the suitcase and come with her on exile.

(As her wardrobe consisted solely of ensembles useless to anyone but a lady of leisure, it hadn't mattered whether she brought tennis costumes or dinner gowns. The more pieces she could stuff into her luggage, she had reasoned, the more assets she could have to sell as a last resort.)

Mrs. Watson was waiting for her in the largely empty room that had once been Miss Redmayne's nursery, in a close-fitting blouse and a skirt that did not narrow toward the knees. "I'd assumed earlier that you must be familiar with the operation of firearms, as you were raised in the country. But are you, Miss Holmes?"

Charlotte nodded. The Holmeses didn't have a game park of their own, but most every autumn her parents managed to obtain an invitation to a shooting party. "Shotguns, yes. Rifles also, for target shooting. One time my father let me fire his revolver."

"Excellent. However, you're not likely to be walking around London, or anywhere else, for that matter, with a rifle. But a lady usually has a parasol on hand, which will serve, in a pinch."

Mrs. Watson handed Charlotte a walking stick. "This is not a parasol, obviously. But I love my parasols too much — and I'm sure you do, too — to subject them to such abuse when there isn't actual danger. Walking sticks, on the other hand, are sturdy things that can take a beating.

"My grandfather was a fencing master. He lived with us for a while in his old age and amused himself by instructing my sister and me in the use of *canne de combat.* I arrived in London confident of my ability to defend myself. But the first time someone grabbed me from behind, I froze. All my practice in swordplay had been somewhat stylized — *en garde, prêts, allez,* and all that. But in real life no one waits for you to be in proper stance, and they are not going to come at you only from the front.

"What you want, then, is to train yourself to overcome that moment of paralysis as quickly as possible, dig your elbow into the kidney of your assailant, and, while he loosens his hold momentarily, turn around and hit him as hard as you can, generating the blow not by flicking your wrists, but by putting your full body behind it."

Charlotte tested the balance of the walking stick in her hand. It was made of malacca, light but strong. "This isn't about Moriarty, is it, ma'am? His agents are not likely to snatch me off the streets."

"No," Mrs. Watson admitted. "As much as you might consider yourself a free woman, Miss Holmes, you are still a fugitive from your family."

"So it's my father you are recommending that I whack as hard as I can."

"Or his agents — while thinking of queen and country, of course."

Charlotte couldn't help smiling. "I feel sorry for the second man who grabbed you from behind, ma'am."

Mrs. Watson winked. "Oh, you should feel sorry for the first one, too. I broke one of his fingers."

Mrs. Watson started with the basic stances. "You need to learn how to stand so that you are steady and connected to the ground — and difficult for anyone to shove aside or push down."

The positions made Charlotte's legs ache, those limbs that never had to do anything more strenuous than a few turns about a ballroom.

"Now the most important thing is to hold on to your weapon," warned Mrs. Watson.

Charlotte gripped harder at the walking stick in her hand.

"Now parry this."

Charlotte raised her stick to block Mrs. Watson. She wasn't sure what the latter did, but the sticks banged together and the next thing Charlotte knew her stick was flying across the room — the thankfully sparsely furnished room — crashing into the mantel with a fierce clank.

And her hand vibrated painfully from the contact. "Ow!"

Mrs. Watson tsked. "You didn't hold on to your weapon, Miss Holmes."

Charlotte retrieved her stick. "I could have sworn I held on with a death grip."

"Granted, your average assailant might not know as many clever ways of disarming an opponent. But a man can still knock away your stick by dint of superior strength, unless you take advantage of leverage. You must become more proficient with your weapon, Miss Holmes."

And becoming more proficient was not a pleasant process.

"Oh, my." Charlotte was already huffing and puffing after a quarter of an hour. "I don't know that I can keep up for much longer."

"Come, Miss Holmes. Think of it as staving off the arrival of Maximum Tolerable Chins. After you exercise, you can indulge your appetite more freely."

Charlotte panted. "Well, in that case, I might find some additional willpower."

With ten minutes to the hour, Mrs. Watson took pity on Charlotte and declared the day's session finished. Charlotte leaned against the wall. Her arms ached — even the one that wasn't holding the stick. Her legs ached. Her whole body ached.

"And you will ache worse tomorrow morning." Mrs. Watson grinned.

Charlotte moaned.

"Now, Miss Holmes," said Mrs. Watson, not even breathing faster, "when you told me about the surveillance that had been put on this house, you mentioned Lord Ingram's observations. Did I miss his calls?"

"No, he didn't come in on either day, though I did meet him as I went out the front door this morning."

"But he did mean to call on us, both times?"

Charlotte hesitated. "It would be reasonable to suppose so."

Mrs. Watson's voice grew taut. "You don't think it's because he found out about his wife's visit to Sherlock Holmes?"

Charlotte patted the back of her neck with

a handkerchief — and shook her head. "There is something else I need to tell you. Lord Bancroft has proposed."

Mrs. Watson's jaw slackened. Then she let out a peal of exhilarated laughter. "I never saw *that* coming. I mean, the man is odd enough, but I didn't think he had it in him to buck conventions to such an extent. But this does improve my opinion of him, that he has such good taste in matrimonial prospects. This isn't the first time he's proposed to you, if I recall correctly?"

"No."

"I like him more and more." Then her face fell. "My goodness, you are seriously considering it."

"I must." Bernadine was as blank and unresponsive as Charlotte had ever seen her. Even Livia, as sensitive and vulnerable as she was, was far better equipped to handle life's vicissitudes. "My disgrace has made things difficult for everyone in my family, but especially for my sisters. Marriage will 'redeem' me enough for me to look after them. And if Lord Bancroft guarantees me enough freedom and intellectual stimulation, which he seems well inclined to do, then I must give it every consideration."

"What — what does Lord Ingram think of it all?"

"I didn't ask him," muttered Charlotte. "But I would not be surprised if he was the one who gave Lord Bancroft the idea."

Inspector Treadles arrived home at almost exactly the same time as his wife.

"Why hullo, Inspector." Alice smiled as they met on the doorstep of their house. "Welcome home. Long day?"

He exhaled. "And how. Strange new case. Fellow was done in, all right, but we have no idea who he is or why anyone wanted to kill him. I've got MacDonald looking to see if someone of matching description has been reported missing, but it might take some time."

"You always get your man," said his wife.

He did, but not necessarily without help. And as he'd stood over the dead man, puzzled by the situation, he'd distinctly wished that he possessed Sherlock Holmes's powers of observation. That he, too, could take one look, and know everything there was to know about a victim.

He kissed Alice on her cheek and said, though without great conviction, "Thank you, my dear."

They let themselves into the house, a wedding present from his father-in-law. He would have to rise to the position of commissioner, with a housing allowance of three hundred pounds per annum, to have any hope of living in such a fine house on his own income.

"Where were you?" It was almost dinnertime, and he wasn't accustomed to Alice being out so late.

"At my brother's." She sighed. "I saw Barnaby only briefly — he was under morphine. But Eleanor is terrified. Barnaby won't tell her what's the matter with him — and he's also forbidden Dr. Motley to say anything to anyone.

"Surely . . ."

"*I* don't think so. But Eleanor is convinced that's exactly what's ailing him — that he caught it somewhere and gave it to her, too. I tried to tell her that Barnaby fears the French disease even more than she does, but she was beside herself. In the end I had to give her some laudanum to calm her down — and so I could leave."

She shook her head. "I'll need to call on them again — at least to make sure Eleanor is all right."

A thought occurred to Treadles. "I'm sure Barnaby will be fine in no time. But what if something were to go awry, what happens to Cousins Manufacturing?"

"Oh, I don't doubt he'll recover, sooner

or later." Alice frowned. "It's been a long time since I read my father's will. But if I remember correctly, if Barnaby were to die without any male issue, the firm would come to me."

And Barnaby and Eleanor Cousins, like Robert and Alice Treadles, had no children.

None that had survived both the womb and the outside world, in any case.

TEN

Ever since Charlotte had run away, Livia had been under an interminable interrogation, conducted by ladies Avery and Somersby, Society's leading gossips. One of the ladies, or both, was always tapping Livia on the shoulder, to ask whether she'd had any news from her scandalous baby sister.

But the moment Livia wanted to find *them,* they disappeared.

Or at least that was how it felt.

She even asked her mother whether the gossips had left town, only to be told that she was an idiot. "Why would they, when everyone is still in London? Besides, I saw them yesterday."

Which was patently false as Lady Holmes had suffered from a headache the day before, took laudanum for it, and didn't leave her bed all day.

But Livia didn't argue. Arguing with her

mother was like arguing with a brick wall. Worse, in fact — at least one could kick the brick wall when one tired of the argument.

"Oh, you stupid girl," hissed Lady Holmes all of a sudden. "Why did you bring them up? You've conjured them."

Livia couldn't locate the gossip ladies immediately. It was only after her mother had absconded that she saw them on the opposite side of the Round Pond. They saw her at the same moment and immediately headed in her direction.

When they were about twenty feet away from where she sat, a miracle happened. The young man, *her* young man, sauntered into view and took a seat on the next bench.

She couldn't be this lucky, could she? No, not her. Never. Some people won prizes. Some had loving parents. Some arrived home before the rain came down and didn't need to go anywhere until the sun was shining in the sky again. Livia was always the one who did get rained on, the one whose skirt got mangled in the wringer, the one who stood in line behind the person who would receive the last ladle of punch.

But there he was in his Sunday suit, neatly turned out and presentable, but not so gleamingly dapper as to make her suspicious. And goodness, was that a reddish hint

236

to his beard — and hair, too? She'd never given a single thought to redheads, but if they all looked like him she would happily praise their existence in the world.

Was it possible — was it somehow within the realm of possibility — that he had come to the park specifically to look for her? After all, they had been in the same general area last Sunday, when they had first crossed paths.

"Miss Holmes, just the person we wish to see!"

Oh, damn Lady Avery and Lady Somersby. Last Sunday he had departed at the faintest stirring from her mother. Surely this time, seeing her surrounded, he would again make himself scarce.

She parried the gossip ladies' questions, a labored smile on her face. Two questions. Three questions. Five questions.

He was still there.

She relaxed a little. When she'd answered seven questions and he still remained in place, she began to grow giddy.

And then she remembered that she wasn't there to meekly suffer through another interrogation: She had been tasked by Charlotte to obtain answers from ladies Avery and Somersby. But how to steer the topic to Lady Ingram without appearing as if she were transparently scheming to do so?

A lesser miracle took place, but still a miracle: Lady Ingram, her children in tow, passed into view, a vision in an apricot walking gown and matching parasol.

"Oh, it's Lady Ingram," she said.

"So it is," murmured Lady Somersby.

Charlotte had become a topic of gossip of late, but Lord and Lady Ingram had been the subject of speculation for years, from the most admired young couple in Society to the most estranged. When there was so much beauty, wealth, prestige, and — at least initially — love involved, everybody wanted to know what went wrong.

Lady Ingram nodded, but her squared-back shoulders spoke eloquently of her desire to be left alone. Livia, Lady Avery, and Lady Somersby returned the acknowledgment and watched as she and her children receded from view.

Livia seized the opportunity. "Do you know what I sometimes wonder? I wonder whether there wasn't someone else before Lord Ingram. That might explain things, might it not?"

"Not for me," said Lady Somersby. "Have you seen him at a game of polo? If I were Lady Ingram, I'd have instantly forgotten whomever I'd been fancying the moment I saw Lord Ingram on a polo pony."

"Oh, you naughty old woman," said her sister.

"Thank you, my dear." Lady Somersby laughed heartily. "That said, I believe you are correct, Miss Holmes. We *have* heard that Lady Ingram, before she made her debut, had hoped to marry a rather unsuitable young man, unsuitable not in terms of personal qualities, mind you, but because of irregular parentage."

"I was surprised," said Lady Avery. "Hadn't suspected that of Lady Ingram. She always struck me as someone with her gaze up, not down, if you know what I mean."

Livia longed to check again on her young man, but she and the gossip ladies had turned as one to follow Lady Ingram's departure and now he was behind her — if he was still there.

She began to scheme how she could extricate herself, but — would miracles never cease? — the ladies spied someone else they wanted to speak to and excused themselves with unholy haste.

She stood in place, waiting impatiently for them to disappear from sight — with Charlotte's scandal still fresh, Livia didn't want them to see her running after a man.

The moment the gossip ladies were well and truly gone, before she could turn around, his voice came, a few paces to her left. "I thought they'd never leave."

Livia felt the tremors in her heart as a pulsing sensation in the back of her head. "Same here," she managed to reply.

But now that she knew he wasn't going to depart before he'd spoken to her, she realized that she wasn't without misgivings about the situation. London was a city of four million souls. Three chance meetings in a short span with the same stranger? Their second encounter could still be explained away as a coincidence. But this one? No, he'd intended for it to happen.

Strangers, especially those of the well-dressed, well-spoken variety who appeared to be gentlemen, were considered a grave peril by Lady Holmes. *Scoundrels and fortune hunters, one and all,* she'd often said. Livia had secretly scoffed at her concern: A fortune hunter would have to be especially inept to come after the Holmes girls, given how little wealth the family actually possessed.

She didn't think the young man was a fortune hunter. But it would be stupid of her not to wonder, at this point, what it was that he wanted.

"May I interest you in a walk — and perhaps a bit of conversation?" he asked.

It was a dangerous proposition. They hadn't been introduced. To take a walk with him . . . Why, even before Charlotte's scandal, Lady Holmes would have locked Livia up without supper for such an infraction.

But Livia wasn't prepared to repudiate all further contact with him, starting this moment — not when she faced eight months in the country without Charlotte, without even a somewhat ally like Mott. The next best course of action would be for her to ask detailed questions.

And pray that she had the ability to correctly judge the sincerity and legitimacy of his answers.

"Yes," she said, turning to him, her heart leaping in spite of herself at the sight of his warm eyes and bright smile. "Yes to both a walk and a bit of conversation."

Monday

Oddly enough, now that Charlotte had warned Mrs. Watson that they were under surveillance, the surveillance evaporated. They observed carefully, but no one loitered unduly near any of the exits of either Mrs. Watson's house or 18 Upper Baker Street.

Still, on Monday, Charlotte took extra caution to make sure that they were not followed, going so far as to enter the de Bloises' hotel and exit from a service door on a different street.

The three women visited two other houses first, per Miss Redmayne's recommendation, before knocking on Mrs. Woods's service entrance. A nervous-looking young girl opened the door.

"Afternoon," said Miss Redmayne warmly. "I am Miss Hudson and this is Mrs. Hudson, my aunt. I study medicine at the University of London. As part of our curriculum, we are required to spread medical knowledge and combat misinformation, especially among those who might not otherwise have access to physicians. May I come in and speak to the staff?"

The girl looked uncertainly behind herself. "Let me ask Mrs. Hindle."

She closed the door, which was opened again a minute later by a brisk, large-boned woman in her forties.

Miss Redmayne offered her hand. "You must be Mrs. Hindle."

"That I am, and who are you?"

Miss Redmayne introduced herself and Mrs. Watson, and reiterated her purpose.

"A woman doctor? Well, I'll be."

"A woman doctor-to-be — I'm still in medical school. May I have your permission to come in? I'd be delighted to answer any questions you might have concerning your health — and to dispense such cures as I have brought with me. Free of charge, of course, all part of our program."

The sound of remedies she didn't need to pay for clearly appealed to Mrs. Hindle. But she wasn't yet convinced. She pointed at Charlotte. "And who is she? A lady doctor, too?"

Charlotte, in a brown wig and a pair of spectacles, kept her face turned to the side.

"This is my sister, Miss Eloisa Hudson," said Miss Redmayne apologetically. "She isn't studying medicine, unfortunately. As you can see, she needs looking after. No one else is home today, so we brought her with us. She is no trouble at all as long as someone keeps an eye on her."

Charlotte had decided to come as a facsimile of Bernadine. People tended to be alarmed about Bernadine at first, if they ever saw her, and then quickly forget her existence.

Perhaps it was Miss Redmayne's amiable yet capable manner that persuaded Mrs. Hindle the final inch. Perhaps it was Mrs. Watson's reassuringly maternal presence.

Or perhaps it was the quality of their garments — Charlotte's father was always suspicious of men of the lower class, even though the only men to ever rob him were two of his well-educated, well-dressed men of business. In any case Mrs. Hindle harrumphed. "Well, I suppose you can come in."

Mrs. Woods truly did run a tight ship. The basement passage was as spotless as any Mayfair drawing room. When they reached the servants' hall, which had two rectangular windows near the ceiling that admitted daylight, Charlotte saw that all the uniforms on the women were also perfectly spiffy.

"I see I needn't spend any time expounding on the importance of hygiene in this house," said Miss Redmayne. "We are fairly swimming in it. Does anyone have any questions? Rashes, intestinal troubles, feminine problems?"

No one seemed to be suffering from any of the problems she named, but it did not take long for the women to be engrossed in a discussion about hair loss, with the seemingly gruff Mrs. Hindle actually quite distressed about her thinning hair, and the younger women chiming in about various female relatives experiencing the same, and Miss Redmayne giving a scientific explanation about follicles and growth cycles.

Charlotte took the opportunity to slip out of the servants' hall and up the service stairs. She bypassed the ground floor: She wasn't interested in the common rooms or Mrs. Woods's apartment. She also bypassed the first floor: That was where she expected to find the bigger, better apartments, beyond what Mr. Finch could afford.

On the next floor she walked the corridor, glad to discover a small sign outside each door, carefully lettered with the name of the resident. *Mr. Lucas. Mr. Kennewick. Mr. Black. Mr. Donovan. Mr. Denham. Mr. Elwin.*

She double-checked the doors to make sure she hadn't skipped one. But no, no sign for Mr. Finch.

She went back to the service stairs and climbed up, only to be stopped by a locked door. Beyond would be the servants' rooms; the door was there to prevent fraternization.

There was no choice but to descend. The first floor had higher ceilings, a finer carpet stretched the length of the passage, and the doors were much farther apart, indicating significantly larger suites of rooms. *Dr. Vickery. Mr. Huron.* Aha, *Mr. Finch.*

The passage was silent, save for the faint sounds seeping in from the street outside. She tiptoed to the door, the soles of her boots sinking into the pile of the carpet. A quick look at the door gave no clue as to what Mr. Finch might be like in person, except that he wasn't a drunkard who scratched the Yale lock with careless efforts.

She put her ear to the door. Silence. Very carefully, she turned the handle. The door was locked.

The moment she let go, someone inside spoke. "Did you hear that?"

A woman's voice.

Charlotte hurried to the service stairs, more quickly than she had moved in ages. She was behind the door just in time to hear Mr. Finch's door open. And then close again.

She stood for a moment against the wall of the staircase, waiting for her heart to stop thumping. Then she made her way down to the servants' hall. No one had missed her departure — and no one paid any attention as she sat down again in the chair nearest the door.

The women were engaged in a rousing discussion about the men they served, their foibles, their odder habits, their sometimes inexplicable requests. Fortunately, it was agreed, Mrs. Woods was an excellent judge of character, and as eccentric as they could be, her gentlemen actually merited that appellation, unlike other men in other residences who liked to pinch bottoms, or worse.

"And she passes on their tips, too," said Mrs. Hindle approvingly. "Not like some landladies that ask for tips for us at Christmas and keep everything themselves."

"But surely not all the gentlemen here are of the old variety," Mrs. Watson prompted, a conspiratorial smile on her face. "There must be some young, handsome ones."

"Mr. Finch is young, but he isn't as pretty as Mr. Denham," said one of the maids.

"But he's a lot nicer than Mr. Denham," said another maid. "Mr. Denham isn't awful or anything, but he's awkward and wants to be left alone. Mr. Finch is pretty enough — and he's always got a smile and a how-do-you-do. Mrs. Woods doesn't like us to talk to the gentlemen, but we are supposed to answer when they say something to us. You take a man like Mr. Black, he's polite and all, but he's been here five years and I've said a thousand good mornings to him, and I'm sure he doesn't know me from a nail on the wall. But Mr. Finch remembers my name, my mum's toothache, and that last time I had a holiday, I went to Brighton to see my cousin. And he's only been here what, three months?"

"Four at the most," said Mrs. Hindle.

"And he's already one of Mrs. Woods's favorites. Brought her a nice wheel of cheddar from his holiday. When I went into her rooms this morning to clean, she was polishing it like it was a big old diamond." The maid tittered, then turned more serious. "But that was sweet of him, that. Most of them don't think of their landladies any more than they think of us lowly maids."

"Bit of a ladies' man?" inquired Miss Redmayne, with a half wink.

"Oh no, nothing of the sort. Proper. But easy to be around. Makes you feel right chirpy after you've had a quick chinwag with him."

Mrs. Hindle glanced at the clock. Miss Redmayne did not miss the signal: It was time for them to return to their duties. "Ladies, thank you for having me. I hope some of the remedies will prove to be of use. Perhaps we'll meet again someday."

More pleasantries were exchanged, with Mrs. Hindle issuing an invitation to her callers to return anytime.

Charlotte pulled both Mrs. Watson's and Miss Redmayne's sleeves. "Cheddar. Want cheddar. More cheddar."

The ladies looked at her, then exchanged a look with each other. Mrs. Watson was the first to react. "I'll serve you some cheese when we get home, my dear." And then, as Charlotte hoped she would, she turned back to the staff, "Speaking of cheddar, did Mr. Finch go to Somerset, the village of Cheddar? I've always heard there are some good sights to be seen in that area."

"Yes, there's where he went," said the most loquacious maid. "Told me about the gorge and the caves."

"Thank you." Mrs. Watson inclined her head. "Ladies, you have been a delight."

"A woman in his rooms?" Mrs. Watson and Miss Redmayne exclaimed together.

They were all three in the former nursery, which Miss Redmayne had jokingly rechristened the gymnasium when she joined Charlotte and Mrs. Watson for Charlotte's second self-defense lesson.

Miss Redmayne, with years of training under her belt, moved with a pantherlike grace. Charlotte's walking stick had flown everywhere for most of the session, though toward the end she did manage to disarm Miss Redmayne once.

"It isn't terribly shocking," Charlotte pointed out, still panting against a wall. "Every sign indicates that he has moved past his youthful passion for Lady Ingram.

What I find odd is the timing: that he has a woman in his rooms in the middle of the day."

"It wouldn't have been easy to smuggle her in, in broad daylight," mused Miss Redmayne.

"Perhaps she's been there since the night before and hasn't left," said Mrs. Watson. "But shouldn't he be at work? You said it sounded as if she was addressing someone."

"What Mr. Finch may or may not be doing with another woman — or with any number of other women — isn't what we have been engaged to find out," said Charlotte. "Lady Ingram wished to know 'whether he has passed away unexpectedly, whether he has married and no longer wishes to continue our acquaintance, whether he has been imprisoned or sent abroad.' At this point we can answer all of her queries. He hasn't died, been imprisoned, or sent abroad. He hasn't married. But by his action it's obvious he no longer wishes to carry on as they had."

"So do we let Lady Ingram know?" asked Miss Redmayne.

No one answered.

The question was settled for them when they went to the general post office and checked Sherlock Holmes's private box.

There was a letter from Lady Ingram and she wished to speak with them at six o'clock that evening.

Mrs. Watson studied Lady Ingram's upside-down image, taking note of her mounting distress.

"I know this isn't what you had hoped to hear," said Penelope, concluding her account, "but it is what we found, Mrs. Finch."

Mrs. Watson flinched to hear Lady Ingram's alias, now that she understood its significance. Even Miss Holmes, she thought, thinned her lips.

Lady Ingram was silent for a long time. It was difficult to tell via the camera obscura, but Mrs. Watson thought she shook. Then she said, "No, I'm afraid this is all wrong. You must have found a different Mr. Finch."

"Even in a city of London's size, there can't be that many illegitimate Myron Finches working as accountants."

"But you never saw him. By your account you've spoken to his landlady and the servants who work in the residential hotel where he lives. But you never saw him with your own eyes."

"We are not acquainted with Mr. Finch," Penelope pointed out. "And you have supplied no portrait or photographs. Seeing him in person would have made no difference to our investigation."

"But *I* know what he looks like. If you'll give me his address, I'll arrange to speak to this man myself. There must be some mistake."

"That is not what you asked of us, ma'am. We were tasked to discover whether he was dead, abroad, or otherwise detained in such a fashion that he could not get word to you."

Lady Ingram's jaw moved. "I thought that would be enough for me. I thought that would be enough either way. But now that I know he's well and nothing untoward has befallen him, now that all my frenzied worries have proven to be nonsense, I — I can't simply let it go. We loved each other. And I love him still. I always will."

Unshed tears shimmered in her eyes. She looked at Penelope. "Please, Miss Holmes. I need to speak to him, face to face. I need to hear from his own lips that we are never to see each other again. I need this. And he owes me as much."

"Mrs. Finch, listen to yourself," Penelope said sharply. "You are a married woman. You have a husband who has treated you with honor and kindness. And here you are, pining after a man who has happily moved on to other things. Nothing but further heartbreak and disillusionment await you down this path.

"Go home. Reconsider. Stop grasping at a past that has already receded beyond all reach."

Lady Ingram bolted from her seat. "You have no idea what we had."

"But I know that you can never regain it, even if you do see him, even if he agrees to more meetings in the future, and even if you forsake your vows and become his lover. You are a different woman. He is a different man. The most you will achieve is a pale, corrupted echo of your youth, a mirage that will console you not at all."

The woman who would never be Mrs. Finch stood as still as a pillar of salt, her fists clenched.

Miss Redmayne held out an envelope. "This is the fee you paid. There will be no charge for this consultation."

ELEVEN

"My aunt tells me I was right in denying Lady Ingram any possibility of reaching Mr. Finch," said Miss Redmayne softly. "But I'm not as sure of it myself."

They were back at Mrs. Watson's house. Mrs. Watson was in her room dressing for dinner, Charlotte scanning the small notices in the back of the paper, Miss Redmayne circumnavigating the afternoon parlor, tapping her fingertips against table corners, mirror frames, and the luxuriant fronds of a large, potted fern.

Charlotte looked at her. "No?"

Miss Redmayne sat down on the piano bench, her back to the instrument. "I can't decide whether I was truly motivated by principle, or whether there wasn't some vindictiveness on my part, an instinct to punish the one who has made a good friend miserable." She looked at Charlotte. "Would you have given her Mr. Finch's address?"

Charlotte thought about it. "Probably."

"And therein lies the difference. You don't wish her to suffer, but I do, at least in part, and I don't like that part of me."

Charlotte had no interest in seeing Lady Ingram suffer, but it was not out of any particular nobility of character: Whether Lady Ingram was in torment and how much did not affect the situation, or anyone else involved.

"I wouldn't have given her the address immediately," Charlotte said. "I would have asked her to come back in seventy-two hours, if she still wanted it."

"Do you think she would have had the wisdom to change her mind? To realize that it's a useless pursuit?"

Charlotte shook her head. It required no powers of deduction to see that Lady Ingram was lost to the persuasion of reason — for now.

Miss Redmayne looked up at the painting that hung opposite the piano: blue sky, blue sea, white marble, and languid, doe-eyed women — a present-day artist's unrelentingly romantic view of classical Greece. "I remember seeing her at the Eton and Harrow game the year she made her debut. She was so beautiful. Truly a vision. But even then we worried a little, my aunt and I, that he loved her more than she loved him."

Her gaze returned to Charlotte. "Five quid says she barges into 18 Upper Baker Street in less than seventy-two hours and demands to know Mr. Finch's address."

Charlotte would wager her last penny on that, almost as sure a bet as sunrise and London fog.

She folded the paper neatly and came to her feet. "The time has come for me to speak to Mr. Finch in person."

Charlotte stopped for a moment as she passed a house in which a *thé dansant* was reaching its apogee. Strains of violin and cello spilled out, the eternally ebullient melodies of Herr Strauss's Vienna. Brightly clad figures passed before open windows, champagne cups in hand. Laughter and the hum of animated conversation served as percussion to the music, with an occasional masculine voice rising above the din to lob a word of friendly mockery across the gathering.

Charlotte didn't go to many tea dances — they were not so fashionable these days — but the scene itself, this elaborate, stylized merrymaking, had figured prominently in her life for eight summers. And now she was a bystander, an outside observer of all that beauty and artificiality.

She understood the charges of profligacy and shallowness pelted at the Upper Ten Thousand, at those whose entire lives revolved around endless arrays of entertainment. But she also knew that for those on the inside, it was the only way they had been taught to live.

Few, in the end, ever truly defied the way they were taught to live.

She resumed walking. It was almost eight in the evening. Mrs. Woods served a plain supper at seven; her gentlemen ought to have dined by now. Chances were, Mr. Finch would be at home. The woman might still be with him, but that shouldn't preclude him from receiving his sister.

Charlotte noticed herself slowing down as she drew closer to Mrs. Woods's street. She wasn't nervous about meeting Mr. Finch, but she also wasn't looking forward to it. In her place, Livia would hesitate because of Mr. Finch's irregular birth. Charlotte had never understood the brouhaha over parentage — it was to the credit and blame of no one what their progenitors had been up to before they were born. Her reluctance stemmed from the indissolubility of blood ties — once the bond was claimed it couldn't be repudiated — and she was not keen on granting a permanent place in her life to a stranger.

She made the turn. Now she was halfway up the street. Three more houses and she would be knocking on Mrs. Woods's door and announcing that Mr. Finch's half sister had come to call. Two more houses. One more.

A young woman bounced up the steps from the service entrance of Mrs. Woods's place. Charlotte remembered her — the most talkative maid in the servants' hall. Even though she didn't expect to be recognized, now that she wasn't wearing either a wig or a pair of spectacles, Charlotte turned her face and pretended to read the playbills stuck to a lamppost.

The door opened again and out came Mrs. Hindle's voice. "Bridget, can you take this basket back to the tea shop?"

The maid went back. "Yes, mum."

"Good. When Mr. Finch comes back, tell him you returned it for him. There ought to be a copper in it for you."

When Mr. Finch "comes back"? From where?

"There better," said Bridget saucily. "It's out of my way."

Charlotte followed her. She was sure she would be found out within a few steps, but

258

the maid paid little mind to a woman walking behind her.

At the service entrance behind the tea shop, she knocked and a waitress wearing a long apron opened the door.

"I got you Mr. Finch's basket. He won't be coming 'round for a bit — got sent to Manchester for work, he is."

"Ah, you'll miss him, won't you, Bridget?" teased the waitress.

Bridget giggled. "I will. I won't lie. Such a sweetheart. And none of that nice-to-you-only-to-reach-under-your-skirt nastiness."

Charlotte slipped away as the two women exchanged their good-byes.

She wasn't familiar with the lives of accountants. Lawyers sometimes traveled for professional reasons, so it didn't seem unreasonable for accountants to be sent to another city for work-related purposes. But Mr. Finch's movements of the past ten days were beginning to appear calculated. He left on his holiday soon after Lady Ingram's notices appeared in the paper. And even when he returned, it was only to leave again.

One might almost conclude that he wished to avoid Lady Ingram.

Charlotte sipped the tea — no doubt Mrs. Woods's best Darjeeling served in her best

Crown Derby china — and sniffed. "Really? Manchester? What sort of business?"

She didn't quite duplicate Henrietta's nasal voice, but the sniff was rather spot-on.

"I'm afraid I don't know, Mrs. Cumberland," said Mrs. Woods, wringing her hands, as if the fact that Mr. Finch failed to inform her of the specifics of his trip were a personal failure on her part.

Charlotte emitted a small sigh, a whiff of air calibrated halfway between magnanimity and irritation, but not before she gave Mrs. Woods's highly chintzed parlor a pitying look. "Of course you can't possibly be expected to know everything. But this is vexing nonetheless."

"I'm sure it must be."

The landlady was nearly simpering — and at the outset she had not looked at all the simpering sort.

Henrietta Cumberland, Charlotte's eldest and only married sister, wielded an interesting kind of power over other women. The Lady Ingrams of the world parted the seas with their unassailable glamour. Other leaders of Society relied on their ability to cull an enviable guest list or pull off the event of the Season. Henrietta was neither elegant nor well-connected, and she presided over one of the cheapest tables in the history of dining.

And yet she had the uncanny ability to put herself into the dominant position in almost any exchange, an inner aggressiveness that discomfited most other women. So they accommodated her and tried hard to please her, rather than risk any unpleasantness.

"Do you know where he is expected to lodge in Manchester?"

"I'm afraid I don't know that either."

"His date of return?"

Mrs. Woods's voice grew smaller and smaller. "No, ma'am."

Charlotte sighed again, an expression of open displeasure. "I imagine you also don't have the address of the firm he works for?"

"Oh, but that I do. It is listed on his application, which I have in my office. If you will wait a minute, Mrs. Cumberland."

Mrs. Woods rushed off. Charlotte relaxed her face from the expression of barely-held-back disapproval that was Henrietta's trademark. Henrietta used this technique a great deal, demanding a series of items she knew she couldn't have, each time responding with greater dissatisfaction, until the beleaguered other party leaped with relief at a chance to prove her own knowledge, ability, or authority.

Mrs. Woods returned, holding two pieces of paper. "This is the list of references he provided. I have written down his employer's address for you, Mrs. Cumberland."

Charlotte accepted the offering. "Let me see his references."

"Of course, ma'am."

Charlotte scanned the three items on the list. Besides the London firm, there was a landlady in Oxfordshire and a solicitor in the same town. "Thank you. I will see myself out," she said, handing back the references.

"Would you like to leave your address, ma'am, for him to call on you, in case he returns before you find him?"

"No," Charlotte said with Henrietta's utter certainty, "I will not be leaving my address. Mr. Finch may be blood, but I cannot receive him at home. Good evening, Mrs. Woods."

"Only eight days since Lady Ingram came to us with her problem — and you are already a bona fide imposter, Miss Holmes," said Miss Redmayne, in smiling approval.

"Much must be sacrificed in the pursuit of truth," Charlotte replied modestly.

She expected Miss Redmayne to find her

ploy entertaining — by and large Miss Red-mayne still thought her involvement in the Sherlock Holmes business an amusing lark. Mrs. Watson, on the other hand, had always felt deeply uneasy about Lady Ingram and Mr. Finch — more so with each passing day. Her response to Charlotte's account of her time at Mrs. Woods's was a fretful silence, broken with a soft gasp.

"I almost forgot," said Mrs. Watson. "A letter from the chemical analysts came on the late post."

"Nothing from my sister?" asked Charlotte, without too much hope. Mrs. Watson would have already mentioned it, had there been a letter from Livia.

Mrs. Watson shook her head, her gaze sympathetic. "No, only the chemical analysts. They conducted every test in their repertoire and Mrs. Morris's biscuits came back negative on all accounts."

Charlotte wasn't surprised — she didn't think Mrs. Burns, the housekeeper, would have pulled such an obvious move on an already mistrustful Mrs. Morris. But she also didn't think Mrs. Morris had made everything up. The latter had seemed a little sheepish in describing her robust constitu-tion, but Charlotte suspected that she was secretly proud of that glowing health and took it as a sign that she had been favored in life.

"Do you know what I think, Miss Holmes?" said Mrs. Watson. "Mind you, I haven't had proper medical training, unlike our future Dr. Redmayne here."

From where she sat, Miss Redmayne sketched a bow.

"But I was married to a first-class doctor and that was a bit of an education in and of itself," continued Mrs. Watson. "To me the symptoms Mrs. Morris described sound like a case of severe allergy. Nothing less, nothing more."

"You could be right, ma'am," said Charlotte. "I'll keep that in mind."

Not all the biscuits Mrs. Morris had brought as evidence were sent for chemical analysis. Charlotte returned to her room, took out the one she had kept in a tin, broke off a small piece, and popped it into her mouth. A dessert biscuit, made with a substantial amount of butter in addition to the usual flour, sugar, and eggs. Charlotte was accustomed to dessert biscuits seasoned with ground ginger and cinnamon and liberally studded with currants, candied peels, and shredded coconut. Mrs. Burns's dessert biscuit was much plainer, no spices, no confected fruits, only a hint of lemon zest.

Charlotte ate another morsel of the biscuit, stale but still edible. She wasn't a true gourmet — not yet, in any case. But she possessed a nuanced enough palate, which confirmed that her initial judgment was correct: There was nothing in this biscuit except flour, butter, sugar, eggs — yolks only, to be accurate — and a pinch of grated lemon zest.

She finished the entire biscuit, scanning the rest of the post that had come for Sherlock Holmes. Nothing was the matter with her. She sat down before her vanity to brush her hair one hundred strokes. No incipient symptoms. She read the chapter on antimony in *Poisons: Their Effect and Detection — A Manual for the Use of Analytical Chemists and Experts.* And felt no different from how she normally did at this hour of the night.

So, no noxious substances in the biscuits. She supposed Mrs. Morris could be allergic to one of the ingredients in the biscuits, but they were such common ingredients that Mrs. Morris would have ingested four out of five when she'd eaten a *tuile* during her visit to 18 Upper Baker Street.

Could she possibly be allergic to lemons?

Charlotte dashed off a note.

Dear Mrs. Morris,
I submit the chemical analyst's report. In brief, they could not find any trace of contaminants in the biscuits.

This does not, however, conclusively disprove your hypothesis.

If it is amenable to you, I would like my sister to inspect the domestic offices of your father's house, preferably when the servants are away on their half day.

Yours,
Holmes

The letter on the desk remained blank. Livia's favorite pen, which wrote with a velvety smoothness, stood in the inkwell. Livia herself sat before the desk, feet on the chair, arms around her knees, rocking back and forth, wishing she were dead.

She really ought to have written Charlotte as soon as she got home from the park on Sunday. But she couldn't. Thinking about any part of that day and all she wanted to do was to whimper in a corner.

Dear God, what a disaster.

And she was so stupid. So stupid. When would she learn? When would she at last get it into her thick, moronic head that nothing good would ever happen to her?

What a disaster.

What an unmitigated catastrophe.

TWELVE

A startled doorkeeper admitted Inspector Treadles and Sergeant MacDonald, led them upstairs to a common room, then rushed off to knock on a door deeper in the dwelling. After several minutes, a man of about thirty-five, well-dressed and well-coiffed, came into the common room.

"Mr. Ainsley?" asked Treadles.

"The name's Temple. I do for Mr. Ainsley."

The valet, then. Treadles introduced himself and MacDonald. "Is Mr. Ainsley at home?"

"He is. But he's never up at this hour, unless he's just come back from a night on the town. Won't you have a cup of tea?"

Tea sounded tempting. Treadles had abandoned his own breakfast when MacDonald had banged on his door, all excited to have come across a missing-person

268

report, filed the evening before, that matched the description of their murder victim exactly. "Yes, thank you. Much obliged."

They followed the valet to a small sitting room dominated by a painting of an African elephant. Temple brought not only tea but buttered toast, muffins, marmalade, and a bowl of strawberries and grapes before running off to wrangle his master again.

"I wouldn't mind having someone to 'do' for me," said MacDonald, helping himself to a muffin.

Treadles couldn't complain. He might not have a valet, but since his wedding, he had never had to worry about how his meals got on the table or whether his clothes were overdue for laundering.

From farther inside the apartment came Temple's muffled entreaties. "Mr. Ainsley, you said you'd be up when I came back. Come now. You've got to get up now. You can't keep a police inspector waiting. What are they here for? I told you. About Mr. Hayward."

"Hayward?" came a sleepy voice. "Wait! You didn't tell me it was about Hayward."

The voice had become much less sleepy.

"I did, sir."

"No, you didn't. Oh, for God's sake, don't

269

open the curtains — the light hurts my eyes. Let me put on some clothes. Make me a cup of coffee, will you?"

"It's already in the percolator. Shall I shave you now?"

"I thought we mustn't keep the coppers waiting."

"But you can't receive anyone looking like this!"

"Trust me, plenty of people have seen me like this and the sun still never sets on the British Empire."

A minute later, a young man with blood-shot eyes, sandy stubble, and the beginning of a paunch came padding out, clad in a heavily embroidered black dressing gown. He shook hands weakly with the policemen and sat down opposite.

"What can I do for you, gentlemen? Oh, thank you, Temple, you're an angel."

"You reported a missing person last night, a Mr. Richard Hayward," Treadles stated, "whose address, according to the report, is the same as yours."

His first swallow of coffee had a marked effect on Ainsley. Already he was more alert, his speech sharper. "Yes, Hayward has the rooms at the end of the hall. Didn't know the police were this efficient. Will you be able to find him soon? He needs to at least

270

come back and take his poor guinea pig."

"Guinea pig?"

"Yes, he has one, which he has almost killed with neglect."

"Oh?"

"Yes, sweet little fellow — Samson's his name, though between you and me, he could be a Delilah, for all we know. But anyway, Hayward and I had plans to dine at this new place last Thursday. He was supposed to come by and have a drink here before we headed out. I waited and waited and he never came. Knocked on his door and no one answered. I figured he must have forgotten and was probably out having fun with other people, so I went to dinner on my own.

"When I came back, I knocked and still nobody answered. Left him a note under the door and told him what an ass he was. Expected him to come by and apologize — or at least explain. He didn't. But what can you do? Some fellows are like that.

"But then Saturday the landlady came and asked if I'd seen Hayward. Said he didn't come by to settle his bills for the week. That's when I remembered I still hadn't seen him since before Thursday. We got a little worried. She opened his door. And wouldn't you know it, the place had been turned inside out. Temple had to go fetch some smelling salts for Mrs. Hammer. And it was only when we were leaving that I saw Samson's cage on the floor, the little fellow starving to death inside. Took Temple the rest of the day to coax him back to life. Excellent nursemaid, Temple. Absolutely first rate."

"Mrs. Hammer didn't report the incident to the police."

Ainsley began to shake his head, thought the better of it, and shrugged instead. "I told her she ought to. But she said she had no evidence that it wasn't Hayward himself who tossed the place. You know how it is — she doesn't want anybody to think anything untoward has happened here. I couldn't force her to. But when there was still no hair or hide of Hayward forty-eight hours later, I thought something had to be done. Happened to walk by the police station and decided to do my duty."

"Is it possible to see the place?"

"Sure, but I had Temple tidy it up. Paid for the week's rent for Hayward, too — in case he fell into an opium den. Wouldn't be nice to come home and find all his belongings already carted off and someone else living there, would it?"

Treadles frowned. "Does he have an

272

opium habit?"

"Not that I know of, but who hasn't lost a week here and there to a lark?" said Ainsley with the sympathetic understanding of one who most certainly *had* lost a week here and there to such larks.

Treadles gave Ainsley a minute to consume a slice of toast. Then he said, "Sergeant MacDonald and I are here not because we routinely investigate missing persons, but because the description you gave of Mr. Hayward matches closely to that of an unidentified murder victim."

Ainsley choked on his coffee. "What?"

"We would like you to come with us and see whether you can identify the body."

Ainsley stared at Treadles, then MacDonald, then Treadles again. "*Jesus.* I mean, pardon my language, but — but surely you aren't serious?"

They convinced him that they were dead serious. A disoriented Ainsley went off to shave and dress — "Mustn't go see him, if that is him, looking like this, you see." Treadles and MacDonald used the key Ainsley had of Hayward's apartment — "Got Mrs. Hammer to give me a key. Samson should be in his own place. It's where he's most comfortable."

Temple had done the best he could, making the place presentable again. But he was no furniture restorer and had piled the damaged chairs in a small room equipped with only a set of shelves and a cot— the valet's room, if Hayward had one.

Clearly someone had been looking for something of value, something small enough to be stowed in a hollowed chair leg — except the ones that he sawed off all happened to be perfectly solid.

MacDonald was by the window, reaching through the bars of the guinea pig's cage to scratch the creature between the ears. "If only you could talk, Samson."

They spent another ten minutes looking through the rooms. And then, with a clean-shaven, soberly dressed Ainsley in tow, they departed for the morgue.

Mrs. Watson had formed the habit of checking for the post at 18 Upper Baker Street in the morning. The first two letters to ever come through the slot had been stepped on as Mrs. Watson and Miss Holmes arrived for their appointments. They were still more likely to get circulars and pamphlets, but thank-you notes and packages from clients had become increasingly common.

Two days ago, they had received a pair of opera tickets, which they had gifted to the de Blois ladies. And three days before that, an excellent bottle of whisky. No one had thought to gift Miss Holmes a plum cake yet, but it was probably only a matter of time.

This morning's post at Upper Baker Street, however, did not please Mrs. Watson as much. It took some self-restraint not to slam it down on the breakfast table when she reached home.

Miss Holmes, already dressed for going out, took a look at the typed address on the envelope and sighed. She finished the poached egg on her plate, wiped her fingers with her napkin, and reached for the letter.

Mrs. Watson knew what it said:

Dear Miss Holmes,

I cede you the moral high ground. I accept your admonishment that seeking the whereabouts of a man who has demonstrated his lack of interest in me is both an insult to my intelligence and a black mark upon my conduct as a married woman.

Nevertheless, I do not care anymore about either my own opinion of myself or anyone else's. I need to speak to Mr. Finch and that is that.

Please, I beg you, give me his address.

Yours,
Mrs. Finch

Miss Holmes rose. "I would have liked to have another muffin before leaving this table, but then again, I always feel the same no matter how many muffins I eat."

They removed to the drawing room, where Mrs. Watson wrote down the contents of a brief note, as dictated by Miss Holmes.

Dear Mrs. Finch,
Mr. Finch is away from London for a fortnight. When he returns, I will make inquiries on your behalf.

Yours,
Holmes

Mrs. Watson sealed the letter. "Do we know for certain that he will be gone that long?"

"Mrs. Woods told me yesterday that he has paid two weeks' rent in advance, so I am perfectly comfortable claiming he will be out for the duration." Miss Holmes checked her watch. "Shall we start our day?"

At least now the corpse had a name. Richard Hayward of London.

Unfortunately, the dead man's friend was a font of non-knowledge. Mr. Ainsley couldn't remember exactly when Mr. Hayward became his neighbor. "Four months ago. Six? It was some time this year." He was at sea as to where Hayward had lived before. "Norfolk, maybe. Or was it Suffolk?" And to Treadles's question on what the deceased had done for a living, his reply was a semi-horrified, "I would never ask such a thing. Why, that would presume he needed to toil for his own support in the first place."

Given Treadles's dedication to work, it was easy enough to forget that for a certain segment of the population, having to earn one's keep was considered a badge of dishonor. One could have serious interests, even callings. But to exchange honest labor for remuneration, well, that was for the lower classes.

"Don't think he mentioned work — never heard him complain about having to get up early. But if I were to be perfectly honest, I can't be entirely sure that he was a gentleman. A gentleman by birth, that is, not that he wasn't perfectly trustworthy and all that."

Treadles understood. Mr. Ainsley meant to say that Hayward had not been a man from the same class as himself.

He went back to the dead man's former lodging, to check on the references Hayward had furnished to his landlady. Only to discover that Mrs. Hammer didn't require references for those tenants who could pay three months' rent up front.

He asked to speak with Temple, the valet, instead. Temple was in the small room where he performed most of his work. Between polishing Mr. Ainsley's boots and ironing the man's shirts, he answered Treadles's inquiries.

According to him — and this agreed with Mrs. Hammer's records — Mr. Hayward moved in the first week of April. Temple remembered because he had learned about it from Mrs. Hammer when he returned from picking up Mr. Ainsley's new summer coats from his tailor, which he always did the first week of April.

Three weeks later, Mr. Ainsley had invited Mr. Hayward to his place for dinner — Temple was sure of the date because he had written down the purchases in his diary, which he gladly showed Treadles. Bottle of claret, bottle of champagne, three bottles of mineral water, veal cutlets, a saddle of mutton, and a strawberry tart and a Swiss roll from Harrod's.

"I do all right with plain baking," Temple

said apologetically. "But fancy cakes we buy."

"I'm saving up for one of those meringue cakes for my sister's birthday," said Mac-Donald. "She's wanted one for ages."

"Oh, those are almost too pretty to eat, they are."

Treadles cleared his throat. "Mr. Temple, do you know where Mr. Hayward lived before he became Mrs. Hammer's tenant?"

"I didn't ask him — he was Mr. Ainsley's friend, not mine."

"Mr. Ainsley didn't think he was born a gentleman. Do you agree with that assessment?"

"I do. I think he went to a proper school — he didn't have a regional accent, if you know what I mean, sir. But I don't think there are enough quarterings in the family. Or any, for that matter."

"How do you know?"

Temple half winced. "Hard to say. I just do. For example, the day of the dinner, he came, brought Mr. Ainsley a marvelous bottle of cognac, and it all went off very well. But when he was on his way out, he tipped me."

The way Temple shook his head, one would have thought Mr. Hayward had performed a handstand in the vestibule.

"Mind you, I appreciated the generosity, but it was only dinner. If he'd stayed with us for a few days and I'd done for him, then, yes, it would have been the right thing. But it was only dinner. And he gave me far too much. So that told me that his money was awfully recent. Not even nouveau riche; that would have implied his father had it. And if his father had it, he should have known what to do with a valet. If you ask me, I think he probably came into some unexpected inheritance within the past few years."

It never failed to surprise Treadles — and dismay him in some way — that a person's origin was so easy to pin down. Here was someone who had exchanged scarcely three sentences with the dead man, yet could offer such trenchant insight on when he had obtained his fortune.

On the other hand, had Temple been able to tell Treadles a great deal of Hayward's inner life, but nothing of his pedigree or lack thereof, it would have been of far less use to the case. He thanked Temple and asked to have the key to look through Hayward's rooms again.

On his way out, he asked, rather casually, "You wouldn't happen to know, would you, Mr. Temple, who might have wanted to harm Mr. Hayward?"

Temple thought for a moment. "I can't say I do. But come to think of it, Mr. Hayward himself might have known."

"What do you mean?"

"My schedule is regular — Mr. Ainsley's, too, if you think about it, even if it does start three hours after everyone else's. So I go in and out of here at about the same time every day, to get what I need to look after him. But occasionally he wants something out of the blue. Or I remember that I've forgotten the bacon when I went to buy everything else. Then I need to make an extra trip. And the odd thing was, whenever I've come back after going out unexpectedly, as I let myself back in, I'd hear Mr. Hayward's door open a crack. By the time I turned and looked, he'd already closed the door again. Every time.

"I didn't think much of it at the time — some people are jumpy. But knowing what happened to him, I can't help but wonder if *he* didn't expect something awful to come his way. Maybe whenever he heard someone in the hall at an unexpected time, he got nervous. And had to make sure it was only me, coming back with a rasher of bacon or Mr. Ainsley's shaving powder, and not someone here to harm him."

Temple thought for another moment, then nodded. "Yes, I reckon he must have been scared."

"Well, that was quick," said Mrs. Watson, as they walked out of Norton & Pixley, Chartered Accountants.

Apparently, Mr. Finch had resigned from his post after only six weeks. Which meant that for the past two months, he hadn't been working — at least not at Norton & Pixley.

Mrs. Watson didn't want to say it aloud, since he was a close blood relation to Miss Holmes, but she was beginning to be convinced that Lady Ingram was entirely mistaken in Mr. Finch's character. Maybe he was well liked at his place of lodging, but at this point, one certainly couldn't call him *dependable.*

"Harrod's, please," said Miss Holmes to Lawson, as they climbed up into Mrs. Watson's carriage.

Harrod's? "Do we need anything from there?"

"We are being followed," said Miss Holmes, settling herself into the seat. "Harrod's would be a good place to get rid of this unauthorized addition to our party. Also, it has been a while since I browsed their cheese selection."

Mrs. Watson's heart pounded. Of course she had steeled herself for the possibility that those who had watched her house earlier would resume their surveillance at some point, but she had hoped much more fervently that all such potentially Moriarty-related troubles had gone away for good.

The carriage didn't have a window in the rear, but she still turned and stared at the burgundy-brocade-upholstered surface, anxiety churning in her stomach.

"Don't worry," said Miss Holmes quietly. "We'll shake them loose before long."

"But they'll simply go back to the house and wait for the next opportunity to follow us."

Miss Holmes said nothing.

They maintained their silence inside Harrod's, marching through various departments and stopping briefly at the cheese counter. But Miss Holmes being Miss Holmes, when they left from a service entrance, she was holding a freshly purchased tin of biscuits.

Only when they were being driven away in a hackney did Mrs. Watson ask, "This is about the wheel of cheddar Mr. Finch bought Mrs. Woods, isn't it?"

Miss Holmes nodded. "Very fine deduction, ma'am. Our little jaunt to the cheese counter confirmed that not only is it possible to buy a wheel of prize-winning cheddar without going to Somerset, it's almost as easy as a trip to the corner post box."

Their next stop was the house of Mrs. Morris's father, Dr. Swanson. When they arrived Miss Holmes announced that they were free of followers, but Mrs. Watson's relief was only momentary.

Mrs. Morris received them with much pleasure. It wasn't the servants' half day but the housekeeper, Mrs. Burns, had leave from her employer to help at the soup kitchen for a couple of hours. She took her maids with her, which left the coast clear for Mrs. Morris to give Miss Holmes and Mrs. Watson a tour of the housekeeper's office, the stillroom, and the stockroom.

"I assume you've been well, Mrs. Morris?" asked Miss Holmes.

"Yes, thank goodness," said Mrs. Morris fervently. "But then again, I haven't had anything that came out of Mrs. Burns's stillroom."

The stillroom was superbly organized; clearly labeled jars of jams, jellies, and preserved fruits and vegetables sat in alphabetic order on the open shelves. There were also jars of crystallized ginger, confected pineapple, and candied peels.

Miss Holmes examined everything closely, especially the candied peels. "There's the making of a good fruitcake."

Mrs. Watson didn't know how she could concentrate on their client's problem. Mrs. Morris had an allergy; Miss Holmes had caught the attention of a man so nefarious that his wife staged her own death to get away from him.

So iniquitous he gave Lord Bancroft Ashburton pause.

Mrs. Morris made a face. "I don't like dried fruits. Raisins I hate above all, but the rest of them aren't much better."

Which might explain why Mrs. Burns's supply of dried fruits had remained so high.

"I'm surprised there is pineapple, though," said Mrs. Morris. "No one in the family likes tropical fruits."

"No?" Miss Holmes ran her hand along several spools of twine.

Mrs. Watson, to distract herself, did likewise. Most of them were made of jute, but the last one felt a little different: stiffer and coarser. Coir?

"I was born in India. But according to my father, India disagreed with everyone in the family. My mother contracted malaria, my father had dengue fever, and I had the most terrible heat rashes. And none of us ever cared for mangos, jackfruits, or what have you."

Mrs. Watson chose not to suggest that Mrs. Burns might be personally fond of confected pineapple. She felt rather sorry for Mrs. Burns. The woman seemed very good at her work. Yet here she was, the subject of a clandestine investigation that could result in her expulsion from the house without a letter of character.

At this point Mrs. Morris's demeanor was the only thing in her favor. She seemed grateful to be taken seriously, but there was no sense of preening, of wallowing in her status as the unfortunate victim. If anything, Mrs. Watson received the distinct impression that Mrs. Morris wished none of this had happened at all.

Miss Holmes pointed to a shallow pan next to the coffee mill. "Mrs. Burns roasts the coffee?"

"She does, and I must admit that she does the roasting very well. I never drink coffee, as a rule, but I will take an occasional cup here."

"Does she keep any ground coffee on hand?"

"No, she makes essence of coffee and mixes it with milk for my father's morning cup; it's almost as good as the café au lait they serve in Paris. But otherwise she roasts and grinds the beans daily, usually before lunch."

"Quite a luxury," said Miss Holmes, sounding impressed.

"I know." Mrs. Morris groaned. "That alone will make it difficult to get rid of her. My father is terribly fond of his coffee and very particular about it. He has no domestic skills whatsoever — not that he needs any — but from time to time he used to grind his own coffee and operate the percolator to his exact specification. Not anymore, of course, now that Mrs. Burns does it so well."

Miss Holmes tapped her index finger twice against her chin. "I've seen all I need to of the domestic offices. Will you invite us for tea — or coffee — when Mrs. Burns is here? My brother would wish me to observe her at work."

"I almost certainly can, but it won't happen immediately. Father and I are going on a short holiday," said Mrs. Morris, perking up. "You see, he still thinks I'm reacting to London and that I'd feel better in a less polluted place. So we're off to the seaside tomorrow."

"I'm sure you'll find it very enjoyable."

"Yes, just like old times. But, in the

meanwhile, I would be delighted if you ladies would stay for tea today. I have some lovely biscuits from Fortnum and Mason."

"We will if we can also make a contribution," said Miss Holmes. "I happened to acquire some biscuits from Harrod's just now and I would dearly love to scc how they compare to the biscuits from Fortnum and Mason."

Mrs. Morris was taken aback — it wasn't every day a guest asked to serve her own biscuits. But she said, "Certainly. Why not?"

Dr. Swanson's drawing room seemed to have been recently redecorated — it was strikingly simple in its ethos. All the patterns were stylized flora and fauna, the furnishings were almost rustic in their appearance, and there was such a remarkable lack of clutter that Mrs. Watson, who enjoyed a bit of old-fashioned clutter — a home ought to give the impression of having been lived in — felt the place was too empty.

"A very modern room," observed Miss Holmes, opening a tin of lemon biscuits and holding it out in Mrs. Morris's direction.

"So they say." Mrs. Morris's lips slanted. She took a biscuit from Miss Holmes's tin. "I prefer how it was before. I can understand not displaying every knickknack my mother ever acquired, but I can't help feeling a little injured on her behalf that they were put into storage wholesale. And it's all Mrs. Burns's influence, I daresay."

"Oh?" asked Miss Holmes with her usual neutrality.

"My father thinks Mrs. Burns has good taste. Oh, but this is a good biscuit. Where was I? Right, I've never heard him say that about any other woman. I tell you she has her claws deep in him, Miss Holmes."

As if they'd conjured her father, the front door of the house opened. A minute later, a man poked his head into the drawing room. "There you are, Clarissa. I hope I am not interrupting."

Dr. Swanson, then. He was a tall man, erect of carriage, with a fast gait and a full head of salt-and-pepper hair. Mrs. Watson had no idea why she expected a doddering old man. Mrs. Morris had told them he was sixty-three, which was only ten years older than her current age — and she had by no means expected herself to arrive at full senility in a mere decade. She could only conclude that even for those who are no longer so young, old age remained an alien land, its residents regarded with both pity and suspicion.

Mrs. Morris introduced her guests as new friends from the charitable knitting society. Mrs. Watson laughed inwardly. Having made theatrical costumes for herself and others, she sewed very well, but couldn't knit to save her life. And Miss Holmes, hmm, she would have to ask Miss Holmes at a later time whether the latter was acquainted with any feminine arts.

Dr. Swanson offered them his hand to shake — he had a strong, but not overpowering, grip. "I would have made coffee had I known Clarissa was expecting guests."

"Ah, a pity. I enjoy coffee very much," said Miss Holmes.

"Our housekeeper also makes excellent coffee, but unfortunately you came on her day to help at the soup kitchen."

Miss Holmes sighed dramatically. "I can only wish my housekeeper had mastered the art of coffee making. Alas, she makes a bitter brew."

"We have been very fortunate in Mrs. Burns. I can't complain about her predecessor, a very conscientious woman. But her coffee had nothing to recommend it."

Mrs. Morris, having probably heard enough talk of Mrs. Burns, placed her hand on her father's sleeve. "I was just telling these ladies about our imminent holiday."

The rest of tea was spent in agreeable chatter about the trip. As Miss Holmes and Mrs. Watson rose to take their leave, Mrs. Morris said, "Oh, your biscuits, Miss Holmes. You mustn't forget them."

"Keep them," said Miss Holmes. "I think you'll enjoy them more than I do."

The rest of Charlotte and Mrs. Watson's day was spent checking Mr. Finch's other two references, both in Oxfordshire. Neither, in the end, proved remotely trustworthy.

The address he gave for his prior residence was indeed a lodging house for single gentlemen, but the landlady had no recollection of having ever hosted a Mr. Myron Finch, let alone written him a letter of character.

The other, a solicitor, had retired six months ago and embarked on a grand tour of Europe and the Levant. He was not expected back for another year and a half, at least.

They returned to Mrs. Watson's house hungry and stiff from their travels — or at least Charlotte was hungry and Mrs. Watson muttering about her aging back. Mrs. Watson received a massage from Miss Redmayne; Charlotte sequestered herself with a sandwich made with Madame Gascoigne's secret-recipe pâté.

They reemerged to meet in the drawing room, both commenting on how much better they felt.

"I can only hope that someday I will prove to be as useful as that pâté sandwich." Miss Redmayne laughed. "Truly, what heroic service it has rendered."

"You are young and ambitious, Miss Redmayne," said Charlotte. "I have already learned that I will never be as valuable as a pâté sandwich."

"In that case I must have a new objective. Aha, I have decided that my goal is never to be as troublesome as Mr. Finch."

"Under normal circumstances, I might chastise my niece for being too blunt. But I'm afraid I agree with her tonight. I am very glad, Miss Holmes, that when you were in need of assistance, you didn't go to your brother."

For Mrs. Watson, this was strongly worded condemnation.

Charlotte remembered that sensation she had from the very beginning, of something being not quite right about this case. If only she knew exactly what it was. "I won't defend Mr. Finch," she said, sorting through the letters that had arrived while they were out, wondering when, if ever, she'd hear from Livia again. "But he is still my brother — and this is a highly irregular situation."

"What do you plan to do?" asked Miss Redmayne.

"I'd like to take a look inside his rooms. That could give me a better idea of what he's up to. Would either of you ladies know someone conversant in lock picking?"

"Funny you should ask," said Mrs. Watson. "When you first met my staff, you warned me that Mr. Lawson had spent some time in a penitentiary. Care to guess what he did?"

Charlotte barely heard her. *A note from Livia!*

"If you'll excuse me for a minute," she said, slicing the envelope open. "My sister might have some information about Lady Ingram to pass on."

But at this moment she didn't give a farthing about Lady Ingram. Livia had written, at last.

Dear Charlotte,
Please forgive me for not putting pen to paper sooner.

I encountered ladies Avery and Somersby on Sunday near the Round Pond. As it so happened, Lady Ingram walked by with her children. Her presence made it easy to pose questions about her. The ladies confirmed that indeed, they had heard rumors that before her debut, she had at one point hoped to marry an unsuitable young man.

Which made me sad for everyone involved.

And now for news you were probably not expecting. After Lady Ingram had left the scene and the gossip ladies moved on to greener pastures, a gentleman came up to me and asked if he could speak with me. He then proceeded to introduce himself as Mr. Myron Finch, our illegitimate half brother.

Two days later I still have not found the words to describe my stupefaction. I do not believe his approach was called for. No self-invitation on his part could ever be called for.

Yet I cannot fault his reason for taking this extraordinary step. Apparently, one of Papa's solicitors had called on Mr. Finch some days ago, when he had been out of town on holiday. It was his understanding, from speaking to his landlady, that the lawyer had not wished to leave a message, as he had come on a private matter of some delicacy.

"I gathered," said Mr. Finch, "that the visit had been in regard to Miss Charlotte — whether she had sought my help in her exile."

"You know about her?" I couldn't help but exclaim.

"I do. Unfortunately, I have not heard from her at all. I hope she is well."

"We all hope so," I told him.

"If you can convey a message to her, please let her know that she is welcome to call at any time. And any assistance that I can render her, I will be more than glad to offer."

With that, he bade me good day and departed. The encounter shook me. I am shaken still. But at least now there is one more avenue of possibilities for you, Charlotte.

Love,
Livia

P.S. Mr. Finch has taken rooms at Mrs. Woods's residential hotel for gentlemen, on Fountain Lane.

P.P.S. Mrs. Montrose's ball is tonight. After that, only Lord and Lady Ingram's ball to go before we leave London. I have had more than enough of the Season, but I do not know how I shall bear eight months without you.

Livia sat at the edge of a group of other wallflowers, hating everything about the evening.

Everything about her life.

She had somehow managed to pen the letter she owed to Charlotte. But what purgatory, having to set down the events of that calamitous day, her skin scalding with mortification, her stomach contorting in nausea and disgust.

Her own brother! She had fallen in love with *her own brother.* And the worst thing was, whenever she thought of him, before the tsunami of dismay crested, she still felt that same sense of hope and excitement.

Which only made everything twice as repugnant.

"Miss Holmes? Miss Olivia Holmes?"

A young woman with a pretty, amiable face stood before Livia.

"Y-yes?" said Livia uncertainly.

"Of course it is you. How good to see you again! Do let us find somewhere quieter to talk — so unspeakably loud in here, isn't it?"

Without waiting for Livia to respond, the young woman took her hand and pulled her to her feet. Livia, disoriented but not wanting to make a scene, let the young woman link their arms together and lead her away from the other wallflowers.

The young woman leaned in close. "I'm a messenger from Miss Charlotte. She needs to see you. Will you come outside with me?"

Alarm trilled through Livia. "Is she all right?"

"Yes, she's fine. But she has questions for you after receiving your letter," answered the young woman. "And I'm Penelope Redmayne, by the way, Mrs. Watson's niece."

"R-right. Enchanted."

Livia could only hope that her unrequited and — Dear God! — incestuous love for Mr. Finch didn't somehow announce itself loud and clear in the letter. It was terrifying, at times, to have a sister like Charlotte.

The streets outside Mrs. Montrose's house were crowded with carriages. They walked some distance before reaching the one that contained Charlotte.

"I'll be quick — we must get you back before Mamma notices that you are missing," said Charlotte, once Livia had taken a seat.

Lady Holmes was an inconsistent chaperone. Sometimes she was far too concerned with her own amusement to keep an eye on her daughters. Other times, perhaps to expiate her guilt, she watched them like a hawk. Tonight she seemed awake enough, so there was no telling which kind of chaperone she would turn out to be.

"You said you were near the Round Pond in Kensington Gardens when you met Lady Avery and Lady Somersby. Where exactly were you with regard to the Round Pond?"

What did that have to do with anything? "On the east side."

"Where the pond meets that grassy avenue?"

"Yes." The grassy avenue extended all the way to the Long Water, the man-made lake that was half in Kensington Gardens and half in Hyde Park.

"Which way did you stand?"

"Facing the water, of course."

"And where did Lady Ingram come from?"

"South of us. The children's governess was carrying a toy boat, so probably they had been playing with it in the pond earlier."

"Which direction were they headed?"

"To the avenue — to go home, I suppose."

"And Mr. Finch, in your letter you said he approached you after the gossip ladies left. Was Lady Ingram gone from the scene by then?"

"Yes."

"So he didn't see them?"

Charlotte's questions confused Livia, but she gave her sister the benefit of the doubt. "He'd already seated himself on a bench near mine as Lady Avery and Lady Somersby made their approach. Since he'd meant to speak to me, no doubt he saw them. I can't be sure whether he saw Lady Ingram, but men usually tend not to miss a beautiful woman in their vicinity."

Charlotte was silent for a moment. "Miss Redmayne, will you light the pocket lantern?"

A match scratched. The sharp tang of sulfur assaulted Livia's nostrils. The lit pocket lantern was oriented so that its light fell on an open notebook in Charlotte's lap.

She drew an oval, which was the actual shape of the Round Pond. "So here you are at its eastern edge. Where is the bench Mr. Finch took?"

Livia put her finger where she estimated the spot to be. "Ten paces away."

"On the north side of the pond, facing south?"

"Yes."

"You are sure?"

Livia nodded. Unfortunately, she knew exactly where he had been sitting.

"And you said Lady Ingram, her children, and their governess were coming *from* the south?"

"Yes."

Miss Redmayne made a small, sharp sound, as if she'd sucked in an abrupt breath.

"How did Lady Ingram look, by the way, when you saw her?"

Livia shrugged. "How she usually appears these days. Beautiful and rather aloof, I'd say."

"She didn't look weary or unhappy or . . . surprised?"

"Not that it was apparent."

"Did she see you?"

"She nodded at us. Very regally."

"And how closely did she pass by you?"

"Fifteen, twenty feet, thereabout."

Charlotte closed her notebook. Nobody said anything for a moment. Then Charlotte blew out the pocket lantern and murmured, "A difficult couple of days for you?"

The gentleness of her voice . . . Livia wanted to burst into tears. *Oh, you have no idea!*

She had elided over her encounter with Mr. Finch as much as possible. In reality, he hadn't immediately confessed that he was her brother — she hadn't wanted to begin their conversation with all the serious questions. Instead, they had spoken for a good quarter of an hour in great animation, laughing together more often than not, and she had been walking six inches off the ground.

Or perhaps it had been six miles. For the crash to earth had shattered everything.

"It was shocking, that was all," Livia managed, grateful for the darkness that followed the extinction of the lantern's small flicker.

She reached for the door. Charlotte put a hand on her sleeve but didn't say anything.

After a moment, she let go.

Thirteen

Wednesday

It was already raining by the time Charlotte reached Kensington Gardens, the sky heavy, the gust cold — another English summer day. Charlotte, in Mrs. Watson's first-rate mackintosh and rubber boots, felt as water-repellent as a duck, marching past those trying to hold open their umbrellas against a wind that changed direction every two seconds.

She arrived at a Round Pond that was largely empty, except for a nanny as well equipped as she and a boy who looked to be the sort to regard a day stuck inside as divine punishment.

Up close, Round Pond possessed the shape of an ovoid mirror with a somewhat ornate frame. At the eastern end, a straight edge roughly one third of the width of the pond met the grassy avenue that gave onto Long Water, a quarter mile away. A bench sat at either end of this straight edge, where the banks of the pond began to curve again.

Charlotte placed herself behind the bench to the north, where Mr. Finch had sat. Farther away there were trees, but the pond was situated in the middle of a clearing, surrounded by manicured lawns that did not in the least impede the view.

Given the distances Livia had described, it was extremely difficult to imagine how Lady Ingram and Mr. Finch had not seen each other. Mr. Finch would have been looking south toward Livia, and Lady Ingram would have been headed northeast and —

Unless their line of sight had been blocked by Livia, Lady Avery, and Lady Somersby and their parasols?

Unlikely, but not impossible. And Mr. Finch wouldn't have been staring in Livia's direction all the time, as he wouldn't have wanted her to think of him as rude or potentially dangerous.

Not impossible, but at some point, the likelihood of a scenario approached so close to zero that it merited no further consideration.

They *had* seen each other.

Then what? They were in public. Lady Ingram had her children and their governess with her. And even if she could order the governess to take the children home, she couldn't possibly have approached Mr. Finch then and there, not with the two most infamous Society gossips standing nearby.

Was that what had motivated her subsequent note, practically begging for his address? Because the sight of him had sent her into an inward frenzy and those chaotic emotions would not stop wreaking havoc until they had a proper face-to-face?

And Mr. Finch, what had been his reaction? It seemed not to have affected his encounter with Livia. But the next evening he had left town abruptly. Could his departure have been a result of his seeing Lady Ingram? A guilty conscience after all?

What about Lord Ingram? Where had *he* been? Sunday afternoons he was usually the one taking the children out for small expeditions. Was he still away on the crown's business, risking life and limb for queen and country while his wife accidentally encountered the only man she'd ever loved?

She must stop bringing Lord Ingram into her deliberations, Charlotte thought. Her reasoning was still valid. What could he do even if he knew? Forbid civilized contact between Lady Ingram and a friend of long standing?

He could despise you, pointed out the part of her that did, from time to time, take human emotions into consideration.

And that, in essence, was her problem.

After leaving the Round Pond, Charlotte stopped by the newspaper office. She had a note that she wanted to place in the papers, or at least, in the one to which her parents subscribed.

CDAQKHUHAAQDYNTVDKKJSGHM-
JNEYNT

It was a simple cipher that she and Livia had devised together when they were little girls, which consisted of replacing the letter B with the letter X and pushing all the other letters down a place. They called it the Cdaq Khuha, for Dear Livia.

DEARLIVIAAREYOUWELLITHINKOF-
YOU

Livia had not been well the night before. She had been on the edge of hysteria, clutching white-knuckled on to her composure. Public gatherings tried her. Under the current circumstances, they tried her even more. But that she was at a ball where she was having no fun wasn't enough to account for her jagged distress.

Even an encounter with their illegitimate brother ought not have affected her that much.

"There you go, miss." The clerk came back with a receipt. "Your message will be in the papers tomorrow."

"Thank you," said Charlotte. "And can you tell me, if I wish to put a notice in the paper without coming in person, how that can be achieved?"

"You can write or cable us with your message, the dates you want it to run, and send a postal order with the correct fee. As simple as that."

"If I wish to put a different notice every day, should I write daily then?"

"I wouldn't advise it. Then every day you'd need to pay poundage on a different postal order, wouldn't you? Better to send in all your messages at once."

"But what if I don't know what I wish to say ahead of time?"

The clerk regarded her quizzically. "Then you must do as you see fit, miss."

"Is there anyone who does that in practice? Send in a different notice daily?"

"No." The clerk shook his head decisively.

She supposed submitting notices in batches made sense in Lady Ingram's case.

She wouldn't miss the pennies for extra poundage, but it would be easier for her to manage the deployment of messages if she did so once or twice a week, instead of every day.

Charlotte pulled out her pocket watch, a man's watch; watches made for women, though prettier, tended not to keep very good time. A quarter past nine. A lady made or received calls in the afternoon. During the Season there were also plenty of other functions — at-home teas, rowing parties, drives in the park — to keep her post meridiem hours scheduled to the minute.

But she had some time in the morning.

The two most recent notes from Lady Ingram had not been sent by courier but from the Charing Cross Post Office. A sensible place, as she could call for letters there, too. And if she had recognized Mr. Finch but was unable to speak to him because the place had been too public, wouldn't she be calling for letters at every opportunity, in case Sherlock Holmes decided to part with Mr. Finch's address after all?

Luckily for Charlotte, there was a tea shop diagonally across the street from the post office. She took a position by the window. Her view of the post office door was partially blocked by a hapless sandwich board man trudging back and forth in the rain, advertising hair pomade. Still, a good enough vantage point, better than standing on the drenched street — or attempting to loiter inside the post office.

Surveillance was boring work. And surveilling Lady Ingram made no sense, unless one was prepared to accept the very damaging theory that she didn't actually know Mr. Finch at all. Charlotte was eminently prepared to accept any theory that fit all the facts, even the seemingly preposterous ones.

But if she didn't know Mr. Finch, why would Lady Ingram be looking into his whereabouts? For that Charlotte had no good, or even halfway coherent, guesses. But first, she must see for herself whether Lady Ingram was truly upset, when she wasn't in front of Sherlock Holmes's representatives.

She asked for a fresh cup of tea and slowly took another bite of her crumpets. Even for someone with her robust appetite, limits existed as to how much she could ingest in one sitting. She was approaching those limits. Not to mention, the chair was rather uncomfortable. And she was beginning to long for a trip to the water closet.

She blinked. She recognized the person

passing in front of the window: not Lady Ingram, but the woman pointed out by Lord Ingram as the one watching Mrs. Watson's house, the day they stumbled across the murder in Hounslow.

Should she follow the woman? Goodness knew she didn't have much experience in these things. And unlike the previous time she performed surveillance — at Claridge's trying to spy on the Marbletons in the middle of *l'affaire Sackville* — she didn't have a widow's veil on hand to keep her identity hidden.

The woman went into the post office.

On the other hand, Charlotte had Mrs. Watson's mackintosh, which she wouldn't be obliged to remove in the post office. And in order to fit under the raincoat's hood, she had worn a hat so small and undecorated it was practically nonexistent.

Not to mention, she did have a letter to Livia in her handbag.

She exhaled, left money on her table, and hurried out. It took longer than she wanted to cross the street, but her luck held at the post office: The woman, standing before the counter, had her back to the door. Charlotte slid over to the stand where telegram forms had been placed for the patrons' convenience and pretended to compose a cable.

A clerk returned from the sorting room and handed a letter to the woman. The woman left the counter and went to the form stand across the room from Charlotte. Charlotte continued to doodle lightly on her form.

The woman finished with hers and approached the next available clerk. Charlotte couldn't hear what she said, but she did hear the clerk's reply, asking for a shilling and two pennies. She was purchasing a telegram. The cost of telegrams had been reduced the year before. It was now sixpence for the first six words, and one penny for each two additional words. The woman had bought a maximum of twenty-four words.

A bit long for a cable, though not extraordinarily so.

Charlotte waited until the woman left before hurrying over to the stand where she had written out the text of her cable. The surface of the stand was not in terribly good shape. The wood had become pitted and grooved. The woman would have put her form on top of a few other forms, so that her pencil didn't poke through the paper.

Ah, here it was, the form that had been directly under hers.

Alas, it was difficult to make sense of the faint indentations on the paper. She went outside, where the light was stronger. Still she could only be sure of two words, *the Lord.*

Charlotte wasted no time before queuing up to the window where the woman had sent her cable. When it was her turn, she said, with some anxiety, "I do apologize, sir, but my aunt thinks she might have made a mistake in the cable she sent just now. She sent it to the *Illustrated London News,* but she actually meant to send it to the *Times* instead."

"If you are speaking of the woman who sent the cable for a shilling and two pennies, you may rest easy, miss. She did send it to the *Times.*"

"Oh, wonderful. My goodness, you wouldn't believe how panic-stricken she was — she was too embarrassed to come and check herself."

"That isn't a problem at all, miss."

"Just to be sure, we are speaking of the one with the biblical verse, yes?"

"Yes, miss."

"Thank you. You've been so helpful."

She turned around, only to see someone else she recognized: Mott, the Holmes groom who had been instrumental in getting Livia and Charlotte's letters to each other. And she was right about his nearsightedness: He wore a pair of wire-rimmed glasses.

This was her day for unexpectedly running into people she didn't mind coming across. Mott appeared equally astonished at the sight of her but did not need her to gesture a second time to meet her at the telegram form stand, putting away his specs as he did so.

"Do you have anything from my sister for me?"

"No, Miss Holmes. I'm just here to see whether there's anything for her from you."

"There is, but I haven't put it in the post yet." She pulled the letter from her handbag and gave it to him. "She can use the stamp."

"I'll give it to her."

"How is she?"

"She is . . . carrying on," said Mott, rather diplomatically.

"And Miss Bernadine?"

"She I don't see. And I don't hear much about her. I can ask for you, next time I'm in the servants' hall."

"Will you do that? Thank you."

She gave him some money for his trouble, walked out of the post office, and returned to the tea shop.

She saw Mott again, leaving a few minutes later, hunched under his mackintosh. But she did not see Lady Ingram, not then, and not for the remainder of the hours she spent at the tea shop, staring out.

Charlotte arrived at Mrs. Watson's house shortly after one o'clock in the afternoon — and for the first time in her life believed that she not only didn't need lunch, but could also do without tea.

She climbed up to her room, closed the door, and sat down heavily before her writing desk. From the beginning she had believed there was something wrong with the state of affairs between Lady Ingram and Mr. Finch. Now, *everything* felt wrong.

The purely logical part of her wanted to investigate both Lady Ingram and Mr. Finch equally. In practice, she must concentrate on Mr. Finch. He was the unknown entity, the one who kept eluding her, the key to making sense of all the incongruities of the situation.

The evening before, when Miss Redmayne asked what she planned to do, she had said that she wanted to take a look at Mr. Finch's room. Now she *needed* to examine Mr. Finch's room. She *needed* to understand exactly what was going on.

Perhaps a bit of Lady Ingram's hysteria was rubbing off on her. Or perhaps it was some of Livia's wretchedness. An urgency escalated in her that had no rational basis — yet felt all the direr and most ominous.

She found Mrs. Watson in the afternoon parlor, reading the paper. "Ma'am, did you mean to tell me last night that Mr. Lawson was once an expert lock picker?"

Mrs. Watson rose, the paper clutched in her hands. "Surely, Miss Holmes, you don't mean to —"

"I do," she said quietly. "Every time we learn anything about Mr. Finch, it only serves to make the situation more incomprehensible. I don't wish to proceed piecemeal any longer. The time has come to find out the truth."

Fear darkened Mrs. Watson's beautiful eyes. Her jaw worked. The paper crinkled under the pressure of her fingers. And then she squared her shoulders and said, "It isn't what I would have advised or wished for, but I've grown more and more uneasy, too — my innards feel like a spring that's been wound up too tight. If you are sure it can be done safely . . ."

"I can't make any promise about the risks — I know nothing of such things. All I know is I fear picking Mr. Finch's lock a great deal less than what I might learn next if I didn't."

Mrs. Watson exhaled audibly and tossed aside the crumpled newspaper. "Then let's not waste any more time."

Mrs. Watson took it upon herself to speak with Mr. Lawson, Charlotte in tow. The groom and coachman had a healthy fear of going back to prison again. But when Mrs. Watson mentioned the amount of the reward she was offering, in exchange for the risks he would take, his eyes widened and his decision was made. He asked for exactly the types of locks they were to encounter, then asked for the rest of the day to prepare. "Haven't done anything illegal in years — not even betting, mind you, mum."

Charlotte spent the remainder of her afternoon acquiring an outfit, in a shade of dark blue-grey, that allowed her to move freely — no fashionable narrowing of the skirts at the knees.

At dusk, the rain stopped, but a peasouper rolled in, turning London into a sea of vapors. Charlotte took this as an auspicious sign: A peasouper would keep both pedestrians and carriages off the streets and send people to bed early.

She and Mr. Lawson left Mrs. Watson's

shortly after midnight, driven by Mr. Mears, who would also serve as their lookout, even though one was scarcely needed under the current atmospheric conditions. At Mrs. Woods's, Charlotte guided Mr. Lawson to the service door, which he opened after a quarter of an hour.

The basement was dark and quiet, the service stairs equally so. Charlotte felt completely unafraid — she had not lied when she told Mrs. Watson that she didn't fear picking Mr. Finch's lock. Certainly it was a great deal more criminal, but in essence the act was no different from stealing into her father's study when he was away.

Once inside Mr. Finch's room, she would discover everything she needed to know.

She led the way up to the first floor. The darkness smelled of linseed oil and beeswax, reassuringly domestic. The carpet in the passage muffled their footsteps. An almost imperceptible glow emanated from the high window at the far end of the passage, light from the streetlamps that had somehow managed to penetrate the fog.

By Mr. Finch's name plaque they stood and listened, Mr. Lawson with his ear against the door. When he was satisfied, Charlotte let some light out from the pocket lantern she was holding. Mr. Lawson unrolled his pouch of tools and got to work.

One floor up someone was tapping slowly on a typewriter. From time to time the house creaked, shrinking in the coolness of the night. And twice there came the unmistakable whistle of a distant train.

But it was quiet enough that the tiny flame inside the pocket lantern seemed to whoosh and crackle like a bonfire. Mr. Lawson's breaths, through a slightly blocked nose, brought to mind the wolf huffing and puffing at the third little pig's house. And his lock-picking implements, which had sounded so soft and gentle in the beginning, now made Charlotte think of her walking stick clashing against Mrs. Watson's.

Mr. Lawson stood up, almost colliding with Charlotte. In the dim light cast by the pocket lantern, his face was tense.

What's the matter? she mouthed.

He put his ear to the door. She did likewise, her fingertips tingling, her heart beating fast.

Silence, deep, wide silence. *Clack, clack, clack* — but that was only the typewriter, still being used. Wait. Was that a footstep? There it was again, closer.

A succession of quick clicks — the unmistakable sound of a revolver cocking.

She and Mr. Lawson looked at each other
— and ran.

FOURTEEN

Thursday

"This is unacceptable. Completely unacceptable," said Charlotte, with an extra sniff for emphasis.

She was back at Mrs. Woods's, this time in the parlor, in a gold-and-scarlet visiting gown that Livia, whose sensibility was better suited to classical Greece, had variously deemed "dire," "ghastly," and "absolutely tasteless." Charlotte hadn't thought much of what *else* the gown could accomplish — her eyes were simply drawn to things that Livia considered "absolutely tasteless." But as it turned out, such an ensemble was perfect for intimidating the Mrs. Woodses of the world, its ostentation translating into stature and authority.

The landlady, who no doubt had hoped not to see "Mrs. Cumberland" again for a millennium or so, was all but wringing her hands. "I beg your pardon, ma'am, but exactly what is unacceptable?"

"Any number of things, Mrs. Woods, any number. Of course you are not solely to blame for them — my brother is a grown man, after all. But I am deeply disappointed nonetheless. I had expected better of this establishment."

"Ma'am, please, if you will only let me —"

"Oh, yes, I will let you know. I visited my brother's firm day before yesterday. He submitted his resignation two months ago — they have no idea where he is. Now this is not your doing. But I also visited the other two references you furnished. The landlady in Oxfordshire has never heard of him. And the solicitor retired six months ago. Did you not check either of those references?"

Mrs. Woods's mouth opened and closed, opened and closed. No doubt in dismay, to be caught at being less than thorough in her selection process. Also, astonishment, at being blamed for Mr. Finch's less-than-laudable conduct.

But this was how Henrietta derived a large part of her dominance, because those she accused of various shortcomings were often too rattled to defend themselves — and too polite to tell her that she was being an unfair arse.

"I . . . um . . . It must have been a very busy week when Mr. Finch applied for a place. And you must understand, Mrs. Cumberland, he's a *most* winsome young man. I never imagined that —"

"That is what references are for, Mrs. Woods, so that we are not so easily guided by mistaken impressions. I am further disturbed to find out, upon inquiring about your place, that according to some sources, you allow overnight female guests. What kind of lassitude is that? Do you uphold no standards here? Is that what my brother has been doing, entertaining women in his rooms instead of going to work, as he properly ought?"

Mrs. Woods's horror was complete. "Certainly not! These are baseless rumors. I am a Christian woman running a most respectable establishment for Christian men."

"Then let me see his rooms," said Charlotte with a severity she did not need to manufacture. "Let me see for myself that it is not crawling with disreputable females."

Mrs. Woods shot up the stairs with the speed of a racing greyhound. As Charlotte followed in her wake, she reflected rather grimly that this was what she ought to have done in the first place. Why break the law when all she needed was to cast a few aspersions?

Thankfully, nothing had happened the night before. She and Mr. Lawson had sprinted down to the basement, out the service door, and into the waiting carriage. Mr. Mears, witnessing their flight, had needed no urging to get the coach moving. And the fog, which had offered concealment when Mr. Lawson had worked on the service door, had quickly obscured them from potential pursuers.

But Mr. Lawson had been sincerely frightened. Charlotte had been sorry to be the cause. And this morning it had taken rather a lot of convincing for Mrs. Watson to let Charlotte out of her sight.

Mrs. Woods stopped before Mr. Finch's door and knocked.

"I thought you said he's out of town."

"Oh, he is. It's a habit, ma'am. I always knock. I don't wish to walk in on my gentlemen without warning and I'm sure they don't wish it any more than I do."

The door opened to a largish sitting room, furnished with oriental motifs that would have been the height of fashion when the regent had been the first gentleman of Europe. There was a smaller room that seemed to serve as a study, with a blank notebook sitting on top of a desk.

Mrs. Woods threw open the bedroom door with great drama. "See, no women here at all!"

She proceeded to show Charlotte the attached private bath with the same trembling energy. Charlotte pushed her lips to one side, as if saying, *Very well, but I remain skeptical in the greater scheme of things.*

What she truly wanted was to have a look at the photographs. At last Mrs. Woods had presented all the spaces in the rooms that could possibly — but didn't — contain a disreputable female. Charlotte, with a very Henrietta-ish tilt of the chin, headed straight for the mantel.

The photographs were small, one and a half by two inches. All were of scenery and only scenery.

Charlotte stared.

"Surely, Mrs. Cumberland, there can be nothing the matter with his pictures."

Except Charlotte had seen these photographs before.

Recently.

When she went through Mrs. Marbleton's rooms at Claridge's, Mrs. Marbleton being the alias of Mrs. Moriarty, née Sophia Lonsdale.

Two young people, who were registered as her children Frances and Stephen Marbleton, had gone around the country, traveling as photographers. During their travels, they had recorded a great many scenic views, which were practically unidentifiable. But *unidentifiable* didn't mean that Charlotte didn't remember what they looked like.

She dismantled the frames.

"Mrs. Cumberland —"

"Shhh."

She was becoming worse than Henrietta. But the give-no-quarter persona worked. Mrs. Woods meekly held her tongue.

It wasn't until she'd taken apart all the frames that she found what she was looking for: In one frame, another photograph behind the one that was on display. And this one did feature people, two men. One standing with his back to the camera, the other looking at it.

Charlotte immediately recognized the person facing the camera. There was a beard, a Newmarket jacket and trousers, even a walking stick, but it was a woman. Frances Marbleton.

She showed the image to Mrs. Woods. "Is this what Mr. Finch looks like nowadays?"

"No, no, that isn't Mr. Finch. But I've seen him before, that's Mr. Carraway, Mr.

Finch's friend."

That would explain the woman's voice in these rooms — Charlotte remembered voices very well, but the only other time she had heard Frances Marbleton, the latter had spoken in a broad Cockney accent, with a nasal twang to boot. And it could very well have been her the night before, cocking her revolver on the other side of the door.

"Mr. Finch is still of medium height, slim build, brown eyes, and hair with a slight hint of red to it?"

"Yes. He's grown a beard in the time he's been here, but yes, that's how I would describe him."

Charlotte set down the photograph.

Were Stephen Marbleton and Myron Finch the same person? She supposed it was possible. She didn't know anything about Mr. Marbleton's life before or after his brief appearance in hers earlier this summer. He could very well have spent most of his life as Myron Finch, illegitimate son of Sir Henry Holmes, unfortunate suitor of Lady Ingram when she was Miss Alexandra Greville, until he'd joined Mrs. Marbleton as an associate of some stripe.

But that was a slender possibility compared to the overwhelming likelihood that he was *not* Myron Finch.

It would explain so much, wouldn't it, if they were two different men? Stephen Marbleton didn't meet with Lady Ingram because he knew nothing of the secret pact between Lady Ingram and the man he was impersonating. For the same reason he remained in a state of oblivious cheerfulness while Lady Ingram lost a little bit of her mind every day. And of course, then they could have stared right at each other at the Round Pond without either seeing any significance in the other.

But why was he impersonating Myron Finch?

And where was the real Myron Finch?

Where was her brother?

Her hand tightened into a fist. Now she knew why she had felt uneasy about the case. Now she understood her urgency the night before, throwing caution to the wind. Now it became rational, her decision to return as soon as possible to the scene of her failed crime and to persist until she had at last gained entry into these rooms.

But was she too late? Would Stephen Marbleton dare to openly impersonate Myron Finch if he didn't already know, with complete certainty, that the latter was not going to barge in and put an end to it?

Assuming that Stephen Marbleton had

truly been away, as he had told his landlady, if Charlotte were Frances Marbleton, staying in a place she considered safe enough, only to hear her lock being picked in the middle of the night, how would she leave? She would first make a sweep of anything incriminating — probably not too many items as they had been at such covert activities for a while. And then, would she leave a message for her cohort?

If she had, knowing that there was outside interest in this location, knowing that it might be searched, she would have done so in such a way as to ensure that it was easily overlooked.

Charlotte remembered the blank notebook in the smaller room. It was still blank when she returned to examine it more closely. But as she scrutinized it from the side, one page near the middle appeared slightly thicker than the rest. And when she opened to that particular page, she saw that it had been pricked with a pin.

She closed her eyes briefly before slipping the notebook into her handbag. "Do inform Mr. Finch that we are most disappointed in him, Mrs. Woods. He will have a great deal of explaining to do."

Charlotte expected Morse code. But when

she held up the notebook page that had been pricked, the dots were in Braille.

Braille.

That in itself would not have been particularly interesting, had she not, only a few days ago, found Braille inside a dead man's jacket.

Slowly she lowered the notebook and closed it, feeling as if she were putting the lid on a casket. She'd thought herself the kind of person who was always prepared for the worst. But knowing that something awful could happen and facing the certainty that it had — that was the difference between reading about *canne de combat* over a cup of tea and a piece of plum cake and the humerus-jarring reality of it, all shaky thighs and labored breaths.

She gave herself half a minute to calm down, then knocked against the top of the hackney. "I wish to alight right here!"

She had been on her way from St. James's to Mrs. Watson's house, but the intersection of Duke Street and Oxford Street had become the perfect place to get off.

Since she was now headed for Portman Square.

FIFTEEN

It was not often that Inspector Treadles wished that an interviewee would be *less* forthcoming. But there was no stopping Mrs. Egbert, the small, grey-haired widow who was frightfully organized.

Upon receiving Treadles and Sergeant MacDonald in her study, she had immediately presented a pile of documents. *I'll ring for tea after you've had a look at those.*

She and her late husband had owned nearly five dozen dwellings in the environs of London. He had passed away six years ago and had left her all the properties, even though they had grown sons. "He knew very well our boys had no head for business. A decent lot, but not a single one of them capable of looking after what we had built."

For a moment Treadles saw not Mrs. Egbert behind the impressive desk, but his own wife, so hardened and efficient that she couldn't be bothered to offer a cup of tea and a bit of pleasantry.

He prayed, for the first time in his life, for his brother-in-law's well-being and longevity.

"The house you are interested in was built in '69," said Mrs. Egbert. "For the first few years, the tenants were a young family. In the winter of '72, the husband and the children all died from influenza. The widow quit the premises that summer. We put the house up for let again and advertised in the papers. Usually those who have an interest in a vacancy write and ask for an appointment to see the place. Mr. de Lacy, however, inquired only whether we would accept a postal order for a year's rent.

"We had no objections at all to a year's rent in advance. Once we had received the postal order, we sent him the keys to the house, to be called for at the General Post Office, as he had instructed. The understanding was that an agent of ours would inspect the property at least once a year — more often should there be cause for concern. And our condition was readily agreed to."

She showed them the letters from de Lacy and the duplicates of letters that had been sent to him, the canceled postal orders, the neat numbers in a ledger that listed all the monies received from the property and all the expenses related to its upkeep.

"That was the extent of our initial contact with Mr. de Lacy. In subsequent years, he sent a postal order, without fail, a month before the period paid for in the previous year ran out. And you can see, each year we wrote him and arranged for a date on which our agent might inspect the house. He always agreed to the time we proposed — and always said that he would be away from London at the time and that our agent should feel free to enter the house using the key in the agent's possession.

"I have here all the inspection reports. Now that I know something terrible has happened, Mr. de Lacy does seem too good to be true. But I have hundreds of tenants, some of them quite irksome, and I was all too happy to overlook a few oddities on the part of a tenant who was never any trouble and always paid his accounts in advance."

Treadles, faced with page after page of meticulous recordkeeping, wished then that Mrs. Egbert were a little cagier. If he had the sense that she was concealing anything, then he would have gained a toehold. But her transparency forced the conclusion he'd been afraid of in the first place: that this was another dead end, as far as his investigation was concerned.

He gave the appearance of studying everything carefully, and even asked a few questions. But in the end, he left Mrs. Egbert's house with nothing to go on — and a spiraling sense of dread that he wasn't even scratching the surface.

That the surface was there somewhere and he was a hundred miles away, trying to feel his way out of a shipping crate.

"Let me see if I have understood you correctly, Miss Holmes," said Lord Bancroft. "You posit that one, Finch is the name of the dead man found in Hounslow; two, he happened to be your illegitimate half brother; and three, he is currently being impersonated by Stephen Marbleton."

He and Charlotte were seated in an eye-watering drawing room: This was the house in which Lord Bancroft had intended for them to live as man and wife, done up in what he gauged to be her taste before the first time he proposed, when he had been certain of his impending success. Charlotte had never heard the whole story from Lord Ingram, but it seemed reasonable to assume that after Lord Bancroft failed to win her hand, he had decided to turn it into a place of business. The crown's business.

Usually Charlotte enjoyed being in the house: Lord Bancroft's estimation of what she liked in terms of decor was barely three percent wide of the mark. But today all she could see was the dead man in Hounslow, his face a mask of agony and shock.

Had that been her first and last look at Mr. Finch?

"Precisely," she said. "If Mr. Finch's former sweetheart hadn't come around begging for help because she was convinced something terrible had happened to him, no one would have known anything about his disappearance and the police would simply have one more unidentified corpse on their hands."

"That isn't entirely true in this case. The victim has been identified as a Mr. Richard Hayward by a friend."

This was news to Charlotte. "Let me guess. Mr. Hayward was new to London, or at least new to this friend. The friend knows nothing of his origins. And the police haven't been able to find out anything either."

"That . . . does happen to be the case."

"Then it doesn't matter by what name the victim has been identified."

"Let's put aside for a moment the name of the dead man. What I do not understand is why Stephen Marbleton introduced himself to Miss Livia. To contact her was to court your attention. The moment you saw him, his guise would be penetrated — which was more or less what happened. Do you mean to tell me that the Marbletons had no idea of the connection between Livia Holmes and Sherlock Holmes?"

Good. He didn't dismiss her theory out of hand. Instead, he challenged it on reasonable grounds and left it up to her to justify her assertions.

It was a sad comment on the state of humanity that his willingness to take her seriously counted as a very large point in his favor, when really it should be considered a bare minimum in civil discourse.

"In Mrs. Marbleton's letter to me near the end of the Sackville case, she specifically wished me success in my endeavors as Sherlock Holmes — given the resourcefulness of that clan, it would be careless to assume that they didn't know I am none other than the disgraced Charlotte Holmes, daughter of Sir Henry Holmes. As for why Mr. Marbleton approached Livia, I can only suppose it must have been a matter of necessity.

"Mr. Finch had been removed for a reason. Mr. Marbleton is impersonating him for a reason. It's possible Mr. Marbleton believed that Mr. Finch's relations knew something — something crucial."

"But you yourself told me just now that no one in your family ever had any personal interactions with Mr. Finch," Lord Bancroft pointed out. "Your father, only via his solicitors. Your sisters, resistant to the idea of becoming acquainted with their illegitimate brother. What could they possibly know about a man they had never met?"

"Sometimes one knows things without understanding what one knows. I, without having ever met Mr. Finch, could be said to have known of his demise for days — I have even examined his body. But until more information came to light, I didn't know what I knew. Perhaps Mr. Marbleton sought a single missing piece, which he was convinced a member of my family might unwittingly possess."

Lord Bancroft's brows drew together — he really wasn't an unhandsome man. "I'm not sure I'm fully convinced of your theory, Miss Holmes, but I'm willing to look into this business with Mr. Finch."

Yet another point in his favor: Not only was he willing to listen, but he was willing to act — even if it would be only a simple command issued to a subordinate. "The real

Mr. Finch, or the imposter?"

"Both."

But she was not finished yet with her theories. She was curious to see what he thought of the next one. "After the conclusion of the Sackville affair, I went to Somerset House and looked up marriage records for Sophia Lonsdale. When I found out that she was married to someone named Moriarty, I asked Lord Ingram whether he knew of the name. He went to you, and you warned him to steer clear of the man."

"I did."

"Officially, Sophia Lonsdale died many years ago. From what I'd been able to gather, it had been reported as a skiing accident. Upon learning that Moriarty was not a man to be trifled with, I assumed that she had begun to find life with him intolerable and had therefore staged her own death in order to escape. But now I'm not so certain.

"What if, instead of a one-sided scheme, it was a jointly planned, jointly executed ruse? Perhaps they realized that she was a potential weakness for him — that his enemies could harm him by targeting her. But if those enemies believed her dead, then that was one significant vulnerability neutralized."

Lord Bancroft leaned forward an inch. "Are you implying that Moriarty is involved in this affair?"

"More than implying, I should hope," said Charlotte. "I am stating it outright. That Vigenère cipher always struck me as excessive. And the Braille on the dead man's garments — ridiculously complicated. Then I remembered the ciphers Mrs. Marbleton presented when she first called on me. They were much simpler, of course, but still had a similarly Baroque feel.

"It may be that for those in orbit around Moriarty, communicating in code is deemed as necessary and indispensable as wearing hats for going out. I posit that the Vigenère code I deciphered wasn't a transmission of vital information so much as a test, to see whether the recipient could find his way to the house in Hounslow. It's my further contention that the dead man, in the Braille he left behind, wasn't trying to signal a detective from the Metropolitan Police but a fellow member of the organization, someone more accustomed to looking for such clues everywhere, especially in unexpected places."

"You think the dead man, Mr. Finch by your contention, was one of them?"

"Yes."

"It would imply that there had been a schism in the organization, that the death was fratricidal."

"Yes."

Lord Bancroft's expression turned speculative. "I'd like for you to be correct. Any division on their part is good news for me."

"But perhaps not for long. After they stamp out dissension, they could become more efficient and more ruthless."

"Or it could embroil the entire organization in upheaval and reprisals." He looked at her. "I'm an opportunist, Miss Holmes. I must be prepared for any and all opportunities."

Such as a time when a woman who had previously turned him down found herself no longer in a position to do so? "Naturally," she replied.

"And opportunist that I am, I must seize the occasion to invite you to remain for luncheon."

Charlotte consulted her watch. It *was* almost time for luncheon, yet another point in his favor for not neglecting his — or her — stomach. "Thank you. I'll be glad to join you."

She must still eat, even on the day she found out that she had most likely met her brother as a dead man.

■ ■ ■ ■

Luncheon was the afterthought among meals. Breakfast was a necessity, dinner had its swagger, tea everyone was fond of, but luncheon usually limped by with a few leftover cuts from the night before, a bit of bread and cheese thrown in.

Lord Bancroft's luncheon, however, featured thin, crispy chicken cutlets, an excellent veal-and-ham pie, an even better cold plum pudding, and an abundance of summer berries to enjoy in a manner Charlotte had never been exposed to before, dipped into a small dish of condensed milk.

She understood condensed milk to be very popular in America, resulting from its ubiquity as rations for soldiers during the Civil War. But here in Britain, condensed milk had something of a dubious reputation. And yet she couldn't argue that a strawberry with just a tiny dot of sweetened condensed milk was utterly delightful.

"I didn't know condensed milk could be put to uses other than feeding infants deprived of mother's milk," she said.

"At home my cook has found an even better use for it," said Lord Bancroft. He looked completely at ease in a dining room that was as gaudy as the drawing room, one step up — or down, she had no way of knowing — from what she imagined a brothel with some aspirations must look like. "Condensed milk, heated gently for a few hours in simmering water, will turn into a kind of milk jam, with a taste rather like very soft caramel."

"Oh, my."

"My reaction precisely." Lord Bancroft studied Charlotte. "I hope this news further tilts you in favor of my proposal?"

"It does," Charlotte had to admit.

Charlotte believed that romantic love was a perishable item, at its freshest and most delicious for a limited amount of time before turning stale, if not outright putrescent. As a woman who put no stock in the primacy of love, she ought to be perfectly amenable to his offer.

Alas, there was the little matter of preference: She infinitely preferred being on her own to being Lord Bancroft's wife. The only question was, at a moment like this, how much importance should she give her own decided preference?

"Good," said he. "Perhaps you, Mrs. Watson, and Miss Redmayne will consider dinner at my house one of these days? It would be my honor to host the three of you."

When he had said that he would not object to her further association with Mrs. Watson, she had assumed that he meant he would not forbid her from slipping out and calling on Mrs. Watson, as if she were conducting an illicit rendezvous. She had no idea he was open to receiving either Mrs. Watson or Miss Redmayne in his own home. "I'll be delighted to convey your invitation."

She was almost afraid to ask whether he had changed his mind about her taking clients as Sherlock Holmes.

Lord Bancroft inclined his head. "And your sisters, are they well?"

Ah, he knew exactly where to press his advantage. This, she approved of. They were, after all, grown-ups in something approaching a negotiation. He was free to remind her, using every means at hand, that she really was in no position to negotiate at all.

Before she could answer, a servant announced, "Lord Ingram to see you, my lord."

Lord Ingram entered, dressed in a grey lounge suit, cut loosely and of very modest material — someone who didn't know better might mistake him for a bicycle messenger. His boots and trouser legs had the telltale splashes, too — too muddy to have originated in London, though, what with the roads and functional sewage system the great metropolis currently enjoyed.

Country mud, then, no more than two hours old.

The papers might be able to tell her which places, within two hours by rail, had the right kind of weather. The papers might even provide clues on why he had rushed back to London to speak to Bancroft in person, instead of using a coded telegraph.

Unlike Livia, Charlotte found the papers wonderfully illuminating. But one had to know where to look — it was often in pieces that didn't grace the front page or sentences outside the first twenty paragraphs of an article that the true significance of the matter accidentally shone through.

Lord Ingram reacted to her presence at his brother's table as she had expected him to, his surprise — and was that a trace of alarm? — quickly and thoroughly contained. "Miss Holmes, how do you do? Bancroft, a word with you."

Lord Bancroft excused himself. The brothers left the room. A few minutes later, Lord Ingram returned by himself and sat down.

"Bancroft sends his regrets, Holmes. Pressing matters, et cetera."

It shouldn't have come as such a relief to hear him address her as Holmes, but it did. *Holmes* meant they were on good terms. Or, at least, normal terms. "Of course. And how do you do, my lord?"

They had not seen each other since the day they discovered the significance of the house in Hounslow. In the meanwhile, his hair had been cut shorter — but the difference was most pronounced in how much more she noticed the bone structure of his face.

"I've been well enough. You?"

She thought of the dust sheet — of herself, with no feelings whatsoever, pulling it back and revealing the body underneath. "Same. I assume I shouldn't inquire into what you have been doing with yourself since you abruptly deserted me Saturday last."

"You can inquire but I won't be able to answer — forgive me. And you, what have you been doing?"

His wife's frantic letter came to mind, as well as the desperate hope in her eyes, the last time Charlotte saw her in person. *No, I'm afraid this is all wrong. You must have found a different Mr. Finch.*

And she had been right all along.

"Interestingly enough, I also cannot answer. I hope you'll forgive me."

Lord Ingram's eyes bored into Charlotte. His mind didn't work in remotely the same fashion as hers: Whereas hers dealt in cold, swift calculations of logic and facts, his relied much more heavily on a finely honed instinct. Good instinct, the way she saw it, was but logic and facts processed by the gut rather than the cerebrum — he might not be able to enumerate each step of the analysis, but that didn't mean the conclusion he reached was any less sound.

"You have done something," he stated. "You are not issuing a general apology, as I was. You are asking *me,* specifically, to forgive *you.*"

She dipped a raspberry into the dish of condensed milk — and left it there. "You are right."

He leaned back in his chair. "And that is all the answer I am to receive?"

His gaze was on her fingers, still nudging the raspberry around in its milky bath. His arm braced along the back of the next chair, a seemingly relaxed gesture that radiated latent power. Beneath the unassuming brown waistcoat and the humble white shirt, his chest rose and fell evenly, steadily — he was waiting.

She made him wait some more, eating the raspberry with the speed of a tired snail — this time not tasting anything.

He raised a brow.

She sighed inwardly. "Strictly speaking I've done nothing wrong. But things are complicated and I'll probably be held to blame for certain decisions on my part that placed my integrity as an investigator above my loyalty as a friend."

"Usually you speak with greater clarity and directness." He lifted his eyes to her face. "Should I understand, from all that verbiage, that you have done something that might be construed as disloyal to *me*?"

She nodded, distracted for the moment by the motion of his thumb, slowly caressing the crest rail of the adjacent chair.

"In the course of your work as Sherlock Holmes?"

She nodded again, still distracted by the way his fingers grazed the notches and swirls atop the ornate chair.

"Be more specific."

With some regret, she looked away from his hand. "I can't. I can't say anything beyond what I've already said."

"You think this will anger me?"

If nodding could reduce extra chins she would have whittled hers down to only one point two. "But it does not harm you in the not-knowing."

Their eyes met, his cool and dark. "Are you asking me to trust you?"

"I'm letting you know that I'm in the middle of something that you will not like, if you knew what it was."

His eyes narrowed. "There are a great many things I don't like. But losing a polo match, for instance, is not the same as my house burning down."

She could only repeat herself. "I can't say anything beyond what I've already said."

He was silent.

"I'm sorry," she heard herself murmur.

Soundlessly his fingers tapped the crest rail on which they rested, each one by turn. "Years ago, you said something to me. I don't remember it word for word, but in essence, you told me that men, even otherwise sensible men, fall under the illusion that they will be able to find a perfect woman. That the problem lies not in the search so much as in the definition of perfection, which is a beautiful female who will integrate seamlessly into a man's life, bringing with her exactly the right amount of intelligence, wit, and interests to align with his, in order to brighten every aspect of his existence."

She remembered that conversation, one of the most disharmonious they had ever held, on the subject of the future Lady Ingram.

"You warned me against believing in that illusion — and I was highly displeased. I didn't say so at the time, but as we parted, I thought that you'd certainly never be mistaken for a perfect woman. It was beyond evident you'd never fit readily into any man's life, and no one could possibly think that the purpose of your life was to be anything other than who you were.

"At the time, those were not kind thoughts. They flew about my head with a great deal of scorn — venom, even. My opinion of you hasn't changed, by the way. But nowadays I think those same thoughts with much resignation but even more admiration." Their eyes met again. His were still the same mysterious dark, but now there was a warmth to them, a deep affection tinged, as he said, with much resignation but even more admiration. "I'm sure I'll fly off the handle and accuse you of all kinds of perfidy once I learn what you've been up to, but let it not be said that I don't know who I'm dealing with. We disagree often, and that is a fact of our friendship."

He reached across the table and took away the berries and the dish of condensed milk.

"But for your penance, and because I'm hungrier than you, these have been confiscated."

She watched him eat. How did preferences arise? Was it due to the arrangement of features or the modulation of voice? Certainly it couldn't be argued that Lord Bancroft was less wise or less powerful than Lord Ingram. Yet one brother invoked in her a bland and rather aloof approval, while the other . . .

"Little did you know, these were forbidden fruits," she told him. "And I will extract payment in exchange."

"Huh," he said in response.

"I believe there is a darkroom in this house. And I believe you, time permitting, develop negatives for Bancroft. I would like to have a copy of a photograph."

"Which photograph?"

"A clear image of the face of the victim from the house in Hounslow."

He put down his fork. "Why do you want it?"

She explained, omitting Lady Ingram's name and general background. He listened with some incredulity. "You understand it isn't likely for the man to be your half brother."

"I do understand that. Yet I am compelled to think so, unless proven otherwise. I'd like a photograph, so that I can show it to those who actually did know him. That way I'll know for sure, one way or another."

"You shouldn't further involve yourself in this matter. If it's as you said, and Moriarty or his associates are involved . . ."

"I'm only trying to find out if he was my brother."

"And what will you do if he does turn out to have been just that?"

"Then I'll ask that Bancroft get to the bottom of the matter urgently. I am not going to rush out and hunt down the killer myself, if that's what you are worried about."

"Is that a promise?"

"Yes."

"So many promises of late." He viewed her with patent suspicion. "Wait here."

He returned a few minutes later with an envelope. "Don't abuse my trust."

"I won't.

She reached for the envelope, but he didn't let go. "This isn't what you apologized for, is it?"

"No."

"You aren't looking me in the eye."

She looked him in the eye.

He looked away, unable, for some reason,

349

to hold her gaze.

She took the envelope from him. "Thank you, my lord. I'll see myself out."

Mrs. Watson was, in fact, a longtime subscriber to the soup kitchen on Great Windmill Street. As a supporter, she had toured the facilities. Based on this meager familiarity, she took for herself the task of finding out when Mrs. Burns would be there again. At first she considered simply sending a note, but in the end she decided to go in person, so that she could speak of some experience as a volunteer when she did meet Mrs. Burns.

She couldn't be entirely sure, but there didn't seem to be anyone following her around — which was a relief. Her luck held at the soup kitchen. The harried woman in charge of the staff took one look at her and said, "It's a good thing we have Mrs. Burns here today, mum. She'll tell you what needs to be done."

Mrs. Watson was already perspiring by the time they were halfway across the large kitchen. She had dressed lightly, knowing that kitchens were infernally hot places. Still, the heat and humidity struck her like a large brick wall to the chest, making her gasp for breath.

"Mrs. Burns" — the woman stuck her head into a room that led off from the kitchen — "I've a subscriber here to volunteer. Can you show her what to do, please?"

Her tone was pleading. Mrs. Burns, behind a pile of turnips, did not appear particularly honored by the request. But she rose from her stool, let the woman present her to Mrs. Watson, and welcomed her. When the woman had rushed off, she asked whether Mrs. Watson could peel turnips with a knife without injuring herself.

Mrs. Watson hesitated. As a child, she had regularly helped in the kitchen at home. But as a firmly middle-aged woman, she had not performed menial tasks for some time.

"If you can't peel vegetables, I suppose I could set you to brushing and washing them, but that's rougher work."

"I've peeled any number of potatoes and turnips, only not recently. May I try a few and see if I've still got the knack?"

Thankfully, those old skills returned quickly — she had once been capable of peeling apples in a single strip. Mrs. Burns did not bother hiding her surprise. Nor did she bother to praise Mrs. Watson for not being a complete disgrace in the kitchen. "Good. We've much to do."

Mrs. Burns did not immediately strike

Mrs. Watson as beautiful. But before long she had already remarked the housekeeper's lithe figure and fine-boned features. She peeled turnips with a seriousness others reserved for prayers — or battle planning.

Mrs. Watson, too, focused on the turnips, until they had reduced the pile by about two thirds. Someone came for the basket of peeled turnips and both Mrs. Burns and Mrs. Watson helped in carrying the heavy container to the kitchen table, where they would be chopped and added to the large cauldrons.

When they returned to their stools in the peeling area, Mrs. Watson judged that it was an opportune time to begin a conversation. "Are you employed here, Mrs. Burns?"

Mrs. Burns shook her head. "I'm a volunteer, Mrs. Watson."

"But not an inexperienced one. Do you come often?"

"Once every week."

"I admire such dedication."

Mrs. Burns shrugged. There was a refinement to her motion. Put her in a proper frock and she would not appear any less a lady than the wives of Dr. Swanson's colleagues. Mrs. Watson had earlier thought Mrs. Morris perhaps overly suspicious. She still didn't know enough of the truth of the situation to judge. But having met Mrs. Burns — and heard Dr. Swanson's praise — one thing became clear: If Mrs. Burns wanted to become the next Mrs. Swanson, she had a very realistic chance of succeeding.

"Would you happen to be in service, Mrs. Burns?"

This provoked a slightly wary glance from Mrs. Burns. "Yes."

"You are sacrificing part of your half day to be here."

"Not today. My employer is away on holiday so my time is my own."

"You didn't take the chance and go away yourself for a small holiday?"

"There are maids in the house — someone must keep an eye on them. And holidays are expensive," said Mrs. Burns with a trace of regret. "The more I save now, the sooner I can leave service."

If Mrs. Burns were scheming to leave service by marrying an employer, would she be so careful with her money?

"You're still awfully young. Retirement must be many years away."

For the first time a spark came into Mrs. Burns's eyes. "Ah, but by my own estimate, and I estimate very conservatively, I'm only three years away from retirement."

"Really?"

Mrs. Watson was amazed. She knew that it was possible for those in service to accumulate decent savings, given that they did not need to spend their wages on food or lodging. But few people in any line of work had the discipline to hold their expenses to only the bare minimum. It was all too human, especially for those whose work was monotonous, to seek pleasure and seek it hard.

"I used to be a lady's maid, and I was very good at dressing hair — other ladies would beg my mistress to lend them my service. I do believe I'll stay in London for a bit and teach some young girls my skills in hair-dressing. But even without that, I should have enough money."

Mrs. Watson shook her head. "That's marvelous."

"I know. Three more years. But sometimes every day can seem that long."

"Are your master and mistress too demanding?"

"My master is all right. No mistress — he's a widower. But his daughter has come to stay with him and she has disliked me from the very beginning." Mrs. Burns pulled her lips. "She hasn't been unpleasant or anything. But you just know when someone would rather you be gone. Her husband is at sea right now — I can't wait for him to come back and for her to leave. Only three years to go — I don't wish to move to a different household."

She tossed a peeled turnip into the basket. "But I will if I must."

Sixteen

"You think your brother is *dead*?" Mrs. Watson and Penelope exclaimed in unison.

Over tea, Miss Holmes had recounted both what she had learned at Mrs. Woods's this day and what she had uncovered the week before, working on a Vigenère code that Lord Bancroft had sent for her amusement, as part of his courtship.

"Lord Bancroft isn't convinced yet. And I don't blame him. There is no direct evidence. There is, so far, no reason why Mr. Finch should have been strangled and left in an empty house, wearing a coat that secretly warns of his killers. So first I must ascertain the identity of the dead man."

Mrs. Watson felt as if someone had laid an icy hand at the base of her spine. "How?"

"I have written Lady Ingram and asked her to call on us this evening." Miss Holmes extracted an envelope from her handbag. "There is a photograph of the dead man inside. I plan to show it to her."

Lady Ingram's hand shook.

Penelope couldn't breathe. The dead did not discomfit her — she'd had too many dissection lessons for that. Photographs of the dead affected her even less. But this evening she could not manage to summon the detachment of a medical student. This evening she was thoroughly exposed to the violence of the death and the potentially just-as-violent effect on the one who loved the departed.

Lady Ingram lifted the flap of the envelope. She let it drop without removing its contents. She lifted it again — and let the whole thing fall to her lap.

"You must excuse me but I'm not sure I understood anything you said just now."

Her voice quavered. The crystal beads on the skirt of her elaborate gown clinked together, a minor symphony conducted by her trembling knees. It was very late — she had sent around a note earlier saying that she would not arrive at Upper Baker Street until near midnight, when she could steal a few minutes away from a ball she was attending — and the lamps of the room seemed to shine too harshly on her chalky face.

"The last time we met, you told me Mr. Finch was doing well. You said he was taking holidays and charming his landlady. Why did you go to the police all of a sudden?"

Penelope had explained the photograph as having been obtained by a contact inside the Criminal Investigation Department, which, come to think of it, was not entirely false. "Since you insisted that we had the wrong Mr. Finch, we decided to take your judgment seriously. What if we did have the wrong man? What if something had happened to the real Mr. Finch? If the worst had befallen him, then the police would likely learn of it, sooner or later. There was no record of Mr. Finch's death. So we made arrangements to see the bodies that had been brought in and had not yet been identified.

"This particular gentleman was young and seemed to have been in respectable circumstances before his unfortunate demise. He was an unlikely sort of candidate for a man missing with no one knowing who he is."

"And where was he found?"

"We're not privy to that — it was a great deal of trouble just to obtain this photograph. But we thought it would be easier for you to see the picture here rather than having to go to Scotland Yard." Penelope paused for a moment. "Surely you have contemplated the possibility."

Lady Ingram looked away. "Of course I have. And after what you said last time about his recent carefree ways, I have wished again and again that he were dead instead. Now — now I think I have cursed him."

Penelope, caught in the undertow of Lady Ingram's despair, felt her own eyes sting with tears. "I'm sorry to cause you such distress, ma'am. Please remember that it may not be Mr. Finch in the picture. We only wish to eliminate that possibility."

Lady Ingram's lips quirked, but without humor. "So my choices are that he is dead or that he is having the time of his life without me."

"I'm sorry."

"No need to apologize. I knew that in the end you couldn't possibly discover anything good. But I held out hope that perhaps there was a one in a thousand chance that . . ."

Her hands balled into fists. She grabbed the envelope and yanked out the photograph. The expression on her face was indescribable, halfway between revulsion and utter euphoria. "This — this isn't Mr. Finch!"

Penelope gulped down air. "It isn't? Thank goodness!"

Lady Ingram tossed aside both envelope and photograph. Her breaths came in like bellows, her eyes tightly shut. "I never thought I'd see the day when I'd prefer that he forgot about me. But here we are."

Penelope retrieved the picture from where it had fallen, shuddered at the dead man's grotesque expression, and shoved it back into the envelope.

To her surprise Lady Ingram took the envelope from her. She pulled out the photograph, flipping it around as it had come out facedown, and stared. After a few seconds she panted again. "I'm sorry. For a moment I was assailed by doubt. What if I hadn't looked carefully enough? What if in my desire for him to be alive I'd made a mistake?"

She gave the envelope back to Penelope. "But no, that truly isn't Mr. Finch."

Penelope wondered if the ordeal hadn't been too much for her. After all, she was a sheltered woman who, despite her heartaches, had never dealt with the rougher elements of life. She didn't know what to say, so she stirred her tea and let Lady Ingram be.

After a few minutes, Lady Ingram rose

360

and winced at the pain the motion must have caused her bad back. "I should go, or my absence will be noticed."

"Of course."

She sighed, a heavy sound. "Last time I was here, you admonished me. I think I finally see your point, Miss Holmes: There is nothing I could possibly gain from the continuation of my inquiry.

"I'm glad Mr. Finch isn't dead. And I hope he is as well as you have described. I'll keep our appointment next year at the Albert Memorial — and every year thereafter. Maybe I'll see him again someday. Maybe I won't. But I shan't trouble you again."

"So he's alive then, Mr. Finch," said Mrs. Watson, still limp with relief. "Or at least the man murdered in Hounslow wasn't him."

Lady Ingram had departed. The ladies of 18 Upper Baker Street had gathered in the parlor for tea and biscuits. Or rather, Miss Holmes partook in tea and biscuits; Mrs. Watson and Penelope each nursed a finger of whisky. The grandfather clock had gonged midnight a while ago, but no one seemed the least bit interested in retiring.

Miss Holmes polished off a madeleine. "I had better send word to Lord Bancroft that facts have laid waste to my brilliant hypothesis."

She appeared as unmoved as ever, but earlier, when Lady Ingram had declared the man in the photograph a stranger, she had let out an audible breath, which had been quite enough to inform Mrs. Watson that she was beyond relieved to be wrong.

"What should we do about Mr. Finch then?" asked Mrs. Watson. Lady Ingram might have come to her senses, but the only Mr. Finch they were able to locate had turned out to be counterfeit.

"You remember Mr. Gillespie, the solicitor Mr. Mears impersonated?" Miss Holmes poured herself another cup of tea. "I stopped by his office this afternoon on my way back and made an appointment to see him tomorrow. Though I haven't a ready story yet on what to say to extract maximum information from him without alerting my father of my involvement in the matter."

"I have an idea," said Penelope. "I can play the part of Lady Ingram — under a different name, of course. My point is I can use the bones of her story, tell Mr. Gillespie that Mr. Finch is missing, and worm out some information."

"I like that idea," said Miss Holmes decisively. She turned to Mrs. Watson. "I didn't have a chance to ask earlier, ma'am, but did you learn anything from going to the soup kitchen today?"

Mrs. Watson recounted her conversation with Mrs. Burns. "It didn't appear that she was at all interested in her employer. Of course, one could make the case that she's canny and careful and wouldn't spill the beans even to an absolute stranger. But she struck me as truthful, bluntly so."

Miss Holmes nodded and made no further comment on Mrs. Watson's observation. They discussed their plans. Mrs. Watson would go back to the soup kitchen on Saturday — Mrs. Burns had indicated that was when she planned to give her time again. Miss Redmayne would beg off accompanying the de Blois ladies on a trip to Bath so she could meet with Mr. Gillespie.

"I will go with Miss Redmayne," said Miss Holmes. "The presence of a friend will help make Miss Redmayne's claims seem more convincing."

"But are you sure it's wise to meet with a close associate of your father?" Mrs. Watson couldn't help but imagine all the undesirable consequences should Miss Holmes be recognized.

"Mr. Gillespie and I have never met," said Miss Holmes. "But even if he does know what I look like, at this point, it's a risk I'm willing to take."

They were quiet for a minute, Mrs. Watson busily planning how to use theatrical makeup to change Miss Holmes's appearance.

Penelope cleared her throat. "I hope, Miss Holmes, it will not shock you to know that I have been apprised of Lord Bancroft's matrimonial intentions."

Mrs. Watson cleared her throat, too, embarrassed to have been revealed as a gossip. But, as Penelope said, it could scarcely have shocked Miss Holmes.

Miss Holmes only waited for Penelope to continue.

"You met with Lord Bancroft today — or yesterday now, since we're past midnight. I'm curious to know, did he press you for an answer?"

"He did, though not in so many words." Miss Holmes sipped her tea and eyed the rest of the madeleines on the plate with a combination of longing and apology. "I believe Lord Bancroft thinks that I am the perfect woman for him."

"You don't sound particularly pleased by that idea," Penelope pointed out.

"To be thought of as the perfect woman for a man isn't a compliment to a woman,

it's more about how a man sees himself —
and what he needs." Miss Holmes sighed.
"Should we marry, either I will be exhausted
trying to keep his illusion intact — or Lord
Bancroft will be severely disappointed in his
choice. Likely both."

Mrs. Watson couldn't help herself. "What
does Lord Ingram think of you?"

"Lord Ingram?" The movement of Miss
Holmes's lips could indicate either a smile
or a moment of ruefulness. "He has always
understood that I am one of the most
imperfect women alive. Thank goodness."

SEVENTEEN

Friday

Livia stared at the pages, amazed.

She was writing Sherlock Holmes's story. And she did so with the mad speed of a convict about to face the gallows.

Two decisions had helped loosen the words. One, she opted not to begin the story with the origins of the crime. After all, the point was Sherlock Holmes. Two, after trying — and failing — to make him the narrator, she chose instead to use the fictional masculine equivalent of Mrs. Watson to fulfill the role.

And that was perfect. Watson was the embodiment of everyone who had ever stared at Charlotte in wonder and unease — and everyone who had ever said *I could have guessed that, too,* after they made Charlotte explain her deduction in painstaking detail.

They'd been to the crime scene. They'd

visited a constable who hadn't realized that the drunken loiterer at the scene was the murderer himself, coming back to find a sentimental item he had accidentally dropped. (Livia hadn't decided what it would be yet. A cameo brooch? A locket? No matter, she could settle on something later.) And now Sherlock Holmes had ordered a newspaper notice about said sentimental item, in order to lure the murderer to him.

But would the murderer come?

Livia yawned. She'd been up since half past four, writing. And now it was almost seven. She didn't want breakfast, but she did want some tea.

She went down to the breakfast parlor, poured herself a cup, and sat down with the paper. Almost immediately she spotted the new Cdaq Khuha message at the back.

CDAQKHUHAGDHRMNSNTQXQNS-
GDQXTSXDVAQD
DEARLIVIAHEISNOTOURBROTHER-
BUTBEWARE

She covered her mouth with her hands. He wasn't their brother? He *wasn't* their brother!

This was the best news she'd had in a long time.

She ran back upstairs, fell onto her bed, and lay there panting, speechless with relief. Thank God. Everything was still wrong with the picture, but thank God her feelings were no longer incestuous.

It was only after a solid five minutes that she sat up and frowned. Of course she would beware, but if he wasn't their brother, then who was he?

De Lacy, the alleged murderer of Mr. Richard Hayward, even if he hadn't been waterlogged, would still have been sizable.

After a good soak in the Thames, it became harder to tell whether he had been strong and burly or merely fat and soft.

Probably somewhere in between. Not someone Inspector Treadles would want to meet in a dark alley; but if he had met such a man in such a place, he also wouldn't have been unduly afraid.

"Interesting scarf," commented Sergeant MacDonald.

The man was indifferently dressed, except for the summer scarf of white and scarlet stripes around his neck, the colors so vivid that the pattern was unmistakable even under a layer of mud.

Inspector Treadles felt the material between his fingers. Silk, no doubt about it, lightweight yet strong. "You read the preliminary report, MacDonald. This is the scarf the pathologist said he'd been strangled with?"

"That's his theory, sir. Said the bruises around the neck point to strangling. But he'll have to open the man up and check the lungs before he can be sure that drowning wasn't the cause of death."

Treadles made one more circle around the slab on which the dead man lay. "Let's speak to some witnesses."

Charlotte had declined Mrs. Watson's offer to make her look splotchy and at least fifteen years older. "I'm going to be sitting four feet across from him, ma'am," she'd told Mrs. Watson. "A face full of makeup might make him pay more attention to me, rather than less."

But now that she was sitting four feet across from Mr. Gillespie, she wondered whether she wouldn't have been better off with "a face full of makeup." He didn't stare at her, but he had blinked rapidly a few times when they were shown into his office. Even though he seemed to be giving Miss Redmayne's recital due attention, he kept rearranging items on his desk, as if he were his own overzealous secretary.

"Are you listening to me, Mr. Gillespie?" Miss Redmayne asked outright once.

The solicitor gave a pained smile. "Of course, miss. Do please go on."

But it would appear that Miss Redmayne's instincts were correct and he hadn't paid the least attention to her, because now that he was forced to, he sat with wide eyes, blinking often, frowning almost as often, even shaking his head a few times, not a motion to indicate negation, but the kind of quick rattle one gave oneself in extraordinary situations to make sure one wasn't dreaming.

Not exactly the sympathetic response one might have anticipated on the part of an older man faced with a pretty young woman's tearful distress.

At the end of Miss Redmayne's account of many woes, he studied her closely. "This is a joke, right, Miss — ah —"

"Miss Gibbons," Miss Redmayne supplied helpfully.

"Right, Miss Gibbons. Surely this is all a prank."

"How could you say that?" cried Miss Redmayne, with a convincing display of consternation.

"Because you are not the first woman to come in and give me this exact story about him."

"What? *What?!*"

Miss Redmayne's voice rose shrilly. The next moment she slumped over into Charlotte's lap.

"Oh, dear. Oh, dear!" cried Charlotte with plenty of fearfulness, though she stopped short of actually wringing her hands.

"Shall I — shall I send for a doctor?" said Mr. Gillespie, with the expression of a man who wasn't sure whether he ought to laugh or drink heavily.

Charlotte was of half a mind to ask the man outright whether he knew who she was, but decided to carry on with the charade. "The poor dear will be so embarrassed. Let's see if she comes to on her own."

They both stared at Miss Redmayne, Charlotte tapping her on the cheeks a few times. When Miss Redmayne showed no sign of "reviving," Charlotte decided that the former meant for her to take over the conversation.

"I tried to warn her, Mr. Gillespie, I did. I told her that it was foolhardy trying to find a man who doesn't want to be found. But you can't tell young people anything, can you?"

"No, you cannot. Not these days."

His expression was more under control. Had he, like her, opted to keep up the farce?

"Was the lady who came to see you a tall, slim, beautiful brunette with dark eyes, about twenty-six, a beauty mark at the corner of her mouth?"

"Why, yes."

Charlotte clutched the buttons of her bodice. "Oh, that cad! We saw him with her one time and he swore up and down it was his cousin, visiting from Stokes."

"I am most distressed to learn that Mr. Finch should turn out to be so faithless. But he is illegitimate, and it was a mistake on your charge's part to hold his character in high regard."

Charlotte sighed exaggeratedly. "Well, she is very young. I hope this will prove to be a valuable lesson to her."

A knock came at the door. Mr. Gillespie's secretary stuck in his head. "Sir, Mr. Malcolm is here and he's in a hurry to see you."

Miss Redmayne, hearing this, slowly sat up. "Oh, my," she said vaguely, "how strange I feel. What happened?"

"I'll tell you later, my dear."

"But wait," said Miss Redmayne to Mr. Gillespie. "Do you have Mr. Finch's last known address? I have need of it."

For a moment Mr. Gillespie looked conflicted.

Miss Redmayne rose and stamped her foot. "You must. I will not leave until I have it."

"Yes, yes, of course. I'm all too happy to oblige."

But Charlotte knew that he didn't oblige them at all. When they had left Mr. Gillespie's office, she told Miss Redmayne that she could give the piece of paper from the solicitor to the next scrap collector they came across.

Miss Redmayne was dismayed. "This isn't the correct address?"

"No," said Charlotte. "But I saw the address in the dossier he took out, ostensibly to write it down for us."

"But he put his hand in front of it."

He had, but a fraction of a moment was enough for Charlotte, looking at the address upside down, to memorize every line.

"That didn't matter," she said. "I say we did well."

The pub was a hard place and smelled of cheap ale and indifferent food. But it was also a good deal cleaner and sharper than it had any reason to be, in imitation of its proprietress, a flinty-looking woman who seemed to have never been pretty but was put together with the precision of a Swiss watch.

Treadles didn't know how he knew, but he was certain the woman had been a prostitute at one point.

He did not enjoy questioning prostitutes, to say the least.

"Mrs. Bamber, the dead man washed ashore not far from the back of this pub. When bystanders were gathered around and one of your patrons declared that he had seen this man in the pub two nights ago and had spent a solid hour talking to him, you contradicted him and said the victim had never been in your establishment."

"I did."

"Are you concerned that if you told the truth, it would lead to trouble?"

"What I told was the truth. I know the regulars who come in. I know the strangers who come in — pay more attention to them, in fact, in case they start a fight or leave me with their tab. Two nights ago a man did speak to Young Boyd for a while. But the dead man? Wasn't him."

"Why should I believe you, Mrs. Bamber, given your past occupation?"

The woman stilled, then flicked Treadles a look of contempt. "If you have no intention of believing me, best not waste my time, Inspector. There's Young Boyd yonder. Take his account. And while you're at it, ask him to read today's headlines for you."

It defeated Treadles why *she* was the one scornful toward *him.* Nevertheless, her look made him feel . . . low, somehow. He thanked her curtly and decamped to where Young Boyd sat, nursing a pint before noon.

"Mr. Boyd, we are interested in your account of the man you met two nights ago."

Young Boyd seemed to fit the description of an amiable drunk — or at least a harmless one. He offered a shaky hand to the policemen and was full of smiles and eagerness — no doubt in the hope of a free pint. Treadles reluctantly motioned for one.

"Fine fellow he was. Big, fine fellow. Kept buying me rounds. Then he asked me, when we were good and jolly, if I could keep a secret," said Young Boyd, the man least likely to keep a secret Treadles had ever met.

"I told him, of course! They could torture me in the Tower of London and I won't say a thing. That's when he told me he was a killer by profession. That he hired out his services and that it wasn't a bad living, but not fancy either. But something went wrong for him and he was 'bout to go on the run.

"So I asked him if he was afraid of the

police. He laughed and said only namby-pambies were afraid of the police. He was afraid of the people who hired him. They wanted the thing done nice and quiet and the police somehow caught wind of him in Hounslow. And now the people who hired him wanted to get rid of him, to make sure the police couldn't find *them*."

"Did you ask who they were?"

"He said they were criminals. But not pickpockets. Not even hired killers like him. They are kings of crime and hardly ever dirty their own hands. The man he killed tried to double-cross them. And they hunted him down. And this fellow, de Lacy he said his name was, he thought his own days were numbered. And gosh if he wasn't right about that."

Treadles had been looking askance at Young Boyd, wondering whether he wasn't simply making things up from what he'd read in the papers — until the name de Lacy dropped from his lips. That, he'd only just learned himself and was *not* public information.

"He told you his name?"

"And said that's just what he was called and not his real name and he wasn't even the first man to go by that name."

"Then what happened?"

"Then he left. I never thought to see him again — thought he'd manage to run away and hide somewhere safe. But this morning there he was, dead as a doornail, all bloated and ugly like."

Treadles tried to glean more information, but Young Boyd began to repeat himself. Treadles signaled for another pint, which only made Young Boyd embroider what he'd already told them.

Sensing that the witness was of no further use, Treadles thanked him and rose.

"By the way, Mr. Boyd," said MacDonald, "would you mind reading this headline for us? You can read, I assume?"

"Of course I can." Young Boyd squinted at the big, bold letters and squinted some more, until he muttered and took a pair of bent specs out of his pocket. " 'The Queen heads to Balmoral.' "

Treadles swore inwardly. "Were you wearing your glasses on the night you met this de Lacy?"

"Course not. Never take them out except to read — and I don't read much. But I can see well enough to find my way here — and I saw his fancy scarf nice and clear."

"I don't know why I should have been so surprised that Lady Ingram didn't tell us everything," said Mrs. Watson, at last giving voice to the cloudburst of thoughts that had flooded her head since she'd learned of Lady Ingram's visit to Mr. Gillespie. "Looking back, it's beyond obvious that she would have held back everything she didn't need to tell us. She was on an illicit mission, after all.

"And it makes sense that she would first go to a solicitor, rather than a consulting detective. It would be only after she had run out of options that a visit with Sherlock Holmes becomes thinkable. But this, of course, means that the address from Mr. Gillespie will lead nowhere."

She tightened her hat ribbons with rather unnecessary force. "Anyway, please don't listen to me blathering on about things you already know, Miss Holmes."

They were back in Oxfordshire. The most recent address Mr. Gillespie had for Mr. Finch had brought them to a picturesque village. Mrs. Watson, a longtime denizen of London, loved the sight of green, open country and the quintessentially English beauty of a hamlet centered around a modest stone church. She had lived in precisely such a place as an adolescent and had found it difficult to overcome the prejudice of the villagers against outsiders, especially outsiders who entertained thoughts of leaving. But it was not in her nature to think ill of all small country settlements simply because one had proved unpleasant. She much preferred imagining that most such places were as lovely in their residents as they were in their scenery, that the peace and quiet of village life coexisted with a spirit of curiosity and magnanimity.

At the village pub she ordered a plate of sausage and mash — steak and kidney pudding for Miss Holmes. The plain but substantial dishes were washed down with the pub's own ale, a light, refreshing brew. When the publican's wife came to inquire whether they wanted anything more, a spirited discussion broke out on whether they ought to have summer trifle because summer was ending or the jam roly-poly in hot custard since neither of them had enjoyed one in a while.

They settled on one serving of each and when the publican's wife returned, Mrs. Watson was ready.

"If you have a minute, Mrs. Glossop, may I ask you a question about a young man who might have lived on these premises for some time?"

Mrs. Glossop's eyes widened. "Are you interested in Mr. Myron Finch, by any chance?"

This time, Mrs. Watson was not surprised. After all, what good would Mr. Finch's address have been to Lady Ingram, if she hadn't made use of it?

"Yes, we are. We are making inquiries on behalf of a client of Mr. Sherlock Holmes's, who is trying to locate Mr. Finch."

The name Sherlock Holmes didn't have any effect on Mrs. Glossop, but she did consider the two women at the table with something between curiosity and alarm. "You ladies are private investigators?"

"My brother is a consulting detective," said Miss Holmes. "Mrs. Hudson and I assist him in his endeavors. At the moment his health isn't what it used to be. Ventures that require traveling therefore fall to us."

"How brave you must be."

"We try not to take on clients who would require too much traveling," said Mrs. Watson modestly. "But in any case, not long ago, a lady came to us worried that Mr. Finch wasn't where he ought to be. Since we haven't managed to locate him in London, we thought we'd try and see whether anyone from back home might have news of him."

Mrs. Glossop shook her head. "I'd like to help, but I don't know anything. And if anybody ought to know anything, that'd be me, wouldn't it? After that man what came a month ago, asking about Mr. Finch, I got curious. So I asked Mr. Glossop. His uncle was publican here before him — and married Widow Finch twenty years ago.

"She had no roots here — just her and the boy in an old cottage on Sweetbriar Lane for ten years before she married old Mr. Glossop. Folks here don't have much to say about her — she kept to herself even after she became the publican's wife. And they know even less about her son. He was sent off to school early. They said he played cricket at school but never played it with the village boys when he came home on holidays. He just looked after old Mr. Glossop's horses and read books.

"The last time anyone here saw him was more than a dozen years ago, at his mother and old Mr. Glossop's funeral — they died within forty-eight hours of each other. A bad winter for pneumonia, that was. Mr. Glossop and I didn't know old Mr. Glossop all that well — we didn't even know he'd died. Quite shocked we were, when we got a letter from his lawyer telling us he'd left us the pub. Mr. Glossop felt bad that young Mr. Finch didn't even get a share in the pub. He wrote Mr. Finch and said that he

381

could come and stay with us anytime."

"Where did he write Mr. Finch?" asked Miss Holmes.

"Oh, at his school. He was at a boys' school near Oxford. And Mr. Finch wrote back all polite like and said thank you very much but he didn't expect to return anytime soon. Mr. Glossop wrote again after a year or two had passed, and again Mr. Finch wrote back saying the exact same thing. And that's the last we heard of him."

Miss Holmes had another question. "The second time you wrote, he was still in school?"

"We wrote to the school's address, but it might have been forwarded. The address he wrote back from was a different one, in Oxford proper. When the man asked about Mr. Finch, I gave him that address. The next time Mr. Glossop and I went into Oxford, we went around, since so many people have been asking about him —"

"Wait." Mrs. Watson interrupted her. "There were still more people asking about him?"

"Oh, I didn't get to that part yet? Right, so after the man came, I started asking the villagers about Mr. Finch. They didn't know anything. The one person I didn't think to ask was my husband — I thought he didn't know any more than I did. It was only later that it came up by chance — and that's when he told me about the two men who came last April to ask about Mr. Finch. I was in bed with a cold that day and he served all the customers. Was a busy few days, too, so he forgot about it completely, until I brought up this other man."

"Would Mr. Glossop be able to tell me if this is one of the two men who came in April?" asked Miss Holmes, holding out a small photograph.

"I can ask him."

Mrs. Glossop returned two minutes later, looking excited. "Mr. Glossop can't be altogether sure but he thinks so."

Mrs. Watson held out her hand for the return of the photograph. It was the one of the young Marbletons that Miss Holmes had found in Mrs. Woods's place, with Frances Marbleton facing the camera.

"Any other parties looking for Mr. Finch? Any ladies?"

"No, nobody else that we know of. And no ladies besides yourselves."

"The man who came a month ago by himself, can you describe his appearance?"

"He was in his forties, I'd say. Medium height. Thin. Patted the top of his head with a handkerchief at one point — he was half bald. Can't remember much of his face — one of those faces, you know."

Miss Holmes nodded. "If you wouldn't mind going back a bit, Mrs. Glossop. You were saying something about the last time you and Mr. Glossop were in Oxford together?"

"Right. We decided to look up the address that Mr. Finch had given us. The place isn't there anymore. I mean, the building still stands, but it's no longer a boarding home. A dressmaker took over the premise. The ground floor is the shop; she and the seamstresses live upstairs."

Mrs. Glossop brightened. "Mr. Glossop bought me a nice tippet while we were there, seeing how business has been good lately."

After leaving the pub, Mrs. Watson and Miss Holmes visited the village church and cemetery. The church registry verified the date of the late Widow Finch's wedding to old Mr. Glossop. The cemetery corroborated the time frame of the couple's deaths. And the vicar, a kindly if rather frail-looking man who had been at this particular living for sixteen years, substantiated Mrs. Glossop's claim that no one had known much about Myron Finch with his own rather profound ignorance on the subject.

"Does it occur to you, Miss Holmes, that there might be something cold in Mr. Finch's character?" asked Mrs. Watson. "I understand that illegitimacy can act as a barrier to friendship, but an entire upbringing in this village and no rapport worth mentioning with *anyone*?"

She had hardly been fond of the village in which she had spent time after she was orphaned. But after she had fled into the wider world, she had maintained a correspondence with a young woman who had been kind to her, until the latter's death in childbirth.

"But I suppose it's possible for him to love one person ardently and to ignore, at the same time, the people among whom he'd grown up," she said, answering her own question.

On their way to Oxford, they stopped by Lady Ingram's ancestral home. The small estate looked trim and spruce — Lord Ingram's fortune at work.

No one at the nearby village had heard of Myron Finch. And no one knew of any romantic entanglements concerning their old Miss Greville. They did, however, confirm that there had been rumors that when the Grevilles went on a grand tour to southern France and Italy, they had in fact stayed at a rather dilapidated house in Oxford itself.

"That's probably where they met," theorized Mrs. Watson.

Miss Holmes did not venture an opinion of her own.

Mrs. Watson was both rather happy and a little sad about it. When Miss Holmes had first become her houseguest, she had made more of an effort to speak. But now, understanding that silence was her natural habit, Mrs. Watson was relieved that she felt comfortable enough to remain silent unless otherwise compelled. But that did not take away from the fact that Miss Holmes, when she did speak, made for fascinating, if sometimes discomfiting, company.

They toured the address given by Mrs. Glossop and confirmed that it had once been a lodging house for young professional men in the city. As they were several hours past lunch, Mrs. Watson expected Miss Holmes to cast her eyes about for an attractive tea shop. Instead, the latter asked, "Have you ever visited Oxford University, ma'am?"

"I don't believe I have."

"May I tempt you with a quick tour? I've never been either."

Of course, Miss Holmes had wished to be educated. She would have been interested in the women's colleges at the country's best universities. "Yes, absolutely."

They spent a pleasant afternoon walking about the green swards of the various colleges, admiring their great façades and punting on the gentle waters of River Cherwell.

It was only on the train back to London that the thought came to Mrs. Watson. "Who do you think that man might be, the one who asked about Mr. Finch a month ago? Do you think Lady Ingram hired someone else before she came to us?"

"I have no idea who the man is." Miss Holmes paused for a moment. "But I'm glad he didn't seem to be Lord Ingram."

Mrs. Watson stared at her. "You think Lord Ingram — you think *he* could possibly be involved in all this?"

"At the moment, the only thing I know for certain is how little we know. Lady Ingram isn't telling the whole truth. Why should we be so confident that Lord Ingram isn't aware of everything that is going on — or has no hand in it whatsoever?" Miss Holmes exhaled slowly. "But, as I said, I'm glad that man did not seem to be him."

■ ■ ■ ■

Inspector Treadles received the pathologist's official report shortly before he left Scotland Yard for the day: There was no water in the dead man's lungs — he had died from strangulation.

He tapped his fingers against the report. There was nothing unexpected in there. And frankly, had "de Lacy" died from drowning, it would be all the same.

If he chose to write the report that he'd spent half the day composing in his head.

Richard Hayward, a young man of perceived means, had been living in London under an assumed name. He had come by his fortune via illicit means. When those illicit means caught up with him, he died at the hands of a professional killer known as de Lacy. De Lacy, upon attracting police attention, feared that he, too, would face reprisals from the same criminal elements who wanted Hayward dead. Under the influence of intoxicants, de Lacy confessed his life's story to Mr. Lucas Boyd of Lambeth, whose testimony is hereby appended.

The truly elite criminal elements had less to do with Scotland Yard than Her Majesty the Queen. If he submitted this particular version of events, his superiors would be more than satisfied. *Well done, Treadles. That's as far as anyone can take a case like that. File it and take a look at this new one that just came in.*

Except he knew that this version of events was, if not an outright lie, then at least a mirage. Someone had gone through a great deal of trouble to make sure that a dunce of Young Boyd's caliber, a half-blind one, too, would tell this tale to the police. Not to mention, this same someone had to kill a man — or at least find a body — and make sure it ended up in the right place for Young Boyd to recognize the distinctive summer scarf.

Yet knowing it for the deception it was, Treadles still couldn't be sure that he wouldn't submit such a report.

He walked into his fine house and closed the door behind himself. The sound echoed in the empty place. His wife would be meeting with a women's group — she'd taken up with them about six months ago. He used to miss her when she was gone. This evening, however, he was glad she wasn't there.

That she wouldn't see him like this, struggling with — and possibly losing to — this desire to appear supremely competent and efficient before his superiors.

The desire didn't originate with Alice, but with Sherlock Holmes — he didn't want a woman to do his work better than he could. But Alice . . . ever since he learned that she once — and perhaps still — harbored ambitions that had nothing to do with their home life, he had not been the same man.

He wanted to be so wildly successful that she would never dream of running Cousins Manufacturing again. He wanted to give her so many children that she never had the time again. But God did not seem to want the latter for them. And the former — would he really write a report full of deception just so he could be one step closer to his next promotion?

He didn't know.

And this frightened him above all else.

It was past eleven and Charlotte was in a bit of a mood. It did not happen very often, but when it did, when that strange restlessness came upon her, she was not very well equipped to handle it: It was something that could not be reasoned away — or crushed under an avalanche of cake.

She paced in her room for a while. Then dressed again and slipped out: She might as well reread *A Summer in Roman Ruins,* and that book was currently gracing Sherlock Holmes's shelves.

18 Upper Baker Street was dark. She reached for a light. The gas flame flared, illuminating the steps.

A small sound came from above. The house cooling down at night and contracting? A mouse in the attic? She climbed up and walked into the parlor.

"Good evening, Miss Holmes."

The stair sconce lit an amber slice of the room and left dark shadows elsewhere. The greeting came from the shadows.

She turned toward the voice. "Mr. Marbleton, I presume?"

A soft chuckle. "I see Sherlock Holmes's genius is real."

"No genius required. We've conversed before, however briefly. I don't forget voices."

She turned on the lamp affixed near the door. Mr. Marbleton stood next to the grandfather clock, a pistol in hand.

"Some tea for you — and Miss Marbleton? Does she need the attention of a physician?"

"How —"

"I can smell blood in the air — and you don't seem injured."

Stephen Marbleton exhaled. "Miss

Marbleton is fine. The bullet only grazed her shoulder. I cleaned the wound with your fine whisky and bandaged it with some boracic ointment."

Charlotte nodded — a doctor would not be able to do much more than that. She entered the bedroom, where Miss Marbleton lay quietly asleep. "Did you give her some of Sherlock's fine laudanum also?"

Mrs. Watson had made sure they had the usual assortment of tinctures and patent medicines that graced a convalescent's bedside.

"I did. Thank you."

She laid a hand on the young woman's forehead. No fever. But then, the wound was very recent. They wouldn't know for some time whether it would become infected. She left Miss Marbleton to her rest, set a kettle to heat on the spirit lamp, and put a few madeleines on a plate. "Have the two of you dined?"

"We have. But madeleines are most welcome. Will you share some with me?"

Most native English speakers would not be able to immediately name the shell-shaped, fluted little cakes. But Stephen Marbleton had a soupçon of an accent — which hinted not so much at foreign origins as significant portions of life spent abroad.

"I serve madeleines for me — you'll need to be quick and ruthless to have a chance at any."

He smiled. She did not return the smile. He was young — younger than she. Left-handed, obviously. Had lived in hot climes not long ago. Enjoyed fiction. Was a little vain about his clothes, but not so much that it interfered with practicality.

"Were you the one who alerted the police about the body in Hounslow?"

The bobbies had gone running to the place because they had received a telegram concerning iniquitous goings-on in the house.

He shook his head a little, but not in denial. "Of course Sherlock Holmes would know that."

The clock gonged the half hour, then carried on with its tick-tocking.

"Thank you most kindly for letting us stay," he said.

"Tell me why you impersonated Mr. Finch," she said at the same time.

He sighed, sat down across from her, and reached for a madeleine. "Mr. Finch has something we want."

"Who are *we*?"

"My family — my parents, my sister, and myself."

"Your mother is Mrs. Marbleton?"

"Yes."

"Your father?"

"Mr. Marbleton, of course."

"And who is Mr. Marbleton, in relation to Mr. Moriarty?"

"They are not the same man, if that is what you are asking."

Charlotte nibbled on a madeleine. "I take it then that you weren't responsible for the death of the man currently known as Richard Hayward. But you didn't learn of it by accident."

"We were watching the house. The house wasn't particularly important — and hadn't been for some time. The man who lived there performed unsavory services for a fee. He'd been working for Moriarty for a while but was the kind of underling happy not to know anything about why he was asked to do what he was asked to do. Nevertheless, he was one of our few leads."

"Your mother doesn't know more about Moriarty's organization?"

"She left him decades ago."

"And she does not cooperate with him in a mutually beneficial manner?"

"Not that I know of."

She eyed him. "Not a terribly reassuring answer."

"I know a great deal of my mother's life. Moriarty has been hunting us for almost fifteen years and we can't afford secrets. Any ignorance — any mistaken assumption allowed a foothold — can lead to disaster for the entire family. That I do not know of something should be a reassuring enough answer."

A strong retort. She would not consider her mind completely put at rest, but the reason he gave was certainly specific enough. She took the kettle from the spirit lamp and poured hot water into the teapot.

"How did Mr. Finch come into anything of value to you? Was he working for Moriarty?"

"He was."

She had hoped, when it turned out that Mr. Finch might be alive after all, that he would also turn out to have no connections to Moriarty. Of course she'd always known that it was a vain hope, but still.

"Since when? And how did he find Moriarty — or vice versa?"

"I don't know when he started working for Moriarty. I do know that Moriarty has a preference for those who are tainted by illegitimacy — they tend to be hungry for success, and ruthless because the world has been ruthless to them. No one misses them very much when they disappear and there's always a ready supply of young, eager men born on the wrong side of the blanket."

"So when you said he has something you want, you mean he has something of Moriarty's."

"That is correct."

"What is it?"

"We don't know precisely. What we know is that a dossier exists concerning plans to be put into motion next year. The plans vanished at the same time as Mr. Finch and Mr. Jenkins, otherwise known as Richard Hayward. Moriarty is extremely displeased about the disappearance of the plans and the betrayal of his subordinates."

"How do you know all that?"

His smile was bitter for one so young. "The less you know about it, the better."

"All right. This Mr. Jenkins, was he also illegitimate?"

"Quite so. I understand he and Mr. Finch attended the same school — and were in the same residence house."

So she was right, in a way, about Mr. Jenkins having been an orphan. What must it have been like, for young men such as her brother and Mr. Jenkins, to feel themselves not so much children of those distant, well-born fathers but bags of refuse that had been carelessly left behind? And was it any wonder that a man like Moriarty had easily garnered their trust and loyalty, at least in the beginning?

"Why did Messrs. Finch and Jenkins abscond with those plans?" she asked.

"On that I do not have reliable intelligence, only speculation."

"And what is your speculation?"

"There might be something in those plans that could be used for blackmail — Moriarty pays well but not so well that a man wouldn't still dream of a fortune."

"Surely, such dreams must be tempered with fear of crossing Moriarty."

"Which is why I'm not entirely sure of my own conjecture. Another possibility is that they wanted to leave Moriarty's service — and believed that having the plans in their possession might ensure their safety."

"Why have you involved yourself in all this? Shouldn't it be your goal to stay away from Moriarty as much as possible?"

"For fifteen years, we've rarely remained more than three months in the same place — and when we did, when we thought we were safe and hidden . . ." He took a breath. "We want something on Moriarty. Something that would make him anxious about *us* instead. Something that would force him to leave us alone, because it would destroy him first."

"And how did you hope to achieve that by impersonating Mr. Finch?"

"We couldn't find him. So we had to hope that he would find us."

"By approaching his family?"

"We thought that if we were blatant in our attempts to contact your family, perhaps it would vex your father enough to send strong words via solicitors, which would make Mr. Finch realize that there was an imposter."

"And then what?"

"We wrote your father three times and gave our address each time. Our hope was that Mr. Finch, after he had heard from Sir Henry, would find us. Then we would offer him a bargain: the dossier in exchange for his safety."

"How can you guarantee his safety? You can't even guarantee your own."

"And yet we are still alive, still more or less in one piece, after years of being wanted by Moriarty. Who else is better positioned to help him keep body and soul together?"

That much might be true. Mr. Hayward-cum-Jenkins certainly hadn't been able to live as long after quitting Moriarty's service.

"Speaking of keeping body and soul together . . . what happened to Miss Marbleton?"

"We went back to my place tonight at Mrs. Woods's. After your midnight visit, her first thought was that it was Mr. Finch. She sent me a cable the next day. As she was trying to slip back into the house, she saw you speaking with Mrs. Woods. Since it was only you, we didn't think there would be *that* much danger in going back. In fact, our main concern was to avoid being seen by Mrs. Woods.

"We wouldn't have anticipated the ambush at all. Fortunately, Dr. Vickery arrived home from an evening out and entered his room while we were waiting in the service stairs for the passage to clear. That was when we saw our door open and close from the inside.

"We still thought most likely it was either you or Mr. Finch. But at least our guard was up . . . Long story short, we were able to shake our pursuers loose, eventually."

"You are sure about that?"

"It happens to be our specialty."

She certainly hoped so, since they were already on Mrs. Watson's property. "Why did you come here, then?"

"I saw the letter my mother wrote you, toward the end of the Sackville affair. She is an excellent judge of character. If she trusts you, then I can trust you, too."

"You weren't concerned that this place might be watched?"

"Tonight Moriarty's minions are watching the railway terminuses, since they expect us to flee."

"I take this to mean that you've been to a railway terminus and found it under surveillance."

"Precisely. Besides, I wanted to ask you a question."

"Go ahead."

"Why are *you* looking for Mr. Finch?"

"I sought him on behalf of a client, an old friend of Mr. Finch's with whom he had a standing appointment."

Mr. Marbleton raised a brow. "Who's the client?"

"I'm not at liberty to disclose that information."

"And the client doesn't know you are related to him?"

"That I can't be one hundred percent sure. Did Mrs. Marbleton know that Sherlock Holmes was related to Myron Finch when she came to see me?"

"She called on you for a completely different matter."

"That doesn't answer my question."

"No, we didn't know. But afterward, when we learned of the connection, we were certain you weren't harboring him, at least not here, as we'd checked the place top to bottom. And it would be demented to hide him at Mrs. Watson's, when you have an empty house here."

Charlotte nodded, checked on the tea that had been steeping inside the teapot, and poured him a cup. "You have one more question, don't you?"

He looked at her a minute. "I suppose I do. Is your sister well?"

"How many times did you meet with her?"

He added sugar to his tea. "Thrice."

"More than necessary."

Did he color a little? "Perhaps. Is she well?"

"Life is not easy for Livia — it has never been. She is an intelligent, discerning woman who believes her intelligence and discernment to be of no value."

"You must have felt the pressure to believe the same."

"Not at all. It took me a great deal of effort to understand that such pressure exists — I am not sensitive to the opinions of others, individually or as a collective. But Livia is. She is excruciatingly aware of what she is expected to be and how different that is from who she is. Not for a moment does she not feel her shortcomings."

Stephen Marbleton took a sip of his tea — he held the cup with both hands, as if he were feeling cold. "Why are you telling me this?"

"So that you understand she is fragile, if you do not already realize that. She will not perish from a little flirtation, but she will suffer."

"Are you warning me away from her?"

"No, but it behooves me to point out the likely consequences, so that should you choose to proceed, you do so in full awareness of them."

She rose. "You must be weary. I will see myself out."

EIGHTEEN

Saturday

Charlotte rose early, took a basket of food-stuff from the kitchen, and called on 18 Upper Baker Street. She wasn't surprised to see her uninvited guests gone, but she was rather impressed at how neat and untouched the place looked.

A note had been tucked under Sherlock's pillow.

> Thank you for your hospitality. We hope to meet again under more auspicious circumstances.

The day Charlotte learned that the woman who had watched Mrs. Watson's front door had cabled a biblical verse to be advertised in the paper, she had sent in a request to consult the archives of the *Times*. The permission had at last been granted.

She had expected the place to be thunderously loud. But the printing presses weren't in use at the moment and the offices of the paper, while bustling, were far quieter than a drawing room on the night of a dinner party.

A large, well-lit editorial room anchored the entire operation, with a sizable oak table at the center and smaller desks arranged along the walls, furnished with every tool and implement to facilitate the act of writing. Next to the editorial room, according to the clerk who led the way, was the editors' dining room.

The archive, just down the passage from the dining room, held every edition of the *Times* since the paper's inception. Charlotte was given brief instructions and then left to browse.

She had assumed the biblical verses would appear weekly. Instead it was three times a month, always on the same dates. She checked the papers from three years ago, but the verses weren't there. When she looked carefully, however, she found a weekly cipher that decoded into a roman numeral, followed by a number. *VIII, 260, XI, 81, XIV, 447,* and so on.

They did not appear to be referring to the Bible. Charlotte got up and walked into the next room, where a dozen proofreaders were working, surrounded by hundreds of dictionaries and encyclopedias. She located the *Encyclopedia Britannica,* volume 8, page 260. The entry was *England.*

The other ciphers also each yielded an entry — if that was what they signified.

But what was the point of all this?

She thought for some time, then took herself to the house on Portman Square and left Lord Bancroft a note.

When, exactly, was the Vigenère cipher you gave me sent as a telegram? The information will be much appreciated.

Mrs. Burns, true to her word, was back at the soup kitchen, peeling carrots. Mrs. Watson tied on an apron and attacked a pile of vegetable marrows.

"Sometimes we have other ladies coming in here to help. But they're finicky. Don't want to do anything too dirty, heavy, or hot. You're all right, Mrs. Watson," said Mrs. Burns, after almost an hour had passed.

Mrs. Watson laughed. "That's probably because I'm no lady, Mrs. Burns. I was a musical theater performer. Even if I married a duke, actual ladies would turn their noses up at me."

Mrs. Burns stopped what she was doing.

"You aren't making fun of me, are you?"

"If I wanted to make fun of you, Mrs. Burns, I'd be telling you how respectable I was, instead of the other way around."

"So you were really on stage, singing and dancing?"

"As described."

"And gentlemen on their knees at your stage door, begging for your favors?"

Mrs. Watson laughed again. "Not on their knees. But yes, there were a few gentlemen here and there who wanted introductions and whatnot."

"Whatnot, eh?"

"Oh, you know it."

Mrs. Burns raised a brow, but her expression was delighted, rather than scandalized. "I hope you had the pick of the litter."

"I had my way of managing that aspect of the business," Mrs. Watson said modestly.

Mrs. Burns shook her head and resumed peeling. "Never thought I'd meet an actress at the soup kitchen."

"I've run into old acquaintances in bookshops, railway stations, and once while walking in the Pennine hills. We aren't that rare — especially not in London."

Mrs. Burns shook her head a little more. Then she looked at Mrs. Watson and said, "I was always interested in the theater. Not in appearing on stage, mind you — wouldn't want all those strangers staring at me. But it'd be . . . freeing, wouldn't it, to be in a place where everybody is, well, I don't know how to say it without giving offense, but —"

"Where nobody is, strictly speaking, all that respectable," Mrs. Watson finished for her, smiling.

"And therefore respect has to be earned, because everyone starts on the same footing."

"If you are looking for an egalitarian profession, I'm not sure the theater is your answer. And the amount of jostling for position is as fierce as anything you see in Society at the height of the Season. But I liked it. There's a certain magic to performing and you can achieve great camaraderie, even if there's plenty of ugly madness, too."

Rather like life itself.

Mrs. Burns didn't reply. In the kitchen, knives thudded on chopping boards and steam hissed from kettles.

Mrs. Watson thought Mrs. Burns's curiosity had been exhausted until the latter said, "Part of the reason I keep thinking of the theater from time to time is because of someone I used to know. He's, well, of a particular persuasion, as they say."

"You mean, his romantic interest lies not with women."

"Yes, that persuasion. He had half a mind to join the theater — thought they wouldn't be so repelled by his kind there."

"He's not altogether wrong. There are more of his kind in the theater than in the general population, I'd say. He'd have found it less lonely — and less dangerous. But that isn't to say he would have been treated well by everyone, or that stagehands wouldn't call him ugly names or make crude gestures when he walked by in his costume."

"No utopias anywhere, eh?"

"I'm afraid not. This is all we've got." Mrs. Watson let a beat pass. "And you, Mrs. Burns, I don't mean to be forward, but you're a beautiful woman. Has there ever been trouble for you in service?"

Mrs. Burns shrugged. "Frankly, I don't think it matters whether a woman is all that good-looking when it comes to these things. A man doesn't suddenly decide, in front of a beautiful woman, that it's his due to have his hand up her skirt. If he's that kind, maybe he's more likely to do it when the woman is pretty. But even if she weren't, he'd have done it anyway to please himself."

A good answer, but not the one Mrs. Watson was looking for. "No trouble on that front with your master, I hope?"

"No, he's all right, Dr. Swanson. Talks more than I need him to, but he's all right."

"What if he falls in love with you someday and comes with a marriage proposal?"

Mrs. Burns chortled. "Oh, there's a thought. If he does that, I'll tell him I prefer looking after him for money to looking after him for free."

"Surely there must be other advantages to being a prosperous physician's wife. You can lord over that annoying daughter of his, for one thing."

"Tempting, but not tempting enough — I'd rather not see her face at all. Besides, I've got someone." Mrs. Burns leaned in. "Her name is Gabrielle — she works for a rich widow with three daughters who want to be countesses. And one of these days we are going to retire to the south of France together."

"Oh," said Mrs. Watson. "So the poor doctor has never had a chance."

Mrs. Burns chortled again. "Now if he were a duke, maybe I'd have considered. I know duchesses go around and take lovers. But a doctor is going to expect me to be all prim and proper. Mind you, I am. There's never been anyone for me except Gabrielle, but old Dr. Swanson would have an apoplectic attack if I told him I'd rather sleep with her than him."

"Or he might ask to join you. You never know."

Mrs. Burns gaped at Mrs. Watson before breaking into giggles. They laughed together for a minute, then started on a basket of potatoes.

"Hmm, the plot thickens — or does it thin?" asked Penelope. Her aunt was taking a nap and Miss Holmes had given a concise account of what Aunt Jo had learned at the soup kitchen — never a dull moment in the Sherlock Holmes business. "If Mrs. Burns isn't the least bit interested in Dr. Swanson, then was Mrs. Morris deluding herself after all?"

"She hasn't complained about her health since she first came to me," said Miss Holmes. "On each of the subsequent occasions we met, she appeared to be in robust shape and glad for it."

"So what do you plan to do?"

"I'll call on Mrs. Morris again and ask a few more questions."

Penelope shook her head, relieved it wasn't her problem. They spoke a bit about the de Blois ladies, who had already sent two postcards from their travels. Then

Penelope decided she'd put in enough small talk.

"Do you really carry suspicions concerning Lord Ingram, Miss Holmes?"

Miss Holmes's face was Madonna-like in its serenity. "Not particularly."

"But yesterday you told Aunt Jo that you thought it was possible that the man asking around after Mr. Finch could be him."

"It could still be someone he sent."

"Surely you don't think he did away with Mr. Finch?"

"I don't. But how can I be certain that he hadn't tried to learn everything he could?"

Penelope tried to imagine Lord Ingram skulking about, secretly gathering information on Lady Ingram's former swain. She couldn't — but like Miss Holmes, neither could she completely dismiss that possibility. He might not love Lady Ingram anymore, but she was still his wife and the mother of his children. Who, except the person in those shoes, could be certain of what he had or hadn't done?

"My father considers himself a clever man," Miss Holmes went on, "and he believes my mother to be of mediocre intelligence. So he signaled his affairs to her in some subtle way. But as far as I can tell, she always knew well before he bothered to send

411

those signals.

"A household can hide many secrets. But Lord Ingram is observant. Perhaps Lady Ingram has been able to conceal everything from him before this summer. But given her frenzy of activity in the wake of Mr. Finch's disappearance, it's not outlandish to suppose he has some idea that all is not well."

"But that man we are talking about — the one you think Lord Ingram could have sent — he visited Mr. Finch's village a month ago. And Mr. Finch's disappearance was more recent than that."

"Lady Ingram is not to be entirely trusted on her version of events. She said she knew nothing about where to find Mr. Finch. But her visit to my father's solicitor showed that she knew more than she told us. If she lied about one aspect of the case, she could very well have lied about other aspects, too."

Penelope sighed. "I wish I could be sure Lord Ingram wasn't involved."

"And he may not be — not actively in any case. But no matter what, if his wife is involved, then he, too, cannot escape entanglement."

Telltale signs of disappointment must have crossed Penelope's face, for Miss Holmes said, very charitably, "Miss Redmayne, I have a medical question. Do you think you might be able to help me?"

It had been years since Lord Ingram had last stepped into his wife's bedroom in their town house. There had been changes — the new clock on the mantel, two small seascapes he didn't remember being there earlier. But overall, the room felt so familiar, he almost expected to meet her gaze in the vanity mirror as she brushed her beautiful hair, a delighted smile on her face.

No, the delighted smiles were from earlier in their marriage. The last time he had stepped into this room, she had smiled, but the smile had been perfunctory, almost forced.

He had wished to make love to her, hoping that physical closeness could bridge the distance that stretched between them, a distance that he could not close, no matter what he did. But in the end, he left after saying good night and little else, so unwelcome had he felt in her private space.

The next week his godfather had passed away unexpectedly. And he had told her that he had inherited only a five-hundred-pound annuity, rather than the fortune that was in his godfather's will. And she had flown into a rage. She had married him because of the expectation he would be a very wealthy man, she'd shouted, and now she had married him for nothing. Now her children had Jewish blood for nothing.

At first he was encouraged by her anger — anger was solid, anger was real, anger was something he could investigate and find out more about. Anything was better than the polite remoteness that made him despair.

What she'd actually said took minutes, hours, days to sink in.

To become real.

They'd never spoken again, except by necessity.

Why, then, was he here, in her room?

His action was the answer he was reluctant to put into words. Half ashamed yet inexplicably compelled, he searched the room with a thoroughness that should be reserved only for those suspected of selling the crown's secrets.

When her room yielded nothing, he searched his study, which he knew she sometimes used when he wasn't home. When that turned up no clues — alas that typewriter ribbons did not retain a legible record of the text last prepared on them — he looked carefully at his collection of books. The maids did dust the books regularly, but it was not part of their daily routine, and it should be possible to tell whether any given volume had been recently taken off the shelves.

The first book that showed unmistakable sign of having been used lately — the dust on top had been flicked off — was a volume on matrimonial law.

He had no particular interest in law. The set of treatises had been a present — and he could recall neither the occasion nor the gift-giver. The pages were entirely uncut, except the section concerning the dissolution of marriages.

Was that what she was up to? Had she been discreetly inquiring into a *divorce*?

NINETEEN

Monday

"Miss Holmes, Mrs. Hudson, what a lovely surprise." Dr. Swanson rose and warmly shook hands with Charlotte and Mrs. Watson. "Clarissa won't be back yet for at least another half hour — she's at the park, taking her morning constitutional. I hope that in the meantime, my company will serve."

Miss Holmes smiled. "It will serve perfectly well."

"Shall I ring for some coffee? Mrs. Burns is at home today and we can all enjoy some of her wonderful coffee."

"We won't mind at all."

They passed time in small talk until a maid delivered the coffee. Dr. Swanson poured ceremoniously and his callers were generous with their praise for the beverage's aroma and flavor.

Miss Holmes enjoyed hers with an abundance of sugar and cream. Then she set down her cup, and said, "You must forgive us, Dr. Swanson — and your daughter, too — for not having been perfectly honest with you at our previous meeting. You see, Mrs. Morris did not meet us at the ladies' knitting circle. Instead, we made her acquaintance when she arrived on our doorstep not long ago to consult Sherlock Holmes, my brother, because she was secretly distraught, fearing that she was being poisoned in her own home."

Dr. Swanson blinked at the name Sherlock Holmes. He recoiled at the word *poisoned.* "That poor child — I had no idea she was beset to that extent. But it's only London. Our very air is noxious. Most are inured to it, but from time to time some become unbearably sensitized to pernicious particulates that are breathed in."

"That isn't what Mrs. Morris believes. She believes that Mrs. Burns intends to get rid of her so she may better pursue you."

Dr. Swanson gaped at her. "But that's ridiculous. Mrs. Burns isn't that kind of woman at all. My goodness, that view is so utterly divorced from reality I haven't the slightest idea how to address it."

Miss Holmes leaned forward. "The only way you can address it is to tell Mrs. Morris the truth."

Dr. Swanson stared at her. "I'm — I'm afraid —"

"You're afraid you know exactly what I'm talking about, Doctor. Your daughter believes that your housekeeper put something in the biscuits to make her ill. But it wasn't the biscuits, it was the coffee she drank, which you had tampered with."

"I didn't put any poison in the coffee."

"No, you wouldn't do that to her. But you wanted her to be unwell enough to leave London. As things stood, Mrs. Morris's hostility might cause Mrs. Burns to hand in her resignation, and you desperately did not want that to happen."

Dr. Swanson swallowed.

"Your daughter has proclaimed to us a profound distaste for tropical fruits. Sometimes people dislike something because they cannot abide the taste. Other times, it's because they react severely to even the minutest quantity.

"My brother considered it a possibility that she is allergic to some variety of tropical fruit. But she avoids them assiduously — avoids even dried fruits that aren't tropical in origin. How then, would it be possible to introduce such an allergen into her diet?

"He was puzzled until I recalled to him

that in the stillroom, which you are familiar with because you used to make your own coffee, there is twine made of coir, which comes from coconuts. It shouldn't be too difficult for you to cut — or grind up — a small quantity so that it resembles ground coffee. The stillroom isn't very bright and in any case Mrs. Morris should have no reason to suspect anything amiss with coffee she'd ground herself only hours ago."

Dr. Swanson gripped the arms of his chair. "Are you — are you going to tell Clarissa?"

"Should we not?"

"Please, please don't. It would devastate her. I swear to you my purpose was not to hurt her. It was as you said, I'd hoped she would leave London."

"You saw how she suffered, yet you still did it a second time." Mrs. Watson could hold herself back no longer. "What kind of father are you?"

"You must understand, after my wife died, I began to think of myself as a man near the end of his life. An old man. I lost interest in things. I stopped reading the papers. I had to force myself to reply to letters when I'd always been a prompt correspondent before.

"And then my old housekeeper retired and Mrs. Burns came. And . . . and suddenly I felt like a young man again. Whereas before I could only see the end, now I saw a future. She is beautiful and cultured. We could attend theater and lectures together. We could travel all over the world.

"I sold my practice so I would have more time to woo her, but she is so proper and inscrutable. Finally I thought she was warming up to me. Then Clarissa came to visit — and never left. And I began to feel quite frantic. She is a gem, Mrs. Burns. What if the tradesmen who come to the house, what if one of *them* wins her hand instead? And then — and then I remembered Clarissa's allergy . . ."

It was an old man who looked beseechingly at Miss Holmes and Mrs. Watson.

Mrs. Watson set her jaw. "Dr. Swanson, there are two things you need to know. One, you were never going to succeed with Mrs. Burns. She has someone and is fully intent on spending the rest of her life with that someone, as soon as they both leave service.

"Two, your daughter is not going back to her husband. Sherlock Holmes had his suspicions. Miss Holmes and I, on his instruction, visited Devonport yesterday. We learned that Captain Morris had brought another woman into his household. Mrs. Morris obviously chose not to accept such an arrangement."

"That — that bounder!"

"She has not been very fortunate in the men in her life," said Mrs. Watson acidly.

Dr. Swanson grimaced but did not dispute her claim. "I'll look after her. Please don't tell her."

"We won't. You are right that it would devastate her — and I'm not sure at the moment how much more devastation she can take. But we will need a signed statement from you, which will be kept in a locked box in the Bank of England. And we plan to call on her regularly to make sure she is all right."

Dr. Swanson swallowed but did as they demanded. It was only as they rose to leave that he asked, "So what *will* you tell her?"

"You may tell her we called and told you of the results of our investigation, which is that this particular batch of coffee beans had been stored with some coconuts. You confirmed for us that she is severely allergic to coconuts, and voilà, mystery solved."

"I still think we should have told Mrs. Morris the truth," said Miss Holmes, as they walked out of Dr. Swanson's house.

Maybe she was right. But Mrs. Watson simply couldn't bear to do that to the poor woman. She had nowhere else to go. The truth would only make her miserable for all her days, that the father she had counted on to shelter her from the husband who betrayed her had, in the end, also betrayed her.

"I'll use the service entrance here," said Mrs. Watson.

Miss Holmes nodded, not belaboring her point. "And I'd better head for the *Times* to keep my appointment at the archive."

After she left, Mrs. Watson sighed and tried to recall the occasions when they were able to help clients without breaking anyone's heart, including her own. She'd been afraid at times, but this sorrow felt worse than any fear.

You silly old woman, she told herself, as she descended to the service door. *It's only because you aren't in any danger right now.*

Actually, that wasn't quite true. Miss Holmes had told her of the Marbletons taking refuge at 18 Upper Baker Street — and of Mr. Finch's confirmed connection to Moriarty. There was danger in the air — and she'd simply stopped thinking about it.

Mrs. Burns answered the bell herself. "Mrs. Watson? What are you doing here?"

Mrs. Watson smiled ruefully. "If you'll offer me a cup of your excellent coffee, I'll tell you all about it."

Mrs. Burns listened to the story with an increasingly incredulous expression, but she did not interrupt once.

"So that's that. Theoretically, this case involves only father and daughter. But I believe you should know."

Mrs. Burns remained silent for some more time. "I did think Mrs. Morris was a bit of an idiot, but she didn't deserve this."

"No, she didn't."

"And Dr. Swanson, I never would have guessed that he had this kind of ruthlessness to him. How disturbing."

"I'm glad you don't see it as romantic."

"Good gracious, no. It's selfish, pure and simple."

"What will you do, then?"

"I believe I'll look for a new place."

"I'm sorry. I know that isn't what you wanted."

Mrs. Burns smiled. "Don't worry about me, Mrs. Watson. I know how to look after myself." She saw Mrs. Watson to the door. "Thank you. I'm most grateful."

"And I'm happy to have been of service," said Mrs. Watson, pulling on her gloves. "By the way, the friend you mentioned earlier, did he ever go into theater?"

"Who? Oh, young Greville? No, his sister

married a rich lordship and that was the end of his hope for a Bohemian life."

The only way to be sure that the newspaper notices Charlotte had singled out were giving keywords to Moriarty's ciphers was to verify them. Now that Lord Bancroft had passed on the precise date the Vigenère cipher had been sent over the telegraph lines, she was at last able to perform the test.

But first, she must find the newspaper notice from that particular point in time. She searched on and before the date she had been given. Because that was a decade in the past, another round deciphering all the coded messages among the advertisements was required. She finally found one that, when decoded, read *C 2 5 7*. A similar message from a fortnight earlier, when rendered into plaintext, said *H 146 6 4*.

She stared at the letters and numbers for a minute. Then she went to the proofreaders' room and asked whether they had a copy of Shakespeare's works on hand. As it turned out, there were two on the shelves, a modern edition and one like Livia's, a facsimile of the first folio.

She looked in the facsimile. Comedies, page 2, line 5, the 7th word. *Earth*. That was not the keyword for the Vigenère cipher she'd solved. She tried the earlier message. Histories, page 146, line 6, the 4th word. *Wizard.* No, not that either.

Was she completely wrong?

Her theory was that almost all communications from Moriarty to his minions — and among the minions themselves — were in code. Such a practice had its advantages but also its share of drawbacks. The same cipher, used too often, became easy for others to catch on to. And when there were defectors, they could give away the secret wholesale.

The solution, then, was to choose a highly sophisticated cipher, and then frequently change the keyword by which the plaintext would be encoded. Which presented problems of its own: Namely, how to broadcast the new keyword in such a way that everyone in the organization learned of it at roughly the same time.

The newspaper took care of the dissemination. But those on the receiving end of the notices still needed a common reference, something that wouldn't be too difficult for them to find. *The Holy Bible. Encyclopedia Britannica. Mr. William Shakespeare's Comedies, Histories, & Tragedies,* otherwise known as the First Folio.

Should a defection happen, those in charge simply changed the book of reference. The defectors could still catch the notices in the paper, but they would be quite at sea as to what the new keywords were.

A complete system. A workable system. And if she were Moriarty, viewing it through the twin lens of paranoia and self-admiration, a near-perfect system.

Then why was this not that system?

She smacked herself on the forehead, attracting a bewildered and somewhat disapproving look from the nearest proofreader. *Of course,* even the most meticulously designed system was prone to human error. What if there had been a mistake on the part of the minion who was supposed to post the clue in the papers? What if some misfortune or inattention had caused a delay in the posting of the linchpin to the ciphers?

She returned to the archive and searched the copies of the *Times* published subsequent to the sending of the Vigenère cipher diagram. A notice dated two days later deciphered to read *T 44 7 9.*

Page 44 of the tragedies brought her to *Titus Andronicus.* She moved her index finger down to line 7. The ninth and final word on the line was . . . *truth.*

And that, indeed, was the keyword to the Vigenère cipher.

When Miss Holmes arrived home an hour after luncheon, Mrs. Watson leaped to brief her on what she had learned. "Mrs. Burns worked in Lady Ingram's household — well, her parents' household to be exact, during the time they lived in Oxford."

Miss Holmes paused only minutely in the removal of her hat. "I must head out soon after tea, ma'am. Will you mind telling me the rest while we practice *canne de combat*?"

Mrs. Watson was taken aback. She and Penelope usually had to remind Miss Holmes, who preferred to remain seated, that she must take the time to hone her self-defense skills. This marked the first time Miss Holmes had taken the initiative.

"Of course."

They changed and met in the gymnasium, where Mrs. Watson put Miss Holmes through the usual opening exercises.

"Come at me a little harder," said Miss Holmes. "And please continue with what you learned from Mrs. Burns."

Mrs. Watson swung her walking stick with greater force. Miss Holmes staggered.

"Oh, come. Don't let an old lady overpower you. Now where was I? Ah yes. Mrs. Burns had been working for Lady Ingram's mother's cousin at the time. The cousin had plans of going abroad for six months with her sisters and they didn't want to take more than one maid, so Mrs. Burns was loaned to Mrs. Greville as a favor, since the Grevilles didn't take their own staff with them to Oxford — didn't want it getting out that they were living in relative squalor nearby, rather than off on a grand tour in Europe."

Miss Holmes parried strongly and ducked under Mrs. Watson's next swing with a flash of agility that Mrs. Watson didn't normally associate with the young woman. "Good! Move those feet!"

"I move my feet. It's the rest of me that doesn't follow soon enough."

"So there Mrs. Burns was, in that odd household." Mrs. Watson went back to her account. "The boys should have been in school but there was no money for it. Their father taught them as best as he could, but he'd forgotten most of his Latin and Greek. She said the boys were ignorant. The younger one didn't care, but the elder one felt bad about it."

"And their sister? You must have asked Mrs. Burns about her."

"Mrs. Burns said that her main impression of Lady Ingram at that age was one of frustration." Mrs. Watson hesitated a moment, almost exposing her weapon arm to Miss Holmes's attack — the girl might be inexperienced, but she knew how to spot an opportunity. She barely sidestepped Miss Holmes's stick. "A frustration that approached rage, at times."

"Lady Ingram would have been about sixteen or seventeen at the time?"

"Seventeen, I think. It was the winter of that year."

Miss Holmes darted to the side and pushed off against the wall to avoid being backed into a corner. "When I learned that my father's first fiancée had jilted him for having sired a child out of wedlock, I thought that fathering an illegitimate son in and of itself had been the cause of that rejection — even though most men are not held particularly accountable for such mishaps. It was only later that I realized what must have happened — that he had impregnated a servant while he was courting Lady Amelia Drummond and she rejected him for his faithlessness.

"Given that he married my mother on the day he was originally supposed to marry Lady Amelia — Mr. Finch is at most a year older than Henrietta, my eldest sister. Which would have made him around twenty-three that winter."

Two young people, both hemmed in by their circumstances. "Do you think Lady Ingram was frustrated because she couldn't be with Mr. Finch?" asked Mrs. Watson. "And do you think Mr. Finch allowed himself to be recruited by Moriarty because of the frustration of not being able to marry Lady Ingram?"

"I don't know when Mr. Finch decided to throw in his lot with Moriarty. Stephen Marbleton wasn't privy to that information."

Miss Holmes lurched to the left, but not fast enough. Mrs. Watson's stick connected with her upper arm. Miss Holmes winced.

"You are tiring again, my dear. You need to develop stamina — which will only happen by devoting more time to exercise." The more mischievous part of Mrs. Watson's mind wondered whether she couldn't stick out a foot and trip the young woman, but the more compassionate side decided that before she did so, she must add some paddings around the room. "Have you noticed, by the way, that in recent years, there has been an undercurrent of anger to Lady Ingram — which hadn't been there when she first came onto the scene?"

"There's always been an undercurrent of anger to Lady Ingram — just as there has always been one to my sister Livia. Except that Lady Ingram disguised hers far better."

Miss Holmes threw up a hand to indicate that she needed a breather. She leaned against the wall, her shoulders drooping. "By the way, ma'am, would you happen to have a weighted parasol — or something similar to that?"

"Mr. Gillespie is out visiting a client — and not expected back today," said his flustered secretary, a young man with a ruddy complexion.

Instead of pointing out that she had seen Mr. Gillespie's walking stick, emblazoned on top with his initials, in the umbrella stand in the vestibule, Charlotte smiled. "I don't need to see Mr. Gillespie. I'm sure, as his trusted right-hand man, Mr. —"

"Parsons."

"Yes, Mr. Parsons. I'm sure you can help me with my simple inquiry."

"I'm afraid I can't either, miss. You see, I — I've been given permission to close the office early — as of this moment, in fact — to meet my — my mother's train. She's coming to town to visit and I don't want her to be alone at Waterloo Station."

His color had changed from pink to scarlet in under a minute. Fascinating how some people's faces betrayed them when they lied, not that she couldn't already tell from the half-finished letter in the typewriter — among other clues on his desk — that he was very much still in the middle of his working hours.

"Of course you wouldn't want her to wait by herself," she said kindly.

"No indeed. But if you'll come back tomorrow, miss, at — ah — ten o'clock in the morning, I'm sure I'll be able to help you then."

She smiled at him again. "I will. Thank you."

The moment Charlotte had solid evidence that she was correct in her conjecture of how those in Moriarty's organization encoded and decoded their messages, she had sent word to Lord Bancroft requesting a meeting. And now they were seated once again in the unrestrained drawing room of the house near Portman Square.

She gave an abbreviated account of her work in the *Times*'s archive room. "I believe I am correct about how Moriarty's system works. But so far, I have only one point of corroboration, a ten-year-old Vigenère cipher. If you, sir, have in your possession more recent examples of ciphers you believe to have originated from Moriarty, I would like to use them to verify that I am indeed onto something."

Lord Bancroft sighed. "Miss Holmes, I must count myself disappointed. When I received your note, I'd hoped that you'd be at last giving me the long hoped-for answer to my proposal."

"Ah," said Charlotte.

"Indeed. It has been two weeks. And we have known each other for more than ten years. I'm persuaded that you can't have any qualms about my character, my finances, or my sincerity in the matter."

"No, I do not."

In fact, on paper they were a nearly perfect match: He had proved himself to be as unconventional and as cool of temperament as she.

"Now that you understand my initial reaction to the point of your visit, let me address your request." He leaned back in his chair. "I'm afraid you have it backward, Miss Holmes. If you have discovered Moriarty's modus operandi, then it's incumbent upon you to disclose said method to me. And I will have my subordinates check to see whether your discovery is valid."

This was not the response she had hoped for. Lord Bancroft was letting her know, not at all subtly, that a woman who wasn't about to marry him could not count on continued access to his work. "Will you inform me of the results? And how soon?"

"Only agents of the crown will be informed of the results. However, I can see my way to an exception."

She knew exactly what that exception would be. She tilted her head. "Do please elucidate."

"I will furnish what you seek, if I have a firm promise that you will shortly become Lady Bancroft."

If he knew of the theories that were beginning to coalesce in her head, he would not be so quick to play games with vital information. But the problem was, she was not ready for him to know these theories.

In fact, it was imperative that he not have any idea of them.

But could she truly agree to his capricious demand? Was it really so important that she must enter reluctantly into marriage — *marriage* — in order to obtain what she needed?

This was where their ideal-on-paper match unraveled. Charlotte was not without a streak of ruthlessness. But if she had cold water flowing through her veins, then Lord Bancroft had glaciers in his. And the thing was, she had no doubt he would hold her to her promise, even though she would consider any agreement to have been extracted under duress.

So on the one hand, decades with a man she would not have chosen on her own, the thought of which made her lungs feel as if they had been caught in a hydraulic press. And on the other hand . . . something far, far worse?

"Agreed," she said, looking him in the eye.

Sometimes one must pay one's debts — and hers were both deep and extensive.

Lord Bancroft allowed himself a small smile. He was surprised, no doubt, but also very, very pleased.

"But," she added, "I stipulate that our accord will only prove valid should what you give me turn out to be useful."

"And how would I know that?"

"Oh, you will know, my lord." She returned his smile, because sometimes she had an iceberg or two drifting through her veins, too. "And since you are demanding so much of me, I will also need to borrow a man who has your complete trust."

The intercepted telegram Lord Bancroft

gave Charlotte — or rather, the copied text, which she checked against the original three times to make sure there had been no mis-transcribing — was dated two days before she had discovered the secret of the house in Hounslow.

Which meant that she didn't need to consult the archive room at the *Times* again — or even work to decipher any additional small notices in the back of the paper: Because of Lady Ingram's inquiry, Charlotte already had all the small notices from around that time recorded and decoded in her notebook.

And the fact that the telegram had a date written in plaintext gave credence to her idea that those who received encoded messages needed to know when it was composed, so they would know which keyword to use to solve the cipher.

The newspaper notices that used *Encyclopedia Britannica* or the First Folio as a point of departure all arrived unambiguously at a single word in those pages. But with the biblical verses, she wasn't entirely sure how to proceed. Since the verses themselves weren't encrypted, it made sense, given the secretive nature of Moriarty's organization, that the keywords wouldn't be words visible in the advertised verses themselves.

But if a verse served as a pointer, what did it point to?

And many among them shall stumble, and fall, and be broken, and be snared, and be taken.

Isaiah 8:15.

She tried the first and last word of the chapter, followed by the first and last word of the Book of Isaiah, none of which decoded anything.

The title of the book? Still nothing.

She rubbed her temples. Of course she was going about it the wrong way: She was solving for a Vigenère cipher. The books in which the keywords would be found had changed at least twice in the past ten years. Yet she was still assuming that the basic cipher form had stayed the same.

What would it have changed to? Since the clues to the keywords now had a less opaque veil over them, it should follow that the cipher itself had graduated to one that was even more difficult to solve.

A Wheatstone cipher? Those, without knowledge of the keyword, were practically impossible. But she did have keywords at hand — or candidates, at least, if her chain of reasoning had been correct so far. She drew up a five-by-five square, divided the letters of the cipher text into pairs, and went to work.

And when she had verified, late at night, that indeed ISAIAH served as that ten-day period's keyword, she laid her head down on her desk.

Then she sighed, consulted her notebook again, pulled out a sheaf of paper, and began to write.

TWENTY

Tuesday

Livia continued to be amazed at herself.

The Friday before, after her euphoria over having never committed incestuous thoughts, not even accidentally, had faded somewhat, she'd worried that the pages she'd produced had resulted solely from the emotional abyss she had been thrown into. That if she felt more like her normal self — not that there was anything enviable about it — she wouldn't be able to pen another word.

But the story had continued apace. The murderer had sent an old woman to claim the sentimental item he'd left behind at the scene of the crime. She'd managed to escape pursuit by Sherlock Holmes. And now a Scotland Yard inspector had come to tell Holmes that they had arrested someone — obviously the wrong someone — on circumstantial evidence.

She set down her pen and flexed her fingers. From time to time she thought longingly of Charlotte's typewriter. But then again, it wouldn't be of as much use to Livia. That thing was *loud*. And Livia's best — or at least her most uninterrupted — writing time had proved to be early morning, before her parents rose.

A maid entered the breakfast parlor, bringing with her the early post. Livia gave the pile a cursory glance, not expecting anything, but the typewritten name on the topmost letter clearly said *Miss Olivia Holmes.*

And when she opened the thick envelope, she discovered not a letter, but a large, hand-illustrated bookmark, depicting a young woman in a white dress reading on a park bench.

Charlotte arrived at Mr. Gillespie's office at the hour specified by Parsons, the secretary. Parsons, his face already a few shades past florid, insisted that she enter into Mr. Gillespie's office.

"I have no business with Mr. Gillespie," she said quietly. "I only need a quick question answered from the diary you keep for the office."

"But I have instructions from Mr.

Gillespie to show you in."

Charlotte folded her hands around the handle of her parasol. "Is that so? If Mr. Gillespie is so eager for my company, he can come out and see me here. You may convey my sentiments to him."

"Will you . . . will you remain here?"

"Of course. You haven't answered the question I came for."

Parsons blinked rapidly, then sidled away, turning back to look at Charlotte every few steps. By and by he returned, and along with him came not only Mr. Gillespie, but Sir Henry, Charlotte's father, with the groom Mott in tow.

"Enough of this nonsense, Charlotte," Sir Henry bellowed. "You will leave with me right now."

"Ah, Father. How do you do? Mr. Gillespie. Mott." Her hands tightened on the parasol. She couldn't be entirely certain of Mott's loyalty in this matter, but even if he were to stand neutral, she still faced three grown men. Mrs. Watson's weighted parasol, however well made, would not prove sufficient to safeguard her freedom. "Unfortunately, Father, I'm quite busy today and must decline your invitation."

"Charlotte." Her name was a growl.

"Yes, Father?"

"Must I tell you specifically what is going to happen if you do not come willingly?"

"I'd like to hear it, but I may find it difficult to believe a man who has been known to break his word."

Mr. Gillespie and the secretary both glanced at Sir Henry, aghast, though she couldn't tell whether they were shocked by the charge or only that such an accusation had been spoken aloud. Mott, though, seemed to be trying not to give in to nervous laughter.

Her father turned almost as red as the secretary. "You come with us or you will be carried out."

"I don't think so."

She reached into her handbag, pulled out a Remington derringer, and cocked it — she wasn't one to entrust her safety to only a parasol.

Sir Henry's eyes widened. Both Mr. Gillespie and Parsons took a step back.

"You will shoot your own father?"

"I will shoot Mr. Gillespie first — not to worry, only in the foot. And *then* I will shoot you, also in the foot. After that I don't believe anyone else will be particularly interested in taking me anywhere against my will." She smiled slightly. "You taught me how to use firearms, Father. You know my aim is excellent."

A knock came on the door. The four men glanced uncertainly at one another. A knock came again. The men remained paralyzed.

The door opened and in walked Lord Ingram. He took a look around the room and tsked. "Are you trying to take these men hostage, Holmes?"

"Hardly, my lord. And good morning to you."

"Have *you* been keeping her?" Sir Henry's voice was high and harsh.

Lord Ingram turned a face of innocent surprise in his direction. "Sir, I am a married man. And unlike some I can name, I have never betrayed my vows. Miss Holmes is keeping herself, in admirable style, too, as far as I can tell."

"I don't believe you."

"Why shouldn't you? Unlike some in this room, I have also never reneged on my word."

Mr. Gillespie and the secretary swallowed in unison. Mott was seized by a coughing fit. Sir Henry, who had now been accused of untrustworthiness twice in the space of five minutes, stared blankly, as if he couldn't believe what was happening.

"Then what are you doing here?" he at last managed to say.

"I am here at my brother's behest. He has proposed to Miss Holmes and would very much prefer that she remain in London until she can give him her answer."

"Lord Bancroft wants to *marry* her?"

"Yes."

Sir Henry turned to Charlotte, looking as if he desperately needed to throttle someone. "Then why haven't you said yes, you stupid girl?"

"For the same reason I didn't say yes to him last time. I'm not enamored of the idea of being married to Lord Bancroft."

"Even though you could —"

"Even though I could make *you* happier, you who have no respect for *my* wishes?"

"Is this all the respect you have for those who raised you?" Sir Henry's spittle flew.

"No, I have quite a bit more respect for you than that. In fact, I plan to send you and Mother one hundred pounds a year."

"You can never repay us for the unhappiness you have caused us!"

Charlotte raised a brow. "I take it you do not want the hundred quid a year then."

"I — I didn't say that."

"Do you want it or not?"

"Y-yes."

"Excellent. But do understand that I'm not giving you this money out of the goodness of my heart. I'll want something in return."

Sir Henry wiped a hand across his forehead. "What? What will you want?"

"You'll see. But don't worry, it won't be anything you'll miss." She smiled, widely this time. "Now, gentlemen, I came to ask a question of Mr. Parsons and I'd like to get on with that. As I said, it will be a busy day for me and there is no time to waste."

"Thank you, my lord," Charlotte said to Lord Ingram, once he had helped her into a hackney.

He shook his head, laughed, and shook his head some more. "At times I have wanted to punch your father, but I'm not sure I'd have shot him."

"Only in the foot," she pointed out, "and only if he refused to show any sense."

"And the poor solicitor?"

"The poor solicitor was a willing party to an attempted abduction." She sighed. Mr. Gillespie's participation was hardly unexpected, but the whole affair still sent a chill down her spine. "The problem is that he believed he was doing something good. That forcing a grown woman to be locked up for the rest of her life figured as part of his duty to her father."

Lord Ingram leaned forward and squeezed her hand. "You know I wouldn't have stood by and let you rot in the country."

The contact of their gloved hands lasted a fraction of a second — and the jolt shot all the way to her shoulder. "I know. I'm all too glad to have you for a friend."

But would he still be her friend, after he had heard what she had to say?

The old silence threatened to descend. On any other day she would have let it. But today she spoke. She asked him about his children. She asked him about the archaeological sites he planned to revisit, now that the Season was coming to an end. She even asked him about the ball he and his wife would be hosting, in honor of her birthday, considered the last major function of the Season. And in turn she told him about her recent cases — as well as Mrs. Watson's attempt to turn her into London's foremost swordswoman, which made him laugh.

The hackney was approaching 18 Upper Baker Street when she said, "I'm glad Bancroft sent you today, since I need to speak with you anyway. Will you come for a cup of tea?"

He regarded her warily but only said, "Of course."

They settled themselves in Sherlock

Holmes's parlor. She made tea and served a plate of macarons, Madame Gascoigne's latest triumphs, light-as-air meringue biscuits sandwiched together with a delicious filling of buttercream.

And now, the moment of truth.

"I asked for your forgiveness earlier. You are about to learn why I did so."

He had been stirring his tea without drinking. Now he pushed it aside, abandoning any pretense of interest in refreshments. "I almost don't want to hear it."

But he had no choice. *She* also had no choice.

"Little more than two weeks ago, Lady Ingram came to me. She was upset. She told me that she had loved someone before she married you and that they had a pact to walk past each other once a year at the Albert Memorial, on the Sunday before his birthday."

His face turned expressionless.

"This year the man missed the appointment. She didn't know what to do because she didn't know how to find him. When she saw the article in the papers about Sherlock Holmes, she decided to consult him. Once I learned that the person she was looking for was Mr. Myron Finch, my illegitimate half brother, I had to carry on until I had some notion of his fate."

He gazed at her. "Did you know who she was before you agreed to see her?"

She exhaled. "Yes."

"I thought so," he said softly, almost inaudibly. Amazing how such quietly uttered syllables could contain so much condemnation. "Go on."

And from there, he did not say another word for the next hour.

When he did speak again, after a silence that lasted twice the duration of the Hundred Years' War, it was only to tell her, "I never thought I'd say this, Charlotte Holmes — or even think it. But I wish to God I'd never met you."

Charlotte hadn't lied about it being a busy day. After Lord Ingram had gone, she traveled by rail to Oxford and called on Mr. Finch's old boarding school, an establishment with no national renown but a modicum of local prestige.

Since her visit to the Glossops' the previous week, she had been corresponding with Mr. Finch's old boarding school. As pretext, she concocted a ladies' charitable society where several of the most admired matrons had sons who attended the school and had been on the cricket team together. The society wished to publish an article about the team's accomplishments in its newsletter, as a surprise to the matrons. Could she, the one responsible for writing the piece, come and see what photographs the school might have?

The response had been unequivocal: *Yes, of course. We would be delighted to share our archival images.*

And now more than a hundred boys clad in frock coats and striped trousers gazed solemnly at her, from a decade and a half ago. "That was Jones," said the headmaster sadly, pointing his finger at one particular boy. "I remember him, Archibald Jones. One of the best batsmen in the history of the school. A shame his father didn't want to further educate him. He would have excelled on many a college team — perhaps even a university one."

Charlotte was busy scanning the tiny print at the bottom of the photograph, listing the names of the boys. There it was, *M. H. Finch.* Fourth row, ninth from the left. But before she could find him in the throng, the headmaster thrust another picture at her.

"Here's another one of Jones, the year he captained the school team."

Eleven boys in the team photograph and one face immediately leaped out at Charlotte. There were no names at the bottom. She turned it around. On the back was written in pencil, *Standing, L to R, T. J. Pearson, M. C. Curthoys, O. A. Murray, G. G. Barber, M. H. Finch.*

Her stomach unknotted.

It would appear that her brother was alive and safe after all.

Lady Ingram exited the modiste's shop, limping. The final fitting had been interminable. The seamstresses had used her as a dress dummy and now her lower back felt as if a spike had been driven deep under her skin.

She didn't much care for fashion — and she disliked spending so much money on fripperies even more. Unfortunately, others expected her to be on display in a new gown, at least at her own birthday ball, so she must waste both time and money to satisfy the demands of Society when she would rather —

An envelope lay on the seat of the carriage. She glanced at her coachman. He stood with his eyes cast down respectfully, waiting for her to climb up. She did, grimacing — the muscles in her back tightened so much they yanked her backward.

Her second confinement had been both

quicker and easier. She had expected to recover fully in no time, but the back pain never went away. Nearly a dozen doctors consulted and no one had been able to do anything for her except prescribe laudanum and morphine — as if she would ever be so weak as to indulge in those.

She didn't even look at the envelope until the carriage had pulled away from the curb. And then only after she had lowered the shades on the windows.

An unsealed envelope, no addressee on the front, a typed sheet inside.

Could it be?

She pressed it to her heart. After all this time, he had at last contacted her. She pulled a pencil from her handbag and busied herself deciphering the message as the carriage turned and swayed.

Trust him to bring a smile to her face: He wanted to meet on the night of her birthday ball. Good thing she didn't give a damn for that nuisance.

She only wanted to see him.

Twenty-One

Thursday

At one o'clock in the morning, during a rousing rendition of Strauss's *Du und du,* Lady Ingram left her overcrowded house via the back service door. That exact moment, in the carriage alley behind the house, an unmarked brougham drew up, unmarked, that is, except for a piece of paper stuck to the inside of the window, with a drawing of a bird.

Not just any bird, a finch.

Her heart quickened. She got into the carriage, hoping to find him inside. But it was empty. Instead, there was an envelope on the seat, with a number on the front, and a key inside.

The carriage took her to a hotel that catered to country squires and their lady wives who wanted to stay in London for the Season but didn't want the fuss of hiring a house. It offered large suites of rooms with front doors on the street, so that one could enter and leave as if from a private residence.

The carriage stopped right in front of the door the number of which was on the envelope. Her heart pounding, her bad back forgotten, she ran up the few steps that led up to the small porch and eagerly inserted the key into the lock.

All the lights in the suite seemed to be on, every room brightly illuminated — and every room, from the vestibule inward, empty. Alone in the drawing room, one hand braced on the mantel, the other against the spot in her back that was throbbing again, she frowned.

Just then the front door opened. She spun around and smiled at the man who entered.

Her smile froze.

Not him but her husband.

"What are you doing here?"

He, like her, was still in his evening finery. His expression made the hairs on the back of her neck stand on end: She'd never seen such a look on him before, not vacant, not blank, only . . . empty.

"I'm here to say good-bye."

"What good-bye?" Her voice was rising — she couldn't control the volume of her speech. "Are you going somewhere?"

"No, you are." He dropped a velvet pouch on the console table just inside the door. "I brought your jewelry."

Through her stupefaction, understanding was beginning to seep through. He knew. He knew everything. It was all over. "How did you know?"

"You haven't been as careful as you should have," he said blandly. "You thought I would never suspect you."

"How long? How long have you suspected me?"

Her voice was still rising, while his remained quiet and even. She hated that almost as much as she hated being found out.

"Does it matter? I know the truth. At least three people are dead because of you."

She heard herself laugh. "They're dead because they chose to do dangerous things. And people who choose to do dangerous things sometimes don't come home."

He sat down stiffly, as if his back, too, bothered him. "Several times when I was abroad, I almost didn't come back. Were you hoping I wouldn't?"

"Does it matter now?"

A trace of sadness shadowed his eyes. "No, you are right. It doesn't matter now. Just go."

Just go? Did he not know her at all? She pulled out the pistol she'd brought in her handbag. "If I leave, you'll never let me see my children again. Better I kill you and carry on as a grieving widow."

He seemed neither surprised nor discomfited at the sight of a firearm aimed at his forehead. "Nobody will believe you a grieving widow. Also, should a gunshot ring out, you'll never leave this place except in custody. There are men stationed both on the street and on the other side of the door leading into the hotel. There are no other exits. You kill me, and our children lose both parents."

She chewed the inside of her lip.

"Not to mention that Bancroft is on his way. You fall into his hands and there will be no public murder trial for you — you will only wish you had one. If I were you, I wouldn't waste a moment."

The pistol shook. Was this really the end? Had she worked so hard and endured so much for *this*? "I have despised you for a long time. Everybody else understands a Society marriage for what it is. But you, nothing less than true love would do for you, would it? Well, I've had enough of your 'gentlemanly' reproach. Long may you rot in hell."

"The carriage outside is at your disposal," he said, his tone as mild as ever. "I wouldn't, however, try to go home and abduct the children. They are already elsewhere."

Her finger tightened on the trigger, the last bit of metal resistance giving away.

He moved not a muscle. "Remember Bancroft. This is your only chance to flee. Once he has you, I will not be able to intercede on your behalf."

Her entire arm trembled. It would be beautiful, the sight of a bullet shattering that thick skull. What wouldn't she give to see it.

A scream left her lips.

He only stared at her.

She shoved the gun back into her handbag, grabbed the pouch of jewels, and ran out. She couldn't allow herself to fall into Bancroft's hands. She couldn't. That would truly be the end of everything. As long as she still had her freedom, this would prove to be only a temporary setback.

A minor defeat before the major victory to come.

Lord Ingram slowly unclenched his hand from the revolver in his pocket.

He, too, was now shaking.

The children had been removed from the town house, that was true. But there were no men outside ready to leap to his assistance, and he would not inform Bancroft of her departure until twenty-four hours had passed.

He owed her this much, the mother of his children.

TWENTY-TWO

Friday

Charlotte sat before her vanity, pinning up her hair and counting her chins.

The doorbell rang. Charlotte had risen an hour earlier than usual, in anticipation of Lord Bancroft's visit. It would appear she had underestimated his impatience.

"Please show him to the parlor at Upper Baker Street," she instructed Mr. Mears, who came to announce their visitor. "Tell him I'll be there in a quarter of an hour."

When she reached Sherlock Holmes's parlor, Lord Bancroft stood before an open window, smoking a cigarette.

"I didn't realize it has become permissible these days to smoke in a lady's parlor," she said.

"My apologies," he said, defenestrating the cigarette and closing the window — though he didn't sound particularly remorseful. "Tea? Your butler insisted on making it."

"Very good of him to adhere to civilized behavior. I'm glad he insisted on some muffins, too, so I wouldn't be dragged out of bed at an ungodly hour only to starve."

Lord Bancroft pushed his fingers through his hair — and for the first time in her life Charlotte saw a smidgen of physical resemblance between the brothers. "Now that you have tea and muffins, will you please tell me what in the world is going on?"

"What did Lord Ingram tell you?"

"Only that you'll explain everything."

"He must have said more than that."

"Very well. At this point, I can't be telling you anything you haven't already guessed." Lord Bancroft sat down and drained a cup of the tea Mears insisted on serving. Charlotte had the sensation he wished it were whisky instead. "Recently we have lost good agents, two men and a woman. It appeared that there was a traitor in our midst, but we couldn't be sure who it was. This morning my brother banged on my door at first light and told me that the traitor was not among our ranks but in his household. And that his wife disappeared the night of the ball, more than twenty-four hours ago."

"That's all he said?"

"And then he left. I have no idea where he is."

With his children, of course. It was the day after they lost their mother.

Lord Bancroft regarded her expectantly. Charlotte, halfway through a muffin, had the feeling she wouldn't get to eat the rest until she had told Lord Bancroft everything. But she supposed the man had been waiting long enough.

"Very well then. Not too long ago, Sherlock Holmes's name was in the papers, in a rather condescending article that insinuated that now all he did was domestic investigations of no consequence whatsoever. In fact, it was the day you kindly proposed."

"I see."

"Within an hour of your departure, a letter arrived at this address, delivered by courier. I recognized the envelope and the typewriter as Lord Ingram's — but as he had no need to write Sherlock Holmes for a meeting, the letter had to have come from his wife. Which told me she had a highly private problem — most likely to do with a man."

"And you agreed to see her?"

"Yes, I did. Or rather, Miss Redmayne did. Lady Ingram gave a heartrending story about a pair of youthful lovers — of which she was one — forcefully torn asunder by greedy parents and the expectations placed on a lady of good birth. And now her sweetheart was missing.

"She told us that his name was Myron Finch and that he was a man of illegitimate birth working in the accountancy profession. I knew of such a man, my half brother, though we'd never met. I even had his address, from a letter he had written to my father earlier in the Season. It seemed a terribly easy case. All I had to do was to visit his place of residence and I would know whether he truly was missing or whether he had simply tired of seeing Lady Ingram only in public and only once a year.

"From the very beginning, however, something about the case struck me as not quite right. I wondered about Lady Ingram's story, about what she wasn't telling us. In fact, after my sister informed me that she had seen Mr. Finch — or the man we thought to be Mr. Finch — and Lady Ingram within easy viewing distance of each other and neither appeared to recognize the other, I did not consider it impossible that Lady Ingram's story had been pure hogwash.

"She was spared further suspicion because that particular Mr. Finch turned out to be counterfeit. In which case, of course she wouldn't have recognized him. And of course he wouldn't have known to meet her for their annual glance of longing at the Albert Memorial.

"But throughout it all, I never fully trusted Lady Ingram. I have always felt, from the very beginning, that she was not the kind of person to love deeply — not in a romantic sense, anyway. So there was always this tension between what I considered to be her character and the story she told of the impossible longing that contradicted everything I knew about her.

"Then there was the question of her choice of private investigator. She didn't go to someone else, she came to Sherlock Holmes, who had worked closely on an infamous case with Inspector Treadles, a man who is well known to her husband. How certain could I be that she didn't know that I was Sherlock Holmes, and that Myron Finch was my half brother?

"If she did know, it would have meant that I was specifically chosen for that connection. And if she knew of that connection, then it meant she knew a great deal more of Myron Finch than she admitted. But just because she was less than forthcoming didn't imply she harbored ulterior motives.

She might have feared that I wouldn't help her if I knew she wanted my help specifically. She might also have felt herself incapable of facing the judgment of others were she to confess how much effort she, a married woman, had put into searching for a man who wasn't her husband.

"My reservations about Lady Ingram were shunted to the side while we tried to understand why Mr. Marbleton was impersonating Mr. Finch. That is, until Miss Redmayne and I spoke to my father's solicitor and learned that Lady Ingram had been to see him. This meant she did know which family he was connected to — and probably a great deal more. But it wasn't until the Marbletons sought refuge here, after having been ambushed at Mrs. Woods's, that my suspicions concerning Lady Ingram began to solidify.

"Lord Ingram first informed me that Mrs. Watson's house was being watched. I had thought that it was Moriarty, on the off chance that our movements might lead him to the wife who had escaped his clutches. But now I began to wonder, what if it was someone connected to Lady Ingram, trying to see if following me would lead directly to Mr. Finch?

"In the days after we first discovered that

our movements were being watched, we acted with a great deal of care. As time passed, we became less careful. There was every possibility that the surveillance had been pared back when we were being deliberately evasive — and then resumed when we let down our guard. And that I had led Lady Ingram to Mr. Marbleton's address without meaning to."

"You'll remember that I had come to you with the theory that the Marbletons were impersonating Mr. Finch in order to get close to the Holmeses, to find out what they might inadvertently know — and that the real Mr. Finch was the man murdered in Hounslow. I had connected the Marbletons to Moriarty because of a similar scheme of codes that they used, and my theory was brought down when Lady Ingram definitively stated that the dead man wasn't Mr. Finch.

"But then Stephen Marbleton confirmed that at least some of my conjectures were correct — namely, that Mr. Finch had worked for Moriarty. That the dead man in Hounslow had been his colleague under Moriarty. And that together they had defected, taking something important from Moriarty at their departure.

"It was quite a leap to consider that Lady

Ingram might be tracking down Mr. Finch for Moriarty. On the other hand, she was perfectly placed. You have no one close to you, so in the short term, at least, she was their best bet, a highly intelligent woman who is bored by Society and antagonistic toward her husband, who happens to be not only your brother but your most trusted ally."

At this, Lord Bancroft downed another cup of tea.

Lord Ingram was tight-lipped and meticulous. But his wife, however estranged, lived in the same household. He kept a diary, which, even if written entirely in code and with everyone important referred to by aliases at all times . . . Well, codes were made to be broken and codes suitable for frequent usage even more so. And should he be away and the diary out of the house, he still wrote his children frequently and the envelopes would give his wife a good idea as to the locations where he carried out assignments.

When he stopped trusting her with his affections, he had believed that would be enough to keep him safe.

Charlotte stirred her tea. "I visited my father's solicitor a second time to find out when exactly Lady Ingram went to see him.

And the answer was three weeks before she came to see me. In Mr. Finch's old village, a man had come asking for his news at about the same time. I could make the argument that she passed on the information to Moriarty and he had sent the man. But that would be only speculation.

"I mulled a plan to speak to ladies Avery and Somersby, to check the age of the rumor that Lady Ingram had once fancied someone unsuitable. But even if I found out, and the rumor turned out to have been recent, it would only give me more circumstantial evidence.

"There was, however, one way to test whether she worked for Moriarty: If she did, she would know how to decode a message from him.

"I spoke to Lord Ingram. He was, needless to say, highly displeased with me, from the first revelation that I'd tried to help Lady Ingram track down her erstwhile beau, to my final suggestion that he do what he could to find out whether she had pledged her allegiance to someone the crown considers an enemy and a threat."

Little wonder. The last time he'd put his wife to the test, he'd found out that she'd married him only for his money.

Charlotte reached for the muffin again.

"And the rest you know."

Lord Bancroft's lips curled humorlessly. "Did it not occur to you, Miss Holmes, to give me this information last we met?"

Charlotte met his gaze squarely. "I owed Lord Ingram an immense debt of gratitude. I do not believe he would have appreciated what you would have done to the mother of his children."

"The mother of his children is now a threat to us all."

"I'm sure he took that into consideration."

At this Lord Bancroft rose, went to the sideboard, and served himself a healthy draught of Sherlock Holmes's best whisky. "I do not know all the rest. I do not know, for example, Mr. Finch's current whereabouts."

Charlotte took a ladylike sip of her tea. "Of that I haven't the slightest idea either."

Lord Ingram had always said that she was the greatest liar he had ever met, a once-in-a-generation talent. Perhaps all the untruths she had ever disseminated had been in preparation for this moment.

"But I can tell you this. I believe Moriarty has already regained his missing dossier. Remember the look on the dead man's face? That's the expression of a man who was told his life would be spared if he'd but give them what they were looking for — only to be strangled for his trouble anyway.

"Not to mention that the last time I saw Lady Ingram, she had changed her mind about finding Mr. Finch — and this from someone who had been nearly frantic before. Which tells me that Moriarty's interest in Mr. Finch had lessened. Mr. Finch might still have a target on his back, but now that Moriarty has his dossier back, he's no longer in such an unholy hurry to find and punish a traitor."

Lies, of course. Lady Ingram had seen the back of the dead man's picture, on which was written the location and the date of the murder, when she had taken that second look. She would have realized who the man was. And that deliberately or unwittingly, Charlotte had linked together Mr. Finch and Moriarty. That was why she had a sudden about-face, renouncing all further interest in Mr. Finch.

And the dead man's expression could just as well be that of a man who had told what Charlotte knew to be the real truth, that his friend was the one who had the dossier, and was then eliminated anyway.

Lord Bancroft studied her for a long moment. Charlotte held his gaze, praying her usual expression of sweet blankness held.

"Sometimes a man must make sacrifices for his country," said Lord Bancroft finally. "My brother did his part — I can scarcely do any less."

She raised a brow.

"Per our agreement, if I reiterated my proposal of marriage today, you were to be obliged to answer in the affirmative. But you are too valuable a woman to waste on matrimony. I would not have Lady Bancroft be concerned with the matters that come before me — but you, you I need in that capacity. You may consider my proposal withdrawn, Miss Holmes."

He took his leave. When she was alone in the room, she sighed. Saved from marriage with Lord Bancroft because he couldn't envision a world in which his wife saved him from a traitor in their midst.

Or because he realized that she had absolutely no compunction about lying to his face while looking him in the eye.

It had been more than twelve hours and Inspector Treadles still didn't know how he felt about the Richard Hayward murder case having been declared closed from above.

On the one hand, damned interference. On the other hand, now he no longer needed to find out whether he was a craven weasel who would lie to make himself look good.

On the third hand — clocks possessed three hands, didn't they? — had Sherlock Holmes had something to do with this? He hadn't seen Miss Holmes except that once in Hounslow. Nor had he heard from Lord Ingram. Yet for some reason, it had ever been a niggling doubt at the edge of his mind that as he trudged through the case, his nose to the ground, they had been investigating it on a far higher plane.

It took him some time to realize that his wife was not next to him in bed. They used to sleep snuggled together, like two kittens in a basket. But for some days now, he'd slept facing away from her, citing a persistently blocked nose that wouldn't let him breathe if he lay in the other direction.

He sat up at the same time she came into the room, fully dressed, her hat already on, her face somber.

"Barnaby died in the night. I'm on my way to see Eleanor. And then I'll have to stop for some mourning clothes."

He stared at her, unwilling to understand what he had heard. "Does that mean — does that mean — Cousins Manufacturing —"

470

"Yes, it'll come to me. But I can't think of business now — there's so much to do." She leaned down and kissed him on his cheek. "Good day, Inspector. I'll see you in the evening."

He remained frozen in place for a long time, then he dropped his head into his hands. She had what she'd always wanted — and he had never felt smaller or more lonely.

Lord Ingram was not at all surprised to see Charlotte Holmes walking up the drive to his cottage on the Devon Coast. The children, who had been playing in the garden, happily greeted her. She patted them rather awkwardly and seemed relieved when they took the sweets she offered and scampered off to enjoy them in their own secret corners.

"I'm afraid all I can offer for your tea is buttered toast," he told her.

"At one point this summer, buttered toast would have been the height of luxury, if I could have afforded any," she said cheerfully. "I'm always happy to have buttered toast."

He excused himself to speak with the cottage's caretaker. When he returned, she stood at the edge of the garden, her hands

on the rails, admiring the view of the Hang-
man cliffs.

"Beautiful panorama."

"It is."

She glanced at him. "How are the children?"

"They seem all right — for now."

"What did you tell them?"

"That she fell ill and the doctors recommended that she be immediately admitted
to a sanatorium in Switzerland."

"Did they ask if they could go see her?"

"They did. But so far they have accepted
that for their own safety, they shouldn't be
near her — risks of infection, et cetera."

She nodded.

The sea soughed at the foot of the cliffs.
Gulls cawed and wheeled overhead. A
breeze blew, filling his senses with smells of
salt, fresh grass, and wildflowers. On the far
side of the small bay, sheep meandered
across green headlands, tiny balls of white
fluff.

She glanced at him again. "And you?"

He half shook his head. "I don't know.
Sometimes I'm glad all the deception has
ended. Sometimes I wish I could have
remained ignorant forever. But then I think
of how she must be faring this minute . . ."

He closed his eyes for a moment, as if that

could shut away the turbulence. The guilt. "I still have my children, my brothers, my friends, all the comforts in life — I've lost nothing except perhaps the last of my delusions about her. But she, she had to give up everything to retain her freedom. And who can say what kind of freedom it will be, serving a man like Moriarty."

"A woman who has nothing left to lose can prove dangerous."

"I'm on my guard — it's a virtual certainty she'll come for the children."

She took his hand and squeezed it. But when she would have let go, he held on. "You know what I meant, don't you, when I said that I wished I'd never met you?"

"I think so. I was the harbinger of the worst news in your life. The one who informed you that your children would lose their mother."

She was too kind to mention that she was also the one to make him see that his wife had been responsible for the betrayal of esteemed colleagues. That in marrying her, he had committed a far greater error than he could ever have imagined.

"I apologize," he said.

"Apology accepted."

He let go of her hand — the caretaker was on his way with tea and buttered toast.

"Thank you for listening to me, by the way," she said, "when you didn't wish to hear a single word."

He would always listen, when she had something to say. That he did not voice aloud, because she already knew.

Tea was laid out under the dappled shade of a large whitebeam. A casual observer would have remarked on the rustic prettiness of the scene. A gingham tablecloth over an old picnic table; the chubby, unadorned tea service; a vase of wildflowers, purple, white, and the palest pink.

He wished he could enjoy the setting. He wished he hadn't been so blind. He wished he could wake up tomorrow and his only problem would be a cold, quietly hostile marriage.

He poured for Holmes and asked, because he'd rather think about something other than the shambles his life had become, "Would you really have said yes to Bancroft's proposal, because he gave you the example you needed?"

"It was a gamble. I wagered that I would prove to be right and rid Bancroft of a great danger to his organization. In which case he would owe me and be in no position to enforce a ridiculous bargain."

Her voice was calm and uninflected, but

he had the sensation that she hadn't been nearly so sure. That he heard a relief equal to that of a mountain climber who had been saved from the ravine by her rope, and who was even now still breathing hard.

"But that's all moot," she went on. "Bancroft has withdrawn his suit."

"He has?" This was news to him. "Why?"

"Apparently I'm too valuable to waste on matrimony — and I thought I had terrible opinions on marriage." She selected a slice of buttered toast. "Now let me ask you something. Were you the one who recommended to Bancroft that he propose to me again?"

"The exact opposite — I advised against it." The memory made him smile slightly. "When Bancroft told me he wished to try his luck again, I said he should court you without asking for your hand."

"Why not?" she asked, spreading jam on the toast.

"No one who asks you to marry him will ever be successful. When you're ready to marry, you'll tap the fellow on the shoulder and make the request yourself."

Her jam spoon stilled. "I understand a little better now how people become unnerved to be known so precisely." The breeze lifted a loose tendril of her hair and pulled it across her lips. She brushed away the offending lock. "But I'm glad someone knows me to this extent."

He raised a brow. "Someone?"

She looked toward the sea, shining and almost as blue as the sky, before her eyes met his. "All right. I'm glad *you* know me to this extent."

Livia couldn't stop talking about her story. "And Sherlock Holmes — *my* Sherlock Holmes — he's taken on a life of his own. I don't think he eats. I don't think he sleeps. He's quite the rude, superior fellow. And for the life of me, I can't get enough of writing him telling other people they're idiots."

"I know someone who would love to tell a great many people that they're idiots," said Charlotte.

"Me?" Livia resisted the urge to giggle, but she couldn't stop the giddy feeling spreading over her. "Goodness, I think you're right."

In the light of the carriage lanterns, Charlotte smiled. "And you aren't particularly enamored of either food or sleep."

It was Livia's last night in London. Somehow she'd finagled permission from her parents to attend an evening lecture. The lecture wasn't the point. The point was to meet Charlotte there and say good-bye to her beloved sister.

They'd sat in a tea shop that was open late until they could no longer reasonably pretend that the lecture hadn't ended yet. And now they were being driven home by Mott. Livia was too bashful — and fearful, and overjoyed — to mention the not-brother who had sent her the beautiful bookmark, so she asked, "Are you sure it's safe for you to be so close to the house?"

"Ah, I see now I haven't told you about my encounter with Father at Mr. Gillespie's office."

As Charlotte recounted what had happened, Livia alternated between gasping and cackling. "So, all that training with *canne de combat,* and you end up using a derringer."

"One must be adaptable."

"And what exactly are you trying to extract from Father with your hundred quid a year?"

"You, of course," said Charlotte softly. "You and Bernadine."

And just like that, Livia's eyes filled. She wrapped her arms around Charlotte. "I'm sorry. I know it makes you antsy to be hugged too long. But I'll miss you badly. And I so want your plan to succeed — and

I'm so afraid of wanting it too much!"

Charlotte patted her a few times on the back. "It'll be all right. We'll find a way."

Livia forced herself to let go. The carriage came to a stop. She wiped the tears from the corners of her eyes and took Charlotte's hands in her own. "I believe you. I believe we'll find a way."

Charlotte had told Livia that Mott would take her home. Mott, however, proceeded directly to the mews, opened the doors of the carriage house, lit the lamps, and drove the brougham inside.

Exactly as she'd instructed him in the note she'd pressed into his hand, when he'd helped her up into the carriage.

The carriage house doors were closed and bolted. Mott pulled off his gloves and opened the door of the town coach. "Miss Charlotte."

She allowed him to help her down and studied him as if seeing him for the first time. "Hello, brother."

ACKNOWLEDGMENTS

Kerry Donovan, Roxanne Jones, Sara-Jayne Poletti, the art department, and everyone else at Berkley for their top-notch work.

Kristin Nelson, who handles everything with aplomb.

Janine Ballard, the best critique partner under the sun.

Jeff Lord, who generously shared his knowledge of historical martial arts.

My husband, who tells everyone he meets about the Lady Sherlock books.

Everyone who has been so enthusiastic about *A Study in Scarlet Women.*

And you, if you are reading this, thank you. Thank you for everything.

ABOUT THE AUTHOR

USA Today bestselling author **Sherry Thomas** is one of the most acclaimed historical fiction authors writing today, having won the RITA® Award two years running and appeared on innumerable "Best of the Year" lists, including those of *Publishers Weekly, Kirkus Reviews, Library Journal,* Dear Author, and All About Romance. Her novels include *A Study in Scarlet Women,* first in the Lady Sherlock series; *My Beautiful Enemy;* and *The Luckiest Lady in London.*

She lives in Austin, Texas, with her husband and sons. Visit her website at sherrythomas.com.